"ACIREMA"

A New Beginning--A Better Way

by

Bill Williams

BADM BOOKS
Pensacola, Florida

Copyright © 1998
By
William Hartman Williams

ISBN: 1-890126-01-2

BADM BOOKS
P.O. Box 2430-1130
Pensacola, Florida 32513-2430

Although some of the characters in this work are real, the story related herein is entirely fiction.

00 99 98 97 / 10987654321

Manufactured in the United States of America.

by

FATHER & SON

ASSOCIATES, INC.

4909 N. Monroe Street

Tallahassee, Florida 32303

http://www.fatherson.com

DEDICATION

This book is dedicated to my parents, Malcolm and Myrtle Williams. No person could ever ask for better parents as there has never been a mother and father who loved their children more.

And to my brother Ronnie and sister Sandi. Many are the cherished memories of growing up together and enjoying a simple but incredibly happy childhood. Each played a wonderful part.

And to four very warm, wonderful, and extraordinarily loving children with whom I am most pleased: Bill Jr., Ashley, David, and Malcolm and their spouses. They made this world a much better place to live by giving me six beautiful grandchildren with whom I am very proud: Justin, Erin, Jenny, Cait, Alex, and Andrew.

ONE

"THE CONTINENTAL BROADCASTING NETWORK brings you this breaking news bulletin. The entire South was shaken this morning when a story came over the AP wire concerning an early morning breakfast meeting at the downtown Pensacola Grand Hotel, Pensacola, Florida.

"Ralph Walton of the Associated Press was the only reporter invited to attend the meeting and filed his report shortly after 10:00 this morning. As soon as it hit the wires, rumors and rumors of yet more rumors to come spread across the entire upper Gulf Coast.

"Taylor Savage, an ultrawealthy businessman, who last year was voted the nation's most eligible bachelor, and is President of Savage Worldwide, announced a plan he has devised which calls for the formation of a new state. Yes, you heard right, a new state. This would be our 51st state and named Acirema, pronounced ASA'-REMA. I get an eerie feeling that you should remember that name, as it may well become commonplace before you know it.

"A move such as this has never happened before in the history of the United States of America, and I place a heavy emphasis on the word 'United.' Obviously, during the Civil War some states either withdrew from the Union or threatened to withdraw. This is not the case with Acirema. No one is talking about withdrawing from the Union. Mr. Savage, and only Mr. Savage at this time, is talking in terms of a number of counties from both Florida and

1

Alabama seceding from their respective states and forming Acirema.

"If this becomes reality, it will hurt both Florida and Alabama since the 19-county combination is prime recreational area in both states. It will take in some 160 miles of Gulf beachfront and 19,468 square miles. There will be 783,624 citizens leaving Florida and 652,767 leaving Alabama. The total loss of residents for these two states will be a staggering 1,436,391.

"The announcement by Savage to a group of personally invited business and professional leaders, movers and shakers, truly shocked those in attendance as no one had an inkling of the purpose of the meeting that called these 20 individuals together. However, the AP story reported those who were in attendance spoke very favorably about the plan and looked forward to the next meeting which will offer more intricate details. CBN is attempting to obtain a list of those in attendance and will interview from the list when available.

"It appears that Mr. Savage has gone to great lengths to establish a plan which may conceivably come to reality and create the state he refers to as Acirema. In his comments he was quick to point out that America needs to change directions, to reverse itself so to speak, and the name for the new state as selected by Mr. Savage is actually the name of **AMERICA** spelled in reverse, ACIREMA.

"There has been no precedence for such a bold move. Therefore, everyone is at a loss for words as to the possibility of success. Mr. Savage is to appear tomorrow night on the national TV show, Laurie Sin' Live, for the full hour, and it's likely the hour will extend into overtime as this most important and interesting news item is on the lips of the entire country.

"Already, there has been a tremendous number of phone calls into the CBN news room since the story broke. CBN contacted Mr. Savage's office in an attempt to schedule an interview, but his spokesperson, Laura Rings, indicated Mr. Savage will have no comments until after the Sin' Show, which should offer an insight into the plans he has conceived. He is expected to make several news shows over the next week or so. It is certain that you will be hearing much more of Mr. Savage in the very near future. The next committee meeting is scheduled for Tuesday, February 6th."

TWO

TAYLOR SAVAGE HAD sent 20 invitations to a group, not all of whom were necessarily the best heeled, financially that is. The 20 men and women were leaders in their special fields of business, trade, and politics and were most defiantly free thinkers.

The invitations included those with business or other special interest along the Gulf Coast of northwest Florida and south Alabama, from Panama City to Mobile and stretching north into Alabama for approximately 110 miles from the intersection of I-10 and I-110 just north of the center of Pensacola.

The purpose of the meeting was held close to his chest and known only to a very few of his closest associates within his company. It was intended to rock the business establishment and send shock waves through Tallahassee and Montgomery. He had spent considerable time developing this plan over five years, and the time had arrived for him to make his splash.

The Savage family were Southerners who had made it big in the business world. Their personal roots ran deep across the South, and their business empire expanded across the globe. Grandfather Theodore passed away year before last and left his fortune to his only son, Ted, Jr. Ted had three children: David, a successful medical doctor in Birmingham; Chelsea, who was married to a criminal lawyer and lived in New Orleans; and Taylor, the apple of his dad's eye, who was President of the family's corporation, Savage Worldwide. Although Taylor was President, his dad remained Chairman of the Board although in name only.

Savage Worldwide had immense holdings in television and radio stations, newspapers, magazines, shopping centers, outdoor advertising, theaters, and three major league sports teams. Ted, Jr., had planned for Taylor to head up the enterprises after he graduated from college, but he had opted to follow his love of flying and entered the U. S. Navy flight program and received his wings at Pensacola. Shortly thereafter he was flying F-18s and had made a serious effort to become a member of NASA's Astronaut Corps.

He graduated from MIT with a degree in engineering and Harvard Law School and assured himself that he was educated well enough to become an astronaut. However, this was one goal where he fell short—quite possibly the only one where he had not found success.

After completing his military tour he joined his family's enterprises. Still the itch to fly needed fulfilling, so he earned his commercial license and later qualified with captain credentials so he could pilot their Gulfstream V, Cessna Citation X, and two Lear Jets although he had been doing so for years without the proper ticket.

With his family's enormous wealth Taylor could do just about anything he desired. A couple of years out of the military, and now President of Savage Worldwide, he wanted to do something on his own. He began working on plans to develop an area with very special concerns and ideas for the family structure and the business community. This took much of his time and considerable dollars from his inheritance. However, he was satisfied with the timetable and the possibility of success.

Unlike most other financially well-off 42-year-old filthy rich men caught up in the middle-age crazies, Taylor had plans, big plans, and all the other interests would just have to take a back seat while he played his cards and put his plans into motion. He had designed his place in history, and the time had come to implement his ideas.

☐ ☐ ☐ ☐ ☐

JOHN PYLE HAD just returned to his desk after a difficult morning staff meeting at PYLE INTERNATIONAL. As President and CEO of his family's shipbuilding firm, with headquarters in Pascagoula, Mississippi, he was almost fed up with the union negotiations and was ready for a few days of rest. He had promised his family a weekend at Pine Mountain, Georgia, at Calloway Gardens. This was always a relaxing weekend of swimming, hiking, tennis, and dining. He was looking forward to leaving early in the morning on the company jet.

His corporation maintained a marvelous, comfortable home on the Mississippi coast overlooking the Gulf where he spent five days each week, then traveled to his family estate in Tennessee each Friday afternoon. His Lear would shuttle him to Nashville to pick up the family and fly to Pine Mountain as soon as the kids were home from school.

His secretary, Susie Gee, a recent graduate of UCLA, had been instructed from day one to call to his attention any correspondence marked personal and/or confidential. His business required him to be on top of some of the more critical issues, and to that end he had made it known to his fellow business associates to address special concerns to his attention and clearly mark the envelope as such.

He asked Susie to bring him another cup of black coffee, and any special mail and to hold his calls. On the top of a three letter stack, all marked confidential, was a letter from Taylor Savage. While Taylor was a friend, but not close, he and his family were well known primarily because of the vast financial holdings of his father, Ted, Jr., and his late grandfather, Theodore.

Among their family's greatest assets were its reputation for upright and honest dealings, a commodity not easily found in today's business community. Therefore, when someone with the stature and leadership qualities of Taylor Savage called a meeting and asked you to be present, you were hard pressed not to show.

The letter was an invitation to join 19 other businessmen and women for a breakfast meeting, Tuesday, January 23rd, at the Pensacola Grand Hotel. The invitation was direct and to the point, stating emphatically this was most important and to please cancel any other plans you may have had for the 23rd. The invitation also noted there was no number for RSVP as no one would be forgiven if he or she did not attend.

"Miss Gee, look in here a moment please," he buzzed.

"Yes, Sir," she said, standing with her ever-present pad.

"Miss Gee, clear my calendar for January 23rd and make all arrangements for me to attend this meeting in Pensacola," handing her the letter of invitation. "There will be no need for me to stay over either the night before or after as the meeting is set for nine in the morning. And keep your eyes and ears open to see if you hear anything about anyone else we know that may be attending. Also, have Harry find out all he can about what Taylor Savage is up to these days. Thank you Miss Gee."

"Yes, Sir, I'll get right on it."

☐ ☐ ☐ ☐ ☐

MARK HOUSTON had just returned from a four-day trip to Las Vegas where he always brought home more than he took with him. From the heart he was a true gambler and cared less about the subject matter of the meeting. He was well aware of the vast holdings of the Savage Group and would attend if for no other purpose than to satisfy his curiosity.

He had inherited his family's asphalt paving business with headquarters in Panama City and had done quite well by expanding the operations to far-reaching corners of the upper Gulf Coast. He knew very well there might be some work for his company since he controlled the industry on the coast, especially if Savage were to announce a development of any sort.

☐ ☐ ☐ ☐ ☐

RAY HAZE, an Air Force Colonel who had retired and then began building a financial empire in the business arena with dealerships in the boat and aircraft industries, banking, television, and recreational vehicles, had also received his invitation to join what was to be a very elite group of individuals.

Taylor Savage knew Haze was always looking for the edge on a deal and could care less whom he hurt as long as he could continue to keep up the public image of being a good and solid citizen on the outside and rotten as a skunk on the inside. His life had become truly a sad one which he covered up with dollars much like a child would pull a blanket over himself to cover and hide from the cold and pains of the outside world.

Although raised in the mountain ranges of Colorado, he retired around the Point Clear, Alabama, area when the military downsized Brookley Air Force Base in Mobile. From his home he worked diligently to put together his business empire by fleecing several active and retired military friends who invested heavily. During the time he was working to establish the enterprise as an active business, he was working overtime to develop a means to rid himelf of his partners and to do so at the least possible cost to himself. Twice he had been a candidate for the governorship of Alabama, finishing third in his first try and making it to the general election in his second attempt. He always retained his interest in politics and knew the day would come when he could take financial advantage of his past experiences.

Although ethics were a real problem between him and some of his business acquaintances, they most often overlooked a problem unless it directly affected their own guidelines for making a buck. Haze had a knack for ending up on top and had made millions by doing it his own way, crooked or not.

The combination of a nasty divorce and a battle with his love for alcohol left him practically null and void. He was able to function in the daytime business world but had a hard time coping at night, especially when alone. Out of necessity he depended on having friends around constantly, but when alone he substituted for lost companionship with white line fever by often staying on the phone late into the night or early morning hours with senseless conversations most frequently with young ladies scattered around the globe.

With this invitation he was looking forward to getting back into the middle of something which he could possibly control, something that might develop into a financial situation where he could quickly make a buck and then dump the deal on a friend who, as usual, would quickly become a former friend.

□ □ □ □ □

MARTIN PARKER, the respected Chairman of the Board and founder of Parker, Adams Law Firm and one of the giants of the legal profession which had roots in beautiful Destin, Florida, had received his invitation and was eager to visit again with his old friend, Taylor Savage. Parker had founded his firm after graduation from the University of Georgia and the University of Tennessee Law School.

He had been born and raised on the Gulf Coast of Okaloosa County and had dedicated much of his life, as other contributing members of the Parker Clan did, to working hard for the betterment of life for everyone who chose to live on the panhandle Gulf Coast. After graduation from high school he had decided the way to expand his circle of friends would be to attend college out-of-state since the majority of those he already knew were attending Florida State in Tallahassee or the University of Florida in Gainesville, with a few attending either Auburn or the University of Alabama.

Over the years he had developed a reputation as someone who possessed all the appropriate credentials and who one day might become President of the United States if he chose to go into politics. His character remained impeccable, and his many friends attested that he was a real man's man and quite the gentleman. While he continued to support several candidates who sought statewide office each election year, he never acquired a desire to be a public servant himself and was most pleased to be known as a "kingmaker."

As his law firm grew, it continued to invite new partners into the association. As with most other large firms, his was simply known by the first two names, Parker-Adams. As the firm grew and new partners came on board, their names became part of the impressive letterhead. However, the firm was still known far and wide simply as Parker-Adams.

Not long ago a young, bright, new intern was studying the letterhead and noted the full partnerships included Martin Parker, Herb Adams, Herman Pruitte, Jim Evans, Robert Ringer, Juan Escopoe, and Richard Miller. He quickly recognized that the first initial of each last name spelled PAPEREM and immediately brought his new find to the attention of the Board. When you place an apostrophe within the word you get PAPER'EM, or "PAPER THEM," which was a common phrase in the law profession for "sue them", "paper them", or "paper'em." The board acknowledged the young man's wisdom but assured him he was employed for better use of his time and that he had better get busy.

THE BATES BROTHERS, Waddell and Boogie, were not of the uptown, run of the mill, popular names, but more realistically described their country upbringing. While they could financially afford to change their name to whatever they desired, they accepted the handle given them by their parents and could not care less what others might think.

Obviously, Boogie was a nickname. It had been bestowed on him in the first grade by kids who were not fond of his real name, which was Beaudreaux. Since early grade school he had been tagged Boogie, and it remained. Waddell was for real.

They made their fortune in the trash and garbage business, starting with three secondhand, or for that matter thirdhand, leased trucks in their hometown of Crestview, Florida. When the Environmental Protection Agency began its enforcement in a serious way, their business prospered and found immediate success.

Outside their primary business they were mostly involved in financial deals that required cash capital but little polished, personal leadership. Their outgoing personalities were such that they attracted an element of friends who mainly could be classified as "hangers on," those who loved to party.

Like someone once noted, sometimes it is better to have a person, or in this case two people, on your side rather than to have them against you. Taylor Savage knew this lesson from a firsthand experience and chose to invite them to become involved in a very special way.

□ □ □ □ □

DALTON BRUCE, a plastic surgeon, always wanted to involve himself with the political element, especially if there was an opportunity to make a buck. This invitation could possibly be a route to financial gain and possible political prominence.

His practice had been extremely successful, and even after three marriages and divorces he still maintained a cash flow sufficient to afford him a very good living. He was overly anxious to have the chance to rub elbows with those in the political arena and was fond of holding fund-raising events from his lavish waterfront home near Deer Point in Gulf Breeze, Florida.

It had been said he would give almost anything to be on a first-name basis with the President if it would provide some reasonable access to the White House. For several years he had sought, unsuccessfully, to have the President, any President, appoint him as an Ambassador to any country.

He thought Savage's invitation might well be his chance to fall into something that would afford him an opportunity to satisfy his personal desire to achieve his longtime political fantasy. Most of his close friends knew his real desire was not politics but to be involved in international personal relationships with the ladies who awaited on foreign shores.

It was common knowledge that all three of his ex-wives would do anything, within reason or not, to prevent his expanding his influence in the political community. Each was prepared in her own personal way to launch a campaign against his goals.

His first wife, now married to a worthless attorney, had been gathering information on him for sometime and was prepared to detail her knowledge of his past drug abuse with the full poison of her personality. She just could not wait to be in the limelight by testifying at a Senate confirmation hearing for such appointment and with little regard, even if her comments hurt their three sons who are all presently in college, one in medical school.

□ □ □ □ □

DURING HIS TWO unsuccessful campaigns for Governor of Alabama, Ray Haze had called on many friends and had those friends call more of their friends, which ultimately had raised considerable funds for his campaign war chest. One of the contributors who was always willing to give more than his share was Mark Houston, the paving contractor from Panama City. He was looking to expand his operations throughout Alabama, especially in the Dothan area where a competitor was financially courting Haze's opponent, who ultimately won the election and became Governor.

After receiving his invitation Haze decided to call a few friends and business acquaintances to see if any of them had been asked to attend. His first call was a strikeout, but his second one to Mark Houston hit its target. The men made small talk, and then Haze came to the purpose of the call.

"I would like the two of us to have lunch and see if we can find a reason for this urgent call by Taylor Savage. He must be up to something, and I would like to know more about it before going in cold turkey,'' Haze stated.

''I think you are right. Why don't we get together for lunch tomorrow. I have to be in Fort Walton for a morning meeting and another in Destin. Could you possibly meet there?'' Houston inquired.

''Sure. I'll fly my one lung over and meet you at noon. Where shall be meet?''

''Why don't I just plan to pick you up at the Destin airport, around twelve noon?''

''I'll be there. See you tomorrow. Goodbye.''

After a hectic week of competitive bidding for construction contracts at Eglin and Tyndall Air Force bases, Houston was ready for a break. His morning meeting with Colonel Wiggins, contracts officer at Eglin Field, finished an hour earlier than he had anticipated, so he stopped by Harry T's for a martini before picking up Haze at the small airstrip. After his first cocktail he realized he had time for a second and wanted a third but decided to wait until they both returned for their luncheon appointment.

The January weather had continued with its daily dose of light rain and early morning fog, but no problem was expected that would hinder Haze's flight over from Point Clear. Almost like clockwork, right at high noon, the blue and white single engine plane broke out of the mist at the north end of the 4,000-foot strip.

''Well, you are right on time. Good to see you again,'' Houston said.

''Thanks, good to see you also. I had some weather along the coast and had to go up to Crestview and down. Glad I didn't delay you,'' Haze said.

''I had an hour to kill after my earlier meeting and stopped in at Harry T's for a martini. Does Harry's suit you for lunch?''

''Sure, that's fine. If I wasn't flying, I would join you in a martini but you had better have all the fun today for the both of us.''

The two men ordered light lunches and Houston had a third martini while Haze finally convinced himself a Miller Light would not hinder his flying ability.

''Houston, it's good seeing you again. How's things in Panama

City?''

''We had a great last year. If this weather will give us a break, the beginning of this year will do well also. I just signed a contract this morning for the rebuilding of runway 18-36 at Eglin, which was nearly $4.1 million, and a contract yesterday for a similar project at Tyndall for a little over $2 million.''

''That's great. Sounds like you are off to a good start in mid-January.''

''And how have you been doing in Point Clear?'' Houston asked.

''Not too bad. The last six months in the car business was a bust. I lost an employee when a vehicle slipped off the transport truck and pinned him under. The insurance is going to cost me a bundle. On the personal side, a female employee filed a sexual harassment suit against me, but I have no problem with that. My attorney found out through depositions this was the third one she has filed in the past two years, against three separate men.''

''Wow! Things have been interesting for you to say the least,'' Houston stated.

''Let's talk about the upcoming meeting. What do you think Savage is up to?'' Haze asked.

''I don't rightly know what to think. He has something up his sleeve and wants several of us there to hear his side of the story,'' replied Houston.

''You know the rumors have been floating around that his company has been showing an interest in purchasing the Grand Hotel at Point Clear. I wonder if this has any connection?'' Haze asked.

''I hadn't heard that one yet. However, I did hear through my contacts with the military contracting officers at Pensacola Naval Air Station that Savage Worldwide was trying to negotiate an offer with the Navy to purchase the old Summerdale OLF just north of Foley.''

''That could be interesting. Wonder what use he would have with it?'' inquired Haze.

''Like we both know, whatever he touches seems to turn to gold. A couple of months ago when he purchased the decommissioned *USS Lexington*, I could not imagine what a private company would do with an antiquated aircraft carrier. I assume he is the only person in the world who owns his own aircraft carrier,'' Houston noted.

''Yeah, that was a surprise. I hear from a couple of retired admiral friends of mine he will be taking possession after the decommission rites are finished, which will be sometime toward the end of this year,'' Haze offered.

''The scuttle is that he will renovate it into a floating hotel with fine staterooms, dining facilities, and something no other luxury liner can possibly offer: an arrival on a cruise ship by jet. Can you imagine how many navy men and women would love to return to the 'Gray Ghost' and bring a romance on board by private jet and land on top deck? And I'm sure he will offer prop plane arrivals as well as helicopter.

''While it cost him millions, I can plainly see where in the long run it may earn him a tremendous profit. He will need a huge berth and docking facilities for supplies; but, as usual, knowing Taylor as we do, he has already found the answers to those questions a long time ago. And when he takes possession, he'll have to go into a shipyard right away to start renovations,'' Houston noted.

After the two decided they had no idea what Taylor Savage was up to, they bade each other goodbye with the intent of keeping their eyes and ears open for any information which might become available prior to next Tuesday's meeting in Pensacola.

THREE

A FEW MINUTES before 9:00 o'clock the special guests began to find their way into the well-appointed, comfortable room which had been set up and arranged to fit Taylor Savage's personal preferences. He wanted to make certain everything was just right for his guests and stood by the door to welcome each with his ever-present warm and friendly attitude.

He had handpicked these exceptional people, some of whom he was acquainted with, knew the background of others, and still others had been recommended to him by a professional search committee. All had proven in the past to be movers and shakers within their communities or held unique abilities otherwise unmatched.

In order to keep it informal, friendly, and close-knit, he had arranged for three round tables, each with seven chairs. All 20 invited guests would be present except for Dr. Bruce, who had to perform emergency surgery that morning. Taylor had invited Ralph Walton, a reporter for the Associated Press, to cover the morning meeting and insisted he have breakfast with the group where he could get better acquainted with all members.

Between small talk and bites of fresh fruit, Savage finally completed a cup of coffee and excused himself from his table guests to take his place at the podium.

In addition to being voted the country's most eligible bachelor last year, he has remained on the best-dressed list since his senior year at Harvard. His business attire was custom-made by the Tom

14

James Company, and every piece was personally tailored from the very finest fabrics available. With his hectic schedule, he had little time to shop for clothing, so the personal touch offered by Tom James was to his fancy. His entire wardrobe was custom-fitted by a clothing counselor in the privacy of his own office and delivered to his home address.

◻ ◻ ◻ ◻ ◻

"GOOD MORNING AGAIN. I want to personally welcome each one of you and thank you for giving your time to attend this morning's breakfast meeting. The first thing I want to say is, today starts a new day in the history of our country. A day that none of you will ever forget. And I promise you we will not stay too long this morning, for sure not as long as some of our meetings will be in the near future.

"You have shown your interest by your attendance. However, none of you should have any idea of why we are gathered. If you do, then I have not done my job properly thus far!"

The room was small and comfortable. Taylor felt very much at ease. He left the podium and strolled between each table and continued with his comments. Those present would quickly learn this would be his normal and personal manner of conducting important meetings, walking and talking at the same time.

"Everyone here is an outstanding leader in his or her chosen field. This is why you were asked to attend this initial conference. With your assistance, patience, and support, we are going to build a new state. Not a state of confusion...but a real state. The 51st State of our Union."

He paused long enough for several of the attendees to whisper to their table guests, "Did he say a new state?"

"Yes, that is what I said. You heard me right. A new state. Not the rebuilding of an existing state but a new state. A brand new state from the ground up.

"For more than five years I have completed exhaustive research for our new state which will be known as ACIREMA, pronounced ASA'REMA.

"My research has educated and proven to me this is quite possible. However, it is only possible if you, each of you, feels compelled to be a part of Acirema.

"After today, should you decide to join with the others of our group, I can assure you that you will be on the cutting edge to make a difference in the way your family will be raised and the atmosphere where your business will be conducted.

"I also can assure you after today your life will never be the same again, so I would like for you to give me your undivided attention because every aspect of our agenda is most important.

□   □   □   □   □

"HOW WOULD YOU LIKE to live in a crime-free, drug-free, Utopian-type society where you and your family can actually walk the streets and not be concerned about the criminal element?

"If there was a land of milk and honey with golden opportunities, Utopia so to speak, we all would want to be a citizen. We can make that happen, right here in Acirema.

"There is no end in sight to the opportunities we have at our fingertips. With your total commitment and hard work we can leave our children, grandchildren, and their grandchildren a new place to live and raise their families in an atmosphere of safety and tranquility.

"However, let me caution you that nothing is free. It always costs somebody something, and that somebody is always the taxpayers. It is always at the expense of the taxpayers, you and I, and again, nothing worthwhile is ever free. A verse in a song recalls, 'Freedom's just another word for nothing left to lose, nothing ain't worth nothing, but it's free'. Well, what we have is 'something' not 'nothing,' and I can assure you if 'anything' is worthwhile it is not free.

"We will have our work cut out for us, but the final result will be something that we all can be proud of, the accomplishment we will make.

"Should you choose not to be involved, then you and I have lost nothing more than a few hours of our time, although I shall not apologize for that loss. I invite you to come along for the ride, as it's going to be a tremendous ride.

"I want to get one special comment on the table and out of the way. Due to my family ties, I am an ultrawealthy individual. I am 42 years old, single, and, as I have said, been blessed with enormous wealth. I split my time between Pensacola Beach and

Amelia Island, Florida, and Raleigh, North Carolina. While I have been privileged all my life, I am not spoiled, not a brat, and I'm well-educated. I know what I am doing and want to invite each of you to be a part of what I conceive to be a very good and special program.

"I bring this up to assure each of you that my plans for Acirema are honorable and straightforward. I want each of our meetings to be exactly that, and for everyone to say what is on his or her mind and to be honest, straightforward, and honorable with all your comments, actions, and intents.

"I intend to give something back to my community, something that is worthwhile. I want to contribute to my fellow man, and to that end I have worked to develop a plan that I invite each of you to become a participant.

"There is nothing within Acirema which I need, want, or require except its success. I have no desire to be an official, either elected or appointed. However, I have the desire to see my plans come full-force forward and to bring our new state into being as the most modern state in the Union, but based on old-fashioned values and principles.

"America must change. Our country has become, in many respects, something that few of us continue to love, honor, respect and cherish.

"Our politicians have let our system get almost totally out-of-hand. They have become politically petrified of the minority electorate and cringe with each comment made by those who have become self-appointed leaders. Those who desperately want to crown themselves as the minority spokesperson, by their antics and comments, project themselves as being interested simply in promoting their own selfish and personal agenda at the expense of the group as a whole. A minority, I may add, who to this day has yet to even reach 13 percent of the total population of our nation; still, they demand more and more attention as though they were in the majority.

"Today and everyday from this day forward, you will hear me speak openly and truthfully. I will shy away from not a single subject. Each will be addressed head-on, as this is the only means, in my opinion, that we have to accomplish our goals. It is the only way that I know to operate my personal life, and that is to be wide-open with total disclosure.

"In Acirema we will welcome all races, bar none. However, we welcome only those, no matter their race, who choose to participate in our society in accordance with, and at the level of, accepting the responsibility of abiding by the laws, rules, and regulations as set forth by a vote of the entire electorate of our new state.

"There are among us those who are sure that individuals who seek to be the leaders of the black community have finally won their goal of bringing our country down to a lower level.

"Let's face it. Although no one wants to admit it, the minorities, with only 12.8 percent of the population, control this nation, and the reason why is simple. Their leaders, some of whom are ministers, control most of our politicians by their continued threat of doing harm to our properties with unwarranted riots and the like. Our politicians must find a better means to correct these problems, and we will in Acirema.

"It is my opinion that we will always have race problems with us, and only we ourselves can react in a more positive way to heal these problems. You cannot legislate them away. That's not going to happen. We all must understand this and readjust our thinking to solve the problems from a new point of view. Integration, as we know it today, is a failure. We must first recognize this as the failure it is and work toward a better solution.

"Former U.S. Senator Bill Bradley of New Jersey said, 'If we are to have racial healing in our country the first step is to engage—to talk openly and honestly with someone of another race'. The Senator is right; this seems simple enough. Doesn't it? That is, until you really break it down and take a long and hard look.

"In my opinion, the road to a more successful relationship between all races has to begin with true and honest facts, not distorted facts. A prime example of distortion is that many of those who want to be leaders of the minorities would have you believe the great majority of poor people in our country are of their race. This is totally false. The greater majority of poor people, by standards acceptable by all, is by far those of the white race and by a gigantic margin of more than two to one.

"The Senator went on to say, 'Racial harmony is in our

economic self-interest. By the end of the first decade of the next century, only about 60 percent of American workers will be native-born whites. Clearly, we will all advance together or each of us will be diminished.'

"I believe the Senator is correct. And I further believe that a large percent of the problems which are counterproductive between the races are generated by pure and simple hatred and the desires by some to start trouble for all, be they black or white. I also like to recall another saying of still another former United States Senator, Alan Simpson of Wyoming, that 'Hatred corrodes the container in which it's carried.'

"Here in Acirema we are going to show the entire nation a change can be made across our country and made effectively. We have got to reverse the trend and direction in which we all are headed. And wasn't it Popeye who said, 'That's alls I can stands, and I can't stands no mo'?

"Enough said. I hope you get the point.

"Over the next several weeks you will hear me criticize the status quo, as I have just done. But let me say upfront, there are many, very good, conscientious lawmakers in our local government, our statehouses and among those we send to Washington. My comments are not aimed at them but at those who seek nothing more than a good job for themselves at the expense of us taxpayers.

"I am often reminded of two old West African proverbs, one from Mali which teaches: 'However long a log spends in the river, it can't become a crocodile.' And one from Senegal that advises: 'The one who sells shadows must lower his prices near sundown.' Are these not real-life descriptions of some of our more well-known politicians?

"Furthermore, we also have some employees of our local, state, and federal governments who are bureaucrats but in spite of that do a darn good job, earn their keep, and care about their performance. However, there are runaway numbers of those who could not care less. These are the ones whom I will be addressing with my comments about the bureaucratic system. It is most important that you understand I am not speaking of every employee in general.

"Our first order of business is to make a change that we all can see here in Acirema. If you will look at the screen behind the podium you will see nothing but a word. That word is AMERICA. Our new state will change America's attitude by reversing the trend that is going on in America today.

"Our new state is founded on the good, clean, wholesome, and ethical values of America and forsakes those attributes which are bad and evil. It is based on all the good aspects that still remain, those which are good in America, and we are going to expand on that goodness in our new state, Acirema.

"We are first going to reverse this geographical section of America by reversing the name AMERICA. As you watch the screen our computer will turn the word AMERICA around and you now see ACIREMA. We will begin to reverse AMERICA's trend with this simple name change that we will adopt as the name of our new State. Acirema will be a state of which we all can be proud, a new modern state built on old-fashioned values.

☐   ☐   ☐   ☐   ☐

"PART OF THE major problem across our country today is that bureaucrats hate changes of any nature. We, you and I, elect our officials to our federal government, statehouses, and local positions. They, in turn, either appoint or keep existing bureaucrats who actually run the government. These people are not elected by anyone. They are 'hirees' of those we elect. They are not beholden to anyone nor in any manner accountable to any voter. And we are going to change all of that, at least here in Acirema.

"With your help and commitment we can change the country by starting over right here at home, right here in the center of Acirema, our own back yard. Since it is so difficult to accomplish changes of existing policies and conditions, we had to find a new method, a new means.

"What I envision is our new state starting from scratch, from ground zero. Beginning with our own new rules and regulations based on what is good for us—today—not based on old worn-out antiquated rules, regulations, laws, and ancient philosophies.

"I want Acirema to be a state which will make free enterprise the number one goal of our Department of Commerce. We will get government off the businessman's back and assist him to go into business. When he opens his company, we will be there to assist him with every effort to make it a major success. We will have an incubator for new businesses and welcome those who truly believe in the free-enterprise system of government.

"And let me tell you, I will be most sincere about leasing from our free-enterprise businesses such facilities as schools and state office buildings, heavy equipment, and even school busses. We can recoup the lease cost from business taxes on company profits which will be paid by those seeking to do business in Acirema.

"With your help we can accomplish what I have worked on for the past five years. Just out of curiosity I would like to see a show of hands of those who would like to begin anew. Start all over again with a new area based on exactly the creation of what we, you and I, the people sitting around this breakfast, would like to see accomplished.

"Don't raise your hands unless you are willing to at least listen attentively to the program which I envision for the future of Acirema. Let me have your response."

With the question every hand but one quickly rose, and then all lowered with a loud round of applause which echoed around the otherwise solemn room. Little concern was given to the negative response of the one person who did not voice her approval. Ms. Hazel Chestnut would soon become known as the lone dissident.

"Thank you for your attention and interest. You have already been here for half an hour, so please continue with your breakfast while I make a few more observations.

□　□　□　□　□

"THE PROGRAM I HAVE written, which you will alter and improve, and if we do our job properly, will be the blueprint for other areas across our country to follow. If anyone really cares about his or her living conditions, he will want to study what we will accomplish here in Acirema. Our Platform will be the manual for the rest of our country.

"Everyone who contemplates ever again voting for a candidate for any office should read what we are all about before casting his or her next vote. And if those who seek an elective office care about being successful in their campaigning, they not only should read what we will have written, but also study it carefully. If we are as successful as I know we can be, then our blueprint for improving our lives is a must read for everyone who will be involved in the political process even to the smallest degree.

"You will be given a printout of what I refer to as 'The Ten Questions.' I feel these are the 10 most essential questions that everyone should ask of every candidate seeking any office whether local, state, or national.

"It would be my hope that anyone who ever considers casting another vote for any candidate seeking public office will carry these 10 questions to him or her and demand an answer before deciding to support the candidate.

☐ ☐ ☐ ☐ ☐

"OUR NEW STATE, ACIREMA, is here. We are gathered in almost the exact center. If you take a map and a compass of approximately 110 miles and center it at the intersection of I-10 and I-110, just north of Pensacola proper, and draw a semicircle, you will include those areas east of Panama City, Florida, north into Alabama and west to the Mississippi line.

"This area has within its boundary everything a family and/or business would need to create a perfect, healthy, economic, wholesome community in which to raise our children and to prosper in the business world.

"Acirema will include 10 counties from Florida and nine from Alabama. The area forms with the Apalachicola River on the east and the Mississippi State line on the west, and includes those areas of Alabama for approximately 110 miles north of Pensacola, making our new state wholly in the central time zone. The counties from Alabama will be Baldwin, Butler, Clarke, Conecuh, Covington, Escambia, Mobile, Monroe, and Washington. Those from Florida will be Bay, Calhoun, Escambia, Gulf, Holmes, Jackson, Okaloosa, Santa Rosa, Walton, and Washington. As you see, we have two Escambia and two Washington counties so one of each will have to be renamed. I suggest we rename Escambia County in Alabama and rename Washington County in Florida. This is certainly open for discussion and can be worked out in our committee work.

"The population of each area coming into Acirema will be

approximately 783,624 from Florida and 652,767 from Alabama making a combined total of approximately 1,436,391. Alabama will contribute 10,676 square miles and Florida 8,792 square miles. Our population will dictate that Acirema will become the 37th largest state. In population we will be larger than Maine, Nevada, Hawaii, New Hampshire, Idaho, Rhode Island, Montana, South Dakota, North Dakota, Delaware, District of Columbia, Vermont, Alaska, and Wyoming.

"Our size in square miles places us as the 42nd largest state and larger than Maryland, Vermont, New Hampshire, Massachusetts, New Jersey, Hawaii, Connecticut, Delaware, Rhode Island, and the District of Columbia.

"We have only one basic problem which we will need to overcome, and that is the secession of these 19 counties from their respective states of Florida and Alabama. However, this is all up to the good people who live in these counties. If their desire is to leave their states and join Acirema, then it is a done deal, an issue that you can count on.

"If they are tired and fed up with what's happening in their state we will be the guiding light that makes the change. Someone once said he was sick and tired of being sick and tired. Well, rather than continue trying to change their state, or their existing bureaucracy, we will heal their sicknesses by building our own new state. A state with a downsized government which will be responsive to the needs of the people and only to the fundamental and basic needs, not a hand-out state.

"Our citizens will live in Acirema because they choose to live in Acirema and to abide by the rules and regulations which they had an opinion in creating.

"What is on the books now, in both Florida and Alabama, has been the law for years, and you and I had absolutely nothing to say about the great majority of it. Now, we, you and I, will create a new set of circumstances we can live with, rules and regulations that are established according to our way of thinking.

□ □ □ □ □

"NOW, YOU NEED to hear this. Pay special attention. The primary reason changes do not come about readily is because they always tend to shake someone's personal ideas; someone's ox always gets gored; most elected officials are taking care of themselves with no or little concern for the people. We have found a means to stop this. We set out to create new rules and regulations for Acirema with our Platform, thereby telling the entire state what to expect and then asking the people to either accept our version of the new state or reject it. No more shall the electorate be guided by what is good for only the special interest groups of individuals which affect the lives of every one of us, black or white.

"We want to accomplish something that has failed in other areas of the nation when previously attempted. It won't be easy, but nothing worthwhile ever is. However, it will be most rewarding. You'll stretch yourself forward and in new directions not because it is easy, but because it is hard. We have a marvelous opportunity before us which can truly change our way of life.

"Our governmental design will reduce many positions of the bureaucracy and place the load squarely on the shoulders of elected officials who must be totally responsible to the electorate.

"Obviously, Acirema will have some bureaucrats. However, I can guarantee you they will be limited in number. Those who are retained in their positions will be accountable for a second and sometimes a third tier of work and responsibilities, based on their ability to perform their duties. Their rate of pay will be commensurate with their duties as assigned.

"In Acirema our employees will operate under our new guidelines, rules, and regulations. Although the system will be new, we will offer a large percentage of career service employees, who currently work for Florida or Alabama, positions similar to the ones they presently hold. These employees will be paid in the vicinity of 50 percent more than their current salaries. However, they will be required to shoulder twice their current load. By this means we can eliminate half the positions and raise the remaining salaries by 50 percent for those who can truly perform their duties as outlined in their job descriptions. 'Incentives' is the buzzword here, and we will offer such to those who can perform at the level which will best serve the citizens of Acirema.

"My plan will also combine several cabinet positions and the responsibilities of each. There is no reason to have a state cabinet such as the one in the State of Florida. Their duties could be divided into at least half their numbers and each become much more effective and efficient.

"To better explain the Florida Cabinet would be a look at the past. One of their former governors denounced the entire cabinet by calling them the seven dwarfs. He said their duties were insignificant, and he urged their positions be abolished.

"Once he announced that he could handle his duties as Governor in the morning hours, then go to a department after lunch and easily fulfill any duties or obligations which might need to be addressed. He suggested that he handle the Department of Education on Monday afternoons, the Highway Department on Tuesdays, and so on.

"While his outlandish attitude was a laughing matter, his perception of the situation was quite on target.

"As noted, we will combine some of the duties of the Cabinet. For instance, we will have our Superintendent of Schools also direct the State Lottery Commission. This will assure that Lottery profits support and advance education as its sole purpose as was intended by the legislature when the Lottery was first adopted.

"The Insurance Commissioner will serve as our Director of Insurance, Fire Marshal, and all Emergency Services including the direction of cleanup programs after disasters such as hurricanes. This office will approve all building permits and administer a single construction code throughout the state. Such a code would bring consistency and stability to the building industry, and the enforcement thereof will limit storm damage which in turn will reduce insurance premiums for every policyholder. And I would think privatizing of inspections would be something we would want to look at closely.

"Under the direction of the Insurance Department will also be the Acirema Department of Law Enforcement. It has been proven that insurance fraud has taken a hold on the American public with the result that the cost of insurance has skyrocketed for every policyholder. If we can reduce the fraud, then the premiums for everyone will come down for both personal and business insurance.

"Our Comptroller will operate as the State Treasurer as well as being the Financial Officer and Chairman of the State Board of Investments including Director of Retirement funds.

"Everything we do within Acirema will be accomplished on the basis that all parties win, win, win. What is good for one needs to be good for another, and everything needs to be good for you, the taxpaying citizens of the state.

"When I think of reducing the size of government I am reminded about a story which happened earlier this year concerning the State Treasurer of Texas. Martha Whitehead was appointed to the position by then Governor Ann Richards in 1993 after Treasurer Kay Bailey Hutchison was elected to the United States Senate. When her appointed term was completed, Whitehead ran for the position and promised if she were elected she would totally eliminate the office and save Texans about $20 million annually. She was elected and did exactly what she promised. Now, the duties of that elected position are under the office of the State Comptroller. This is an example of someone elected to a public trust who not only kept her campaign promises but also understood there was no need for the position in the first place. I congratulate and applaud Ms. Whitehead for this most unselfish decision.

□ □ □ □ □

"IT IS NOT OUR intent to create a Utopia where everything is simply wonderful. However, it is our plans to create a new state free of crime where everyone's family can live in safety. And to do this, we are going to have to build it with a new and different kind of politician and attitude.

"We already have all the natural geographical elements within our area. There are no better beaches in the country, or the world for that matter, and we have world-class fishing on the coast and in our beautiful lakes and streams. Our labor forces are very good, and we most assuredly can count on retirees from the various military bases to enforce our requirements.

"I have developed a master plan which redefines where we are going and exactly how we plan to get there from here. Let's talk a minute about our seceding from Florida and Alabama. First of all, this is a major problem to hurdle only if we choose to make it such. The very simplicity of it is, those who reside within the counties that will make up Acirema will vote in a referendum that will establish the fact that a simple majority wants to secede.

"Let me pose a few questions for you, and I'll give you the answers as we move forward.

"Who will fight our plan?

"The remaining counties of each state.

"Why?

"Because they would like our area to remain a part of their state whereby we can continue to fund their tax base and continue to pay the exorbitant cost of their form of operating their gigantic governments.

"Can the secession be done legally?

"Of course it can. As free Americans we can live where we want to live and adopt our own rules and regulations.

"If we choose to change the name or the boundaries of a geographical area, it takes those within the area to support that change. The citizens who pay the taxes have the right to make the choice. For instance, if in say the State of Montana, the citizens wanted to rename the state, they could do so and choose whatever name they wished. The people own the land that makes up a state. The 'State,' as such, owns nothing. Nothing at all.

"Likewise, we in Acirema can secede from Florida and Alabama and adopt our own rules and regulations to perfect a form of life which suits the majority of our citizens.

"Can the Federal Government object?

"Yes, of course it can. It can object to whatever it wants to object to. However, again remember we the people own the land that makes up the state. The federal government can do just about anything it wants to do. We are not a hostile group. We are simply a number of people who want a better life for our children and a better place to conduct our businesses. We do not present the problems the feds had at Ruby Ridge, Waco, or Four Corners. This is not an issue whatsoever. What we want to do is redesign a section of the country to better control our living habits and our way of life, free from crime and corruption.

"And I'll make you a bet that our program will cause a number of other areas around the country to take a long, hard look at what we are doing, and it will start a chain reaction in terms of similar programs. The net result would be either more divisions of existing states, or the elected officials of several states would change their policies to become more in tune with what we advocate. In any case, the result would be most positive and satisfying and, for sure, much better than what presently exists in many states.

"What about state-owned lands, buildings, and improvements by the governments of Florida and Alabama that fall within our Acirema area? What will happen to them?

"Let me answer that with a question. Who owns those facilities?

"We do. The taxpayers.

"And do we, the taxpayers, own other lands, improvements in other areas of Florida and Alabama that will not become a part of Acirema? Sure we do. However, what is owned currently is not owned by the state. It was bought and paid for by those within this region who funded the projects.

"What I am saying is, this is our 'stuff' and does not belong to a fictitious entity which we are referring to as a 'State.' Anyway, if Florida and Alabama do not like what we are going to do, and they want to come get 'their' improvements, so be it. Let them come. They can either come get them or make a deal that we both can accept and live with.

"While we will be relieving Florida and Alabama from some of 'their' assets, we are also relieving them of much of 'their' continuing cost of maintenance and debts on such assets. It is more than a wash; it relates to a trade-off.

"For instance, think of a bridge like the Beach Bridge from Gulf Breeze to Santa Rosa Island. Everyone thinks it is owned by the state because it was built with 'state funds.' Where did these funds come from? This is our bridge. We the people of this area own the bridge. It is not a state asset. We paid the taxes which built the bridge. It is ours.

"If the truth were known, much more of our taxes that are paid into the funds of Florida and Alabama are used on many statewide improvements in all sections of the states, not just our area. And because of this we are being rooked.

"I can assure you, our area, the area that everyone will come to know as Acirema, has not received back a dollar of value for every dollar of taxes paid. All you have to do is look around at the public improvements of roads, bridges, infrastructures in such areas as Birmingham, Montgomery, Miami, Jacksonville, Orlando, Tampa, the Gold Coast. It is not fair, and we are going to start using the taxes generated here in our own region and not send them away to be used in some distant metropolitan areas.

"What is happening to this area is similar to what is happening on the federal level with gas and fuel tax revenues. Florida is a donor state which gets back less than 77 cents for every dollar sent to the federal government from gas taxes collected here in Florida. Florida's gas tax is funding road improvements in other areas of the country which do not enjoy the influx of tourists who spend large sums of dollars on gas and oil.

"From our donor states our taxes are used to subsidize the citizens of several other states. For instance, it has been reported the State of New Mexico receives some $3,000 more per citizen from the federal government than it sends to Washington, Virginia some $2,700 per citizen, and $2,200 for each citizen of Mississippi. People, we have a plan to stop this. We can stop this. We will stop this.

"We are going to involve ourselves with a new system of government whereby we will become independent of the federal government. There is not one reason we in Acirema have to depend on the wasteful, bureaucratic system offered by the United States federal government.

"There are a number of ways to cut the line of dependency to which we have all grown accustomed. There is no reason we should continue to send our hard-earned dollars to Washington to provide jobs for a number of bureaucrats who could not care less about the amount and quality of service that we receive in return.

☐　☐　☐　☐　☐

"RECENTLY, UNITED STATES Senator John McCain of Arizona noted that the federal government, through the Federal Emergency Management Authority (FEMA), was giving away your hard-earned tax dollars to citizens in certain areas based on nothing more than their zip codes. Just think about this for a moment. Isn't that horrible?

"The Senator also noted that FEMA had funded a very expensive athletic scoreboard at Anaheim Stadium. He wondered, tongue-in-cheek, if those who could not read the one which was replaced may have been exposed to some sort of trauma, thereby causing this drastic spending of our dollars to come to their rescue. People, we cannot afford to send Acirema's tax funds to Washington to splurge on such as this.

"While performing before an audience, which included President and Mrs. Clinton, singer Bernadette Peters opened her act with a comment directed toward the President. It went something like this: 'These are the best years of our lives. We may not know it at this moment, but they are. And we thank you, Mr. President.'

"Comments like these scare me. If these are truly the best years of our lives, what are our children going to do? How can they possibly afford to do as we did during our youth? How can they afford a home? Where will they live? How will they maintain safety for their families? I read a report just last week where an economics professor was estimating that a four-year college education 20 years from now will cost the family between $160,000 and $200,000 per child. How is the average family going to be able to fund this enormous cost? People, these things frighten me and they should frighten each of you.

"We are going to do something about these situations. These are the first two steps we are going to take. First is ceasing to pay the federal gas tax, and the second is drafting a working plan that we will present to the federal government as a substitute for all of Acirema's citizens pertaining to the elimination of Social Security taxes on wages.

"While I will not get into the hard numbers this morning, let me ask this question. After you have worked all of your life and are ready to retire, if you had a choice of receiving approximately $700 per month from Social Security, provided the system is not completely bankrupt by the time you retire, or receiving a nest egg of possibly $2.5 million, which would you choose?

"This is not a hard decision. What we have in mind is to become less dependent on the federal bureaucracy and at the same time offer a system which will better take care of our elderly when they need it most. All this baloney about the feds wanting to assure all Americans that they receive an equal share upon retirement is foolishness. Those who can earn more, work harder and perfect a better savings plan should receive more in their retirement years. Isn't this what our country is all about?

"Equality counts for some things but not everything. We will always have with us the weak and those we need to care for, but not at the expense of overburdening some of our taxpayers while others pay nothing toward this problem.

"I know exactly how we can better put our taxes on wages to use for the retirement years. Of course, Big Brother thinks he has to force us to save by sending to him part of our salary, and that is not the answer. We can have rules and regulations which will make it mandatory to deduct funds from wages throughout the working years but not waste the larger percent by using it to pay the salaries of federal bureaucrats. We will invest these funds here at home in a more meaningful way and earn a much greater amount of interest on such investments.

"When we present our program, one of the first things we will hear from the federal government is that it will threaten us if we don't do exactly as it dictates. In the past it has always kept the states at bay by threatening to 'cut off federal funds.' Well, if we don't want and/or need any of its 'federal funds,' then we won't have to concern ourselves with its threats.

"There is so much that we can do, and I am ready to get on with it. Don't you think we can make Acirema so strong along the Gulf Coast that Castro will have to attack the North? I do!

"There is nothing that will halt Acirema from making fantastic headway with our new Department of Commerce. If ever an area had everything necessary to provide a perfect vacation spot for families, we have it.

"While Disney may possess all the wonderful rides and Hollywood-type showcases, they cannot compare with the beautiful natural beaches of Acirema. We can develop this area to be the envy of all with everything anyone could possibly want when speaking of summer water sports, including swimming, sunbathing, fishing, boating, skiing, etc.

"Obviously, both Florida and Alabama will want to keep their prime waterfront. However, it is not theirs to keep or to even think in terms of them making any such decisions. The decision will be made by those who seek to live here in Acirema.

"Now, I would like to take whatever time is required for each of you to stand and tell us your name, your company name, your association in the community, and where you are from. You can be as brief as you like or take as much time as required. Let me first acknowledge Mr. Ralph Walton from the Associated Press. He is the only media person that was invited this morning, but you can rest assured that in meetings to come we will be inundated with reporters.

"Mr. Wright, would you like to be our first member to introduce yourself?"

"Good morning. This has been most interesting, and I appreciate the opportunity to meet with this group. I am Andrew Wright and was associated with Regions Power company for over 23 years. I live in Cantonment, Florida."

"Thank you, Mr. Wright. If each of you will follow suit, let's continue to go around the room."

"I am Bob McGuire, a Baptist minister from Monroeville, Alabama. I appreciate being here this morning and gladly offer my services to begin all future meetings with an opening prayer."

"Thank you for coming Reverend McGuire, and I apologize for failing to call on you before we began our breakfast. It will not happen again, I promise."

"Next please."

"My name is Bryan Berns, and I am the Airport Manager for the Mobile Airport. It is a pleasure to be with you this morning. I am most interested in what you have said thus far and look forward to future meetings. However, while I am interested to learn the complete details, I have personal reservations and questions which need to be addressed. The idea is, at this time, just an idea. A good idea. However, just an idea. Don't forget this. There will have to be a great deal of salesmanship to both the people of Florida and Alabama."

"Thank you for your observations, Mr. Berns. You are right. We have our work cut out for us, and we want to be able to lean on your personal and business experience to help us make this become a reality. A reality we all can be proud of. Next."

"My name is David Hickman, President of Hickman & Hickman Engineering. Our home office is located in Gulf Shores, and we have regional offices in Tallahassee, Montgomery, Atlanta, and Houston. I, too, am pleased to be present."

"I am Hazel Chestnut, President of People on the Move, and we are located in Brewton, Alabama. I would like to hold my comments until all others have been introduced if that's okay with you, Mr. Savage.''

"Surely. Thank you, Ms. Chestnut. Next''

"My name is Hilman Duncan, Sheriff of Covington County, Alabama, with headquarters in Andalusia. This is quite an undertaking. I look forward to more details at the next meeting.''

"Thank you, Sheriff Duncan. Mr. Pyle.''

"I am John Pyle, President of Pyle International. We are shipbuilders and operate our primary facility from Pascagoula, Mississippi. I am most interested in what has been said today, especially with the area of Acirema having good ports in Mobile, Pensacola and Panama City.''

"Good morning, Mr. Savage and all. I am Howard Tufts, and I'm very pleased to have been asked to attend this meeting with such dignitaries. I am staff director for the Alabama Senate Highway Committee and previously served as Secretary of Insurance under the last two Governors of Alabama. I think this program has much appeal and look forward to hearing more about your ideas in detail.''

"Thank you, Mr. Tufts. Next please.''

"I am James Warthon, Admiral, U.S. Navy, Retired. I currently live in Jackson, Alabama. I am most interested in the idea of Acirema especially since it includes the areas of Pensacola Naval Air Station, Whiting Field in the Milton area, Eglin Air Force Base, Hulbert Air Force Base, Tyndall Air Force Base, and several military Outlying Fields, OLF's if you will. I, too, look forward to learning more details.''

"Thank you, Admiral. Our next member is Mr. Cole Williams, President of the University of West Florida. I have spent considerable time with President Williams and know of his interest in the improvement of this area of the country. President Williams.''

"Thank you, Taylor. It also is my pleasure to join with all of you in learning of Acirema. This is a most interesting concept and has much appeal. I look forward to meeting again and hearing more specific details.''

"Thank you for your comments. President Williams, the next person to speak is sitting on your left and is a student at your University. Sir, please stand and tell us about yourself.''

"Good morning, Mr. Savage. My name is Lou Atkins. Thank you for including me with an invitation. I am most excited about the possibility of Acirema. As a student at the University, I am always interested in change. I guess I have not been subjected to the bureaucracy as have many of you, but according to your comments something needs to be done and done quickly. My home is Bonifay, Florida, and I have lived in Pensacola since enrolling at the university three years ago. Thank you again for the invitation.''

"I'm glad you were able to attend, Lou. Okay, who's next. Mr. Houston.''

"Good morning, Taylor, it's good to be with you again. Let me tell you that you have bitten off a mouthful, but I really think well of what I have heard thus far. For those whom I do not know my name is Mark Houston. I am President of Upper Gulf Coast Paving Company and our home office is in Panama City. I look forward to working with all of you and finding out more about the plans for Acirema.''

"Thank you for coming, Mark. Now, a longtime friend of mine, Mr. Martin Parker.''

"It's been good meeting all of you this morning and I've enjoyed your comments. Thanks for including me in your invitation. As I look around the room, I can see that I am the oldest and, therefore, in all probability have seen more changes in my lifetime than many of you. I am amazed at the possibility of Acirema. I look forward to working with this group and want to learn as much as I can about your plans and to do so right away. I am the Chairman of the Board of Parker-Adams Law Firm, and our offices are in Destin, Florida. Thank you again for inviting me to participate.''

"Thank you, Martin. It is good of you to attend our first meeting, and we also look forward to working with you to make Acirema a reality.

"As in any format where changes in government are contemplated, the political atmosphere has to be strongly analyzed. Our positions have to be exactly on target. Our next guest has much experience in the political arena. Peaches.''

"Thank you for those comments and for the invitation to join such an important movement. I look forward to working with this most prestigious group of individuals. As you mentioned in your opening remarks, none of us knew of the reason for this meeting.

I think this is most adventurous and certainly within the realm of possibility. My name is Peaches Lamont, and I operate my business from my hometown of Mobile. I am very interested in working to see this become a reality.''

"Thank you, Peaches. Our next guest is someone who does not need any introduction. As a former Governor of Florida for eight years, he is widely known. Governor Daniels.''

"It's good to be with so many of my friends whom I have known for a number of years. I do appreciate the invitation and feel this will be a great opportunity. While I do not want to dampen the spirits of anyone or the comments which have already been made, I do want to make sure you all know the opposition from both Florida and Alabama will be monumental. The two states will be losing some of their prime real estate, tax base, political contacts, and some very fine citizens. However, with that said, from what I have heard this morning you are on a track that will obviously satisfy the citizens who are fortunate enough to live within the boundary of Acirema, and I look forward to offering what assistance I can. Thank you for your invitation and your kind remarks.''

"Thank you for coming, Governor. Now, let's hear from Mr. Haze.''

"Good morning, Taylor, it's great being with you and these good folks. Your comments have been well taken by me personally and, from the comments I've heard this morning, accepted by the group in general. I am Ray Haze, President of Haze Enterprises, Point Clear, Alabama. Your subject matter is very, very interesting, and I look forward to doing my part to see if we can pull this program together. Thanks for including me.''

"Thank you for your comments, Ray. Next please.''

"My name is Sister Anna Smith. I am the Administrator of the Holy Heavens Catholic Hospital in Mobile. I fully understand the subject matter and think it has a good deal of appeal to at least everyone gathered here today. My first question is, what can I do? Where would I or my Hospital fit into your plans?''

"Thank you, Sister. You will learn in due time what a great role you and your hospital will play. Thank you for coming this morning and please come to the next meeting for many more details.''

"Okay, Mr. Bates, your turn."

"Good morning, Taylor, and good morning to each of you. I am Waddell Bates, President of Bates Brothers, Inc., Crestview, Florida. My brother, Boogie, and that's his nickname, is Vice President of Bates Brothers. I'm glad to share this time with all of you. Mr. Savage, you have really got something here which not only will change this part of the south but also the country in general and obviously every map of America. I feel good about the positive prospects and look forward to working towards its implementation."

"Thank you, Waddell. And now, last but certainly not least, let's hear from Mr. Hartmann."

"Look, you don't know how good it is to be last this morning. I have marveled at the comments made by each of you, and I, too, feel very optimistic about the chances of Acirema becoming a reality. I look forward to working with you. My name is William Hartmann, President of Hartmann, Inc., and we are located right here in Pensacola. You may call on me for any assistance that I may offer."

"Thank you, Mr. Hartmann. I want to announce that our missing person, our twentieth member, Dr. Dalton Bruce, had to cancel this morning. His nurse called our office and explained he had to perform emergency surgery and could not make it but assured us that he would be at the next meeting.

"Today, when we adjourn, you will be issued a preliminary copy of our Platform which gives broad details of major subjects. In the front of each document is a list of committees and committee members with a designated committee chairperson for each. I would like you to take your copy of the document, and I would ask the committee chairs to be in touch with their committee members and meet one day next week to review the Platform. I would like for each chair to be knowledgeable enough on each subject to comment on those subjects assigned to your committee at our next regularly scheduled meeting on February 6th.

"During your first committee meeting, I would like each committee to nominate three additional members from outside, which will increase each committee to seven members. I have a couple of other people that I would like to make known for the purpose.

"Now, that just about does it for this first meeting. I trust you are better informed now than you were a couple of hours ago. I apologize for the clandestine invitation which I sent, but it was done in this manner for two reasons. First, it was imperative the subject matter be guarded until we all could sit down together, and, second, I did not want the media to have your name and start bombarding you with questions before you even had knowledge of the subject.

"I note that Mr. Walton has been busy filling his pad with notes. I would imagine you will be hearing of this meeting about the time you return to your cars and tune in to WCOA. I have not asked Mr. Walton to keep any of your names from the press. Therefore, you may be contacted, and, if so, speak your own mind and answer any questions that you choose to answer.

"Again, thank you all for coming. Rather than open the floor today to questions, of which you must have plenty, let me ask you to attend the next meeting which is scheduled in two weeks. We will again meet in this room, and breakfast will be provided. I have purposely scheduled our meetings to be held on Tuesdays and trust this meets with everyone's approval.

"If you could hold your questions until the second meeting, I feel certain many of them will be answered at the next presentation. When you leave this morning, my special assistant for this project, Miss Laura Rings, will give each of you a business card with a phone number especially designated for this program. If you have any questions that cannot wait until our next meeting, please let Miss Rings know. She will see to it you get your answer.

"That's it. Thank you for coming, and I'll see you in a couple of weeks. Meeting adjourned."

"Wait, please. Mr. Savage, I wanted to address the group. Did you forget?"

"Yes, yes I did. Please forgive me. Ladies and gentlemen, let's have it quiet for a moment. Ms. Chestnut wanted to make a few remarks. Go ahead, Ms. Chestnut. The floor is all yours."

"Thank you, Mr. Savage, and members of the committee. I have sat here throughout your various and sundry comments and have been totally amazed. However, I'm afraid I am amazed and in a totally different frame of mind than are most of you.

"First, I have no idea who may have suggested my name for

this committee. Had I an inkling as to the subject, I would not have wasted my time; rather in all probability, I would have formed a boycott of the building.

"I can't believe that any of you are serious about trying to accomplish the goals outlined by Taylor Savage. What on earth has become of your support for your own home state, the place where many of your mothers and fathers were born? What about your heritage?

"If any of you, any one of you, thinks this can be accomplished without bloodshed, you are sadly mistaken. Understand me and understand me good, the people of this area, especially those in Alabama, will not stand for this. They will not give up their lands without a fight, and I mean a good fight.

"Taylor Savage, you carpetbagger, if you think you can bring your wild ideas to our area and create such dissension as you are planning, you've got another think coming. You're nothing but a rich man playing with the lives of thousands upon thousands of good-hearted souls who may well take your teachings hook, line, and sinker. We will never, never, you hear me, never, allow such as you have described to come into reality. Someone is going to get killed before this is even started good, you mark my word."

With that she stormed out of the room amidst catcalls and boos and the wave of goodbyes of most hands.

"Ladies and gentlemen, I apologize for this distraction. Obviously, she is not in favor of our program, wouldn't you agree? Let's learn from this and let it be a lesson to each of us as this will happen throughout our campaign. Certainly we do not expect everyone to approve of what we will do. Some of those who think otherwise will voice their opinions in different ways, and I assume some will follow the lead of Ms. Chestnut.

"Again, thank you for coming today. This concludes our meeting. See you in two weeks."

LAURA RINGS, THE divorced mother of two charming and highly intelligent high school girls, as of late had been searching for something which would make the world sit up and take notice of her. Laura was a well-educated, beautiful redhead whose husband, general manager of a pharmaceutical company, had decided a couple of years ago to trade her in for a younger model. No one understood his line of reasoning especially since Laura was closer to 30 than 40.

She had yet to forgive him—or, for that matter, forget him—and still carried his torch but lived her life through a number of men just to show him she, too, was still young, attractive, and could have whomever she wanted, no matter the age. And she did—and did often.

She had taken a job in real estate although her alimony and child support payments were most sufficient for her and the girls to live comfortably. The only reason she worked, as everyone knew, was to give herself an opportunity to be in a position to meet the next one in line, and the line was always very long.

She had been attracted to Taylor Savage for some time but only through his reputation since she had not had the opportunity to meet him. Someone had suggested to him that he consider bringing her on board to improve the attitude of the male board members who, from time to time, lost interest in attending committee meetings. She was a real looker, a class act whose elevator actually did go to the top floor.

Taylor was looking for a special assistant for the project and did not want to move someone from Savage Worldwide. He had his office contact her and set up an interview. He was most impressed with her business talents and her desire to mix, mingle, and meet with people.

His reputation was impeccable as was his knack for getting right to the point of the subject matter. He let her know from day one the purpose of her employment was that of special assistant and did not involve anything of a personal nature. She assured him she understood, but Savage, even with all his wisdom, apparently did not notice the twinkle in her eyes.

FOUR

"HELLO, AND WELCOME to the 'Bosch Lemoreaux Program' coming to you from beautiful downtown New Orleans. Today we have some fantastic news developing. This morning, multibillionaire Taylor Savage met with a group of 20 movers and shakers at the Grande Hotel, Pensacola, Florida, and literally shook the eyeteeth of the political establishment throughout Florida and Alabama, not to mention the entire federal establishment.

"In his address to this group, and none knew the reason for the meeting until his announcement, he bombshelled them with news that they had been selected to serve on a committee which would assist him in designing the 51st State of the United States.

"Mr. Savage, President of his family's business, Savage Worldwide, and the only company to own its own aircraft carrier, made known his plans to annex nine counties from Alabama and ten from Florida into a new state which he suggested be named Acirema. He insisted that America needs to reverse its direction and the first step was to reverse the name 'America' into 'Acirema,' thus the name of what may be our fifty-first state. This is a play on words to call attention to the fact America has gone astray with its many factions and policies, and the trend needs to be reversed. I personally agree that something big has to be done.

"The following are some comments made by a few newspapers this morning as the story made front-page news in every major paper across the nation, and all are seeking an interview with Mr. Savage.

''The *Tallahassee Democrat* led with headlines stating, 'Billionaire Wants His Own State. The *Montgomery Advertiser* said, 'Our 51st State Coming Soon.' And the *Birmingham News* announced, 'Alabama May Lose 700,000 People.'

''An article in the *Democrat* by Weston Carey said, 'The idea has much merit, and he expected other regions across the nation to pay special attention and many might follow suit. The article went on to say a new state could be formed if the majority within its proposed boundaries were in favor and voted for such a move in a referendum. The article continued by saying, 'The proposal is unlike a state trying to secede from the Federal Government, but more resembling a large county within a state that wishes to subdivide itself into two separate counties.'

''The story in the *News* spoke in tones of losing almost 700,000 people from Alabama. With the success of Acirema this would be true as well as a similar number from Florida. Quite possibly, the net result of this development not only might create a new state, but also have a lasting effect on all the other 50 states to get themselves in a better position to face the future before a similar thing occurs within their boundaries.

''The proposal of Taylor Savage caught everyone off guard. In his opening remarks, he indicated this had been in the planning stages for five years, and he had the groundwork completed and ready to move forward.

''The Governor of Florida, Brandon Woods, said in his prepared statement this morning this was a most unusual concept. However, he conceded that a portion of a state could secede should the majority of the region in question feel motivated to do so, and he agreed with the legality of a referendum to set in motion the actions necessary for the establishment of the new fifty-first state.

''These are just a few comments, and I personally believe that his concept may very well have some merit. Mr. Savage is to be on the Laurie Sin' Show this evening where it is expected he will communicate other information.

''We are going to take your calls on this most ingenious plan which is certainly a new and unique means of accomplishing some major goals of which many are interested.

"Now, let's take the first call from Howard in Montgomery, Alabama. Thanks for calling, go ahead, Howard."

"It appears to me that Mr. Savage wants to take away the prime lands of our state, and I'm not sure we want him to have them. But, on the other hand, if those who reside in the proposed area of what may become Acirema vote to annex and join up, there is little anyone else outside the region can do about it, nor should they want to do anything about it.

"You know some states started to leave the Union during the Civil War and they were permitted to do so, or maybe not permitted as much as they were not stopped from doing so. Good luck to Taylor Savage, and that's my comment."

"Thanks for your call, Howard. I'm going to reserve my personal comments, and as you surely imagine, I do have some, until we have a chance to hear from a few more callers. Here is Miss Hudson from Milton, Florida."

"Thanks for taking my call, Bosch. I am a first-time caller, and it's a privilege to speak with you and be on your show."

"Thank you for calling."

"I think Mr. Savage is the only person that I've heard of who is willing to take the bull by the horns and do something positive. I look forward to hearing more of his detailed plans. It makes little difference to me if I get my mail addressed to Milton, Florida or Milton, Acirema. However, it does make a lot of difference to me if there is a way through which my family and I can better our lives. If such a way is available and possible, I'm all for it. Let's face it, what we are now doing is not working. It's not right, and I personally am ready for a change. Crime is forever on the rise so much so that I'm afraid to even leave the safety of my own home, and sometimes I don't even feel safe even when I'm inside it."

"We now go to Miami with Sam on the line. What's on your mind today?"

"I don't know what all the disturbance is about. Let them have that hick part of north Florida and all of Alabama as far as I am concerned. Those are the most backward people that I have ever seen. They ain't nothing but a bunch of rednecks, and now this Savage guy comes along and wants to deliver them. Reminds me of Moses. Let them follow him. They'll learn their lesson, and when they do, let's not dare take them back in.''

''And Sam you're in Miami, right?''

''Yea. That's right,'' he responded.

''Well, what about all of the foreigners down where you live. How you feel about that?'' Bosch inquired.

''Hell, they need to go to. Maybe Savage wants to come down here and take a few thousand loads up there with him. That'll suit me just fine.''

''I'd say it looks like you have your mind made up. Thanks for calling, Sam. Our next call is from Marcus in Mobile, Alabama. Go ahead, Marcus.''

''It's time someone did something with some vision. I think what Mr. Savage is presenting is just amazing, and I hope the bureaucrats and legislators of Florida and Alabama don't start in lambasting him like they do with all other issues that have merit. The bureaucrats and politicians have had their turn for a couple of hundred years, so move over and let someone do something who has a view of what is needed for the future of every one of us. Thank you.''

''Well, thus far most callers have been positive and support Taylor Savage's program. This was sprung on Florida and Alabama very suddenly this morning, but obviously most have made their minds up with little more than the small amount of information available. I wonder if this acceptance falls into the category of 'Anything is better than what we now have?'

''When you start telling people you can become more effective and efficient with their taxes and actually show them a proof-positive way to do so, you are onto something and singing on the same page with the citizens.

''When you completely eliminate the political way these two states have operated for hundreds of years and offer a new and specially designed substitute, then the people are sure to follow you. This is what Taylor Savage apparently has done, and apparently he is going to be successful.

''What amazes me is Acirema will be starting over from scratch with a totally new, complete, and comprehensive agenda, and the Platform can be either approved or rejected after those of the 19 counties have had the opportunity to decide their own fate.

Let's take another call. This one is from Jim Harris in Biloxi, Mississippi. Go ahead, Jim, and thanks for calling.''

"I can't think of any good reason why Mr. Savage would stop at the Alabama-Mississippi state line. My goodness, let's talk about taking in a few more miles of the Mississippi Gulf Coast. We too would like to have an opportunity to restart our lives, and this sounds like a fantastic idea and offers us a means to do so.

"And if the Mississippi Gulf Coast could be included, why not get rid of those gambling boats at the same time. In fact, the State of Florida should rid itself of those harmful one-armed bandits before the criminal element becomes involved in the state as has happened in Louisiana and most likely will happen here in Mississippi. Gambling boats represent everything that is bad for the country, and they should be eliminated as quickly as possible.

"So I say to Taylor Savage, I wish you all the luck in the world, and please don't leave Mississippi out of the planning."

"Well, Mr. Savage, you've got others to contend with outside of Alabama and Florida. I wonder what you're going to do about them? What is real interesting is that we have a non-politician in Taylor Savage who apparently wants nothing but to change directions of the current political atmosphere in these two state governments. This is a sobering thought, and I believe the citizens will pay careful attention to his comments and quite possibly flock to this new idea which was created outside the normal realm of standard political activities.

"I've been advised by staff that Taylor Savage is on the line. Good morning, Mr. Savage."

"Hello, Bosch, thanks for taking my call. I hope that I am not intruding on your other callers."

"Listen, you are the man of the hour and maybe the man of the century. Everyone in the country is talking about what you have suggested. It appears you have really shaken the eyeteeth of the establishment with your Acirema program. Where did you get such an idea, and do you really think that you can pull it off?"

"The idea has been cooking in my mind for several years, and I feel reasonably sure we can pull it off. Bosch, the people of this nation are crying for leadership and a change in direction. For someone to come along without a personal political agenda, such as myself, I certainly feel that we can be successful in our endeavors and be of great assistance to approximately 1.4 million people who reside within the 19 counties that will become Acirema."

"If you are successful with your plans, will this have an effect on the rest of the country?" asked Bosch.

"Surely it will cause a change, if nothing more than changing the face of every map that is printed in the future. Bosch, there is so much that needs changing and not just in the area we will call Acirema. There are major changes that need to be made in our federal legislation, and we are hoping that our leadership in a small section of the country will give our elected officials in the Congress the intestinal fortitude to break away from their traditional ways and step up for the people.

"Bosch, can you believe our nation has as high unemployment as we have, although granted there are many who would not work if you handed them a job. Yet the Congress continues to allow foreigners into our country to work at a lower cost per hour wage rate which creates even more unemployment for Americans.

"We have many on welfare who should have never been on the rolls in the first place. At least the President has now signed a reform bill that is intended to take a good percentage of them off the welfare rolls and force them to find employment. However, our brilliant government sends millions of our jobs to Mexico and other foreign lands, reducing the possibilities of actually changing our welfare conditions here at home.

"And can you believe that we have a class of foreigners in this country, and get this, a large group of them who are not even American citizens, yet they collect welfare. Isn't that incredible? Our taxpayers are paying welfare for some foreigners who live here, live off of our land, are not even American citizens, and we foot the bill for their upkeep.

"And still other classifications are those who work in our country for 11 months each year, go back to their home country for a single month, then return to this country to work here for another 11 months. Because of this, they are not liable for paying taxes. None at all.

"These are some things that we, as a new state, may not be able to do anything about because these are federal issues. However, you can count on our new United States Senators and Congressmen working on a solution to these types of problems and to do so every day while they are in Washington in the halls of Congress. The Congress will definitely hear from our members. After all, it's our money that is being spent to pay these enormous, exorbitant, and completely un-American expenses.

"Sometimes it's hard to comprehend the reasons why our elected officials do the things they do. I think for the most part members of the Congress are listening to a group of eggheaded, pinko, round-mouthed, baldheaded, flip-flop wearing, liberal advisors—who, by the way, are being paid by us, the taxpayers—who advocate and advise the Congressional membership on an agenda which is directly opposite of what we believe. And our Congressional delegation is giving little attention to their constituents who offer a more commonsense approach and who sent them to Washington in the first place to voice the opinions of the folks back home.

"So often our members of Congress feel they have to go along with the majority leadership and vote as they are told, often forgetting their constituents who sent them to Washington in the first place to represent the views of their constituents. They placate the leadership of the Congress so they can advance to a more powerful position and then be in a better role to make even more drastic decisions which totally reflect ideas that are adamantly opposed by their back-home supporters.

"And they have the nerve to forsake those who sent them there to do a job which is supposed to reflect the positions of those back home. Sure, they come home and talk to the people and make promises. Then they return to Washington and vote in accordance with the dictates of the leadership of their party in exchange for a promise of a better leadership role in the party at some future date. What really makes it sickening is our elected Senators and Representatives understand just exactly what the folks back home want and need. Still, they deliberately continue to vote their own personal desires and that of their party leadership and not the wishes of their constituents.

"Bosch, I got off the subject a bit and started talking of Washington's problems. However, we are going to change our little corner of the world at the local level in our new state by sending to Washington Senators and Representatives who will vote the desires and wishes of those who elected them to do a special job for the citizens of Acirema.''

"Well, I really like what you are saying, but before we part, tell me about the dissident who apparently was one of your committee members.''

"That was an unfortunate situation. I do not want to dignify it other than to say there will be those who do not favor what we are all about. There are going to be those who feel their homeland, their mother land if you will, is going to be taken from them. We have our work cut out to make sure they understand our program. To make sure they are educated about what we will do for them, each and every one of them.

"Other than that, let's just say we had someone who had been recommended to us and who, after learning what our agenda was all about, disagreed with the concept. I'd just as soon leave it right there.''

"I have no problem with that. Listen, Taylor when can you come on our show for an hour?'' asked Bosch.

"I prefer to do it after our next full committee meeting and wait until after the Florida Cabinet and the Alabama Cabinet sit down together and discuss whatever they feel they must discuss. I have also heard they are going to Washington to speak with the President, or at least his people, about the issue. Let's wait until these things have passed.''

"And when do you think these will take place?''

"Oh, you can bet they are on the front burners, and I know our opponents are working day and night to counter what we expect to accomplish. I think it would be safe to schedule an hour on your show for February the 23rd. Does that suit you?''

"Let's see, that's on a Friday. Friday is our open forum day, but let's do it. Friday, February 23rd. You're on! And Taylor, I really look forward to that hour. You have a most interesting concept. I'll have my people talking with your people and set it up. And many thanks for calling.''

FIVE

"GOOD EVENING, THIS is Laurie Sin' Live. Welcome to the show. Tonight we have as our only guest Mr. Taylor Savage who yesterday morning in Pensacola, Florida, made known his plans to entice the southern portion of the State of Alabama and the northwest portion of the State of Florida to secede from their respective states and form our Fifty-first State, which Mr. Savage suggests be known as ACIREMA.

"Good evening, Mr. Savage, and welcome to Laurie Sin' Live."

"Good evening, Laurie, and thanks for inviting me. It's a real pleasure being with you."

"Obviously there is much to cover, and I really don't know where to start. What in the world did you do down South yesterday morning to stir up such a fuss? Do I understand that you want to form a new state, our 51st. Is that correct?"

"Laurie, I want to answer that question. However, let me make this as the first comment on your program. Don't ever let anyone tell you the mess we currently have across this great country of ours cannot be corrected. It can be. All we need is a group of elected officials, and mind you I did not say politicians, but a group of citizens who want to make a change in the direction that we have been headed for way too long.

"Now, back to your question of what we did yesterday morning. You are absolutely correct with your comment. I want to build a new state and want Acirema to be the most modern state in the Union and base its success on old-fashioned values. A state that is crime-free and developed around a new atmosphere from

48

present-day politics, a state which will not continue with the old worn-out, antiquated means of doing political business as usual. A state that will commence its Statehood with a downsized form of government. A government that is responsive to the needs of the people and only those needs which they cannot meet or do for themselves.

"We are dedicated to reducing or eliminating as much government from our lives as possible to the extent government is only big enough to offer assistance when citizens are in dire need. Like someone once said, we have substituted the image of the American Eagle with that of a mother hen. We seek to change directions within Acirema, and for the first time we are going to get government off our back. And I am dedicated to making Acirema the most conservative, politically speaking, state of our Union. Laurie, we are going to do that. This I promise you."

"It appears to me, Mr. Savage, that you have bitten off a mouthful."

"Maybe from first glance it might well appear that way. However, you can be assured that I have done my homework. What I propose has a large base of support from the attendees of our first meeting yesterday in Pensacola, and I am most certain of its practicality and benefits for all concerned."

"What caused you to design such a concept?"

"Well, Laurie, I have an engineering degree from MIT and a law degree from Harvard. I guess this, coupled with my military flight training and my pure love for that area of the country, brought many factors together that led me to make a decision to put together something that I personally could be proud of. At the same time would be quite beneficial to a couple of million citizens who will live in Acirema as well as the several million who will visit the area each year."

"What is the purpose?"

"The main purpose, the primary purpose, is to create a crime-free atmosphere where good people can live safely and raise their families and conduct their business without fear of having to be armed everywhere they go. We are going to build Acirema based on using a common-sense approach to government, heavy on the free enterprise system and strong on local home rule. And built around the concept that bigger is not always better. We are going to have a streamlined government, one which is manageable.''

"Are you describing a police state? Is this what Acirema will become?"

"Absolutely not. Why should you even suggest that? I resent the fact that you even made such a comment about the remotest possibility that anyone would think in terms that we may be referred to as a police state when we simply want to enact rules and regulations to protect our citizens."

"Please accept my apology. I did not mean it to sound apparently like you took it. So you think you can create such a place as you have described?"

"Laurie, with the help of those gathered with me for breakfast yesterday morning, and with the will of the people who will reside in Acirema, I know that we can accomplish the task before us."

"Are you interested in being the first Governor or maybe a United States Senator?"

"In my opening remarks over breakfast, I told those gathered that I had only one interest and that is to see Acirema develop and the area prosper. I have not one inkling of interest for public office, either elected or appointed. I do think it a worthy cause for those who choose to fill elective roles. However, it simply is not my cup of tea."

"So you are saying tonight that you will not be involved in a political sense. Is that what you are saying?"

"Let me make myself perfectly clear on this. I will most definitely be involved in a political nature inasmuch as I will do everything possible to ensure that our elected officials are the very best available to fill the positions of authority. But again, I personally will not be a candidate for any office, either elected or appointed.

"And since we are on the election questions, let me tell you about one of the tenets of our political structure which is the complete elimination of the word 'elect.' This word will not appear on any campaign material, including print, radio, or television. We will substitute the word 'hire' in place of 'elect.' After all, we are 'hiring' these people to operate an office for the general public. They are our employees and work for us. Therefore, they are 'hired' to do a job. If they do the job correctly, we will consider renewing their contract for another term. It's that simple.''

''And where will the funds come from to get this venture off the ground?''

''I plan to have the Savage Foundation foot the initial bill to get us to the point of creating our statewide Platform and the mailing out of petition ballots to all citizens so they can voice their opinions and decisions about leaving their respective States of Florida and Alabama and becoming a part of Acirema. After we are successful in that endeavor, then we will structure a financial contribution format to raise the funds to take us through to Statehood.''

''Who are the members of your committee? Can we obtain a list?''

''Certainly, you can have a list. I should have brought one with me, but rather than try to mention each member by name and occupation and chance leaving someone out, I had just as soon wait until tomorrow and fax you a list. By the way, a complete list was on the AP machine last evening and in most papers this morning.''

''Who appointed the membership?''

''I did. But it wasn't an appointment as much as it was a selection process.''

''You selected all 20 members?''

''Yes.''

''And did you know all of them before making the selections?''

''No, I did not know them all. Some I was quite familiar with, some I knew by reputation, and others were suggested by a professional service.''

''Will you or the committee be grooming someone on the committee for political offices such as the governorship, the U.S. Senate or other offices? And will the members of the committee be permitted to run for public office inasmuch as they had a hand in creating the Platform?''

''Of course they will be permitted to run for office. Why shouldn't they? And no, the committee will not endorse any one candidate for office over another. Individual members of the committee most likely will endorse candidates in every race. However, this will not be a combined or unified effort of the committee as such.''

"And will you endorse individuals in some races?"

"Sure. I have done this for years now, and I see no reason to cease. I want the very best candidates available to run the State of Acirema, and to that end I am most dedicated."

"And what would you imagine would happen if say two or more members of the committee sought the governorship of this new state?"

"What I would imagine would be that one would win and the others would lose."

"You know that is not what I am asking. Would you choose between one of those running? And, if so, wouldn't that have an effect on the committee as a whole? Wouldn't that weaken the togetherness of the committee in continuing its efforts?"

"Laurie, I can support whomever I choose just like every other member of our society. And to speak of weakening the committee is moot because by the time we are down to qualifying for the first elections the committee will have finished its job and disbanded."

"Okay. What will it take to make Acirema become a reality?"

"It will take a lot of hard work and much cooperation from both Alabama and Florida. Although their governments will fight us, and we expect a good fight, there is no way they can win. Law provides if people in an area wish to disassociate themselves from their respective state, so be it. Although it is not written into law as I have stated, and for obvious reasons, but the Constitution will prove that I am correct. By the way, a couple of our committee members who will have a great deal to do with the development of Acirema are Florida's former Governor, Prescott Daniels, and my longtime personal friend and well-known attorney on constitutional law, Mr. Martin Parker, Chairman of the Board of the Parker-Adams Law Firm of Destin, Florida.

"Do you think Florida and Alabama are going to make a formal objection?"

"Certainly I do. Wouldn't you?"

"Well, if I were Governor Woods of Florida or Governor Foxworth of Alabama or a member of their Legislature, I surely would form a steadfast, hard-line objection. Can they deter you? Can they stop you from doing what you have in mind?"

"No. While there will be those who raise objections, the decision will be made by the citizens who reside in the 19 counties that will make up Acirema. There are 10 counties in Florida and nine in Alabama. You see, we are not going to ask Florida and Alabama for their permission. This is not necessary. We don't have to. We are simply going to draw a new boundary around a certain area and form a new state government.

"Obviously, we are not hostile people such as was encountered in Waco or Ruby Ridge. Nor are we comparable to the uprising of the Branch Davidian group or the recent actions by those who called themselves the Republic of Texas. We simply want to work out our problems and remain a state within the Union and support the kind of lifestyle we believe in. Over the years Americans have thought in terms of seceding from the Union. Texas has a past history of such actions, and we have the group who wished to set up the state of Westsylvania during the Whiskey Rebellion. There have been many groups throughout the United States who sought independence from the Union. We are one, and we will succeed.

"Laurie, let me say at this point, I want to be careful not to go too far with details tonight as I feel committed to bring these points to our next committee meeting, and it would be most unfair if our membership had to learn of intricate details second hand. Please understand."

"I understand. Okay, give me a couple of reasons why the citizens who reside in the 19 counties that may make up Acirema would want to consider accepting your plan."

"Sure. Let me give you just one reason, the primary one that will affect every citizen in Acirema. Let's say you live in another state. Pick one. It does not matter. Let's say Michigan. You could have been born there or moved there in recent years; neither makes a difference in this example. What is important is the laws, rules and regulations in Michigan pertain to every one of its citizens. For the most part hardly anyone living today had anything to say about them. Sure you elect your Senators and Representatives in your State House, but you have little say-so about the legislation that shapes your state. That's not the way it is supposed to be, but that is the way it is.

"I want to make this point very clear, so listen carefully. You do elect your Legislators and surely you can lobby for change. However, if anyone has gone through this experience, it's like pulling hens' teeth; in final decisions the Legislators are, by and large, going to do what they want to do. And their decisions are often made because of tremendous pressures applied by the imbedded bureaucrats and arm-twisting efforts by effective and popular lobbyists.

"My point is simple. You have little or no say in old, worn-out, antiquated laws that affect you. In Acirema it will be absolutely opposite. Let me tell you how it will happen.

"We, our committee, will expand and improve on the Platform which I have already written, and it will be the blueprint for Acirema starting with the first day. All new rules, regulations and laws. Certainly, we cannot detail every decision because changes will have to occur as our new state grows. However, each citizen will know the basics of what we propose from day one. With this information and knowledge in hand, studied and digested, we will call for the referendum vote.

"If the majority of the citizens don't like our State Platform, and don't get this confused with a candidate's platform, if they don't like our State Platform, on referendum day they have the opportunity to vote against Acirema becoming the 51st State. On the other hand, if they like what they see and hear about the Platform, then they will vote for it. It is my personal commitment to make sure the people have all the facts, and that is my intent. I personally feel we will be successful.

"There is no way a state, any state, can perfect the changes that I envision with the political structure that now exists. In every direction the politicos would fight every issue because each issue would have an effect on some political group. No one wants to lose, and no one wants to give up his or her position in the political hierarchy. It just could not happen with the system as we now know it.

"What we have to do is accomplish our goals based on a program as designed. Start all over from scratch and design a system before any group with significant political pressure has an opportunity to get its grasp on the controls. This is our plan, and this is what we are going to do."

"Tonight, can you offer a couple of examples of some changes that will take place, changes that you are going to propose for Acirema?"

"I can, and I will. However, keep in mind that as I said earlier

I do not want to disclose too much at the present time until our committee hears my plan firsthand. But let me give you a couple or three ideas.

"First, welfare will be limited to two years, maximum. After then you either find a job, or you stop collecting. Period. Surely, we will have those who are sick, weak, and/or old, and we must take care of them. We will not be paying people, of any color, to have babies and collect welfare.

"Second, we will use corporal punishment in our schools for infractions. But those who create major infractions, such as bringing a weapon into the school, will be expelled immediately and not allowed back into the school system, ever. We are going to run our school programs with good, reasonable, common sense. That's all, just plain common sense.

"We plan to have a number of charter schools. These schools will create not only a fantastic opportunity of competition between the students for better grades, but also competition among the groups of individuals who chartered each school. Every two years recertification will be required, and those most competitive will survive the process.

"Let's face it, there have been a large number of well-meaning individuals and groups of individuals who are very much concerned about the education of our children. These folks have put in countless hours trying to find a solution, and nothing seems to be working. We have got to find the answer, and the answer does not lie within the realm of doing all the things that we have been doing for years on end.

"We must find new and effective means to accomplish the education of those in the classroom who come there to learn and improve themselves. To make themselves ready for the era that is not somewhere off in the distant future but is here now, today. We are not at a crossroad where we can afford to choose one direction or another and continue to make efforts but fail in those efforts. We must succeed.

"It is my belief that we have to turn away from old antiquated methods by moving our education system beyond the monopoly of what we now know as school systems operated by the state and federal governments. We must break that monopoly. The wave of the future is to do so with private, chartered schools. Schools which are not depressed by the Federal Department of Education. This is the only reasonable and sensible means of accomplishing our goals of better educating our children. And, by the way, I also think the Federal Department of Education should be completely eliminated.

"In Acirema we intend to educate our children and to do so in an atmosphere where they can study and learn without disruptive students in their classrooms. In keeping with law and order in our schools, we plan to offer one classroom in every school to either the city, county, or state governments to use to conduct their training sessions for their future law enforcement officers. This will do two things. It will generate, perhaps, 30 officers on each campus at all times and will also free up floor space that was previously dedicated to classrooms at the local Police Stations, Sheriff's Departments, or the State Law Enforcement Bureau whereby this space can better be used for the purpose intended, the business of stopping crime, which should be their only objective.

"Laurie, our entire process is based on common sense. Nothing more, just plain common sense.

"Let me give you a third idea. Now, I fully understand these comments are somewhat strange to those who may be listening to your show, but I urge each of your viewers to hear me out. We are going to cut corners in every respect, and we have designed a variety of means to do that. Take an example of a single piece of equipment that is used in the construction industry. This machine hardly is noticed by anyone and gets little attention or interest, but let me show you what I am talking about as it relates to what we are going to do in Acirema. Would you have any idea what a front-end loader is?"

"Yes, it's one of those machines that loads sand and stuff like that."

"You are right. There are a variety of manufacturers; Caterpillar is one of the major ones. There are also a variety of models with each having a different price range. For this example, let's use the cost of $75,000 each. Now, Laurie, can you even start to imagine our elected politicians even thinking in terms of talking about a front-end loader and the associated cost. This simple example will magnify just exactly what we are going to accomplish within Acirema. We are going to get down to the nuts and bolts of every cost item.

"Within the boundaries of Acirema I count no less than 50 cities which are large enough to require the use of repair and maintenance equipment. Most would have at least one front-end loader. There are 19 County Road Departments and 19 school boards within Acirema.

"Additionally, you have Universities, Colleges, Junior Colleges, Bridge Authorities, Authorities such as the Santa Rosa Island Authority, Water Management Districts, Housing Authorities, etc. I think you see what I'm speaking of. It would not be hard to find in excess of 100 front-end loaders within the total of all of these entities. For this example, let's use 100 loaders at the price of $75,000 each. That's a total cost of $7,500,000 to the taxpayers of these nineteen counties that will soon become Acirema.

"Let me carry this a bit farther. It would not be difficult tonight for me to find 300 dump trucks, 500 pickups, and 200 automobiles being paid for by these same taxpayers. Add these figures up with a commonly accepted cost and you have $31 million. Laurie, that's $31 million in this 19-county area. And guess what? I would bet you each piece of equipment that I have detailed is used less than 25 percent of the time. Most of the time it is in an equipment yard just in case it is needed. What a waste.

"What we will do in Acirema is make use of the high-tech computers that we all have come to love. We will sell half the equipment and take that $15,500,000 and invest it somewhere. With as little as 5% interest it will earn us $65,000 each month. To the legislators of such big states, such as Florida and Alabama, this is chicken feed. At least these two states spend taxpayers' money as if it were chicken feed.

"We have a plan to save countless millions for the citizens of Acirema. You realize it matters not whether the savings is at the city, county, or state level. Each cost is paid by the taxpayers, and if we can find a means to reduce the cost of government, everyone wins.

"Getting back to our computers, we will use them to schedule and shift equipment around from place to place where it is required and make the maximum use of every piece, everyday. It really matters not who owns the equipment. It could be the state, county, or city. However, we all will be better off when the savings start to take place. We will purchase a number of lowboy tractors and trailers to supplement those already owned by some of the cities and counties and shift the equipment around where it is needed. Again, common sense.

"All you really need is employees who are motivated to work hard for their salaries and to have the interest of the taxpaying citizens foremost in their minds at all times. I know just how to motivate these types of individuals, and we will show you the entire program as we progress.

"You have no idea what little cooperation is currently being shared between the state, counties, and cities. It is called a lack of communication, and it would literally make you sick. Laurie, those were just three examples of what we are going to do in Acirema.

"And while we are on the subject of lack of communication just last week there was a story in the news about the military and the cost and availability of equipment and supplies, etc. It seems as though the Army in the earlier part of the year was in bad need of a certain caliber of ammunition and were without knowledge of the fact the Marines had an oversupply of the same item. This did not come to light until after an annual audit by the Auditor General; then the facts became known. The news story reported the Auditor General made a comment pertaining to this specific item, and he laid the blame directly on the lack of communication between these two agencies. This is often the fact and in this day and time with all the computers and high-tech equipment, it is a shame something like this is occurring—and probably many more times annually than any of us would like to believe."

"Well, you indeed seem to have some interesting facts. Let's move on to another subject. What about the political structure of Acirema?" asked Laurie.

"Again, I don't want to discuss much detail, but let me give your viewers something to think about. A maximum of only two months' politicking for any office, statewide or local. A unicameral legislature. Election day will be on April 16th, the day after tax day. Get the idea?"

"Now, that's interesting, especially tax day elections. Why this?"

"In my opinion that is the very best choice of days. The voters will be tuned in to their true feelings about the cost of government, and what better time would there be than to ask them if they are willing to extend the contract for their hired employees for another term or replace them with a different choice.

"Laurie, our committee can make these rules, regulations, laws, and guidelines right now and present them to our citizens for their consideration. Florida and Alabama, or any other state for that matter, cannot make corrections like this because each change would have a drastic, direct, and personal effect on their current officeholders. Therefore, those who are already on the public payroll would not permit such rules to pass or changes to be made because it would affect them personally.

"On the other hand, we do not have any officeholders to fight us about what we are creating, which is good, solid, and meaningful legislation that is good for every one of our citizens. We do not have to be concerned with whether or not it is good for current officeholders. We are free to create our rules and regulations for the benefit of our citizens without pressures from anyone. Other state governments simply do not have this opportunity."

"You may have something there. Taylor, I keep getting this eerie feeling while sitting here talking with you, listening to your ideas and watching your positive mannerisms, I keep seeing another Ross Perot. Do you think in terms of conducting yourself along those lines, and has anyone else asked you about any resemblance?"

"Laurie, the only resemblance is that we are both very fortunate to have financial means to accomplish dreams. I don't see myself with the same ego as Ross. However, I'm not sure that some of his ego wasn't developed in order for him to seek the Presidency, if you know what I mean.

"Like I have already made very clear, I have no desire whatsoever to become involved with the political process as a candidate for any office. However, like Ross, I do have some ideas and dreams that I want to accomplish, and I will conduct myself in the manner to accomplish those goals."

"Okay, let's continue. Have you given any thought as to where you think the capital of Acirema will be?"

"Yes, Pensacola. And we are going to build our capitol on the campus of the University of West Florida."

"Why Pensacola?"

"Because it is completely central, and I designed the concept of Acirema around the most central point of the state. The founding fathers of Florida did a horrible thing by developing the City of Tallahassee as their capital. It is located in northwest Florida where only 15 percent of the state's population reside. Over the years there has been much conversation about relocating it to a more central area, perhaps near Orlando. However, we all know that is not going to happen. In Acirema we simply will not make a mistake like Florida did. Even Alabama has a much more centralized location in Montgomery.

"Laurie, unlike what happened in Florida, where they chose a location for the capital and then built the state, we are going to do it all at the same time and do it in Pensacola, the most central spot.

"And by the way, I bet you didn't know that Pensacola was the very first city in our country, did you?"

"I've always heard that honor belongs to St. Augustine. Am I wrong?" she asked.

"Well, yes and no. Pensacola was first founded in 1559 by Ponce de Leon, but devastated by a hurricane shortly thereafter. It was not until 1565 when Spain commissioned Pedro Menendez de Aviles to come to Florida where he settled the first permanent city which is now known as St. Augustine.

"Obviously, Pensacola, and Florida in general, is the cradle of American history. Pensacola has existed under five flags: Spanish, French, British, American, and Confederate. In 1821 after transfer of flags and sovereignty, General Andrew Jackson set up the Florida Government with Pensacola as the capital. Just 40 years later, in January 1861, Florida seceded from the Union. So you see, we will not be the first to secede. Anyway, it's been a long time since Pensacola was the capital of a state, and I think its time has come once again.

"It's strange but Pensacola, even with its extraordinary historical past, is often overlooked as the magnificent city it has become. In recent years it has received more than its share of horrible, unwarranted press. The great majority of negative stories have centered around abortion clinic bombings or the murder of those who have chosen to assist with abortions. On the other hand, the area has produced many great athletes in every sport, but it seems the reporting of these positive stories are hard to come by.

"And quite often that area of northwest Florida is even left off the map, as often as not by state agencies that have faulted in this respect. The business community across that part of Florida can and will attest to the fact that most of the area has been treated as a red-headed stepchild. We plan to change that.

"Some of Florida's closest knit families, the cream of the crop, the salt of the earth, reside in that area, an area I am proud to say that has not been overpopulated by foreigners or misfits.

"The area has a long and proud history of families of early settlers who remain convinced that Pensacola is still the first settlement in the New World regardless of the claims coming from St. Augustine that challenge those facts. In short, this area of 19 counties will at long last obtain its just rewards and show the entire nation its capabilities as soon as we reach Statehood," preached Savage.

"Well said, but let me change the subject a bit. While doing research for your appearance on this show, I certainly did not want to forget to ask you about the *USS Lexington*. So the audience will know what I am speaking about, the Lady Lex, known often as the Gray Ghost, was decommissioned last year by the United States Navy, and the Savage company purchased it. Now, my question to you is, what are you going to do with it since you are the only person on earth who owns his own aircraft carrier?"

"That is true. Savage Worldwide does own an aircraft carrier. When I earned my wings in Pensacola, I landed many times aboard the LEX. When it came available, I thought it would be a good investment and therefore the acquisition."

"Now, answer my question. What are you going to do with it?" she insisted.

"It is our plan to completely renovate it with well-appointed staterooms and magnificent restaurants. We will be a cruise liner which will offer something that no other liner can claim, and that is the opportunity to fly on deck in a jet aircraft, spend whatever number of days you have reservations, and leave in the same manner. Obviously, you can come and go by using our helicopters as well."

"And when will the LEX be delivered to you?" She inquired.

"While it has already been decommissioned, it will not be turned over to us until late December this year."

"How will you actually take possession? Where will you put it, and how many men will you employ to bring it to wherever you will home port it?"

"The contract calls for the Navy to deliver it to us. We have a contract which states the delivery date can be delayed up to an additional six months if we desire. However, we expect to take delivery in late December this year."

"Ultimately, where will it be delivered, and where will it be ported?" she continued.

"Well, stop and think for a moment. Both Pensacola and Mobile have great ports. Pascagoula has a shipbuilding and renovation facility. There could be other opportunities for a port within the area of Acirema such as Panama City. Why don't we wait a few months to answer that question."

"Okay, let's move on. Your company is heavy in television stations, radio stations, newspapers, theaters, shopping centers and probably several other sources of ownership. Will Savage Worldwide be developing within Acirema?"

"I certainly hope so. We plan to, and I hope that everyone hearing my voice tonight plans to look into what we are going to do and bring his or her business to Acirema. Just because I have written the master plan for this movement does not mean that I will not be an investor. We invite everyone to come on in. The water is going to be just fine.

"In fact, Laurie, I hope to make a major announcement of an investment which our company will make in Acirema during the next Acirema committee meeting. Stay tuned. I think that you will like it."

SIX

SINCE THE INITIAL announcement, every national news program, all major papers and news magazines, and every radio talk show focused its primary interest on Acirema and its architect, Taylor Savage.

From all accounts the preliminary acceptance was overwhelmingly favorable with an approval rating of more than 82 percent in every poll conducted by ABC and the *Washington Post*. Savage had realized from the beginning the tremendous potential of the project as he assembled all the component parts but was most pleased to hear of the polling results and the program's outstanding acceptance. However, there was little doubt the positives in the poll would slip as the liberal press began to give coverage to the handfull of dissidents.

The State Cabinets in Florida and Alabama each had called a special meeting with Acirema as its sole agenda item. Governor Woods of Florida had even suggested a joint cabinet meeting between the two states, something that had never been done before. Each state thought this to be a good idea but wanted to wait until after Savage's next general assembly meeting which was scheduled for February 6th. They agreed on a joint meeting date of Thursday, February 15th, and flipped a coin with Alabama winning, so the meeting would be held in Montgomery.

☐ ☐ ☐ ☐ ☐

LAURA RINGS HAD her hands full with scheduling Savage's appearances on the network television shows as well as radio talk forums. During the few days since the first announcement, he had

63

already given personal, one-on-one, interviews to six major papers in Florida, three in Alabama and also the *Washington Post*, *New York Times* and, of course, all 18 papers which were owned by Savage Worldwide operating under the trade name of "The Savage Group."

After 10 days on the news circuit, he was ready for some leisure time. The agenda for the second meeting was almost ready. While his staff labored to complete the finishing touches, he flew to Goldsboro to pick up Sheery Goss, his longtime companion who lived on Amelia Island but was visiting her parents in North Carolina, and off they went to northern California.

They were en route to attend the winter performance of the Navy's precision flying team, the Blue Angels. The Blues spent the winter months in California while retaining their permanent home in Pensacola.

After a fast-paced weekend, they returned Sunday evening to his home in Raleigh where Sheery made herself comfortable while he made an appearance as a guest on a local television show that highlighted area businessmen and women who had made a difference in the Carolinas with the development of special social programs. Midday on Monday they boarded the Gulfstream V for a flight to Pensacola with a stopover in Atlanta where he huddled with some company executives at the Atlanta Airport Business Center to discuss Savage Worldwide operations, not Acirema business. Sheery stayed in Atlanta, checked into the Hyatt Regency, and met the next morning with the new owners of Santa Anne Condos, Amelia Island, Florida, the same group she had worked for at Clearmont in Gulf Shores, Alabama.

Sheery and her partner, Darlene, had just celebrated the third year of their new business, a home and commercial decorating service which they had named "Ess-Dees." She had pleased the owner of Clearmont with her ideas and schemes and was working towards tying down the contract for "Santa Anne" as well as a contract for four other condos he would be constructing during the year.

Savage arrived in Pensacola just past 6:00 in the evening and went directly to one of his favorite restaurants on the upper Gulf Coast, Skopelos, where he was to meet with the editorial board of the *Pensacola News Journal*. They had been trying to arrange a meeting since the first announcement, but this was the first opportunity he could fit them into his chaotic schedule. He dined with the six members in a private room where they all could relax and talk of his plans for Acirema.

After dinner he was driven to his spacious home on the bayside of Pensacola Beach where Voncile, his housekeeper, and his two blue-eyed Siberian Husky dogs, Hot and Toddy, welcomed him home. Voncile and her husband, Kory, lived in a guest house next door. She took care of his home and often prepared his favorite dishes while Kory served as handyman, runner, and sometime driver.

Normally, his first order of business when returning home was to walk the two Huskies along the pristine white beaches of Santa Rosa Sound, but tonight the bitter cold January weather forced their camaraderie to be contained on the roomy redwood, cedar deck overlooking the Sound and facing the south shores of Gulf Breeze just across the bay. While Hot and Toddy would have thoroughly enjoyed frolicking in the cold, it was way too rough for Savage to endure.

□ □ □ □ □

TUESDAY MORNING CAME early, and Savage was up, ready to face the day, and most excited about this morning's second General Assembly meeting. When he arrived at the Pensacola Grand Hotel, the media had already clamored around the front entrance with each spouting a variety of questions while a small band of sign-carrying objectors had assembled, and their handmade signs made it very difficult to access the building.

Hotel security had already alerted the city police, and two officers were on the scene with more on the way. With the arrival of flashing patrol cars, the nonconformists slowly moved away from the front door and let Savage and his staff pass.

Savage, well aware of the dangers of short sound bites, quickly announced he would have no comment but invited each to come into the committee meeting after the private breakfast and assured them that no business would be conducted until the doors had been opened to the media and the public in general. He also welcomed those who were in opposition to the movement but assured them they would be removed if they acted in any manner which would delay the purpose of the meeting.

□   □   □   □   □

WITH BREAKFAST OUT of the way, Laura Rings opened the double doors while hotel personnel swung open the folding wall partitions which separated the middle dining area from two other large rooms on either side. With this open invitation, the media rushed in to establish an upfront advantage from their competitors. Cameras and video equipment were quickly assembled and set up. None of the reporters even took time to notice the committee had provided coffee and breakfast finger foods on a rear table. The band of dissidents, perhaps eight to ten, quickly positioned themselves between the podium and the tables.

Savage stood and gently opened the meeting. "Thank you all for attending this morning. Today, we have a full assembly meeting, everyone is present, and for this I am most appreciative.

"I would ask you folks who seem to have an objection to our position to move towards the rear of the room so I can speak directly to those of our committee."

Apparently they had elected Hazel Chestnut as their spokesperson, and she dug in quite hard. "Mr. Savage, you need to realize that we are not going to allow you to take the position which you seem determined to take. We are here to protest this movement, and protest we shall."

"Ms. Chestnut, I have no problem with your wanting to make your point. In fact, you have already made your point. Now I would ask you to please either retreat to the rear of the room or leave the building so our committee can conduct its business."

"Mr. Savage, apparently you do not understand what a protest is all about. We are going to be right here. Right here in your face, and that's the way it's going to be."

"No, Ms. Chestnut, that's not the way it's going to be. Now, if I have to summon the law to have you forcibly removed, I will do exactly that. You are welcome to remain as a member of the public and observe this meeting if you like. However, if you persist in disrupting our meeting, you will be removed. Is that clear?"

"Then you will just have to remove us because we are here to stay,'' she lectured.

"Ladies and gentlemen, let's take a short break, and we'll get this cleared up, once and for all."

Savage left the room, and in less than two minutes there were a dozen or more uniformed city policemen who took each agitator from the conference room; all were led directly into the back of a waiting paddy wagon and swiftly off to city jail.

Returning to the podium he continued, "Now, perhaps we can continue with our meeting in peace and quiet. You should expect some protest at each meeting. However, we plan to deal with them as they occur. Please do not be alarmed.

"The past two weeks have been filled with much media exposure which you have witnessed, and I am sure tonight's news will feature what we just went through. Some of you have been approached by various media and have been exposed to exactly what will now and forevermore be just the beginning. So you may as well get used to it.

"I tried very hard to prevent saying anything on the media circuit over the past two weeks that would give world exposure to our program without first bringing it to your attention. I want to apologize to each of you if anything was revealed that you may have heard for the first time. I thought I could protect exposing new thoughts while talking with the media. However, I am sure that I erred a few times, and for sure it was not intentional. It is my intent to discuss with you every aspect of Acirema either prior to it being revealed in the media or to do so at least at the same time with the media present.

"As you can see this morning, we have with us what appears to be a representative of every major news organization world-wide. We welcome them, and our only personal request is that they treat this meeting, and all future meetings, with honest reporting. As long as our comments are reported as intended, we will enjoy cooperating with the media 100 percent. So I say to the media, everyone, we welcome you.

"Now that the membership of the Acirema Committee is known, each of you will be continually bombarded by media questions. Be on the alert and careful, because what you say as sound bites is often misquoted and ill-used. Someone once said if you always tell the truth, then you don't have to worry about remembering what you said. If each of us will accept this as our guideline, then our mission will surely be accomplished.

"Two weeks ago, I briefly outlined the program of Acirema. Today, I would like to get into some basic details but certainly do not intend to cover them all. We will get into more minute details with our committee reports.

"Let me plant a thought in your mind. There will be numerous people who will challenge us. We do not ever want to be tagged as a committee that adheres to what I refer to as the 'Three Bad C's' which are Criticize, Condemn, and Complain.

"We do not intend to be a committee that will just find fault in government without offering a solution. This is why each of you is here. You, individually and collectively, have every ability and a vast world of experience, everything which may be required to find solutions to any problem that may hinder Acirema from becoming a truly great state. So please accept my challenge to find not only an answer to the problems we may face, but strive to always find the correct and best answers to these problems.

□ □ □ □ □

"AGAIN, IN OUR FIRST meeting I touched on general ideas pertaining to the formation of Acirema. This morning let me offer some thoughts whereby you can start to adjust and alter the basic concept and outline of the Platform when attending your various committees. My comments today will not try to detail all the subjects that we will address, but are offered to give you some basic ideas. Ideas to start your brains in motion whereby you can begin to understand the enormous potential of what we plan to do. We have a fantastic opportunity, and we will succeed.

"What I have proposed sounds like a gigantic undertaking, and it's not as simple as I seem to be making it out to be. However, we, the people in this room, will lead the way, but those who live within the boundaries of Acirema hold the reins and have complete control over our success or our failure. The final vote at referendum will send us down one path or the other.

"This morning we will set some of our goal dates. There is no reason we could not have our Platform printed and ready to mail by April 23rd. If this is accomplished, then we could count on mailing the Referendum Petitions to all voters on Independence

Day, July 4th.

"The Petition forms, the election ballots of the referendum, will be due back in our headquarters on August 5th. After verification of victory we would set the dates to commence statewide campaigning for 60 days beginning September 26th, and our first election date will be November 26th. And that's right, you heard me right, only 60 days of campaigning. This is ample time for any candidate to get his or her message across to all voters and continue to be bound by the Platform designed by this committee.

"What I want to do this morning is outline the basic format of several subject matters and then let your committees fine-tune each. Now, let me give you the outline of the Platform pertaining to the election of the Governor of Acirema. The details of this subject will be addressed in a separate committee which I will chair. This committee will be composed of the five chairs of the five standing committees.

"The Platform provides for a Unicameral Legislature, one body. There will be a total of 29 members. There is simply no reason to have a larger number as this would only increase the cost of government. Each of the 19 counties will have at least one member. The larger counties will have more as determined by their population. Mobile County will have five as will Escambia County, Florida. By the way, as mentioned previously, we very soon are going to have to deal with the renaming of two counties as we have two Escambia and two Washington counties, one each in Florida and Alabama.

"Each two years one-third of the Legislature stands for election. Each major party, and we could care less how many parties are involved as long as they follow our guidelines of party establishment, will nominate an individual to represent its party for the Office of Governor. This is not unlike what the parties are doing today in both states. All parties will conduct their own in-house procedure to determine their nominee. Each party must have its nominee selected the day before the first day of the 60-day political cycle commences.

"The electorate does not actually vote on a person for Governor. The party with the majority number of members elected to the Legislature wins the Governorship, and their nominee is inaugurated. With this process there will be little, if any, dissension within the ranks of the Legislature and absolutely no gridlock. If the balance of power shifts with any election of the Legislature, the controlling party's nominee becomes the new Governor.

"The party controls who its nominee will be. Therefore, it is possible a Governor's term could be for only two years based on the will of the party or due to the voters who may seek a change based on the performance of the current Governor's administration coupled with the performance of his party's dominance of the political issues during his or her term. The Platform provides that no Governor shall serve more than six consecutive years.

"While some may question the reasoning for our system based on, in their opinion, the fact that it is not good for the Legislative Branch and the Executive Branch to be of the same party, I completely disagree with that argument.

"Think in terms of what we often have in many of our existing states, and most of the time at the federal level of government. After elections we often have a Chief Executive diametrically opposed to the makeup of the Legislature and everything that branch of government is trying to accomplish. The result is a standoff, a complete and total gridlock of the government and possibly even a shutdown of government as we recently witnessed twice at the federal level.

"For those who would argue that what we propose is not a good system, I would simply answer the charge by saying our system will allow two years of harmonious political activity between the Governor's Office and the Legislature, and if the people wish to make a change they can do so every two-year cycle. To me this is much better than to have a complete breakdown, shutdown, gridlocked government for the term of at least four years and possibly eight.

"And while we cannot demand it, we, this committee, will ask the first elected Governor, and those who follow him or her in office, to bring on board a variety of individuals who more resemble the population makeup of Acirema. All too often, an incoming Governor brings into his administration too many Ivy League, know-it-all, yuppie-type individuals who simply do not fit in with our way of life. We need folks in the Governor's office who have had to meet a payroll and who understand what we, the people, are all about.

"There are several unique planks in our election Platform. For instance, our system will afford an opportunity to every voter to cast either a positive or negative vote in every election for every office. Contrary to past elections where voters did not want to vote for anyone running in a particular race, they will now actually have an opportunity to vote against someone whom they think would do a horrible job and, therefore, reduce the positive votes which that candidate may have picked up from others. This will give a much better, more qualified selection of those who are standing for election.

"Our approach in this regard will greatly increase the number of voters who actually go to the poles to vote. In many of our national elections the turnout is 30 to 40 percent at best. An old friend of my father, Scott Kelly of Lakeland, ran for Governor of Florida twice in the '60s. He always contended that while folks might like to see you elected, they often would pass up the opportunity to vote. However, if they opposed you, they would turn out in droves and go to the polls in the middle of a hurricane just to vote against you. Using this scenario, we will turn out the vote and select better candidates at that.

"How often have you been unable to decide between two candidates and not wanting to vote for either, but finally did cast a vote for one of them simply because there was no one else in the race that you really preferred. Well, we are solving this situation with the possibility of a negative vote

"And every candidate who seeks any office in Acirema will file, at the time they qualify, a complete personal résumé.

"In Acirema the word 'elect' will become taboo and will not be used in any political campaign advertising. Where the word 'elect' was used in the past, it will now be substituted with the word 'hire.'

"Later this morning I will speak of 'The Ten Questions.' These are questions that I feel should be asked by every potential voter of every candidate who seeks any office, local, state, or federal. We will address the Ten Questions in a few minutes.

"I would like now to open the floor to questions which we will take at the end of each subject matter we address. I'm afraid that we will waste quite a bit of time by taking a large number of questions at every break, so why don't we first take any questions from our committee members and then limit each subject matter to maybe three questions from the media. It is not my intent to limit questions from the media, so please understand that I will be available after the meeting today to answer any questions that we do not get around to during this period. Now, are there any questions from the committee?''

"Yes. I have one," said Peaches Lamont. "Being in the political management business, I am concerned about giving statewide candidates only two months for politicking. Do you really think this is sufficient?''

"Peaches, first let me ask each of you committee members to state your name when you ask a question. I think by the end of today the media will know and recognize each of you, but for this morning's session please announce your name. I know they are very anxious to learn more about each of you. So ladies and gentlemen for your information you just heard from Peaches Lamont.

"Now, to your question. I certainly feel the 60 days is sufficient. If everyone is in the same boat then no one has an advantage over the other. I would anticipate a candidate preparing television scripts, radio commercials or print materials beginning anytime he or she wishes. However, I want to restrict any form of advertising taking place prior to 60 days before any election date. I fully realize just how much the general public dislikes seeing commercial after commercial for several months during a long and drawn-out political season.''

"I have a question. I am John Pyle of Pascagoula, Mississippi. You did not mention a campaign cap on spending. Do you envision a cap?''

"I'm glad you asked that, John. Yes, this is most important and thanks for reminding me to hit the high points.

"We will have election reform, but it will be known in Acirema as 'Hiring Reform.'

"For any statewide race, no candidate shall be permitted to collect and/or spend more than one dollar per total number of residents of our state. Presently, that would be about $1.4 million. This will be a total cap including both primaries, if necessary, as well as the general election. There will be a cap of $100 per contribution from individuals, companies, and corporations, as well as PACs.

"The United States Congress often talks in terms of campaign reform and campaign finance reform. However, have you listened to their comments? Every time they speak of the subject, somewhere in their speech is the thought, 'We need an overhaul to campaign funding, and much is needed to be done pertaining thereto.' Yet, if you listen closely and read between the lines, you know they are not interested. These same elected individuals who get on the stump and tell you how bad we need reform are the exact same folks who could legislate it into law if they really had a desire to do so. To me it is a sorry situation when those who are sent to the Congress think so little about their constituents to make such a comment that totally insults the mentality of the voters back home.

"To say they want reform when they, themselves, are the only ones who can vote it into law is talking out of both sides of their mouths. It's like your wife saying she wants to bake you a cake but your daughter's mother won't let her. The Congress will remind you that the United States Supreme Court will not permit restrictions on how much a candidate for office can collect and/or spend, and the Court states in its opinion this is a hindrance to one's freedom of speech. What we really need to reform is the United States Supreme Court. Maybe we can tackle that next.

"In America we have about 270 million people. Historically, about 900,000 each year give more than $250 each to a variety of candidates. Now, do you think it fair that one person out of every 300 should have that much control of the issues which govern all our 270 million lives?

"And by the way, we are going to restrict those who choose to give to candidates who are running for statewide offices here in Acirema. If you are not a registered voter within the state, then you cannot contribute to any candidate. We do not need to have out-of-state influences coming into Acirema with high-powered dollars to try to change the clean atmosphere that we are working so hard to accomplish. This rule is very simple and easy to implement. If you do not live here in Acirema, you are restricted from contributing financially to any campaign.

"It seems to me when one-third of one percent of the people

control the lives of the remaining 99.67 percent that would be what constitutes the restriction of freedom of speech of the entire nation's population. But there goes the Court again, protecting the minority element with little or no regard concerning the majority population of the remainder of the country.

"If the Court feels our restriction on capital funding is an act against our freedom of speech, then we in Acirema will support only those candidates for public office who volunteer to abide by the planks of our Platform relative to campaign finance reform.

"Any more questions from the committee? If not, then we will hear from the media. Yes, sir. You in the blue coat, red tie."

"Mr. Savage, I would like to know about the *USS Lexington* that you discussed on the Laurie Sin' Show some 10 days ago."

"Sir, I have no problem answering that. However, I would like to try to stick with the subject matter while we are concentrating on the election process. Could your question wait for a few minutes?"

"Certainly, then will you tell me about the Lieutenant Governor position. Is there going to be a Lieutenant Governor within Acirema?"

"Thanks for your question. In most states who have Lieutenant Governors, their role is primarily ceremonial, similar to the Vice-President at the federal level. It is my suggestion that we do not have a Lieutenant Governor and the President of the Legislature shall serve in the line of succession should that become necessary.

"Again, I want us to think in terms of creating a smaller government and cutting out all the fat at every level. To have a Lieutenant Governor would mean another staff, a private secretary, another vehicle, another person on the payroll, retirement funds and pensions for him or her as well as the staff. It just goes on and on. We are committed to work for the people in this endeavor, and we do not want to start overloading our budget with such nonsense."

"May I inquire," said a nice-looking, well-dressed man who appeared to be a local television anchor. "As I understand it, it is your position to print your Platform, mail it out to the potential voters in all 19 counties, and at a later date mail them a petition for their signature. Is this the ballot you have been discussing? Or will there actually be an election with the voters casting a vote either for or against Statehood for Acirema?''

"It is our intent to educate all the voters within the 19 counties as to the Platform we are writing. This Platform will be mailed to each voter. We later will mail each a petition to sign which is, in fact, their vote. The petitions will be counted by the local Supervisors of Election in each county and the totals made known which will verify the results. If we get 50 percent plus one more vote then Acirema is on its way to Statehood. Does that answer your question?''

"Yes, Sir.''

SEVEN

"OKAY, WHY DON'T WE tackle something easy this time, say the Platform position on prisons and the death penalty. As in every plank of our Platform, I have written my general opinion of the subject matter and this assembly can build on my ideas.

"Let me begin by giving you some startling statistics. Every prison in the country exceeds its capacity by about 40 percent. It is said today there is one prisoner on the inside for every 167 free men and women on the outside. That's a lot.

"A very clear example that will give you a better idea would be to examine any college campus with a good-sized football stadium. Think of yourself sitting in the stands with 80,000 other fans. Based on this ratio of 1:167, for the number of fans in the stands there are another 480 inmates in prison. Think about this for a moment. That is an astronomical number, and it's growing daily.

"We have another problem that is fast approaching which will have a horrendous effect on every one of us. If you think the prisons are overcrowded today, just wait a couple of years from now and see what happens. The President has signed the welfare bill, and I want to make sure the entire country understands that I support it totally; this is a good beginning to make those who are too sorry and lazy get off their asses and try to find work. But let me give you a warning: somebody had better start looking into this situation and do so quickly. It's a huge problem that is approaching like a freight train out of the night.

"When the magic date comes around when thousands are eliminated from the welfare rolls, this is not automatically going to make them more ambitious. They will not necessarily start looking for a job. What is going to happen is, it will create a tremendous amount of crime. Where thousands of welfare recipients have been somewhat content, thus far, to sit back and let us pay taxes to feed and house them, when their welfare is eliminated they are going to be in deep doodoo. There are going to be more break-ins, more robberies, more crimes of every description. These people are not going to let those who have accomplished something in their lifetime continue with their way of life when they, the former welfare recipients, go hungry or without. They are simply going to take what they need and worry about the consequences later.

"It is sickening to pick up a Sunday paper from Atlanta, New York, San Francisco, Birmingham, or any number of other cities and open to the classified sections and find thousands upon thousands of jobs that are available with few or no takers. This is frightening.

"I got a little bit off the track from the subject of prison and the death penalty issues and involved you with comments pertaining to welfare. However, a good deal of the time they go hand in hand.

"Let's go back and discuss gain time for prisoners. This is simply wrong. Look at the message which is being sent. It says to the prisoners they have committed a crime, were found guilty by a jury of their peers, and sentenced accordingly. Yet if they behave a little bit, they do not have to pay the penalty in full for the crime that was committed. Generally speaking, gain time is an evaluation of time given to a prisoner of 20 days off their sentence for each 30 days they have no disciplinary action against them.

"In my opinion that kind of thinking is way too late. Don't you think criminals should pay for their crimes in total? I do. Our liberal judicial system has created this problem, and our soon-to-be former Legislators have passed laws thus approving. Does it make any sense to sentence someone for a crime and then tell that convict he only has to serve 50 to 60 percent of the sentence? I think not.

"Prisons are built supposedly to assure that inmates are punished. The victim or victim's family does not think it so wise to let the offenders out early. Why doesn't someone listen to the victims? Victims did not get a percentage off from the crime that was committed against them. They received the maximum of the crime, the full brunt, no discount, no reduction, no percentage off!

"Here in Acirema we have to build whatever number of facilities that are going to be necessary to house such criminals and keep them off our streets and away from our children and families. Across our nation many innovative County Sheriffs have gone to great lengths to erect tents to house several classifications of prisoners. These tents are most uncomfortable—as they should be. No television, no air conditioning, no heat, etc. A large percent of our inmates not only could be, but should be, incarcerated in this manner. Sheriff Duncan, maybe you can comment on this within our committee assignments," stated Savage and then continued. "The major portion of our Platform of Acirema is built around the idea of safety for our families. In order to provide that safety, we have designed many programs that are reduced in cost so that more funds will be available to build what is necessary to accommodate our needs and to house as many prisoners as is required. Whatever it costs, we shall and must be willing to pay.

"It will be our position to adopt the 'one trial, one appeal' concept. Period. One. That's all. We will not continue to pay, as Florida and Alabama do, for long-term incarceration of prisoners on death row. They are there to be executed, not to be housed year after year.

"They have been found guilty and sentenced, and that's it. Our Acirema government will function around one of the planks of our Platform which is to carry out the death penalty in a swift and effective manner. If a criminal in Acirema commits a capital crime, he or she must be willing to forfeit his or her own life and to do so at an early date.

"Let me tell you about an agency that functions in Florida. It is called the Capital Collateral Representative. This is an agency funded by taxpayer dollars to the tune of approximately $5 million annually, and also receives matching federal funds, all of which comes right out of your and my pockets in the form of taxes.

"The sole purpose of the agency is to bottleneck the criminal justice system and to do everything in its power to prevent the execution of inmates who have been given the death sentence by a jury of their peers. Again, this is its sole purpose, nothing more. And I have often wondered just how Florida Senators and Representatives have the audacity to stand before their constituents back home while knowing their votes were helping fund this liberal group of attorneys when it is a known fact that more than 78 percent of the population supports the death penalty.

"This is absolutely unrealistic to me. Wouldn't you think the members of the Legislature should adopt a common sense approach and vote the will of the people who elected them and sent them to Tallahassee? And this includes not only the capital punishment issue but all other criminal justice issues as well.

"Their Legislature has provided taxpayer funds in excess of $25 million to CCR over the past 10 years with the present-day level of funding at approximately $5 million annually. This is not a Democratic or Republican issue, nor is it a black or white issue, but an issue which needs to be seriously addressed by the Legislature for the benefit of every citizen in Florida.

The taxpayers of Florida, every year, pay the expense of their judicial system to convict hardened criminals who have committed capital crimes such as rape or have taken the lives of our mothers, fathers, sisters, brothers, or our children. And the Legislature continues to use our tax dollars to keep these society misfits alive and prevent the very judicial system which convicted them with a jury of their peers from administering punishment as prescribed by our laws.

"It is time we Americans get back to some of the old-fashioned values that our parents and grandparents accepted as everyday ways and means of conducting their lives. Let me tell you a story which details a perfect example of how things were back then, back when criminals were actually punished for the crimes they committed on society. This is a shining illustration of how we have let our criminal justice system get out of hand.

"In November 1932 Franklin Delano Roosevelt was elected President of the United States. After a long, grueling campaign, the President-elect took a much-needed vacation. Upon returning to Miami from a cruise, he had a couple of hours to spare before he was to board a train back to New York and decided to greet a group of supporters with a short speech at the Bayfront Parkway. This was on February 15, 1933, some 64 years ago.

"The Mayor of Chicago, Anton Cermak, had also been vacationing in the Miami area and wanted to speak with the President-elect, so he was advised to meet Mr. Roosevelt at the park. After a short speech of only 143 words, Mayor Cermak came to Roosevelt's side. At that moment, a small man of only five feet and 105 pounds took an $8 pistol from his pocket and opened fire. Several were hit; the President was not; Mayor Cermak was.

"The would-be assassin, Giuseppe Zangara, an illiterate, unemployed New Jersey mill hand who had been in Florida seeking work, was immediately arrested. He was arraigned before Judge Collins the next day, February 16th, on attempted murder charges. Mayor Cermak died on March 6th. The charge was changed to murder, a trial was held, and the transcript was sent to Florida Governor Sholtz on March 11th. The Governor signed Zangara's death warrant and set his execution for the week of March 20th. Sheriff Hardie took him from the Dade County Jail to Raiford State Prison on the same day the Governor signed his warrant. Zangara was executed for the murder of Mayor Cermak on March 20th. The time which elapsed between the shooting and the execution of the murderer was only 33 days, and just 14 days after the Mayor died. This is what I speak of as 'old-fashioned values.'

"Today, murder is still murder as it was on February 15, 1933, and crime is still crime as it was on that date. The death penalty was in effect at that time as it is today.

"What happened on February 15, 1933 was a pure and simple act of murder and the State of Florida exercised its privilege of justified punishment in accordance with the laws of the state. Today, our liberal judges and justices of our courts have painted us, the law-abiding citizens of this nation, into a corner and wrapped us tightly with comments such as 'criminal rights.'

"Now, if you want to believe as I do that those who have committed major criminal acts should forfeit their rights, all of their rights, then we can change the system throughout America. I believe that it would make a great deal of difference if a person who goes into a convenience store or into someone's home, office, or business and knew if he committed a murder that within 33 days he himself would sit in 'Old Sparky' and forfeit his own life. I know for sure he would have second thoughts before committing the crime.

"There remain among us a few skeptical individuals, and I may add they are in the minority, who continue to voice their opinion that capital punishment is not a deterrent to crime. Regardless, and with assurance, the criminals who have embraced 'Old Sparky' would offer a countermeasure to this point of view.

"Recently, a professor, an antideath penalty activist and chairman of the University of Florida's sociology department, issued a statement and report proclaiming his study indicated the death penalty was not a deterrent. He further pointed out the cost of an average execution in Florida was approximately $3.2 million and compared this to the average cost of lifetime incarceration, approximately $600,000.

"The quoting of cost is a typical liberal statement designed to make us taxpayers convince ourselves that we should choose the lesser cost of punishment. However, the reality of the situation is that the cost of executions is high simply because the liberal activists continue, time and again, to hold up procedures of capital punishment with unwarranted stays, which is the culprit that drives the cost to extreme levels.

"For a moment, let's take the professor at his word, assuming the cost of an execution here in Florida is as high as he says it is. If the liberal judges of the courts of this state were shaken up, the public made more aware of what is going on, and the longevity of death row inmates could be reduced by half of their present duration, then I figure the state of Florida could save you taxpayers approximately $587 million.

"What the public does not understand is there are 461 circuit judges in Florida. This is the trial level court which hears capital criminal cases. In last November's election about half of them were up for reelection, 228 to be exact. Do you know how many went unopposed? All but one. There were 227 circuit judges who did not have any opposition. Why? Because lawyers are afraid to challenge them knowing if they do and lose the election, they will have to practice before a judge who was once their political opponent. That is a sick situation. By the way, the one judge to have a challenger lost the seat.

"What I am saying is judges think they are there for a lifetime and can hand down any liberal opinion they wish and cannot be removed from office. In Acirema we will change this lifetime expectancy and in so doing have a much more balanced system of justice.

"I promise you the comments and beliefs of all liberal activists, such as this professor and liberal judges, further instills in the minds of criminals the attitude which all liberals champion. If they had their way, capital punishment would cease in its entirety, and this would prove to be the biggest mistake of all. Our society would experience a wave of criminal activities unlike anything we have ever known.

"It is true that only one person is guaranteed never again to commit a heinous crime after sitting in 'Old Sparky.' That within itself is satisfying. However, the real deterrent does not come with the actual execution but with the swiftness in which our society administers the penalty. I can assure you if we were to return to swift and final justice, as it was administered to Zangara for the murder of Mayor Cermak, this would surely do more to eliminate and deter capital crimes than anything else our politicians could possibly dream of or adopt through the legislative process.

"You see, it's not a question of deciding if capital punishment is a deterrent or not; this may be debated for years on end. But it is a question of responsibility by those who formulate our laws, our Legislators, to assure themselves that swift and final punishment is the true answer as a deterrent. In Florida the criminals and misfits of our society think little of the consequences of their acts because they have been given a battery of legal minds, funded by you taxpayers, who are protecting them at every turn, thus the CCR.

"A short scenario goes like this. The criminal commits the crime, is found guilty by a jury of his or her peers, is sentenced to be executed, and then comes the bottleneck. The bottleneck in Florida is twofold. First is the CCR and its overly zealous liberal executive director. And second is liberal judges.

"It is not hard to comprehend that if the Governor of any state has the authority to execute a criminal, he certainly has the authority to remove or alter the attitude of a state employee such as the director of the CCR. If the Governor would remove this cog in the system—and it is my belief that he could find the legal means to do so if he so desired—the system would then flow in accordance with the original intent.

"When the CCR was first formed in either '85 or '86 at the urging of Florida's Attorney General, it was for a good, reasonable, and responsible purpose. We all believe it necessary for those on death row to have legal and proper representation which was the purpose, pure and simple, for the origination of the CCR. That within itself was a good idea, but now it has truly gotten out of hand and totally defeats the original intent.

"The criminal, through this group of liberal, extremist representatives, has been assured and fully understands that if he is caught and convicted of a capital crime, the worst thing that could happen is a few years behind bars with three full meals per day, a place to sleep, color television, recreation room, library, medical and dental care, no taxes to pay, no rent to pay, no payments for child support, no alimony payments. Get the idea?

"When the warden at Raiford State Prison asked Giuseppe Zangara if he would like to speak a last word, he simply answered, 'Pusha da button.' I say to each of you and to every American, if we exercised more persistence and expediency in pushing 'da button,' we would have a hell of a lot less criminals walking the streets of this nation, and our homes and businesses would be much safer places.

"During the early '60s, someone once remarked that the race to the moon and the exploration of space was no longer a race between Americans and Russians. It was simply Germans on each side playing rocket ship. Somehow, this comparison seems fitting since we have a large contingent of attorneys on either side of the death penalty issue, and, as usual, the taxpaying public is picking up the cost of both sides.

"No one is against legal representation for those on death row. However, what is so objectionable is the undue delay of the sentences set forth by a jury of their peers. Taxpayers are sick and tired of learning of delays because defense attorneys have convinced the courts that their client was underprivileged during his or her early childhood days. Sometimes even arguing the reason for the criminal activities came about because no one ever bothered to take them to a McDonalds, or they never had a color television, or some other nonsense such as this.

"There seems to be no end to the countless number of excuses that causes execution delays, and many of our liberal courts are eager and more than pleased to bargain for time for these killers. It is time we get on with executions, the due punishment as prescribed by the laws of our state.

"As we begin to 'hire' our judges, let's do it right from the get-go. Let's hire only those who want to control crime based on our way of thinking. Let's hire those who will abide by the laws of the state and not create new laws themselves.

"In Florida the legislature passed certain guidelines as represented by SS 924.055 that clearly outlined dates and times certain for their courts to act timely pertaining to capital crime issues. Do Florida judges abide by this law? Of course not. Can you think of anything more appalling than when judges themselves do not adhere to the laws of their state?

"While we all have friends who are legislators, attorneys and judges, we must be more selective and choose only those who have a proven conservative approach to the death penalty and capital crime issues. We will not hire a Judge who wants to hide behind 'guidelines' but only those who have the intestinal fortitude to stand on their own two feet and dish out punishment in accordance with the crime committed. It makes me ill when I read about a judge who offers an opinion that a murderer was underprivileged as a child and, therefore, was not accountable for his actions. This is simply hogwash and nonsense.

"Seldom does anyone want to get down to the real root of the judicial problem and for a variety of reasons. Let me tell you what our society is experiencing today and what I think the real problem is. Everyone wants to talk about crime issues, but few have the guts to do what is right in our courts of law. You fix the problem by voting out the liberal judges and justices of the courts. After they are sworn in, they think they are there for life no matter what decisions they make. There is no way a judge can be approached by the man on the street to discuss any issue. This is wrong. Judges have to answer to no one. Former Vice-President Dan Quayle was absolutely correct when he spoke out about 'ending lifetime jobs for judges.'

"One of the reasons judges continue to enjoy lifetime jobs is because attorneys are afraid to oppose them for obvious reasons. When was the last time you heard of anyone conducting a political campaign against a judge. This is unreal. They are treated as if they are gods, but they aren't.

"I suggest here in Acirema that we hire the proper type individual to conduct our courts from day one. Then I suggest that an independent group, a public service type association or interested group, form a task force to review every opinion pertaining to capital crimes or criminal justice issues that are handed down by every judge and make their opinions readily known to our citizens on a monthly basis. The purpose of this evaluation and monitoring, which we may want to refer to as 'COURTWATCH,' is to have a political impact when the judges are again up for their renewed confirmation before the electorate.

"In Acirema we intend to start off with the right system. All judges and justices of the Supreme Court, Appellate, Circuit, and County courts will be elected. They will have a maximum term of office of only eight years. The election will be partisan in order to have a real race between the parties for these most important positions. Perhaps the race will not just be between Democrats and Republicans, or other parties, but will evolve into races between conservative and liberal philosophies. We also will have a recall provision for Judges as well as all other elective office holders.

"Likewise, this same task force should make known the voting record of every one of our legislators if they vote to take any actions that will prohibit a swift and final punishment of inmates who have been given the death sentence. It stands to reason if a Legislator is not for just punishment as handed down by our jury system, then he or she apparently must be against it!

"And wasn't it General Colin Powell who said during the Gulf War, 'If you cut off the head, the snake will surely die'? The same is true here. If our Legislature does not fund liberal programs whose intent is to prolong the life of those who are sitting on death row, then the mission of such programs will surely cease to exist.

◻ ◻ ◻ ◻ ◻

"NOW, LET'S ADDRESS the health issues relative to those within our prisons. The AIDS disease of inmates has grown to outrageous proportions, and the exploding population of prisoners has created a horrendous problem. One which is very costly. The Supreme Court has ruled that those operating our prison systems cannot be deliberately indifferent to inmate health needs.

"It is reported the annual average cost of treating prisoners with AIDS is approximately $2,500 each, and a lifetime care cost is projected to be in excess of $100,000 each. With the possibility of new drugs that will continue to increase the life span of AIDS victims, the cost will skyrocket to new proportions.

"Just think in terms of the predicament we, the law-abiding citizens are facing. For example, let's use a young male, maybe 25 years old. He is on drugs, has no job, is on welfare, has contracted AIDS, and has no funds to battle his disease. As others have done, he has a choice. He simply walks down the street and shoots a completely innocent stranger in the head. Arrested, taken to jail, a trial occurs, and he is committed to life in prison.

"We taxpayers have to pay for his incarceration including medical, dental, health care, a place to sleep, television, air-conditioning and heating for the place he will sleep each night, the use of a library and other recreational activities. This is truly a sorry scenario. What we have created is a new and different type of welfare system hidden behind the veil of incarceration. We have got to change the system, and in part it has to start with our appointment of Justices to the United States Supreme Court and trickle down to our state and local courts.

"Another health issue that needs addressing, although not yet as important as the AIDS issue, is that of prisoners being permitted to smoke inside our prisons. We all know that statistics have proven that smoking causes health problems and often death. Again, why should we, the taxpayers, continue to let prisoners smoke, then pay the huge medical bills for their care and maintenance. This is foolish. So we won't. We in Acirema will do something about this problem.

"In Florida the Governor spends countless hours and many taxpayer dollars chasing underaged teens who are caught smoking. I think they even have passed a law which fines the kids $25 if they are caught smoking. This is okay, and I'm not critical, because we should be strong and effective in our education of the horrible results caused by smoking. Our children should be well-aware, and perhaps this is a means to do so. However, I am under the impression the Governor has chosen an easy means to get his name in the paper and to show his influence to the voting public.

Often, elected officials seem to choose the easier laws to enforce and shy away from those that really take hard, critical planning and manpower to enforce. Why doesn't our Governor issue an executive order this afternoon to stop all prisoners from smoking immediately. He can do that, assuming he wanted to.

"We also will strongly support the 'Strike Three And You're Out' program. In short, we have to get very tough on our prisoners. There are so many improvements which could be made if only our Legislators had the intestinal fortitude to make these tough decisions. In Acirema we will 'hire' only Legislators who believe in our point of view.

"Once I was told—and this may or may not be true, but you will get the idea—that in Las Vegas, which is often called Sin City, at the local city level they have a city ordinance which is an automatic six months in city jail if anyone is caught pilfering through someone's automobile. You get caught, and there simply is no defense. You go to jail for six months. The locals have been known to often leave their vehicles unlocked. However, they greatly fear other more serious crimes, as we all do. The point is, we can be tough no matter the degree of infractions of our laws.

"In Acirema we are going to make our prisoners pay for a portion of their cost of incarceration, if not all of it. There is a way. When they are convicted and sentenced, we, the state, will confiscate their personal possessions. All of them. We will find means and ways to make them pay for their keep, and we do not believe this will constitute double jeopardy.

"And there is no reason we should pay for costly items such as gasoline to power lawn mowers when the old-fashioned push type will do just fine. Anyway, there may be an opportunity to manufacture a simple push model within the prison system, possibly through our PRIDE programs.

"Many years ago the Skinner family of Duval County leased prisoners from the state and from other counties around the northeast Florida area and used these prisoners as employees in their fields as laborers. This is something that we need to look into. This income will assist in defraying the cost of prisoner maintenance.

"For those convicted of rape, I think it prudent that we administer chemical castration. If these animals are prone to rape we need to stop it and do so shortly after their incarceration.

"And I don't know why Alabama gave in to the liberal element that forced them to change their minds about the chain gangs. I think a program of this nature is suitable punishment for those within our prisons. Second, when chain gangs are seen working the roadways, it just may have a bearing on some juvenile who is considering crime as his or her vocation. I would like to formulate a program that will bring first-offender juveniles into the prison system to tour the death chamber and to have the opportunity to actually walk through the chamber and do a 'hands on' experience of touching the heavy wooden arms of 'Old Sparky.'

"And to take it even further, each time an execution is scheduled, we should bring a first-offender youth group into the prison and let them witness what will happen to those who have chosen a life of crime. You can bet they would take this firsthand experience back to their friends and neighborhoods and it would be the talk of their group. I am convinced this will have a great effect on their future conduct.

"Let me also comment on something that gets little attention in the press but is very common and will get much worse. I have always been a football fanatic although I had little to cheer about while a student at Harvard. We did not have the quality of programs that is prevalent in other parts of the country, certainly not here in the Southeast. Since spending much time in northwest Florida, I have adopted Florida State University as my team to follow, and I really enjoy their brand of ball. Bobby Bowden is a first-class individual as is his coaching staff, and they conduct as clean a program as any in the nation.

"While I do not pick on any team, as they are all guilty, you may well be surprised to learn of the number of athletes with criminal records who are recruited by coaches and supporters, and it is getting worse with each passing season. I completely agree with the coaches who think in terms of giving young folks a second chance. However, I also completely disagree with their attitude that winning comes before everything else. I am afraid many, and that certainly does not mean everyone, have adopted the line of thinking that you have to be prepared to lose if you look past the opportunity to sign athletes with criminal records. If you really want to shake the sports world, then call your local paper and ask for a reporter to do a story on the roster of the major college teams in reference to the number of players who have any form of criminal record.

"Now, let's shuck right down to the cob, as Paul Harvey is fond of saying. Many want to discuss the inequity of black inmates. Data and statistics show a much larger percentage of the prison population is black. This seems to also reflect the same as the numbers on death row. However, it is just the reverse. In Florida the number of whites on death row is just about twice the number of blacks.

"Often we find the liberal elements of our society crying unfairness in our courts pertaining to minorities. I do not feel this is necessarily correct. It seems their statistics point to the fact that a black on white murder is more likely to draw a death penalty than any other crime. Why on earth is this even a statistic which is discussed. If someone murders someone else, then the death penalty should be administered and done so swiftly.

"In Florida as of today, there have been 36 executions. And guess what? Of those 24 were white men and 12 were black men. A ratio of two to one. Still, the liberals want to scream 'inequities.' They simply do not know what they are talking about.

"And are you aware of the so-called 'Racial Justice Act'? This is a part of a United States Congress house bill which, in effect, would establish racial quotas for the death penalty. Can you imagine such a thing as that? If a convicted murderer could establish that previously convicted murderers of his race had been sentenced to death in disproportionate percentages or that the victims of murders resulting in death sentences come disproportionately from one race, then the state would have the burden of proving that the disproportion was not the result of racism or the convicted murderer could not be put to death no matter how heinous his crime.

"People, we have got to get a handle on this group of liberals operating out of Washington. We have to act and do so now!''

"Let me interrupt you for a minute, Taylor," said Hilman Duncan, Sheriff of Covington County, Alabama. "You have spoken of those who think in terms of inequity for the black criminals. Obviously, I am a black man, and I want to make something very clear. When those who think they speak for the black community say the blacks are not treated fairly in our judicial systems, they are far off base. I, for one, do not believe this to be true at all. Today, here and now, our records, data, and stats prove that two out of every three blacks born across the country are raised by a single parent. When are the blacks—and I may add, many, many whites as well—going to learn they have to function and participate in this society at a more effective and personal level of commitment.

"What the leaders, or at least those who assume themselves to be the leaders, need to do is bear down on black men and women to be responsible parents and to take care of the kids they bring into this world. As we all know, data reveals to us families who are together, a mother and a father who really care for their kids, and it matters not if we speak of the white families or the black families, all families who truly care for each are responsible for only a very insignificant percentage of the crime across our nation.

"And let me expand on Taylor's point. I have seen those who are convicted of capital crimes have their liberal attorneys stand before a judge or jury to explain their client had a horrible childhood and should not be judged for his or her actions. This is a bunch of baloney. If you do the crime, if you do a capital crime, you should be ready, as Taylor has remarked, ready to forfeit your own life. That's all I have."

The entire assembly stood and applauded the Sheriff's remarks and Savage commented, "Thank you so very much for your observations and comments, Sheriff. That was very well said, and I do appreciate your attitude and your commitment to serve with us on this committee. Thank you again."

□ □ □ □ □

"LET'S MOVE ON TO our first committee report. This will be an agenda item dealing with education and schools in general. Our chairman for this committee is Waddell Bates. Mr. Bates."

"Thank you, Taylor. Our committee met last Thursday and made a decision to address only one of the subjects that had been assigned to the committee, but we did take the liberty to associate the school issue with the Lottery issue since they are so very closely related. This morning I will bring you up to date on our findings and recommendations. Is this the format you have in mind, Taylor?''

''Yes, that will be just fine. If each committee will stick to a single subject matter with each report I feel it would become clearer as to the direction we are going to take.''

''Thank you, Taylor.

''We have come up with some recommendations, and obviously some are more important than others. Some will seem trivial. However, those type issues are often the ones which cause a great deal of difficulty. We have assembled a written plan which is not complete, but I'll give you some of the highlights.

''We are going to stop crime in our schools. There is no way a young person can attend school and, at the same time, be concerned for his or her safety. Corporal punishment will be administered by our principals and only by them at their level of authority.

''Any student caught bringing a weapon, such as a gun or knife, or for that matter any other items that could inflict pain and/or suffering on another, will be immediately suspended. He or she will never again be allowed to attend a public or charter school in Acirema.

''Those who have been suspended may elect to attend adult classes which will be conducted at a new facility which we recommend building, or for that matter, rebuilding at the Ellyson Industrial Park. There is an abandoned barracks building that was used by the Navy that will do just fine.

''Taylor, we totally endorse your comments pertaining to the allocation of a classroom at each school for training officers for the law enforcement agencies of our 19 counties. Let me expand on your original comments as discussed in our subcommittee.

''Within each of our counties there are several agencies or organizations which need space to train or expand their continuing education for their members. Some which come to mind are the Sheriffs' Departments, City Police, Highway Patrol, Department of Law Enforcement, Shore Patrol, and others. Each of these organizations meet frequently and require classroom activities for continuing education for all of their members. Each group is a law enforcement agency. Each person attending is an officer of the law. What we envision is bringing these groups onto each campus, and their presence will bring to each school approximately 30 officers to be there around the clock for their personal training. Their presence will make a much better atmosphere and to a large degree ensure that our children are safe in their school environment. Their presence will do wonders for the school system.

"In part, and in relationship to safety of our children in schools, and keeping in mind the reduction of crime, we will have our students dressed in school uniforms during regular class hours. This will denote and highlight those who are not students and, therefore, have no business in the area of our campuses.

"We had much discussion about charter schools. The premise of Charter Schools does not work unless you get the parents of the students deeply involved. And if we get the parents involved at a top-notch level, then we really don't need to have as many Charter Schools as we once thought necessary.

"It is our intent to get the parents involved with our education system, and we are determined to educate our students and to do so in a quiet and nondisruptive class atmosphere. We will promote charter schools throughout Acirema and recommend that we also continue with our normal system built around new rules and regulations which we shall recommend for adoption.

"Every student who resides in the State of Acirema will have his or her choice of schools. There will be no cross-town bussing of any sort. The size of classes will be reduced to the extent that teachers can have total control over their students. We will begin a program whereby we promote local businesses across the state to advertise on our school buses. This will generate income by the elimination of the cost of purchasing the buses as each will be sponsored by individual companies. However, we will continue to have the expenses of operations and maintenance.

"There will be a program introduced whereby fast-food restaurants such as McDonalds, Hardees, and Burger King, along with sports equipment firms such as Nike and Reebok, would sponsor all of the schoolbooks within our system. In return, they will have an advertising on the back cover. This would save our state millions annually. We also will sell all school heavy maintenance equipment and join the state, county, and city pool to use their equipment as needed.

"Our recommendations include our State Superintendent of Schools also be the Director of the Lottery. Not only would this insure lottery funds find their way into the school system as intended, but also it would totally eliminate many top positions that are way too costly.

"It would be our estimate that no more than 15 additional personnel added to the School Superintendent's staff could manage the entire Lottery program. The combining of these two agencies would be a shining example of reduction of duplication that is necessary if we are going to accomplish the goals which we have set for Acirema to be a world-class state.

"We do not believe there is a need for a Board of Regents to administer our colleges and universities. This will be a function of the State Cabinet with the Governor being the Chairman.

"Taylor, these are a few of the concerns our committee has addressed thus far. As we meet, we will continue to alter, add to, and expand on the role of the Superintendent of Education.

"I have our report in written form. I suggest that we make this report and all committee reports available to the media."

"This is my thinking also," said Savage. "I'll have LR make copies and pass them out. Thank you very much, Waddell. That was a good report.

"People, I know that we are on the right track, and with the continued support that our committee chairs will offer, we will complete our mission and educate those who choose to reside in Acirema. The tremendous potential we have will offer every citizen a new experience in the way they choose to live their lives.

"Now, we've already covered a lot this morning so why don't we stop for a break. If the media wishes to talk to anyone of you or to me, this would be a good time to do so. Why don't we take 20 minutes, then come back and break again for lunch around noon."

The media flooded toward Savage, and those who didn't find elbow room cornered other committee members with the thought of capturing a sound bite for their noon news programs. Someone from Channel 3 stuck a mike in the face of former Governor

Daniels. "Governor, this is quite an undertaking by Mr. Savage. Do you sincerely feel that it has a chance of passing?"

"Well, you speak of passing as if in a law or a bill before a legislative body. This is not the case here. Passing would mean we, the people of the 19 counties, approve a referendum, and I feel there is a strong possibility we will," replied the Governor.

"Mr. Savage hit hard on the fact that both Alabama and Florida have had, as he put it, hundreds of years to rectify the situation and have done little about it. Since you were Governor for eight years, that seems to be directed somewhat partially at you and your administration. Any comment?"

"Certainly. A lot has changed since I took office more than 16 years ago, and you have to remember I have been out of office for more than eight years. What has happened since then is an almost universal disregard for law and order by those on the fringes of criminal activities.

"More and more juvenile criminals and those who feel compelled to start a life of crime have come to the point that life behind bars is probably better than life on the streets. This attitude has got to cease. Many young folks who are now getting into trouble think prison life is acceptable and actually a part of their society. You would be surprised to learn the percentage of young criminals who have been raised and taken to prison to visit with older brothers, uncles, aunts, cousins, or perhaps their mother or father. It truly has become a way of life for so many of them.

"I believe passage of Acirema to Statehood will be the best thing that could happen to our society. Other areas around the country will either follow suit with our leadership or straighten out their own problems within their own state boundaries."

"Thank you, Governor, for your comments."

The same reporter who had questioned Savage earlier about the *Lexington* could not wait to get another shot at him. "Mr. Savage, can you tell me about your acquisition of the Lady Lex?"

"Sure, I can tell you. As I said on the Laurie Sin' Show, we have acquired the Gray Ghost and will convert it into a great cruise liner with heavy emphasis on accommodating those who have a love for the Navy."

"Do you expect it to be in port much of the time or underway?"

"Obviously, we would like it cruising most of the time as that is our mission and purpose for the purchase. We will, however, have port days and schedules where landlubbers can visit our gift shops as well as dine in a variety of restaurants. We will have three distinctly different, full-course restaurants which will be decorated around special themes. There will be a couple of drop-in, smaller, deli type facilities also.''

''Who will have the contract and where will renovations and upgrading take place?''

''I will use facilities within the State of Acirema. It may be in the Port of Mobile, the Port of Pensacola or perhaps Panama City. Savage Worldwide will use every conceivable facility within our new state in order to increase our job base as well as our tax base.''

''How often or what percent of the time do you expect the Lex to be underway, on cruise?''

''We have established our own travel agency and would wish to have the Lex cruising about 75 percent of the time. We can accomplish this as we will have the ability to shuttle passengers to and from the ship while it is underway and, therefore, do not have to come into port as other liners have to do.''

''What was the price you paid for acquisition?''

''The Lex was declared surplus and for that reason had little value. What can you do with a vessel that large, especially if you have no place to port it?''

''That was a nice answer, Mr. Savage, but that did not answer my question. What did you pay for the Lex?''

''The final figure will be somewhere around $8 million.''

''And what do you estimate the cost of renovations to be?''

''We think we will have a total of perhaps $80 million in the ship when it is ready for our first cruise.''

''That's quite an investment. Are you sure you can recoup such expense?''

''Nothing in life is guaranteed. Certainly, it is our plans to recoup and make a profit. Otherwise, why would we have made the purchase?''

Another reporter broke in, ''Mr. Savage, I hear rumors that your company is looking at the possible acquisition of the Point Clear Hotel. Is this correct?''

''Sir, we are looking at several things. I have recently invested in Clearmont Grande at Point Clear and have every intent to invest heavily in real estate not only along the Coast of Acirema but inland as well. Maybe even some farm lands. Doesn't Savage Worldwide Farms sound interesting?''

"Will you actually go into farming in a big way? As you know, there are large tracts of great farm lands in south Alabama."

"You know farming can mean a lot of different things to different folks. Take for instance the aquatic farming of seafood. And I'm sure some of you are aware of, or at least have seen, the many horses on the landscape at ocean front in California. I wonder why we don't have such beautiful animals running the coast of Florida and Alabama, or running at a track nearby. You see farming could be a number of different things to different people."

□ □ □ □ □

THE COMMITTEE HAD returned to the room and was ready to continue with the morning's session.

"While Waddell Bates is wound up, I want him to continue and give his report concerning his Committee on Agriculture. Waddell."

"Thank you again, Taylor. Our Agriculture Committee also met this past week, and it is a pleasure to give you a report on just one facet of our agriculture agenda. Each of you fully understands the enormous opportunity which we have in Acirema pertaining to the vast amount of farm land scattered across the 19 counties. In every county we are blessed with large tracts of farm land, even in the coastal counties. And we, you and I, and the citizens of Acirema are going to take full advantage of it.

"A new airline, known as Overnight Delivery Express, will specialize in rapid delivery of produce and horticultural products. We will be in great shape to promote those products which can be grown right here at home and get them delivered virtually all over the world in fresh, first-class condition.

"It shall be our utmost responsibility to protect those who are willing to risk their all in the business of growing produce and horticultural products. We need not discuss the importance of their products as we all understand the necessity of fresh fruits and vegetables along with plants and flowers grown for our use as well as the use of millions around the globe.

"I want each of you to know something that may shock you. Do you know that both Florida and Alabama have a bureaucratic set of laws which dictate that any dealer in products that are grown in either state has to have a license and a bond to purchase the products from the source, that is the growers or producers.

"That does not sound too farfetched until you realize what it means. Let's take, for instance, your local farmers market, like the Farmers Market on Old Pottery Plant Road. Do you know that Mr. Barney has to pay the State of Florida a fee and obtain a bond in order to have the 'privilege' of purchasing fruits and vegetables grown in Florida.

"The law when first proposed was to assure that the farmer and/or producer got paid for his products because they have such a short shelf life. If a trucker comes into the state and purchases three large loads of watermelons and takes them north with the commitment to pay the grower by the 10th of the following month and does not pay him, there is nothing the farmer can collect. Most likely the melons have been consumed and the farmer has nothing to reclaim. For this purpose the law is not all that bad. However, if the farmer has a good relationship for many years with those he usually sells to, then he is satisfied that he will get his money due on all sales. But these two states demand that the dealer still purchase a state license and be bonded.

"A part of the problem is that the farmer, the grower, and the producer have to sell their products when they are ready. Therefore, they certainly cannot wait until those who are licensed come around to purchase the products. So they sell to whoever needs what they have grown with little regard for the laws of the states. This puts the producer, farmer, and/or grower in a hell of a fix. He breaks the laws because he has to sell his products before they spoil, and it really doesn't make sense to him that someone has to pay the state a fee, which is nothing more than a tax, in order for him to sell what he has grown.

"In Acirema we are going to protect our farmers as we are going to protect all who are in any type trade or business. We will establish a Consumer Protection Director, a one-person operation with one secretary, who will be given authority powers of enforcement. We will attach any assets, including vehicles, accounts receivable, etc. from any person who purchases by check and the check bounces. There are many ways to accomplish this, and in Acirema we will consider this a crime and will punish accordingly, even first offenders.

"We will also urge those who purchase produce and horticulture products to take advantage of buying from those producers who have elected to use a check guarantee system. In this way everyone who produces products within Acirema will have full protection. We do not need to require those who want to purchase produce and horticulture products to have a license and bond to do so. We will adopt a common sense approach.

"Taylor, this is just one of the many items that we will address in our Agriculture Committee."

"Thank you, Waddell. I did not have any idea these two states required this type of license. It does nothing more than place barriers between those who want to purchase and those who want to sell, and the final results are simply increasing the prices to the consumer. Thank you again, Waddell."

"Taylor, while I'm up and talking, let me bring another thought to the full committee that our Agriculture Subcommittee is working on. Would it be okay to continue?"

"Certainly. Take all the time you wish. I find your reports most interesting," said Savage.

"Thanks. Our subcommittee has brought together a program that fits like a glove and will do well for the citizens of Acirema. The closeness relative to marketing agriculture products, our Acirema Commerce Department and the Acirema Lottery have something in common which led us to come up with a joint sales and marketing idea.

"While other states gear their Lottery program based on you either win or lose, we in Acirema are going to base ours on the theme of win-win-win. We have found a formula that is good for everyone and we want to tell you about it.

"THIS PROMOTION CAMPAIGN will have a tremendous effect on several factors here in Acirema. We have designed it to assist the farmers and producers by increasing the sale of their fresh fruits and vegetables, generating special interest in our Acirema Lottery games, and giving to those who choose to play the lottery a dollar's worth of value for each dollar they spend.

"In most every Lottery across the country the player pays for a ticket, and if he or she does not win the Lottery or a portion thereof, he is simply out the cost of a ticket. Here in Acirema we are going to tie all of this together where everyone who plays is a winner-winner-winner.

"This promotion, as I envision it, will generate approximately $5 million in sales of fresh fruits and vegetables each time we promote through the Acirema Lottery.

"I trust that each and every one of our committee members will fully understand the monumental benefits of promoting any item when it's combined in some manner or form with the millions of tickets we project will be sold each week by our Lottery. One of the best attributes of this promotion is that it is tied together as a joint effort between four Acirema agencies or departments, namely the Lottery Department, the Commerce Department, the Agriculture Department, and our School System.

"You who currently live in Florida may remember last summer when the Florida Lottery joined with Universal Studios for a promotion and gave away 50, if my memory serves me correctly, it was 50 Jeep Cherokees. This was a most successful campaign and was the promotion that got our Subcommittee's attention pertaining to the possibility of a four agency joint effort here in Acirema. I believe what we can do will surpass the success level of the Jeep promotion.

"There is no question that a promotion through the Lottery will touch millions of Aciremans. We have projected that every normal week our lottery can expect to sell some 2.5 to 3 million tickets, on a second week rollover some 3.5 to 4 million, and on a third week rollover 4.5 to 5 million. Obviously, a fourth week rollover could produce in excess of 10 million.

"For the purpose of this presentation, I am going to assume that in a given week we are talking about 2 million players which will mean 2 million coupons promoting the purchase of fresh fruits and vegetables from Acirema. We will promote through two or three supermarket chains, but today I will simply use the phrase 'Supermarket' without designating any particular one. I will also use a redemption value of $1.00 per coupon. To redeem, the consumer will have to purchase at least $5.00 of fresh fruits and vegetables that were grown here in Acirema. One coupon will be issued automatically at lottery terminals when each ticket is sold, no matter the value of the ticket. We suggest that each coupon have a redemption date of a full year. This will soften the tremendous demand during the weeks of promotion and spread it over a longer term.

"A successful campaign and promotion must have a level of accomplishment and satisfaction for everyone. A properly designed promotion will give every player, all four state agencies, our farmers, producers, growers, retailers, etc. the benefit of financial gain at the highest level of acceptance.

"While our subcommittee certainly does not have all the answers yet, I feel the following comments are on track pertaining to offering an element of success. Each week that we air the promotion, it will generate some 2 million coupons worth $1.00 each to be presented to the supermarket. Assuming only a redemption ratio of 50 percent, this will generate and trigger sales of $5 million in fresh fruit and vegetables. And this can happen as often as we decide to use this means of promotion.

"Since our promotion is direct and geared to sell only fresh fruits and vegetables grown in Acirema, this will create maximum inter-est for the supermarkets to label these items with 'fresh from Aci-rema' stickers. It will also prod the retailers to better display 'fresh from Acirema' literature in their produce section. Our promotion will assist Acirema producers and growers to sell a much larger percentage of their products within the state and, therefore, greatly reduce their shipping costs, which in turn will increase their potential for profits right here at home. Again, we are doing all we can to keep our dollars flowing and our profits at home!

"Every time a ticket is sold by our Acirema Lottery, the player has the opportunity and chance to win the Lottery or at least a portion thereof. However, with this promotion program if the player does not win, he or she can redeem these coupons for a like amount of dollar value on food products at the local participating supermarket. Our promotion gives to each and every player $1 of value for each $1 spent on lottery tickets. Period. End of report. They are given a value for every dollar invested in the Lottery. This is good, genuine, valuable consideration for every player.

"Because of the public's acceptance of our program and its

success I project it will produce no less than a five-percent increase in ticket sales which will produce an additional $100,000 cash value to the Acirema Lottery. Again, good, valuable consideration. Each week of our promotions, and I suggest one per month for four months to be held during maximum growing season, the supermarket(s) will be exposed to no less than two million players who will be instructed to redeem their coupons at the supermarkets.

"Our chosen supermarkets will win big time and make our promotion efforts most worthwhile and beneficial to each of them based on the following:

(a) The influx of individuals who come into the stores to redeem their coupons will eliminate the retailers' shrinkage and loss of produce. They will be 'giving away' $1 in merchandise but selling $4. If we assume they double their cost to establish their retail price, then the actual promotional 'loss' is only 50 cents. This 50 cents as compared to the overall $5 value is only 10 percent. This is far less than the percent of shrinkage (produce lost) that is the acceptable norm.

(b) The vast numbers of players, while redeeming their coupons, will purchase thousands of dollars of other products and, thereby, generate thousands upon thousands of dollars of additional sales for the supermarkets.

(c) The supermarkets will show tremendous profits in their produce departments by increased sales of Acirema fresh products in the approximate amount of $5 million with each promotion.

"Every ticket purchaser receives a $1 value for every $1 spent. With the redemption at the supermarket the consumer receives $5 of fresh fruits and vegetables for a cash price of only $4, thus a 20 percent savings on his produce needs. This program will have tremendous appeal with the general public and offers all concerned a great opportunity. It will accomplish a major mission for all four Acirema Agencies, our producers, growers, and farmers—and does so in a manner where everyone wins.

"Taylor, sorry to take so long, but this is the kind of program and innovative idea we are looking at when Acirema gains Statehood. Thank you for your time."

"Thank you again, Waddell. That is going to do wonders with the promotion of four agencies and will certainly help our farmers sell their products right here at home. And the amount of funds that are going to be generated for our school system from the lottery will be tremendous.

"There is no doubt in my mind that our committee members have caught on real quick and fully understand the possibility of all the advantages of Acirema, and how each of us can truly make a change. Thanks again, Waddell.

□ □ □ □ □

"I MENTIONED TO you during our first meeting that I would give to each of you an insight into what I feel are the 10 most essential questions that everyone should ask of every candidate who seeks any office, whether local, state, or national.

"I trust that you will give your undivided attention to these questions, and I urge the media to carry them nationwide whereby everyone will have an opportunity to write them down and use them each time they go to the polls to cast a vote in every future election.

"I would hope our electorate would look at every race as individual and not political party related. We would be better served not to vote for someone simply because he or she is a Republican, Democrat, or otherwise, but to do so because the candidate is the best person for the position. These questions should be asked of everyone in every campaign without regard for party affiliation.

"Laura will hand each of you a copy, but for the benefit of the media let me quickly go through them.

"First question: Will you publish a complete personal resume' at the time you qualify to run for this office?

"Second: Will you resign your elected office if you ever fail to keep the promises you made during your campaign?

"Third: Will you annually provide a copy of your tax return to be made public, and, if this is not acceptable, will you provide a documented statement of your income and the source of same during the past year?

"Fourth: If this position which you seek is a full-time position, will you serve in the position full-time and not involve yourself in other business activities?

"Fifth: Will you return your phone calls, answer your mail,

administer this position? And will you keep your appointments and be on time to meet with your constituents as their time also is very important? During a campaign when candidates seek office, they are ever so humble to ask for our votes. However, after they are in office, it is almost impossible to get a one-on-one appointment with them. Can you agree this will not be the manner in which you conduct your office?

"Sixth: Will you make all of your decisions pertaining to the operation of this office in the Sunshine, that is to say, in public, so to speak?

"Seventh: Will you make sure the bureaucrats in your office carry out the policies you support without any personal regard for their own individual positions on the issues? And offer no excuses as to why you cannot effectively carry out your position by blaming the results on the bureaucracy? And, furthermore, will you dismiss any bureaucrat who does not carry out your commitment to the voters who have hired you?

"Eighth: In your campaign for this office, will you promise that you will not make any statements, promises, or commitments that are so vague they cannot be fulfilled or make promises or commitments which you do not have the least intent of fulfilling?

"Ninth: Should you decide to seek another office while currently holding an elected position, will you, as soon as you qualify for that office, resign the office which you currently hold whether or not the law of the land requires you to resign the position?

"And tenth: You should make a list of 10 common items and ask the candidate to give you an immediate verbal response as to their normal cost. For instance, they could be grocery items such as a loaf of bread, a gallon of milk, a pound of sliced ham, a large can of frozen orange juice, or a pound of real butter, etc. Or it could be something such as the cost of repairing a flat tire, a standard car wash, the cost of dry cleaning a man's two-piece business suit, the monthly cost of delivering the local paper to your front door, or perhaps the per hour cost of your baby sitter.

"This question should be asked openly, and a response from the candidate should be immediate. You need to structure your own list of items whereby they would better reflect the cost of items in your geographical home region. Obviously, you would not ask a candidate who is running for a county commission seat in the Miami area about the hourly rental cost of ice skates or snow skis.

"The purpose of these questions is obvious. We need good, down-to-earth men and women who have not lived their lives in an ivory tower without benefit of the day-to-day activities which we all must endure. You may recall once when a candidate was running for President, someone mentioned the scanner devices which total up the cost of your food items in your grocery store, and he had no idea what they were even talking about. This is what I mean! Ivory tower and all! I hope you will ask these questions often.

□   □   □   □   □

"NOW, LAST WEEK WHEN I had the privilege to appear with Laurie Sin' on her show I remarked that I may have a major announcement to make today concerning an investment that Savage Worldwide will make in Acirema. I was asked earlier about that comment by a media representative, and my answer was that I wanted to save the announcement for the full committee.

"You may recall during our first meeting when we went around the room, and each of you stood and introduced yourself, and I was very pleased to hear the comments of Admiral James Warthon. In his remarks, he mentioned he was very interested in Acirema and noted his interest was directly tied to the fact that our Air Force had facilities within Acirema, namely Eglin Air Force Base, Tyndall Air Force Base, and Hulbert Air Force Base. He also noted the Navy's presence at the Pensacola Naval Air Station and Whiting Field in Milton. Furthermore, he mentioned the several Out Lying Fields, OLF's, which the Navy owns that also are within our boundaries.

"Well, last Friday I was advised that our company was going to be awarded a contract after we had offered a bid for one of the OLF's that was to be declared surplus by the Navy. The location in particular is the Summerdale, Alabama, Out Lying Field, which is a few miles north of Summerdale, which is a few miles north of Foley. Our company has almost completed negotiations with local landowners for surrounding parcels that will provide us with the largest major airport facility in the United States. Our north-the largest major airport facility in the United States. Our north-south runway will allow us to take off and approach over the Gulf of Mexico thereby greatly reducing the possibility of endangering those living within the general area of the field. Our plans call for three parallel north-south runways, each being 14,000 feet in length.

"There will be a complete shopping complex with multi-screen movie theaters, a major hotel complex, as well as a major hospital corporation with the latest facilities. Our jet aircraft can bring those in need of emergency care directly to this facility and waste little time doing so.

"There are plans to construct a convention center and a world-class recording studio. One of our country's top recording entertainers will be building the studio and will make the announcement in the very near future. While we do not know for sure at this point, we are negotiating to construct an international auto race facility on the northeast quadrant of the property. These plans may or may not materialize.

"We plan to have a 5,000-acre ranch that will serve as breeding facilities as well as stockyards in order to expedite the shipping of cattle and horses to countries who wish to purchase from our cattle farms. In this regard, I plan an extensive program that will furnish financing to many countries in South America so they will more effectively have an opportunity to purchase the cattle raised right here in Acirema for their farms and personal consumption. This will be a major income producer for the cattle farmers and ranchers of Acirema.

"In Florida there have been trade negotiations going on for-ever concerning how the state could assist cattle producers with foreign sales, but little has been done about it.

"While that state is sitting on its rear end when it could have been using state funds to promote trade relations that would help everyone, we are going to do everything we can to take a good share of the market from them.

"One of the things we are going to do is to invest some of our retirement funds from the Department of Administration to assist foreign countries to be in a better financial position to purchase cattle from our people. Normally, the funds would be just sitting in an account invested in some safe but low-income-earning market when they could be earning real bucks and helping our ranchers at the same time. It really makes a good deal of sense if you stop and think about it.

"As I explained on the Sin' show, our company is going to invest heavily in real estate both on the coast and inland. This piece of land will offer Savage Worldwide an opportunity to build a world-class airport that will exceed the Alliance Airport in the Dallas-Ft. Worth area. It will be greater in size and services. We have chosen the name of Acirema International Global Airport (AIGA). This will be a facility that will function by serving the entire globe with the latest in transportation needs. When you purchase a flight ticket and leave from AIGA you will be assured a safe flight. Our high-tech facility will include every piece of equipment necessary to detect any possibility of a terrorist bomb or harmful materials as small as a golf ball.

"We will have a tunnel-type facility where every car, truck, van, delivery equipment, tractor trailers, and every type vehicle conceivable will be required to drive through. This equipment will detect any items which may possess a potential harmful factor that would be intended for an aircraft. Our detection tunnel will be constructed in an area that will make the determination of any problem known well before a dangerous vehicle can get close enough to the airport to do any real damage if, in fact, a bomb or other device is detected.

"For years people on the upper Gulf Coast have spoken of a world-class facility between Pensacola and Mobile. With the opening of AIGA, both the Pensacola Airport and the Mobile Airport can be closed and that valuable land used for a more economical purpose. In both cities the current air traffic is not only loud and annoying, but also very dangerous to those who have built their homes nearby.

"With the opening of AIGA we will stand alone as the leading distribution center for major corporations who choose to send their products around the globe. We will be the headquarters for some of the world's largest freight forwarders as well as inter-global shipping centers. Our business center facilities will not be matched by anyone.

"And Savage Worldwide is currently working on plans for what possibly could be the world's largest aqua-farming operations. We plan four locations. There will be two operations inland and two offshore. The locations will be Mobile Bay, Perdido Bay, one offshore south of Orange Beach, and the second just south of Ft. Morgan. Through our operations of AIGA, we will be able to ship fresh seafood around the globe. International trade will be our long suit, and the very freshest of seafood will be our goal. In the bays around Orange Beach, Bon Secour, and Bayou LaBatre, we will establish inshore aqua farming of oysters and scallops. Offshore we will be heavily involved in fish and blue crab farming.

"When the State of Florida passed the no net laws in 1995, it killed the little man who depended on the waters of that area to help him feed his family. Our aquatic farming operations will employ many who are already accustomed to this type of work. These misplaced and forgotten people can earn a decent living by doing work they enjoy and at the same time know they are supplying the world's population with all the fresh seafood that would be required.

"At AIGA we will market worldwide the abundance of fresh produce and pecans grown in Acirema, that portion which is now south Alabama.

"We are talking with a major airline carrier about breaking its contract with the Atlanta Airport and home basing in AIGA. They are most interested because of the heavy traffic and waiting conditions that are always present when flying out of Atlanta. Furthermore, here in Acirema we seldom will have an icing condition to contend with. Our proximity to Pensacola and Mobile with their great ports, the closeness to Interstate 10 plus the major advantage of rail traffic, not to mention the intercoastal waterway, will make our facility head and shoulders above all others.

"Our plans include construction of the AIGA four-lane highway from the airport to connect with Interstate 10 somewhere in the vicinity of the Loxley exit. This will expedite traffic during the hurricane season should our residents need to evacuate more quickly. It also will serve to bring the 50,000 employees who will work in the many areas of AIGA to their jobs each day.

''NOW THAT WE HAVE been through our second full meeting and have listened to some committee reports, I trust that each of you feels as good about our position and potential as I do.

''I think for all of your good, hard work thus far, you deserve a social event. I would like each of you to join with me on Friday night, February 16th, at 8:00 o'clock for cocktails and dinner.

''You are welcome to bring your spouse or a date. I had intended to try out the new Quack & Tail Restaurant on Santa Rosa Island, but I just can't get away from Flounder's. They sure have great food. If any of you need directions, please call my office and Laura will be glad to assist you.

''Okay, our third general committee meeting is scheduled for two weeks from today, on the 20th. What I would like to do is use that as an open day of discussions and for each of you to bring up ideas of items pertaining to any subject that you would like the full committee to consider. We will report the committee findings on our fourth meeting scheduled for March 5th. For sure, I will be with you on the 20th as I have several more ideas to come before the committee, and the media as usual is invited to attend.

''Thanks for coming today. We stand adjourned.''

EIGHT

AFTER THE SECOND GENERAL Assembly meeting, the plans engineered by Taylor Savage were much clearer. The media did a good job in defining the various positions which had been detailed by Savage and various committee chairmen. As usual, Acirema was the headline story across the country and remained constantly on everyone's lips throughout Alabama and Florida.

Thus far, there seemed to be few, if any, obstacles which would cripple the fast-developing opportunity for Acirema's success, and certainly no major mine fields.

Upon reading the transcripts of the second committee meeting, which Savage quickly made available, Governor Lance Foxworth of Alabama and Governor Brandon Woods of Florida and their Attorneys General gathered with their legal councils and had a lengthy conference call.

The purpose of this second conference call was to discuss again a joint cabinet meeting between the two states, something which had never happened and would itself make history. With all their brains functioning at full capacity they were still stumped as to their options, if any.

With politicians being politicians and playing the role to the hilt, neither staff could come up with an agenda suitable to all. Governor Woods was serving his next-to-last year of his last term as governor and could not succeed himself for a third term. Governor Foxworth was looking forward to running for a second term in an election just another year away.

Their personal terms of office presented a very different set of circumstances for each Governor and greatly altered the approach each would take. However, they did have one thing in common: many problems to solve for their respective states. Apparently, each state would lose approximately 700,000 people. Alabama would lose about 10,676 square miles of real estate while Florida would lose about 8,792 square miles. Alabama would lose more acreage of fresh water lakes while Florida would suffer the loss of many miles of pristine Gulf frontage.

Their number one predicament was trying to satisfy those who lived within the boundaries of Acirema when Savage's marketing and campaigning strategies were pointing out, and rightly so, that both Florida and Alabama had had the opportunity for hundreds of years to make things right and acceptable. His position was made very clear, and many wondered why things had to get so far out of control that a movement like the one he planned had even the slimmest chance to be successful.

There was no way the 1.4 million residents would elect to stay within their current geographical and political boundaries when such bright and innovative opportunities were developing at such a fast-moving pace. In part, and very frustrating to both states, was the fact that the entire program developed by Savage was sprung on them with such quickness and intensity. Savage had been making these plans for more than five years, and the states had now been aware of it less than 10 days.

□ □ □ □ □

BEFORE THE TWO Governors would set a joint meeting between their two state cabinet officials, they decided it would be wise to approach Savage to see if he would sit down, just the three of them, and discuss Acirema in more detail. Governor Foxworth asked Governor Woods to set up the meeting, and he would attend it no matter when or where.

It was later in the afternoon before Governor Woods' secretary was able to track Savage down as he had flown to North Carolina for the funeral of a close friend, a distant cousin.

"Hello, Taylor, this is Brandon Woods. Sorry to learn of the death of your friend, Marvin."

"Thank you, Governor. Thanks for your kind remarks. How

have you been?''

"Fine, just fine. Things are going about as well as can be
expected here in Tallahassee as we prepare our agenda for the
upcoming legislative session. I have been seeing a lot of you on
television and in all the papers. Seems as though you are quite
busy.''

"Yes, Sir, we have a very full plate right now. What's on your
mind?'' Savage asked as if he didn't know.

"I had a long conversation with Governor Foxworth recently,
and we decided to call a joint session of our States' Cabinets to
discuss Acirema. But before we all sat down together, I thought
it might serve us all well if you, Governor Foxworth, and myself
could take some time to chat. Would you be amenable to this?''

"Governor, I have no problem whatsoever with doing that.
When would you like to meet?''

"How about over the weekend? Could this fit into your
schedule?''

"This weekend I will be at Seaside visiting with a friend. I
could arrange to meet with the two of you there if you would like
to come down to the Gulf on Sunday afternoon.''

"That's fine with me, and Governor Foxworth said he would
alter his schedule to fit ours. What time Sunday would be good for
you?'' inquired the Governor.

"Why don't we get together at 2:00 in the afternoon?''

"That'll be great. I'll be in Tallahassee all weekend and leave
from here. It's only a short flight down from Montgomery. We'll
be seeing you on Sunday.''

"I'll look forward to it. Call my office and ask for Laura. She
will give you directions to the location. Governor, there is one
thing we need to discuss before we sit down together. I'll only
agree to do this if we all understand up front that we can say
exactly what's on our minds. I will not hold anything back and
expect the same from both of you.''

"You couldn't have said it better. That's the way we should
approach this. With a complete open mind and everything on the
table. This is a most important subject, and we all need to speak
our piece.''

"Thanks for agreeing, I'll see you on Sunday around 2:00
unless I hear differently today.''

"See you on Sunday, Taylor. Have a good weekend."

☐ ☐ ☐ ☐ ☐

SHEERY, TAYLOR'S LONGTIME companion, had recently completed some decorating projects for three homes in Seaside and fell in love with the area. She signed a one-year lease, with option to purchase, on a lovely pink and white stucco home on the Gulf close enough to the water that you could throw a baseball from her upstairs balcony into the emerald green surf.

Although the weather was still very cool, she and Taylor were looking forward to slipping out of the second-story master bedroom onto the cedar deck and into the hot, steamy sauna that she had just installed. They had planned a special do-nothing weekend of loafing, just simply relaxing. She was to fly to Goldsboro for a four-day visit with her folks and was scheduled to leave around noon on Sunday, so he would have the quietness of the home all alone to have a real man-to-man discussion with two of the South's most popular Governors.

☐ ☐ ☐ ☐ ☐

THE TWO CHIEF EXECUTIVES arranged their schedules where both would fly into the Destin Airstrip, and Governor Woods would have his security driver, a Florida Highway Patrolman, pick them up and drive them down the road to Seaside, a short 20-minute trip. They arrived on time and were greeted by Savage with a warm welcome.

"Good afternoon, Governors. Glad you both could make it. Have a good trip down?"

"Yeah, just great. This is fantastic weather and a great time to be visiting on the Gulf Coast," stated Governor Foxworth.

"Thanks, for agreeing to meet with us, Taylor. I appreciate it. This is really a majestic view. Seems as though we should be able to see all the way to Cuba. These clear days on the Coast just can't be beat," noted Governor Woods.

"Tell your driver he is welcome to sit on the downstairs deck and enjoy the Gulf or stare at the television in the den. Why don't we three go upstairs and sit on the patio where y'all can make yourself at home. How about something to drink?"

"Not yet, maybe later," they both countered.

The three VIPs went upstairs through the master suite and onto the deck. From a distance a person would be hard-pressed to tell either one of the three men from the other. Each was six feet tall, within an inch either way, and slender with dark well-groomed hair, and all nearly the same age as Savage.

"Why don't we get right to the purpose of our visit? What's on your mind?" Savage asked.

"Governor Foxworth wanted me to call you and set this meeting up so we could have some time to exchange a few ideas, a meeting of the minds, so to speak. You have already made it abundantly clear that we should speak our minds, and that's what we want also, and with no hurt feelings or apologies necessary when we do."

"Taylor, Governor Woods has known you longer than I. I guess we haven't seen each other since we talked at the Vulcan Steel open house for our Alabama Legislative Day in Montgomery three years ago. It's good of you to meet with us.

"What I want to know is whatever possessed you to come up with a program like Acirema? And by the way, like the program or not, Acirema is a grand and honorable name."

"Thanks," said Savage, welcoming his first question and very eager to offer a response. "Governor Foxworth, things have gotten out of control. I know it, and the two of you know it. You see, I have no reason to do what I have suggested except in an effort to be helpful to about 1.4 million residents of your two states. There is nothing I want except success for the program.

"You folks, both of you, and all the previous Governors before you, have had only one thing in mind, and that is being elected and reelected. It reminds me of when I first joined the Jaycees back in North Carolina. There were three attorneys running for the Presidency of the local chapter. One night several of us, all members of the board of directors, were discussing who we thought would be best for the job. Someone remarked that Jim did not want to be President; he just wanted to 'have been President.' Meaning, of course, he wanted the title only and did not welcome the work or the responsibilities. This is the feeling I think much of the country is having today about those we have hired to run the offices of our state and federal governments."

"By your comments, are you assuming that the two of us are

not interested in anything except the title of the job?'' asked Woods.

"Not exactly. However, what I am saying is very few elected officials these days have any real concern for their duties. They really don't want to work at creating a better place for their constituents to live and operate their businesses. They want to do all that is necessary to get elected, and then it's the same old rotten worn-out means of conducting government as usual. They continue not only to let, but also demand, that bureaucrats carry on running the government in the same chaotic manner that we are all so familiar with. This nonsense we are going to stop.''

"So this is your main concern, the bureaucracy?''

"No. It's just one of my main concerns. When was the last time either of you mentioned the word bureaucracy in a speech? When have either of you said that you would eliminate the bureaucracy that is truly crushing the life out of this country, including these two states? And the primary question is, why don't you, or better yet, why hasn't the leadership of Florida and Alabama done something about it before now?''

"You know full well we can't fire those with longevity in our civil service systems no matter what reasons we may have,'' responded Governor Foxworth.

"This is where we differ. We can. We will. Just you watch and see. Those who will manage the government in Acirema can. Just wait and see.

"Don't you realize people are sick and tired of the kind of attitude and leadership that you are displaying even now as we speak?'' said Savage.

"We are going to be in a position from day one to start Acirema with a streamlined government. We won't have to worry about reducing the size of government because we are dedicated to not letting it get out of hand in the first place.

"I know the two of you understand that a bureaucrat fully realizes the larger he or she can make his bureau or agency, it will create more dollars that he or she can request for next year's budget. It is never a function of how they can become more efficient, but how they can spend more dollars. The larger they can increase the size of their bureau makes for a more important person of themselves in the eyes of their superiors.

"It is most sickening to learn at the end of a fiscal year that a bureaucrat rushes around to spend whatever remaining funds that are in the budget because he does not dare leave an ending balance, not even a single dollar. In this way their comments to the administration can truly testify they have totally depleted their funds, so in the coming year more dollars are surely needed. Each of you know exactly what I am saying.

"The more money they spend and the more personnel they hire are the guidelines for their personal promotion and the so-called increased value of their own job security."

"Why is it that you are so adamant about wanting to create Acirema?" Governor Woods inquired while trying desperately to change the subject of Savage's rampage against bureaucrats.

"You mean after I just finished with that statement you still want to ask a question such as this? I can't believe it. Anyway, I'll be more than pleased to respond. First of all, Governor, you need to understand that I, Taylor Savage, did not want to create anything. You and the people who manage the governments of your two states have brought this on yourself. I am attempting to make things work better, that's all.

"Government is simply not responsive to the needs of the people. Politicians don't seem to really care about the average taxpayer and certainly don't care about the exorbitant cost of government, which has gotten way out of hand. And I want to change all of that.

"Remember the movie 'Network' where one of the characters leaned out of the window of a high-rise building and shouted, 'I'm mad as hell, and I ain't gonna take it any more.' Well, that's where our citizens are today, and you polished politicians with egos twice as big as your ass can't seem to understand it. You both are way too busy thinking about the next election and how you are going to stay in office.

"Let me give you an example. For Florida to have the audacity to think it is doing its citizens a favor to pass a law where prison inmates will now have to serve 85 percent of their sentences is a joke. Why is a law even necessary? These criminals have been given a term of incarceration by the courts which follow the laws of the state, and folks like yourself have sat on your ass and not provided the necessary funds and leadership to operate your prison systems to provide the necessary beds and proper efficiency so funds would be available to keep criminals behind bars until their time is served in full.

"Governor Woods, in Florida last November, you released some 450 hardened criminals who had been convicted of murder, rape, and other capital offenses. Then you turned around the following March and released another 600. Did you think it more political, that is, easier on your administration, to release smaller amounts at two different times rather than to release perhaps 1,000 at one time?" asked Savage.

"You need to stop playing games with your citizens. If you are going to be a chief executive, then have the guts to be a stand-up guy. If you are going to be in charge, then be in charge. Stop playing politics with people's lives and their emotions. To release only one criminal before he serves his full and complete sentence is too many. Why can't you understand this?

"You are not a stand-up kinda guy who will create the appropriate amount of space required for incarceration. Therefore, you pass a law to let these murderers and rapists out early. What a cop-out! Where do you get off with crap like this?" Savage continued.

"It is my understanding that 'gain time' is earned when an inmate behaves himself for a full month. And when this occurs, he is credited with 20 days off his sentence. Isn't that the formula, Governor?" Savage demanded.

"Yes, those are the correct numbers which direct our 'gain time' program," answered Woods.

"Well, have you ever stopped and considered the feelings of the families of the victims? How do you think they feel about you and your administration when you release a murderer who had gone into a convenience store and blown away their 17-year-old daughter who had to work part-time after school? What about them? Is there any wonder what the general public thinks about politicians?" Savage asked.

"It's all in the problem with the tax structure and the funds we have to run our facilities. That's the reason for the 'gain time'" answered Woods.

"That's a bunch of bull crap. You two people set, or at least approve, the spending of tax dollars in your states. You are the primary authority. Why haven't proper funds been provided to keep our citizens safe?'' Savage preached.

''We probably will not be able to cut taxes in Acirema, but we are going to greatly reduce the cost of government in several other areas whereby we will be able to use more dollars in our prison system to insure that our citizens are safe from those who need to be behind steel bars.

''Each of you has received transcripts of our first two general assembly meetings, and you probably have seen me on the Laurie Sin' Show. If you will take the simple example where I discussed the cost of front-end loaders that are purchased with either state, county, city, or some authority funds, you will remember I pointed out where we in Acirema could save more than $15 million on these purchases alone. As small as Acirema will be and save that kind of expense and do it on only one item is incredible. When are you going to come out of your pearly white towers and get down where the rubber meets the road and have a look at the real side of life?

''Why not do what former Governor Bob Graham did and work at a common labor job at least one day per month. That is where you will find out what the common man faces every day of his life. I hope that I am not being too hard on you guys. You see, I have nothing to lose. I am beholden to neither of you as compared to those who work for you and have to be 'yes' men and women all day, every day.

''Getting back to the prison inmates. We're going to cut the cost of government and use those funds to make Acirema a safe place to live, to raise our families, and to conduct our businesses. We are going to keep those who have been given prison sentences behind steel bars for 100 percent of their terms. Period. End of report. That's the way it's going to be. We are going to change the system as it is today. The shabby system which each of you has helped create.

''It's frightful the way you folks have let the cost of government get out-of-hand and you could have done something about it a long time ago, well before it was too late. And now, it's too late when someone, or a movement such as I have suggested, comes along with a better means of doing something good for the citizens who pay for the cost of government, including your salaries, I may add. I am dedicated to solving these problems before they have an opportunity to get a chokehold on Acirema.

"You know what your real problem is? Let me tell you. It is your concern about me, Taylor Savage, someone who needs neither of you, someone who will stand up and tell the world exactly like it is. That is what this is really all about and what you both are shaking in your boots over.

"You both need to understand I am going to accomplish what I have set out to do. There will be no stopping until we see Statehood for Acirema. Therefore, I suggest we start talking about what the results will be after Statehood rather than continue talking about why."

"Okay, let's approach it from that standpoint. Let's assume the referendum is successful. What are you going to do next?" asked Governor Foxworth.

"That question can be answered better with another question," stated Savage. "After the positive vote of the referendum, are you two going to continue to fight the results? I need to know that answer before I can answer your question.

"If you are going to continue to fight us, then we are going to take one route. If you recognize the people want Acirema and you are willing to work with us, then we are going to take a totally different approach," assured Savage.

"In my opinion if the people speak in a positive vote on the referendum to create Acirema, then it would be vain and arrogant for us to fight their decision," responded Governor Woods.

"That also will be my position," said Governor Foxworth.

"Well, at least now we have a meaningful starting point for the remainder of this meeting. So to answer your question and assuming we are successful, we then will start our political process of hiring officeholders to administer Acirema. And mind you I said 'hire,' not 'elect.'"

"I need to add something at this point," said Foxworth. "You need to understand that we in Alabama are going to do everything we possibly can to see to it your referendum does not pass. Is that fair?"

"That is most fair. I would expect nothing less. You should fight for the position that you feel better suits your personality. But let me remind you that the funds which you will use to fight Acirema's Statehood must come from sources other than taxpayers' funds. Is that understood?''

"I can see your point. However, I don't know that I agree with you,'' said Foxworth.

"Well, let me make myself quite clear. If you intend to use taxpayers' money to fight something the taxpayers themselves want to do, I'll wrap it around your neck and strangle you with it. I'll make damned sure that neither of you ever wins another election in your state, ever. That is my position, and you should be aware that is the way it is before you start down the wrong path.''

"That's some mighty strong words, Taylor,'' said Governor Woods.

"Governor, you agreed with me that we could speak our minds. Like President Truman said, 'If you can't stand the heat, get the hell out of the kitchen.' And along that same line, Governor Foxworth, I note with great interest how adamantly you are against Acirema, much more so it seems than Governor Woods. Is there a special or personal reason?''

"No, not really, no special reason. However, I feel strongly that it's not the correct step to be taken, and I will voice my opinion as such and fight it to the very bitter end.''

"And there is nothing of a personal nature which would stir your resentment and objections more so than should be that of Governor Woods?'' asked Savage.

"I don't have any idea what you're getting at. Why don't you come out and say what's on your mind, Taylor?''

"Governor Foxworth, Governor Woods is presently serving in his next-to-last year of office, and since this will complete his second term and Florida statutes will not let him succeed himself, he cannot stand for reelection. On the other hand, I note that you are about to complete your first term, and you are eager to run for your second term. Is this correct?''

"Your facts are correct. However, I have not announced my intent to seek a second term, but your assumption is most likely correct.''

"And Governor, I note your home is in Atmore, Alabama. Is that correct?''

"Yes, my home is Atmore.''

"And if we are successful with our plans for Acirema, then

Atmore will become a part of Acirema. With this being true, you could not seek a second term as Governor of Alabama if you, in fact, lived in another state. Isn't that correct?''

"To follow your line of reasoning, that would be correct. However, I would simply move into another city in Alabama, perhaps Montgomery, and run from my new home city.''

"Then if we are successful, you are stating that you would move from Acirema into Alabama where you could seek another term. Is that what you are saying? Am I to understand this to be true?''

"Yes, that's what I would do should I decide to run at all.''

"You would move from Acirema into Alabama, from one state into another. Is that what you are saying?''

"That's correct. How many times do you want me to answer the same exact question.''

"And do you agree at this time your true home is Atmore, Alabama, and that you are a temporary resident of Montgomery because that is the location of the Alabama Governor's Mansion?''

"This is true.''

"Then, Governor, let me inquire as to how you will change your home address from Acirema to Alabama and seek a second term as Governor when the Alabama state statutes plainly note that you must reside in Alabama for seven consecutive years to satisfy the residency requirements before seeking the office?''

"Well, Uh! Why don't we cross that bridge if it becomes necessary. Anyway, we can make allowances for that. Adjust the law.''

"Governor, I just want to impress on you and Governor Woods that we are most sincere in becoming successful in our intent to assure Acirema receives Statehood, and we will accomplish that fact by using every available legal means to do so.

"Let me point out here and now. Your attitude about doing whatever is necessary to be able to seek office for another term is a part of the problem with government today. And you don't even understand it, do you? You don't even see it, do you? Why should the people trust you with the kind of attitude you have. Like I said earlier, it appears that far too many politicians are only interested in getting elected and then reelected with little concern for the purpose of the office which they seek.

"It is little wonder the voters don't think positively about their elected officials. Governor Woods, right here in Florida the people have voted time and again against gambling, yet you and your administration have seen fit to allow gambling boats to operate from docks within the state and use state waters to accomplish exactly what the people have voted against. This is a ridiculous way to treat those who have trusted you with their support. You are making a mockery of the people who elected you to office.

"And let me tell you and point out just how inadequate some of your state Agencies are, as well as some agencies not associated with state government. Time and again your folks leave the entire panhandle of Northwest Florida off the state map and many other publications. Your bureaucrats have treated this end of the state like a red-headed stepchild, and those who live here deserve better promotion for the area from the Chief Executive of Florida who's supposed to be Governor of the entire state.

"I would expect that the fewer number of voters, due to our population in this end of the state, has something to do with it. Wouldn't you imagine? Isn't it true that you court the more populated areas of central and south Florida and only come around these parts every now and again when you feel compelled to do so?"

"Anyway, shall we get back to what our positions should be after Statehood is achieved?" asked Savage.

"I agree," said Governor Woods. "What about the state buildings of our two states which could end up in Acirema? What would you propose and intend to do about them?" asked Foxworth.

"Well, obviously, you can't come get the buildings can you? Or can you? Anyway, they don't belong to Florida or Alabama. They belong to the taxpayers who have paid taxes to provide a working place for state employees to gather while doing state business. They do not belong to the state, neither state. They belong to the people of the region who have paid for them. The people aren't going anywhere; neither, I assume, are the buildings," answered Savage.

"And what do you think should happen to them?" Foxworth continued.

"Let me put it this way. I feel the buildings and all equipment that were formerly used by employees of either Florida or Alabama should become a part of Acirema in total. Should you not see it this way, then we will abandon the structures and you can try to rent the space. Would that make a lot of sense to you?''

''I don't see how we can simply give away state buildings and equipment,'' stated Governor Woods.

''Again, these are not state owned,'' said Savage. ''They are owned by the people of this region who paid taxes to build the facilities so the state workers could have a place to work and assist those who reside in this region. They are truly owned by the people of the region,'' argued Savage.

''You have made your point. Perhaps we need to move on to something else. What is going to happen to the state employees who work for our two states?'' asked Governor Foxworth.

''Well, speaking of employees, let's first talk about affirmative action. I do not believe in affirmative action because on face value it is not fair to anyone. What I believe is that everyone should have a shot at every job, no matter their race. I don't believe in quotas but do believe solidly in the fact that we will hire, and in this case retain, those ultimately qualified to fill all positions. Some employees may not be retained in their current positions but could possibly be offered other jobs which may become available, assuming they are fully qualified.

''Those who are qualified and fit into our work program will be retained. Those who are not retained in their current position, and again if they are qualified, will be given first refusal of new slots which may open. We will have several new positions in our prison system.

''It is our intent to limit the number of our state employees to a figure equal to one half of one percent of our total population. This is far less than half, and perhaps a third, again based on population, of the number of employees required by each of your two states,'' preached Savage.

''That would only be about 7,000 employees. And you think you can operate a state government, even a small state like Acirema, with such a small number of employees?'' asked Governor Woods.

''Yes, I know that we can. We do it in our own business. We do it every day of the week. In fact, the Acirema Platform states that for each employee we keep in a position we will let another one go. If the employee we keep can assume the duties of a dismissed person, then he or she will take on the duties of both positions and will receive a 50 percent increase in pay.

"You see, we, the citizens of Acirema, are not becoming a state so we can put people to work. That is not at all our objective, not our goal. We are not going to become a state just to create state jobs for a bunch of cronies. We are going to become a state and hire those who are most qualified to operate our state government. Our government is going to be only as big as is necessary to take care of the problems which our citizens cannot solve themselves. We will function, and function efficiently, with a small government. I know this is foreign to both of you, but this is what we are going to do.

"While we are eliminating a number of positions, we can overcome the 50 percent increase in salary by keeping good, productive employees and pay their salary from the savings we create with fewer employees. Also, the elimination of the long-term cost of insurance, pensions, retirement funds, and the like will assist us in reaching our projected goals.

"We are going to be big on offering incentives. This is something both of you have failed miserably in your own states. Every working man and woman needs to have an incentive to get up each day and go to work. This is a built-in objective of ours. Our plan will be woven around our employees doing the very best job they can do, and if they do their job properly they will be rewarded for their efforts and their efficiency.

"Let me give each of you an example that may or may not fit your own style of governing. I wonder if either of you has ever taken the time to walk through your office and spend a small amount of time with each employee. I do not mean your staff office, as you see them several times each day. I mean those working for you who are located down in the 'bowels' of government. Those who are possibly in other buildings away from your kingdom. Have you ever done that?

"For instance, when someone is elected to a cabinet position, say Attorney General, then he or she has hundreds of employees in the agency who are the real workers, the guts of the operation, so to speak. I cannot think of a bigger put-down for an employee of the department, someone who may have really wanted to see this new AG elected and in a small way did everything he could to help his cause and insure his election during the campaign and then for the next four years the AG would not once take the time to come around to the various divisions and meet the 'working class personnel.' Do you actually think that employee would vote for him again when he is up for reelection? I don't.

"There have to be incentives in government, and we expect to show those whom we will hire to work in our government an outline of what they can expect based on their personal performance of their job duties."

"I would like to change the subject and ask another question, kind of like thinking out loud," said Governor Woods. "Provided the referendum vote was positive in favor of Acirema, I have already stated this afternoon that I would not stand in the way of your plans. Governor Foxworth said basically the same thing. Now, what would happen, and I'm only thinking out loud, what would happen if I helped deliver the votes for our 10 counties to your side of the equation, and I resigned as Governor of Florida and sought the Governorship of Acirema?"

"Wow! That would be a most interesting set of circumstances," said Foxworth.

"What you would have to do, as I see it, would be to declare this is your intent and do so very soon. Well before the Platform is printed and mailed out to those who reside within the 19 counties," answered Savage.

"And why is that?" inquired Woods.

"Simply because if you don't, it would have a distinct odor of politics as usual, and this is exactly what we are going to overcome. If you want to run and if you are a citizen of Acirema, then we welcome you as we would anyone else who seeks the Governorship. However, the people would not take your candidacy seriously if you waited to see if the referendum was going to pass or fail before you made up your mind."

"I think it's time to have that drink you offered earlier," requested Woods.

"Sure, what would you two like?"

"A beer is fine with me." answered Governor Foxworth

"Same here," allowed Woods.

"Why don't you two knock around your thoughts, and I'll give you a few minutes before I return."

Savage left the two Governors alone. No sooner had he closed the door behind him when Foxworth continued, "He's one hell of a smart fellow, and I sincerely think he knows exactly what he is doing and where he is going with this program."

"Yeah, you're right. What are we going to do?" asked Woods.

"As soon as we return to our offices in the morning, we should call our two Cabinets together, and while doing so we need to include the leadership from both houses of our Legislatures as we are going to need all the tricks we can pull from the hat," noted Foxworth.

"There's no doubt about it. Do you have a means in Alabama to find a poll and research team and a way to pay for their services?" asked Woods.

"Sure. I can get about anything done that I want in Alabama. What do you think we'll need?"

"It would be well if we had an early poll taken the middle of next week and see the results before we have our joint Cabinet meeting and then another poll about a week later."

When Savage returned, he had three cold Brookman Beers and three frozen mugs.

"Hoppy Brookman is on our committee, and I assured the membership that both Savage Worldwide and I were dedicated to supporting those who will be doing business in Acirema. Hope you two enjoy the Brookman."

□ □ □ □ □

AFTER A COUPLE OF beers, the three decided they had little more to discuss. They knew Savage had put together a masterful plan and was determined to see it to a successful conclusion. Each man had decided for himself that nothing would change the longer they visited, and there was no reason to continue with conversations which could possibly create an atmosphere of anger or say some things that did not need to be spoken.

"Taylor, we thank you for your willingness to sit down with us, and your hospitality is much appreciated," said Governor Woods. "From all indications it appears that you are on a course that you are determined to follow. Therefore, I wish you luck in your endeavor.''

"Governor, I do appreciate your comments. Obviously, my program does not concern itself with either of you personally, although it will affect both of your states.''

"We understand and I want you to know there is not going to be any hard feelings of a personal nature,'' said Governor Foxworth. "We feel what you are attempting is not good for either Florida or Alabama, and we will do whatever we can to halt you. But if the referendum passes, we will cease any and all objections.''

"That's fair,'' Savage responded. "I wouldn't expect anything else. I realize we have different opinions. However, we can disagree without being disagreeable, and I trust that after the results are in, we will again have the opportunity to sit down over another Brookman, beer that is.

"Before you leave let me share something else with you. Our country is without a doubt the very best place on this entire planet to live, but we do have problems which need to be addressed, and we all must pull together to solve them. You know the average man on the street is not getting a fair shake. While he is in the majority, he is not being treated like many other 'more special' groups of individuals. Take for instance, if the owners of two small businesses get together and agree they just simply are not making enough profit for their efforts and time spent and they discuss raising the price of an item or a service, then they could be hauled into court for price fixing. A crime which should never be overlooked in any capacity no matter how large or small.

"Now, I want to be very clear in what I am saying here. I am not accusing anyone of anything, but by way of example consider this. If there were three large manufacturers of a product with each having his very own design and engineering departments or divisions, each operating in a different atmosphere, and perhaps in very different geographical locations of our country, with each company being driven by a stern, hard-nosed board of directors and well-paid executives, you would think their final product, when leaving the assembly line, could cost a considerably different amount, given these vast and different circumstances.

"Still, for some unknown reason, their products are almost exactly the same price when they become available to the consumer. Is this just a coincidence? Or, is there a reason that Fords,

Chevrolets, and Plymouths cost the consumer within a few dollars of each other? Ever thought about that?

"When a story like this comes about, the radio and television networks have a field day. All major networks will go to great lengths to showcase wrong doings or the intent of wrong doings as did ABC in the recent Foodliner charge. And you will remember the courts and a jury saw right through their evil minds and greedy needs to pile up Nielsen ratings, etc., and awarded Foodliner a tremendous judgment.

"Should not networks, all networks, be as pure as Caesar's wife? If they are daily searching for news stories to bring to the public's attention, shouldn't they clean up their own houses and be above and beyond reproach? What, or who, gives them the right to break laws to obtain a story?

"Now, let's look right into the networks' own backyards. Since the advanced stages of our vast computer industries have so perfected their products, we now can do wonders. With computers we can precisely control all facets of the television marketing and advertising industry. In years past television viewers, especially since the remote control became commonplace, quickly jumped from channel to channel every time a commercial appeared on their screens. To react to this, all the big boys of the television industry sat down and formulated a set of rules and regulations by which today they all abide. They adopted a format whereby all the major networks would stop their programs at the same precise time. Now, when you channel surf, you will only find more commercials and not another show.

"Could this not be considered a form of collusion? Did they not get together to sell their products and capture the entire viewing market with this scheme? Somehow or another, doesn't this seem to be wrong? Couldn't it also be considered price fixing?

"In short, they think their misdeeds justify a sound and positive means to an end. This is the same attitude and way that many, and I do mean many, politicians think. Often it matters not what they do or say as long as they can garner enough votes to be elected because in their heart of hearts they feel they ultimately can and will be the best person to hold the office they seek, regardless of what it takes to get them there in the first place."

"You're wound tight today, Savage," said Governor Foxworth.

"Well, I've got a right to be. Wasn't it Popeye who said 'That's alls I can stands, and I can't stands no mo.' I'm beginning to think that is the way most of us feel," Savage reminded them.

□ □ □ □ □

WITH THAT, ALL three men rose and walked to the railing to look over the still waters of the emerald green Gulf and the sugar white sands. They stood there silently as if each were thinking how much they would miss not having this area to revisit, much as if someone had purchased it and was ready to move it to another location.

Walking downstairs Governor Woods asked, "Who do you see as candidates for the Governorship provided your program passes its referendum?"

"It appears to me we may have at least three Democratic candidates and thus far only one Republican. I would not be surprised if Former Governor Daniels, Hoppy Brookman, and Andrew Wright may qualify for the Democrats and Ray Haze for the Republicans. I have also heard rumors that the Chairman of the Mobile County School Board may have an interest. His name is Clay Wingate, and I think he is a Republican."

"Yes, he is. I've known Clay for several years, and he is a very fine gentleman, a real class act, a straight shooter. He originated the One Thousand Black Men for Alabama Organization," said Governor Foxworth."

"I've heard this also and look forward to meeting him soon. Do you both know the four candidates I just mentioned?"

"Yes, I do," said Governor Woods. "I appointed Brookman to a commission, the Northwest Florida Water Management District, just two years ago. I've known Wright for many years as he chaired the lobbying efforts for Regions Power Company. And as you both know, I was Governor Daniels' Lieutenant Governor for eight years, and in that capacity I met Ray Haze on several occasions."

"Well, for me I know Haze better as I had to face him in the last two Republican primaries. I've not had the privilege of meeting either Mr. Wright or Mr. Brookman. However, he does brew a fine beer. I've known Governor Daniels for several years," recalled Governor Foxworth.

"So that you may get a feel of the quality of men, and I hope women, who will seek either the Governorship or U.S. Senate from Acirema, let me tell you about the background of a couple of them. In the mid-'40s, Anthony 'Pop' Brookman originated and built a small brewery on the north side of Niceville, Florida, and did quite well during the early heydays of Eglin Air Force Base and the development of Hulbert Field. His brewery produced and distributed Brookman Beer and Ale and dominated the market along the coast from Panama City to the Mississippi State line and provided a growing family of four boys and twin girls with a college degree and a prosperous life. I know a lot about the Brookman family since my father and Pop Brookman were long-time friends.

"Two of his sons have moved to California and involved themselves heavily in the foreign car market. A third son and one of the twin girls were tragically killed in a private airplane crash on a return trip from Vail, Colorado, in the early '70's. The remaining twin married a dentist and lives with her family on the outskirts of Lookout Mountain, Tennessee.

"Harry, the youngest son, whom we all know as Hoppy, took over the family business after graduating from the Citadel and immediately decided to expand the operation, which now enjoys a large market across the entire Southeast. Hoppy is very much interested in Acirema simply because he understands the tremendous potential for our new state, which would depend a good deal for its survival on tourism and vacationing families.

"He feels the potential we offer would be a Mecca for the rich and famous, and he is simply going to get his share of the pie. I am sure the closeness of Acirema to the gambling casinos of the Mississippi Coast and the sports activities from Atlanta, New Orleans, Jacksonville, and Birmingham are also a great drawing card. What we are going to accomplish in Acirema is a natural project for his company to support. Since I first revealed our plans, he has spoken to me about what I think in terms of his being a candidate for statewide office. He would make an outstanding candidate for either the Governorship or the United States Senate.

"About six months ago Andrew Wright was given his dismissal notice by Regions Power Company after being a tremendous asset to them for more than 23 years. He thought about it for some time, then decided not to fight the termination although he was sure he would win the battle in a court of law. As I understand it, he had uncovered some facts that tied some of their executive officers to something illegal, but I have no idea what it was about. He apparently knows the entire story, knows where all the bones are buried. To me it was a real stupid thing on their part to fire him since he had full knowledge of their every move, and if anything was done illegally he must be aware of it. Anyway, the firing was their decision, and I don't think he ever forgave them.

"Wright is a made-to-order Chamber of Commerce type individual who would do well in the political structure of Acirema. It was rumored two years ago that he was a likely candidate for a Florida statewide race, but that it never materialized.

"After our first meeting, he came up and said that although he, along with all the others, had not known the purpose of the meeting when he arrived, he was absolutely amazed at the concept and that he was ready to allocate as much time as need be and was totally dedicated to do whatever he could to make our plans a success. He was most delighted with the tremendous prospects for Acirema.

"He lives his life to sit at a table and be in the midst of the future plans of almost any deal, to be involved with the movers and shakers, and to that end he is going to do very well in the near future. If I was running a campaign for him, our theme would be 'Vote Wright the first time.' I don't know who coined the saying, but he is forever quoting, 'Don't get mad, get even.' In my opinion, he has waited for several months to have the opportunity to get even with Regions Power—and his time may be nearing.''

With that the two Governors bade Savage goodbye, saying they would be talking with him soon. Savage quickly packed only a few items, leaving most of his things behind. He and Sheery had a complete wardrobe at Seaside, Pensacola Beach, Amelia Island, Raleigh, and Goldsboro. He was off to Pensacola Beach knowing it was going to be a fine afternoon to walk Hot and Toddy.

ON THE TRIP BACK to the Destin airstrip, the Governors had an opportunity to talk openly. Governor Woods assured Foxworth it was perfectly okay to talk in front of Captain Wilcox who had been driving for him for more than six years and was completely trustworthy.

"What do you think we should do next?" asked Foxworth.

"Let's go ahead with our joint cabinet meeting and explore all of our options, assuming we have any! I think it prudent if each of us spends some time with our legal staff as well as our United States Senators and whoever the President will send to us to assist," said Woods.

"Well, you are going to have to deal with the President's men since he is of your Democratic Party. Our two Alabama Senators, as you know, are of separate parties. However, I would think they will be with us together on this issue. Something that worries me is that Senator Wells is from Mobile, and we may have a problem, especially if he likes the idea of Acirema inasmuch as it may well be his future state," said Governor Foxworth.

"If he does, then he will be in the boat with what I fear will be the great majority of those within the boundaries of the newly proposed fifty-first state. Anyway, he will have to consider that he will be losing his Senate seat should the referendum pass, and looking on the bright side if it does, then you as Governor of Alabama will get to appoint his replacement which may well be yourself. That's one way to assure yourself of a great political seat even if the worst happens and we lose the referendum."

"But with me being from Atmore and that area being annexed into Acirema, I wonder how I could appoint myself since I would not truly be a citizen of Alabama once the referendum passes. You reckon my temporary residency in Montgomery would hold up as a residency requirement? Anyway, Senator Wells, as you know, is a Democrat, and his party is certainly not going to roll over and let me have a free ride without a deep, hard-fought court case."

"You know I've got a gut feeling that Taylor Savage has already taken this into consideration during the five years he has been developing this program," said Woods. "Let's face it, if the referendum passes, he gets rid of you, a second-term governor, and a United States Senator both because of residency requirements. It looks as though he is in this to clean house and has started at the top and at your expense," said Governor Woods.

"Yeah, if Wells and I both fight the secession issue, there is no way either of us could possibly stand for election from the State of Acirema, the state that we would actually have to call home. And if we lose the referendum, it is most unlikely that the balance of the voters from Alabama will have enough confidence in us to reelect either one of us to any office," said Governor Foxworth.

"Looks to me as though you both are between a rock and a hard place, in a real pickle. I may well consider throwing in the towel and help them secede and make a run for either the Senate or the Governorship of Acirema," said Woods.

"I've got a real sick feeling down deep inside that Taylor Savage could not care less about anyone's political future. These are our own personal problems that he will not have to deal with, and while we are spending our time fighting him we had better pay a lot of attention to our own little red wagon," stated Foxworth.

NINE

WHILE TAYLOR SAVAGE and the two Governors were in heavy debate over how to handle the possibility of Statehood for Acirema, Ray Haze was busy entertaining Peaches Lamont at Point Clear.

It had been often said that Peaches would make the Mayflower Madam seem like a Baptist Sunday School teacher. However, her reputation in the field of political promotion and marketing could not be surpassed. While those on the inside knew of her personal activities and ambitions, of which some snubbed her and others could not care less, she did have the knack of getting things done, was very successful in the political arena, and had produced a winning record with only one loss out of the 12 campaigns she had managed over the past six years.

In recent months she had tempered her ways of the past and was most often seen with Ray Haze, who was fond of staying around his home spread, hanging out in the hot tub, and doing very little of showing himself around his hometown turf. He always preferred to take his personal, social affairs out of town and often out of the country. This suited Peaches just fine as she was always packed, willing, and ready to travel.

On weekends she usually arrived at his home around 6:00 on Friday afternoon but not before calling at his insistence. He always explained it away by saying a business meeting may be in progress, but she was well aware of his habits and shenanigans and did not buy this excuse at all. It was only a short drive from her condo in Mobile to Point Clear, which was most convenient considering the many times she was sent packing before Monday morning.

As it would often happen, their weekends would commence with dinner and dancing at the Point Clear Hotel, late night after-dinner drinks at 'The Cove,' and a midnight swim back at his place. Midnight swimming in the bay on hot summer nights or in the heated pool during the winter months became weekend commonplace. When they arrived back at his home this winter night, the weather was very cold, but they faithfully fought it off with B&B and hot buttered rum drinks while settling into the steaming hot Jacuzzi tub rather than a swim.

Most Saturday mornings began with the usual big breakfast including all the fatty foods that could possibly be found to aid in maintaining and satisfying his plump stomach and her constantly hanging onto his arm to satisfy his ego and manhood.

This Saturday, after the normal routine, they would take an afternoon and overnight cruise on his 97-foot Broward yacht to Pirates Cove on Perdido Bay. A night on the boat always made Haze feel his oats, especially if there were plenty of Vodka and OJ. With *Many Places* safely anchored in a shallow cove on the south side of the bay, they relaxed on the open rear deck and discussed the role each would play in the development of Acirema.

Haze had wanted very badly to become Governor of Alabama, but his second consecutive loss had assured him his chances were slim to none. With the creation of Acirema, it just might well be the ticket he had been waiting for, the chance of a lifetime.

He had already been in deep conversations with Doc Howard, the political pollster for his previous campaigns. It was easy for Howard to print out a computer listing of the results of the last election which, as they both remembered well, Haze had lost only one of the nine counties that was destined to become part of Acirema. Haze had carried Mobile County by a large margin. In fact, his numbers were almost 61 percent in that county, and there had been three other candidates in the race. History indicated that no one had ever received that large a percent of the Mobile County vote and still not been elected Governor. Something had gone dreadfully wrong in Birmingham, Montgomery, and Tuscaloosa and caused his ultimate loss in the general election although he had won both Republican primaries.

Peaches insisted if he was to consider a race for the governorship of Acirema, he had better start immediately to lose some of the gut he had acquired and get into fighting shape. She knew for sure, due to the limited time restraints before the first election and only 60 days provided for campaigning, that any candidate who already had name and face exposure, as did Haze, would be far ahead of all others from day one.

Neither Haze nor Peaches had heard of anyone mentioning the possibility of Prescott Daniels, the former Governor of Florida and an Acirema committee member, having any interest in the race. However, they thought he would be a very formidable candidate should he show such interest. He certainly had name recognition equal to, if not exceeding, that of Haze.

The television market along the upper Gulf Coast overlaps between Pensacola and Mobile. While Daniels was Governor of Florida, every news event making headlines in his state was telecast over the Pensacola ABC station which encompassed a large area all the way across south Alabama to the Mississippi line and totally blanketed the entire Mobile County market.

Likewise, during Haze's two campaigns, all his commercials had been seen across Pensacola and all the way to Panama City carried by both the CBS and NBC stations of Mobile. Also, the large market of several cable television companies throughout the area carried commercials of each campaign without regard to it being an Alabama or Florida election.

Both Peaches and Haze agreed it would be a very fast-paced and most interesting race should he and Daniels become challengers for the first Governorship of Acirema. They were sure each had maintained his original backers and could count on early support, while a third candidate would have to literally start from scratch.

They discussed what would happen to the sitting state Legislators of both states who would lose their seats due to the annexation of their districts into Acirema. She thought many officeholders might consider a run for the new Acirema unicameral Legislature. He thought otherwise because they would surely fight Acirema's referendum alongside all other Legislators in Florida and Alabama. If Acirema was successful, then their leadership roles and abilities would suffer greatly, and their support to run for the newly created seats would be totally diminished.

◻ ◻ ◻ ◻ ◻

WITH THE ISSUES OF the Platform becoming clearer with each meeting and the committee hearing firsthand reports about the opportunities which lay ahead, several members had found themselves interested in the search for someone they ultimately could support for their first Governor. It was most interesting when a couple or three committee members made known that they themselves might have to look at the opportunity real close for their own possible race as a candidate. Everyone agreed that Former Governor Daniels and two-time Alabama candidate Haze seemed to have the lead in name recognition which would be most important given the brief time frame of the initial election.

Standing in the background, as Taylor Savage had predicted, were two other possible candidates, Andrew Wright and Harry 'Hoppy' Brookman. Both would have to be considered dark horses with Wright being the darkest simply because of Brookman's wealth; he would have no financial problem mounting a very formidable campaign.

The support Haze commanded in previous campaigns in eight of the nine Alabama counties which were destined to become part of Acirema would certainly make a positive impact on his race should he decide to enter the contest. And of those mentioned thus far, he was the only Republican candidate.

The polls would surely place Wright at the bottom of the list of the four. However, it appeared he might gain the support of Taylor Savage. And for sure, he would work hard on his campaign, as it would be a star in his crown if he were successful—if for no other reason than to have an impact on the permitting process of his former employer, Regions Power, which was expected to reveal plans for a new power generation plant to be built on the Perdido River separating Florida and Alabama.

◻ ◻ ◻ ◻ ◻

ALTHOUGH NO ONE HAD completely made up his mind to be a candidate, all four men had commenced to court the leadership of their respective parties. With a crowded field, nothing would be automatic for the Democratic candidates, and each who qualified to run in the primaries would receive a very warm and courteous audience from all the mainline movers and shakers throughout all 19 counties.

On the Republican side, if no one but Haze got into the race, then he would become their nominee with little fanfare and at a considerable savings of funds which could be put to much better use against the Democrats in the general election of the legislature. Haze had already calculated that each Democratic candidate would spend a good deal of the allowable $1.4 million, should he be fortunate enough to raise that maximum amount, in his attempt to eliminate his competitors. In so doing they would cut each other up so bad it would, perhaps, diminish their ability to mount a formidable campaign to assist the party in the general election.

When the election planks of the original Acirema Platform were distributed at the end of the first committee meeting, Haze noticed a subsection dealing with the cap on collecting of funds for campaigns and quickly made a mental note. Although he was sure that Taylor Savage would challenge him, he would accept the challenge and if necessary take it all the way to the Supreme Courts if Savage tried to identify the cap as a rule that was meant as a cap on spending and not just a cap on the collection of contributions. There would be quite a difference as it related to interpretation.

Taking the Platform at its face value would mean he could collect and spend only $1.4 million. However, it did not address the fact that a cap may or may not include any of his own funds that he might wish to spend. Wouldn't this be outside the rules of the Platform, he wondered, and couldn't he spend as much of his own fortune as he desired?

☐ ☐ ☐ ☐ ☐

THE ENTIRE FLORIDA CABINET boarded an early flight on Thursday morning to Montgomery for the scheduled 10:00 o'clock joint meeting. Governor Foxworth had arranged to have three Alabama Highway Patrol officers chauffeur the seven members to the State Capitol. When they arrived, a horde of reporters covered them like the dew covers Dixie. Governor Woods, as spokesman, made a short statement that no comments would be made until after the joint meeting of the two State Cabinets and invited the media to sit in on the meeting.

The Florida Cabinet mixed and mingled with the Alabama delegation introducing themselves to one another over coffee, juice, and rolls. Although their intent was not to discuss the issue until they sat down in an official capacity, still there were comments, questions, and opinions on everyone's lips. With the informal gathering over, both Cabinets took their seats behind the massive table with each state official sitting next to his counterpart.

Governor Foxworth opened the meeting and introduced his Cabinet to Governor Woods, who in turn introduced the Florida Cabinet. A general discussion took place which came close to being a heated conversation and debate on several occasions. In summation, this historic meeting finally came down to the pure fact that there was really nothing much either state individually or collectively could do if the referendum passed and the people of the intended new state boundaries wanted to exit Florida and Alabama and become the state of Acirema.

In a joint effort to reach some formal conclusion, both cabinets voted unanimously to have the two Governors and their four United States Senators meet with President Clinton's advisory people to see what could next be done. With that being agreed, they voted to recess the meeting until such time as their Senators could report back on their efforts in Washington. Governor Foxworth made a final comment and called the question of adjournment without allowing any consideration for the media to participate in questions and answers.

Before a second was offered on his motion, a reporter from the *Birmingham News* stood and demanded to be heard. Governor Foxworth acknowledged him.

"Governor, I am Ted Hooks of the *Birmingham News*. Don't you think it somewhat out of line that you and this historic gathering of the two Cabinets of two states don't conclude your conference by taking questions from the media? And I have more than one to ask."

"Mr. Hooks, this was not to be a press conference. However, if my colleagues want to entertain some questions, I certainly do not object. Members, would you like to field some questions?''

Governor Woods immediately stood and commented, ''I don't think our delegation has any problem with seeing what's on the mind of the media. Sure, let's have a little give and take session.''

With that Governor Foxworth opened the floor to the media, and instantly many hands went up and questions were shouted toward the officials. ''Mr. Hooks, why don't you have the floor first. What's on your mind?''

''It appears to me this joint conference seems to have no answers to Taylor Savage's program, and you want to pass the buck forward to our United States Senators and the President. Would you like to comment?''

''Quite frankly,'' said Foxworth, ''I feel from what was learned here this morning we have little in the way of a solution and need to look into whatever federal actions are available.''

''Okay, but wouldn't your inquiring of federal assistance be playing right into the hands of Mr. Savage inasmuch as these two Southern states, including both Governors and both Cabinets, have once again decided to turn to Washington for help, assistance, and a means to solve local problems?'' the panel was asked.

''I don't think you can classify our current position as turning to Washington to assist us. I feel we, and quite frankly the entire nation, is up against something here that needs the attention of all the citizens of our country,'' responded Woods.

''Yes,'' continued the inquiring reporter, ''but for years you and your colleagues have preached and begged for more local authority, more home rule, and more states' rights. Now, look at what you advocate. Isn't this the primary reason Taylor Savage wants to create a new state? One which can handle its own affairs?''

''Again, Sir, I think we are up against a lot more than what you are asking about. We have some serious problems that will need the attention of both our state governments and the federal government as well,'' answered Foxworth.

''Okay, let me ask something of a different nature. Do you two Governors see a problem being formed as it relates to the dissidents, the nonconformists? Will this be a problem across the region that may well become Acirema?''

''Let me answer that,'' spoke Becca Rawls, Alabama's Attorney General. "We have some very strong-willed folks living in Alabama, and I am sure Governor Woods will attest to the same in Florida. I expect there may be a groundswell of disenchantment across both states, and I certainly feel the large majority of those who have been polled will most likely reduce greatly in numbers. I do not see this movement being a runaway, and consequently the closer the vote, the more problems I expect will erupt across these 19 counties."

"And that presents another interesting question," said the reporter. "What form of enforcement would you use to calm such an outbreak? You obviously could not use the National Guard from either Florida or Alabama. Wouldn't it have to be a function of the President calling out federal troops should a massive disturbance occur? And again, wouldn't this be a situation where the two of you Southern Governors would once again call on Big Brother in Washington to bail you out of trouble? And still again, isn't this exactly what Taylor Savage is trying to avoid, that is the dependency of Big Brother continually looking over our shoulders?"

"Sir, we have an abundance of problems which our joint Cabinet needs to consider," said Governor Woods. "Rather than continue to speculate on answers to your many questions, at this time I suggest to all concerned that we take a few days to digest what has been talked about today and meet again in the near future."

After closing the meeting, the two Cabinets in private agreed that nothing much had changed, and the meeting produced little in the way of answers they were seeking. Before the Florida delegation boarded its flight back home, they all agreed to keep the lines of communication open, to fight the movement with whatever sources they could find, and to get back together in a week or so.

TEN

FRIDAY EVENING WHEN Taylor Savage arrived at Flounder's, about half the committee and their wives and/or dates had already gathered. Over cocktails they made small talk about how much publicity they were getting and how the national news media kept Acirema at the top of every broadcast and on the front page of every daily paper. Several of the members were most interested in finding out more about the Acirema International Global Airport and its stage of development. Mark Houston cornered Savage and was in deep discussion about the possibility of a future negotiated contract to do all the earth work and asphalt paving.

Over the course of the night and throughout dinner, adult beverages too often loosened up a few of the members and made them begin to feel some special closeness to Savage. While he was a most charming man with a great personality, he cared little about people who tended to hang all over him and tried to get too close, especially those he knew very little about personally. They would soon realize in the coming months that each was selected for the committee assignment for a very special and specific reason. Savage had his ducks all in a row long before he mailed out the first invitation asking them to serve in this historic capacity.

Over the next several weeks each would have an indication what role Acirema would really play in his or her everyday personal and business life. Roles which would enhance their personal life in a financial way, all honest and above board, without a trace of corruption.

Before the night was over, Savage had dropped a subtle hint to John Pyle asking what equipment it would require to dry-dock the LEX either in the Port of Mobile or the Port of Pensacola. The question was phrased in such a manner that suggested Pyle may want to consider either opening another ship repair and maintenance facility in one of the two Acirema ports or to actually move his entire operation from Pascagoula to an Acirema port facility.

Savage Worldwide had already made known that all renovations to the LEX would be done within the State of Acirema, and that contract alone would be somewhere between $75-80 million. This hint was only the first of many that would become commonplace among those who would develop a business association with Savage and his company.

□ □ □ □ □

WITH DINNER COMPLETE, Savage extended an invitation to anyone who would like to drop by his home for an after-dinner drink. Ray Haze and Peaches Lamont, Mark Houston and his wife Dawn, Hoppy Brookman and his wife Liz, and Laura accepted. Laura would help serve inasmuch as Sheery was not able to make the trip down from Goldsboro and would not arrive until late the next afternoon.

The weather was quite cool but very nice on the bayside deck where everyone paid a lot of special attention to Hot and Toddy. After an hour or so Houston insisted they had to leave as it was a long drive back to Panama City. Peaches and Haze took off for Gulf Shores, and Hoppy and Liz headed for Niceville.

Savage had remarked privately to Laura a couple of times during the evening that he had a hard time being around Liz because she was so very hyper. Always getting up and sitting down, back and forth, never relaxing, causing him to remark to Laura that he thought ''she would make a tranquilizer nervous.''

''Now, Taylor, she wasn't that bad. Why don't you just relax, and I'll clean up the bar and kitchen,'' she volunteered.

''Don't bother with it. Voncile and Kory will take care of it in the morning,'' he insisted.

She took the hint that it was time for her to leave but decided to ask anyway, "I would like another White Russian, if it's okay with you."

"Sure that's fine. You want to mix, or would you like me to do it?" he asked.

"Oh, don't worry, I'll fix it myself. What would you like? Another brandy maybe?"

"Yeah, that'll be fine. Why don't you bring them to the deck? This weather is just exceptional, too nice to sit inside."

They relaxed in lounge chairs and first discussed some future Acirema plans, then slightly drifted off the subject into more personal and sometimes intimate thoughts.

"I could use another Russian," she said with a question showing in her voice.

"You know where it is. Help yourself."

"Would you care for another?"

"How about pouring me a glass of chardonnay. If there's not one open, I'll come do the honor."

□ □ □ □ □

LAURA AND HER TWO daughters lived in north Escambia County in an area known as Cantonment, about 20 miles from Pensacola Beach. Midway through her fifth drink, she got the nerve to ask, "It's a long way home from here. Think I could use a guest room for the evening?"

"Now, Laura, you know that's a problem that we don't need to have, but you've probably had too much to drink and I hate to see you drive like that. What about your daughters? Won't they be expecting you?"

"They are with their dad this weekend. But it's okay. I'll leave. I don't want to infringe on our business relationship."

"Well, I'm not pleased that we got ourselves into this situation, but you can stay downstairs in a guest room under one condition."

"And what would that condition be?"

"As soon as you wake up in the morning, you need to leave. Don't concern yourself with saying goodbye, and don't worry with the bed. Voncile will take care of it. Why don't you use the room at the end of the hall on the right. Do you think that you will be okay to drive home in the morning?"

"Sure, don't concern yourself with that. I'll be perfectly all right by then. And thanks for your understanding."

"Good night, Laura."

"Good night, Taylor. I'll see you Monday morning at the office."

□ □ □ □ □

MONDAY MORNING WAS not going to be a good day. Laura had received a call from a former friend who insisted he come for a drink on Saturday afternoon and did not leave until shortly before the girls arrived from their dad's around 6:00 on Sunday evening. He was an old flame, and memories from the past and more bottles of wine than she cared to remember made the morning somewhat difficult.

She fixed the girls a light breakfast and hustled them out the door for school, as usual reminding them to drive safely. Their father had given Joyce a new Mustang for her 16th birthday six months ago, although in Laura's opinion Joyce was still in the learning stages of driving, and she cringed each time Joyce started the engine.

For Laura the trip from Cantonment to her office in downtown Pensacola, even via the I-110 express route, was a lengthy one, even on good days. This morning, with ears still ringing, it seemed that she had been driving for hours. Today was going to be especially hectic since her plate was full organizing the committee meeting scheduled for all-day tomorrow. When she arrived at Savage Worldwide offices on Cypress street, she was most surprised to see that Taylor was already at his desk. It was still a quarter 'til 8:00, and his being here this early was indeed a very rare occasion.

She immediately thought of Friday night and her staying over at the beach and wondered if this had any bearing. Did Sheery question him about the party? Was she concerned that I stayed over? Did he even tell her that I had? Or worse did he not tell her, and she found out on her own? She conceded to herself that his being here so early could not be a good sign no matter what may or may not have occurred over the weekend.

She would simply act as though nothing was wrong. "Good morning, Taylor. How was your weekend?"

"Oh, it was all right I guess. Can you make a pot of coffee?"

"Certainly, right away."

While waiting on the coffee to brew, she decided to let him bring up anything that might be the matter. She assumed he had already picked up the morning paper from the mail room area when he came in.

When the coffee was ready, she took him a cup with the regular fixings of one Sweet and Low and one cream. Walking into his office, she noticed the absence of the paper that always lay on the front right-hand corner of his desk, if he did not have it in his hands. Again, she held back and did not ask any questions. He thanked her for the coffee without making any other comment or gesture. He was not himself at all this morning, she thought.

She returned to the coffee lounge, and while preparing herself a cup of hot tea, Donna, the bookkeeper, arrived. "Good morning, Laura. Isn't this weather nice? How was the party Friday night?"

Before she could answer she noticed a newspaper in her hand. "Is that our morning paper?"

"Yes, I picked it up downstairs when I came in. Why did you ask? I always bring it up."

"Donna, what time does the paper usually arrive each morning?"

"Don Allen, our maintenance man, is always here by 6:00, and the paper has already been delivered by the time he arrives. What's the matter? Something wrong?"

"Oh, no. Nothing at all. Thanks. I'll get with you in a little bit and go over some figures that Mr. Savage will need before noon."

Laura walked back into her office and quietly sat down, turned her executive chair around and stared out over the harbor of Pensacola Bay. She knew that Taylor would have picked up the paper had it been here when he arrived so the answer was very simple. He had arrived at the office before 6:00 this morning. She now knew that something was really wrong, and it began to unsettle her nerves.

□ □ □ □ □

SAVAGE HAD NOT LEFT the privacy of his office all morning nor made any of his normal inquiries. In fact he had shut his door, signifying another sign of an apparent problem. Laura heard his private line ring once and could not help but gaze intently at her phone and his private line light, which was on less than a minute when the call concluded.

Savage abruptly left his office and walked to the front of Laura's door. "I'm going flying. I'll be back after lunch."

Without any hesitation, the words flowed from her lips without thinking. "Do you want some company? Would you like for me to come along?"

He just stood there and looked at her for what seemed like forever, then spoke very gently. "No, thanks. I just need to get away for awhile. When I return, I need to meet with you and Donna about the figures for the Theater Complex in Dallas. Make sure she knows what I want to see. Goodbye."

"Taylor, I can tell something is bothering you. Please be careful, and if you need a friend to talk with, you can always count on me."

"Thanks, Laura."

◻   ◻   ◻   ◻   ◻

WHEN TUESDAY ROLLED around, Taylor Savage was again in high spirits and eager to face the committee with new and challenging ideas that would make Acirema the dream State of the Union. No matter the degree of problems he was facing, he was always pumped up when he stood before the committee. He felt most assured and very comfortable by knowing his plans would surely survive and change the political structure of the entire nation.

As usual, the horde of news print reporters, radio, and television media dominated the front entrance of the Pensacola Hilton. And once again, Savage welcomed each into the committee hearing after the breakfast hour with the normal comment that no committee business would take place until that time.

While the committee members finished breakfast, he made his way to the podium. "Good morning. I hope that you are all feeling well this fine morning and ready to undertake another step towards guiding us to Statehood for Acirema.

"I want to tell you all just how much I enjoyed Friday evening at Flounder's. When you spend as much time as we have spent together, it is very good to be able to let your hair down a bit. I did enjoy being with each of you, and this morning I bring you an apology from my friend Sheery who was unable to make it to Pensacola in time for the dinner. She sends her regards and says that she is looking forward to meeting each of you in the very near future.

"At the end of our last meeting, I suggested that we use this session of our committee meeting to open the floor to a variety of ideas from each of you. I am sure the press and media will be delighted that we will cover a more diverse number of subjects which, needless to say, will give them much more to tell the world about what we are planning for Acirema. And while on the press and media, I want to take a moment to thank each of them, maybe with only one exception, and that person would know of whom I speak, for doing a magnificent job of reporting to the world what has been going on behind these walls here at the Hilton.

"I can't help but think something is wrong with our world of politicians who always have some unkind words for the media. With the fair reporting that has been done thus far, pertaining to Acirema, I certainly feel that some of the blame, if not most of it, relative to 'bad press' reporting would have to lay in the hands of the politicians themselves. It would appear to me that if our politicians would always come clean with their thoughts and ideas and not try to cover their tracks all the time, then maybe, just maybe, the press would see the greater majority of them in a brighter light.

"Okay, this morning let's start right in with any comments that any of you may like to make pertaining to any subject which you feel should be addressed in our subcommittees and then brought to the full committee for amendments and inclusion within our Platform. As you stand, I will introduce you for the benefit of the press and media. Who would like to go first?

"Yes, first we have Sister Anna Smith, Administrator of the Holy Heaven Catholic Hospital of Mobile. Thank you for standing Sister Smith. What do you have for us this morning?"

"Mr. Savage, do I understand that we can speak on any topic relative to either the planks of the Platform or items which we feel would be beneficial to the operation of our new state government. Are these the guidelines which we are to follow?"

"Yes, Sister. Anything that you feel that would be beneficial to the subcommittees to address and thereafter bring to the attention of the full committee."

"Thank you, Mr. Savage. As Administrator of our hospital, several times each day I have to speak with various agencies within the state government of Alabama. Obviously, the majority of these matters concern some form of health issues. These could be conversations with their Department of Health and Rehabilitation pertaining to rules and regulations, their license board pertaining to our staff and license requirements, and a variety of subjects such as those.

"Having to deal with the bureaucracy is a real headache, and I want to point out a couple of items. First and foremost is the use of electronic mail, or voice mail if you will. This is without doubt the most wasteful instrument within state government—or in any business or home for that matter. I would dare say the phone companies are the only ones who really like these programs, and they are making a killing on fees, especially long distance fees.

"You can never get a person on the phone, and when you do the chances of them having the correct answer to your question is remote. However, as unpleasant as it is to have a human tell you the wrong answer, it beats having to deal with a recorder.

"And speaking of telephone etiquette, let me tell you, when you call a governmental agency—be it local, state, or national—and ask to speak with someone, the receptionists will buzz their station and if they are not there will return to tell you she or he is not at his desk and could you call back. They do not have the interest in their job to look around the corner to see if he or she may be standing in the hall, getting a sip of water, or speaking with a co-worker. They simply want you to call again. This wastes so much time, is very expensive if you are calling long distance, and, most of all, we are letting our bureaucratic employees make decisions that upper management is totally unaware of.

"I would like for our state government to have real live people who are courteous, well-mannered, knowledgeable about their duties, and feel their responsibility is to assist the person who is calling. As you have put it so well, they are the taxpayers' employees and should treat everyone with the utmost respect.

"I also would like for everyone who works in our state

government to give his or her full name to the person calling for a variety of reasons. It has happened to me several times when I finally get a supervisor on the line and explain the problems that I had with two or three of his employees, who had no earthly idea of the answers to my questions, and then to have him ask me for the names of the employees was too much. I had no way of knowing.

"This is just a few of my very personal experiences with dealing with state governments. And one more thing while I have the floor. You may imagine that I do only a limited amount of flying. However, recently I was in conversation with a friend whose job requires almost constant travel. He was explaining in detail how the frequent-flyer program works with all major airlines, and I was amazed.

"I have to assume that within our state government there will be a good amount of flying on state business by way of commercial flights. I would like to see us establish a policy whereby the traveler receives, perhaps, 25 percent of the flyer mileage and our state travel pool the 75 percent balance. Acirema can set up a fund with these combined travel certificates and use them to transport our children who may be required to travel long distances for medical reasons and whose families may not be able to afford the cost.

"I would think a good name for such a program would be the Acirema Charitable Travel Service or ACTS. In addition to the frequent-flyer miles received, we will also campaign to have corporate and individual donations made to the fund. If it is set up under a 501-C3 program, all donations would be deductible. That's all I have today. Thank you Mr. Savage."

"Thank you very much, Sister Smith. That program is a great idea, and I certainly see no reason that could not be accepted as something which we would want to establish immediately. I also know exactly how you feel about the phone service from a personal, first-hand experience, many times over. I trust the committee will make strong recommendations as to these points.

"And I would like to add that I have often thought it would be a good practice if a government would choose a single day each week, perhaps Wednesday, where every employee with management status would be required to be present in his or her office. On this one day the public, the taxpayers who are funding their salaries, would have the assurance they could be contacted and they would not 'be out of the office' so to speak.

"Okay, Hilman, you're next. People, this is Hilman Duncan, Sheriff of Covington County, Alabama."

"Thanks, Taylor. Good morning to all. It's good that we have this open dialogue. I think we all will get much from the comments made here this morning. What I would like to propose is a curfew for our children under age 16. I have done considerable study on the question, and, while we have little trouble in our home area, I can see this as a potential problem in Acirema especially with the hundreds of miles of beach area and the natural habits of teenagers during the summer and holiday seasons.

"I would propose a statewide law prohibiting those under the age of 16 from being on the streets between the hours of 11:00 at night and 7:00 in the morning during weekdays and midnight and 6:00 in the morning on weekends.

"Furthermore, I think that we should consider some restrictions for our 16-year-old drivers during special hours, seven days per week. We all fully understand the number one freedom that every teenager enjoys is his or her right to drive a vehicle. I would feel most comfortable with a law that takes away the driving privilege of any teenager for a period of one year should that person be found with any amount of illegal drugs in his or her possession or found to be concealing a weapon of any description.

"And while I am standing, let me make another comment relative to our prison system. There are various items that we need to tackle pertaining to prison reforms, and I don't want to forget to address the important fact that quite often our first offenders are housed in a cell right next to violent criminals. This should be corrected, as I am more than convinced violent criminals and their attitudes have a long and lasting effect on those who are sent into the facilities for the first time.

"And, Taylor, if I may, I would like to make another suggestion. I would like to see Acirema create a statewide citizens' academy similar to those which are active in some communities. This type academy would conduct a series of courses, and we would urge all our citizens to participate. They will be designed to educate our public about the policies, procedures, rules, and regulations of our law enforcement officers. It would detail both the difference and similarities between the various branches of enforcement, such as City Police, Country Sheriff Deputies, the Department of Law Enforcement, Highway Patrol, and in this area we should include the Military Police.

"The establishment of the academy would assist in bringing together officers of the law and the general public. What we have to understand is that we are all in this thing together. We all have as our major objective eliminating crime in our area, and we should all pull together to get the job done. These would be my recommendations at this time."

"Thank you, Sheriff. Now each of you can see and understand fully why we very carefully selected such a variety of individuals, each of you, because you all have expertise in various fields. Each of you has been specially selected to offer your experience, and in this way we can develop a program which will be the very best possible for our new state. Thank you, Hilman. Thank you very much for your points."

From the back of the room Cole Williams stood. "Taylor, I am going to have to leave early this morning and would like to make a comment before I do."

"Certainly, go ahead President Williams. This is Cole Williams, President of the University of West Florida."

"I'm sorry that I will have to leave early and will not be here to review the many remaining interesting ideas that I know will be presented. However, I trust when I turn on the news this evening in Plano, Texas, I will see an overview presented by all of the media gathered this morning.

"I would like to leave an idea with you about making better use of our public buildings. We can start with our school buildings and work from there. It seems to be there is a tremendous amount of waste of resources when we build schools that are basically used eight hours per day and only nine months per year. These buildings could be used for a variety of other things if only our school boards and our city, county, and state officials would work more closely together to chart a plan for this purpose.

"In addition to the buildings themselves, such things as tennis courts, basketball courts, football fields, swimming pools, and other recreational facilities would be better used and serve the communities should we develop a means to share these facilities and to make the most use of them for the benefit of the taxpayers.

"There is no reason why our state office buildings have to be restricted to use only for state business. At our University we have fine facilities which could be made available for the use of any number of occasions.

"These are just a few of the things which I feel we can do that will better serve those who foot the bill in the form of taxes paid.

"And I want to comment on another subject that has been in the news lately. Over in Tallahassee, there is a wealthy individual who has been trying to make a personal donation of $5 million to Florida State University. Perhaps you have read where this person has made available these funds to the University to insure that students are aware of the vast government regulations which daily affect the free enterprise system of government. He expresses real concern about and is assured that inappropriate and ineffective governmental intervention and the current regulatory climate is counterproductive to sound economic growth.

"It is his intent to fund a project to create what will be known as The Center for the Study of Critical Issues in Economic Policy and Government. He believes, as I do I may add, the center would be in a unique position to assist the American economy by developing a new application of public choice to local governments in the formation of a new political economy.

"He wants to do away with the stringent, oppressive, and rigid governmental regulations which have a devastating impact on economic developments. In short, he insists The Center teach today's students about economic development as it relates to our free enterprise system of government and to better understand just how much more effectively free enterprise could function without the ever-increasing, massive, bogged-down bureaucratic rules and regulations.

"Now, all of that is good, but let me tell you the rest of the story. The liberal, left-wing professors and administrative staff at the University have intervened and do not want anything to do with his gift. They have insisted and have campaigned against the University accepting the $5 million donation.

"On the other hand, there are those who can't wait to receive the funds as these will motivate new creative energies and new schools of thought directed towards public choice as an alternate way of approaching the problems associated with the vast network of red tape designed to restrict free enterprise and development in general. The opinion column of the *Tallahassee Democrat*, one of the most liberal in the state I may add, had several comments and stories on the subject. Most of them questioned should a rich man, who can afford to give such a large gift, be allowed to control what is taught in our universities.

"One of FSU's liberal law professors even referred to the gift as 'tainted.' How ridiculous this is. What we really have concerning this potential financial windfall is an opportunity to have a free exchange of ideas. To me, much of the meaning of 'public choice' is a reflection of all sides of the political spectrum, a well-rounded mixing of both conservative and liberal ideas. How in the world could any intelligent, thinking person be against this?

"During this episode, much has been said about gifts with 'strings attached.' My goodness, what better comparison do we have than from our own government concerning education loans directed towards individual students provided they follow a specific field of study. Is this not a 'strings attached' gift? And why shouldn't a benefactor be able to direct his or her gifts as he or she sees fit?

"Taylor, I can assure you of one thing. If someone wanted to give $5 million to any school in Acirema, he or she would have a lot less problem doing so than what is being experienced at Florida State.

"I didn't mean to be so long with my comments. Forgive me. Again, I apologize for having to leave early. However, this meeting was something which I could not get out of easily. I hope you all have a great day, and I look forward to discussing your ideas in our subcommittee meetings."

"Thank you, Cole. Those were very good comments, and I agree with them totally. And by the way, if there is someone who would like to contribute $5 million to the education of our students in Acirema, please give me a call and you media people feel free to quote me on that. Thank you again, Cole. Have a good trip, and we will see you at our next meeting.

"I see the hand of Prescott Daniels. You're next. Governor

Daniels hardly needs an introduction. He served as Governor of Florida from 1981 through 1988. It's good to have you with us this morning, and I look forward to your comments, Governor Daniels.''

"I hope that I can add something to those who have already expressed some very good ideas. What I am concerned with this morning deals with illegal immigration. In Acirema we will not be too concerned about our borders for that purpose. However, our borders concern me about the possible off-loading of drugs and other contraband.

"As each of us knows, illegal immigration is a problem throughout our country. We simply cannot permit an influx of foreigners into Acirema. We do not need to assume the tremendous expense of upkeep for those who are not legally within our boundaries. Not only is it most costly, but also it greatly reduces the number of jobs that our own people will need. I urge all businesses within Acirema to work with us and not hire those who are in this country illegally. This also goes for homes where domestic help is hired.

"Let me give you some figures pertaining to immigrants who are legal and arriving on the shores of our country each year. About eight percent of this group settles in Florida. Over the past five years Florida has taken in more than 258,000 of them. And during this same time frame another 200,400, who originally settled in other states, chose to change locations and move down to Florida. Florida is obviously much larger than will be Acirema. However, we need to establish policy from day one and to stick with these rules and regulations. For sure, we will want to accept a policy to deny state aid to any foreigner.

"Although our section of the country is more remote than is south Florida, we still will be a magnet for newcomers to our shores, and our proximity to Cuba, Haiti, and other potential foreign trouble-spots makes us the first choice of refugees when new upheavals break out in those regions.

"There is no way we can get into the intricate details of this problem this morning. I just wanted to make you aware of the potential and that we need to spend considerable time working on our policy.''

"That's scary," said Savage. "Within our company, I have

personally worked on some areas of our immigration policy at the federal level. I know of what you speak. Thank you, Governor Daniels for those observations.

"Okay, who's next? I see Reverend Bob McGuire raising his hand. The Reverend is a Baptist minister from Monroeville, Alabama. Thanks for standing, Reverend. What's on your mind?"

"Not long ago a member of our congregation came in to see me to discuss what he had recently encountered during a strategy session by a candidate for a statewide election in Alabama. This church member has a longtime interest in politics and has been deeply involved in numerous campaigns over several years. It seems the candidate was asking for advice and guidance relative to an issue and requested that each campaign member respond as to how he, the candidate, should handle the issue. Obviously, he was seeking a position which would give him the very best advantage in the race and at the polls.

"Earlier the candidate had expressed his personal feelings about the issue, and then he stated that he did not want to let his feelings make the decision but wanted to adopt the best position to gain the most votes. With this, my friend immediately got up to leave but briefly explained his position before doing so. He told those attending that he could not participate in a political campaign where the candidate thought so little of himself that he was willing to disregard his personal feelings about an issue in exchange for a position which would offer the best political advantage.

"While we cannot dictate within our Platform the positions of those who choose to run for office, we can, however, make sure that we as educated voters choose the candidates that we are sure have a built-in set of values that will not be swayed depending on which way the winds of the polls are blowing from day to day.

"We need to attract candidates to run for office who have a sense of worth not only for the community they wish to serve, but also a sense of worth for themselves and their moral character. And don't you ever think that character is not an issue."

"Reverend, thank you for your point of view. It is well-taken, and I do appreciate your frankness. Perhaps this is an example where the 10 questions could be very helpful."

"I would like to speak next," said Lou Atkins. "I am a student and Student Body President of the University of West Florida. I would like to urge our committee to strongly consider that all same-sex marriages be prohibited within Acirema. We truly do not need those types of relationships in an area where we are doing our best to build a strong, family-oriented atmosphere. I really don't know what else to say about my position on this, but I feel strongly on the issue.''

"Thank you, Lou. That was brief but well-spoken and to the point. I, too, feel very strongly on the issue and would like the committee to make this a very distinct plank in our Platform," responded Savage.

"May I address the committee?" asked Martin Parker.

"Certainly, counselor. Ladies and gentlemen, this is Martin Parker, Chairman of the Board of Parker-Adams Law Firm of Destin, Florida."

"Thanks, Savage. Since our first meeting on January 23rd, I have had the privilege of attending each session as well as several subcommittee meetings. Over the many years I have enjoyed practicing law, I think these past several weeks have been some of the most inspiring, mind-opening, and innovative give-and-take sessions that I have ever experienced. There has not been one meeting that I have not been amazed at the comments made by our committee members. And not one that I haven't received new inspirations for the future of Acirema and our entire country.

"After the initial meeting I told Taylor that his idea of Acirema had much merit and that I was willing to do my part in any way to assist and see that it becomes a reality. I still share those feelings, and with each passing day I know that we are making tremendous headway toward what will be a fantastic future for a great state.

"Today, I want to submit a couple of suggestions that are not offered as critical in any manner. What I see here is a committee built around you people who are full of enthusiasm and potential of gigantic proportions. Over the past weeks every one of you has expressed some magnificent ideas that will lead to the formation of Acirema. However, let me warn you that this committee is simply a committee which has the power to suggest what Acirema is going to be about but our elected, or 'hired' if you may, Legislators will and should make the law of the land.

"While we can write the Platform, and, true enough, we can

admonish those who seek office to adhere to the planks of such a Platform, we cannot dictate that they must adhere to our course of actions or comments in meetings such as this. I think it most necessary that we continue to write our Platform, but let us keep in perspective the reason and purpose of the committee and not lose the fact that we are here to develop guidelines of what we would like to see happen and that we ourselves cannot make them happen although we can have a tremendous effect on the ultimate outcome.

"I trust that my comments will not dampen the spirit of you who have worked so diligently. I just want to make certain that no one leaves any meeting with the thought in his or her head that what we have proposed and approved is, in fact, going to be the law of the land. This is just not the case. Again, those whom we elect to our Legislature will enact legislation that will be the law, rules, and regulations that set forth the guidelines for our much-desired Acirema. Thank you for your attention."

"Very well said, Martin. While we are all working very hard to establish our position and intent for the outline of Acirema, we do want to keep in mind that what we are suggesting is a written Platform that we will ask those who seek office to adopt as their position on the issues. What we are writing at this time is the Platform that we will mail to every voter in the 19 counties that will completely outline our position on the issues and give all of them a basis for making up their own minds as to whether or not they approve of our action. If so, they will vote yes on the referendum, or if not then vote in the negative. Again, thank you Martin for your comments. They were well-delivered and well-taken. Okay, who will be next?"

"I would like to make a comment," said James Warthon. "This is in regards to the comments made a few minutes ago by Governor Daniels. It goes hand-in-hand with his comments relative to the immigration of both legal and illegal immigrants. I want to make sure that Acirema adopts English as our primary language." Before he could continue, the entire committee gave a loud round of applause. "It is a sad situation when we even have to consider a comment such as this. However, it seems the day has come that we must make our intentions known and known to everyone.

"Even to have to discuss this is difficult for me. To think in terms that we have to make a declarative statement to that effect is most disturbing.

"While I have no problem with those from other nations coming into our state, I do have a great problem with those who think we have to cater to them and to do so in their native tongue. If there are groups of people who choose to adhere to other languages among themselves, so be it. However, they will need to have full knowledge of our English language in order to become stable, useful, and active participants in our communities throughout our state. Thank you for the opportunity to speak my mind on this matter."

"I think you are exactly correct in your assumptions and the perspective you have offered. I personally agree with you 100 percent and, from the reaction of the committee, I am sure we are all singing on the same page. Thank you, Admiral. And by the way, for the benefit of the press, that was retired Admiral James Warthon who resides in Jackson, Alabama. Again, thank you, Admiral. Who would like to be next?"

Standing, Peaches Lamont spoke. "Let me make a couple of comments. My name is Peaches Lamont. I am President of Political Winnings, Inc., with offices in downtown Mobile. This morning I would like to address the political situation pertaining to those who would seek office in Acirema.

"During the past few years we have seen a tremendous increase of personal charges, attacks, and negative comments and activities aimed at those who have made a decision to become public figures. There is no question that a large percentage of these activities have been created, developed, and brought on in some manner by the media themselves. With the ever-expanding competition for news stories within their business world, in many cases they have become creators of news stories, sometimes stories which are not newsworthy at all, rather than reporters.

"This morning I would admonish the media to reconsider their daily activities pertaining to the issues of politics, especially politics as they relate to Acirema. If we, our committee, will adopt the attitude that we will cooperate fully with those in the media who are worthy of consideration, based on how they report the facts, and that we will offer no cooperation whatsoever to those who slant the news, then we can truly get our story spread across the nation in a true and reliable fashion.

"Recently, we have seen the media completely destroy some individuals who in all probability would have made good and faithful public servants. I would like to see the media make a diligent effort to adopt a hands-off policy pertaining to the reporting of any subject matter relative to private or personal affairs of any and all candidates. While character is surely an issue in every race, what is personal and private, what is done behind closed doors, is no one's business but the principals involved.

"Character assassination should be completely eliminated. Who among us lives in a glass house without a hint of wrongdoing? This is an area that has devastated many individuals, and for sure it has eliminated some very fine people who had the ability to offer good leadership to our nation but would not subject themselves to the piranha-feeding frenzy that is often present in news stories.

"So, let me make myself very clear. There are many good and qualified reporters in the media. I am not speaking of the media as a whole, but speaking directly to those who feel they must drag someone down to make a story interesting."

"Thank you for your observations, Peaches. Why don't we take a break and return in 20 minutes."

THE COMMITTEE worked tirelessly over many days and nights to mold and perfect the wording of the Platform. After lengthy discussions, some of which were heated, the Platform was unanimously accepted and adopted by the entire committee and received the blessings of Taylor Savage.

ELEVEN

THE TWO GOVERNORS and four United States Senators met in Governor Woods' suite at the Mayflower in Washington to discuss their plans for their early morning meeting, which had been scheduled for the small conference room at the Department of Labor. The Governors had invited Taylor Savage to join them since he had been very helpful in making available all tapes and transcripts of all of their committee meetings. He thanked them for the invitation but declined, saying the time had come for each party to paddle its own boat and to take its best hold, both offensively and defensively.

After consuming several cocktails from the privately stocked bar in their suite, they caught a couple of cabs to their dinner reservations at Maison Blanche, a favorite spot of the upper echelon of government officials and just down the street from the Old Executive Office Building. Before, during, and after dinner and over several more drinks, as hard as they tried they could not find one viable solution to the impending problem, the well-structured plans of the Acirema movement.

THE FOLLOWING MORNING the weather was normal for Washington in late February, damp with light snow and bitter cold. Upon their arrival at the Labor Department, they were greeted by Walter Scott, Deputy Director of the Department. Also present were Harold Lukes, Department of Justice; Susan Batten,

Department of State; and Ralph Dupont, Senior advisor to the President.

The meeting had been arranged by the senior Senator from Florida, Bilinda Hansen of Miami, a Democrat who was serving in her third term. She made the formal introductions, then turned the meeting over to Governor Woods. After several comments by Woods and Governor Foxworth, they asked for open opinions from the representatives of the Federal Government. All were well acquainted with the issues, as it was one of the most innovative programs to come along in many, many years. They needed little lecturing on the pros and cons as each was ready to make known his or her position—which reflected the position of the Department Secretaries as well as that of the President.

Walter Scott from Labor began. "This is not a division of a state considering secession from the Union. As I see it, they want to have more local control and to start all over again with a new set of values which they feel are absent in their association with either Florida or Alabama. For some of us it appears to be a refreshing new idea."

"To me it seems like a division of an existing political and geographical area, nothing more," said Harold Lukes from the Justice Department. "Without question there are many items that will need clearing up if their referendum does pass. There will be a number of questions that will have to be addressed. However, I personally do not see it as a great hurdle to conquer."

Senator James A. Doyle, the junior Senator from Florida, spoke up. "It seems to me that all of you folks are on the Taylor Savage side of the equation. This is really not why we are here. I want some directions as to how to stop the program and stop it dead in its tracks. We can hear all the attributes of Acirema from Savage. Now, let's get down to what we can do to stop this insane idea."

"Senator," spoke Ralph Dupont, "I understood the purpose of this meeting was to get some ideas, including what we thought to be the position of the Federal Government pertaining to the creation of Acirema. Is that correct?"

"Sure, that's correct. But am I to understand that all of you are on the side of Taylor Savage. On the side of creating Acirema? I want an answer to my question."

"Not exactly. However, we are here to tell you like it is. To tell you how we feel about it and what we think can and probably will happen. Isn't that fair?" asked Dupont.

"Yes, that's fair. Let's continue," said the Senator in a sharp, grumbling voice.

Lukes again spoke up. "To tell the people within the boundaries of what may become Acirema that they cannot do this would create much more of a problem. To tell you the truth, we cannot find a real reason to prevent what they are trying to accomplish. Before we can tell them they can't do it, we first must have a good and sound reason why they can't.

"The President's position is that he is for all the people. Period. And that means all the people. Those who may choose to become citizens of Acirema would not make themselves outcasts or foreigners, just people who want to make a drastic change in their personal lives.

"I do not see them as different from our ancestors who longed for a change when they packed up their families and headed out west. Isn't this the same thing that Taylor Savage's Platform is all about?"

"So you are saying to us that your Democratic President is supporting the Savage plan? Is that what you are telling us?" inquired Senator Bennett.

"What we are trying to tell you is that we, just like you, have searched for a solution. One that will accomplish and satisfy both sides of the issue. There are no solutions. The President's position is simple. He is for Americans, all Americans. And to put it bluntly, it would not matter to him if we have 50 states or fifty-one states. We are all Americans.

"As we all know, the President is just now starting his reelection campaign. I don't know if Taylor Savage considered this particular time as the most beneficial to spring this on the country. However, I suspect he did and knows just exactly what he was doing with his announcement in January. The President is simply not going to alienate 1.4 million potential voters, and that's not hard to understand. Anyway, he has his hands full with a certain Senator from Kansas at this time.

"The referendum will take place on August 4th around the time of the Democratic and Republican conventions, just 12 weeks or so before the general election in November. The President will not take sides on this issue but will work with whichever side prevails in the referendum. Assuming the referendum is successful, the electorate of both Florida and Alabama will still vote in this year's general election in their current state elections as Statehood for Acirema will take a few months to complete. Assuming success of the referendum, I would expect Statehood would follow swiftly.''

"It appears to us," said Miss Batten of the State Department, ''that with the passing of the referendum there is not a question of Statehood. Unlike Alaska and Hawaii, which had to learn the rules and ways of America, we are dealing with free-born citizens of the United States who simply want to make a change to better themselves. Their plan is well written, and Mr. Savage has, by all indications, crossed all the t's and dotted all the i's.

"I do not see it as a matter of not granting Statehood. They are already adhering to all the terms and conditions of every other state of the Union. These citizens have been paying federal and state taxes all of their lives, and there is no question of their individual United States citizenship.''

"And you are telling this group that it appears that everything is in order, and if the referendum passes, Statehood will be granted automatically. Is that what you are telling us?'' asked Governor Woods.

"What we are saying is we can find no means to prohibit them from accomplishing what they have set out to do. Yes sir, that is what I am telling you,'' argued Scott.

"And what will happen if other areas of our nation decide to follow suit and want to break from their respective state or states?'' asked Governor Foxworth.

"If other areas follow suit and their plan is as comprehensive as the Savage plan appears to be, then I would have to assume we would have several new states in our Union. It seems as if this may be Savage's game plan. You know, it may be just what is necessary to bring our American way of life back into full focus. From what I have gathered, these folks who are in the boundaries of what may become Acirema want a new change of direction and are tired of having to fight the old, worn-out, antiquated rules, regulations, and laws of Florida and Alabama. Isn't that about it?

Doesn't that sum it up?'' asked Susan Batten.

''Yes. That just about sums up Savage's position. You are right. That is what they are claiming,'' responded Governor Foxworth.

''What will be the result of our federal programs where the percentage of returned funds from various sources such as gas tax revenues, school funding, and social programs such as care of the elderly when these funds are based on the population of each and every State? Ours, both Florida's and Alabama's, will be greatly reduced when each state loses close to 700,000 people,'' asked Senator Bennett.

''It appears to me this will have a big effect on your funding. However, from the Federal Government's standpoint, the funding will be the same, the pie will just be divided differently. And let me add something at this point. A memo came down from the Federal Elections Commissions with a comment on the ''Ten Questions'' which were outlined in Mr. Savage's program, and they think it has much merit,'' said Ralph Dupont.

''The Ten Questions are nothing more than just a means to set up a candidate, to put him in a box, to make him tell a lie when he or she would rather slide by an issue without making a decision,'' responded Governor Woods.

''I think that is exactly the point. I feel a candidate who pledges to uphold those questions would make a better candidate and ultimately a better public servant. He or she will have to take a stand and make his positions and decisions public. I feel this is a part of election reform that has been long overdue,'' added Dupont.

''Let me inquire of you Federal folks,'' said Governor Foxworth. ''What about the buildings, the structures, the roads, the bridges that are within the boundaries of what may become Acirema? What will happen to them? Will we get refunded for the construction expenses of those items? Will Acirema return the cost of construction to either Florida or Alabama?''

''While reading Mr. Savage's Platform, he addresses that question head on, answered Harold Lukes. ''He states, and is probably right in his assumption, that these assets are not owned by the state but are owned by the people of the region. I personally do not believe it would be too hard for a major accounting firm to establish that the taxpayers of the geographical area in question had remitted taxes in excess of those necessary to pay for such items as you have described. And, furthermore, if you aren't careful,the same accounting audit may well reveal that a good portion of the taxes paid by those residing in that region has gone to make vast improvements in other areas of your states."

"Should the referendum pass,what opportunity would we, our two states, have in filing a stop order with the Supreme Court?" asked Senator Hansen.

"I don't see where the United States Supreme Court can involve itself with this issue. Now that I have said that, the Court often involves itself with issues they really have no business in becoming involved in the first place. They are on the bench to interpret laws and not to create them, which they often try to do," responded Lukes. "Like we said earlier, if the referendum passes, it would appear it is tantamount to Statehood.

"With the passing of the referendum and their written Platform which details their plans for the election of their State and Congressional members, the President feels this is a decision he could support because in the purest sense of the matter the people of the region will have spoken, and that's exactly what democracy is all about."

"What will be the outcome for those members of the Congress who are now serving a district that represents, in whole or in part, the area in question?" asked Senator Doyle.

"They will lose their seats. However, I believe Acirema's Platform certainly addresses the fact they can stand for election within the new state," answered Miss Batten.

"But what about the residency requirements which will state you have to be a citizen of the region for so many years, etc.?"

"This is something their committee will need to work on. Certainly, there will be provisions to provide otherwise since that would exclude everyone who wishes to run for any office for the first time. I would expect those who are now holding offices, either state or national, would be grandfathered in."

"Okay, what do we do next? Where do we go from here?" asked Senator Bennett.

"It would be my suggestion the six of you go back to your states, gather up your Congressional House members, and do everything you can to stop the process, provided that is what you want to do. From our perspective and from the President's point of view, what Savage has planned and the purpose of his intent is legal, and therefore he will continue being President to the same number of people, the same number of individuals, no matter if they reside in 50 states or 51 states,'' said Ralph Dupont.

Senator Bennett continued, "You know, all you folks are really concerned about is the reelection of your precious President. You care little about the real issue that we are so very concerned about. It's pure and simple politics, that's all. Anyway, you really have nothing to worry about concerning the reelection of President Clinton. Haven't you young bucks heard the old adage which confirms the candidate with the most hair on his head wins all Presidential elections. You have nothing to worry about. This has been true over the ages, with the only modern exception being President Eisenhower back in '52.''

THE MEETING ENDED, and all felt their time had been totally wasted. The two Governors, independent of each other, would rally their troops back in their state and do whatever they could from their home base. Only one of the Senators, Van Wells of Mobile, would be affected by the passing of the referendum. It appeared the other three were not too concerned although they had to make an effort and put up the proper front. Since their home base was not in the area of consideration for Acirema, the net results, if the referendum passed and Statehood was granted, would be their geographical area would be smaller and more manageable. And smaller seemed to be the buzz word of the day, at least in Taylor Savage's mind and plans.

TWELVE

"HELLO, AND WELCOME back to our second hour of the Bosch Lemoreaux Show. This hour we are privileged to have Taylor Savage with us, through telephone communications, for the entire hour to give his comments and to take your calls.

On the morning of January 23rd, just one month ago today, Mr. Savage shook the eyeteeth of the political world by announcing his intention to create a new state government, our 51st state, if you will. His intent is to have nine counties from Alabama and 10 from Florida secede from their respective states and form what he has suggested will be a new state that will be named Acirema. He insists that America, and the road we are now traveling, must be reversed, and he is starting his venture by reversing the name of America, thus Acirema."

"Welcome to our show, Taylor. Where are you speaking to us from today?"

"Thank you for having me on your show, Bosch. It's good being with you again. I am speaking with you from the studios of WCOA radio in Pensacola, Florida. The entire staff sends you their best."

"Tell the good folks at WCOA radio that we appreciate them very much. They have carried our radio program for several years, which makes them a very important part of our radio family. Taylor, as you know, we have had thousands of calls since you made that first announcement about Acirema one month ago today. For the most part, the larger percentage has been in your

167

favor. What has been happening since we last talked?''

"Much has happened. The Florida Cabinet has visited with the Alabama Cabinet in Montgomery, and that in itself is an historic event. Both Governors and four United States Senators have visited in Washington with the President's chief advisors including Department advisors of several Federal agencies.

"These are all very historic events. However, we intend to make more history of gigantic proportions with the acceptance of Acirema. Bosch, I am very pleased and acknowledge those who have commented favorably in the news media including the responses from your callers,'' replied Savage.

"I was somewhat surprised when the delegations from Alabama and Florida met with the President's people. From all reports it appears the President and his advisors seem to be leaning heavily on your side of the issue. Is this the way you see it?'' asked Bosch.

"Yes, this is exactly the way I see it. The President, through his advisors, has made known he is President of all the people, and if it's the wish of those who will be affected by the formation of Acirema to break away from their past and make a new start, he will not stand in their way. It also appears he is most pleased with the entrepreneurial spirit of what we are going to accomplish.''

"Well, that's the way the President is. I don't know how in hell he thinks he can govern 51 states when he can't even govern 50.''

"Bosch, that's your opinion,'' noted Savage.

"Yeah, and I'm welcome to it. Right?''

"Certainly, you are,'' Savage replied and continued. "Bosch, this country has an itch that very badly needs scratching. Across our country is a silent majority which thirsts to change their personal lives. It's most apparent our politicians are not providing what is necessary to get this magnificent country back on track. I know that's an old, worn out comment. However, it is a fact and very true. Perhaps, just perhaps, someone like myself can lead this 1.4 million people down a path which will affect the political structure in such a way it can start to make a significant difference not only for the people of Acirema but also for our entire country.

"Everyone speaks of wanting a change to occur, but few positive changes are happening. We, our movement, can have a lot of effect on many things, but obviously we cannot improve on all things. Millions upon millions of people say they want government out of their way, off their back, out of their lives. People don't want government to be involved as much as it presently is in their daily lives and their personal decisions. However, it seems that people only want to say these things and take no action to make them happen. Then someone like myself comes along with a vision, a true plan to change the course we are traveling, and some politicians still have the nerve to want to fight the issue. Isn't that sick? Isn't something wrong when we have a chance to alter our lives for the better, and some still insist on fighting us?

"Let me talk about some thoughts that are bugging a large percentage of people across the country. Some are more significant than others. However, no matter how large or small, they all are important. Obviously, there are many things that we would like to change at the state level. However, they are ingrained in the Federal structure and Federal bureaucracy, and we can only attempt to voice our opinions through our new members to Congress who will be representing our new state.

"This is an example of a Federal problem about which we can only voice our opinion and objections, and we will do just that through our Senators and Representatives. We have a tremendous amount of waste in our welfare system. We have countless numbers on the rolls who should not be and some who truly need our assistance. The cost of welfare is horrendous, and we, at each state government, should make every effort to take care of our own program and do so by keeping in mind these expenses are being paid for by our own taxpayers.

"I wonder if your audience knows that our Congress allows, permits, and sanctions welfare payments to foreigners who are not even citizens of the United States. Can you imagine that? And another group that gets special attention are people who come into our country and work for 11 months, then return to their home in a foreign country for a single month, then return again to America and repeat the same steps. By doing this, by taking these steps, none of them are subject to the liabilities of paying taxes on their earnings. This is preposterous. Where in America can an American earn wages that are not subject to taxes?"

"And you know what, Mr. Savage, it's the President's fault that we have the problem with immigrants. Isn't that the way you see it?" harked Bosch.

"It's not his alone. It's the fault of every elected official at the Federal level. We have Congressmen and Senators who are quick to offer lip service as to what they will do when they get to Washington. However, little more than old campaign promises and lip service come about."

"I agree with that totally," said Bosch, "and someone once wrote 'A man that would expect to train lobsters to fly in a year is called a lunatic; but a man that thinks men can be turned into angels by an election is a reformer and remains at large.'"

"That's a very good point, Bosch. So many people think wonders will come about with the election of a person.

"Anyway, let me speak of a few more things on a more minor level, but most important. Things that are really bugging the general population of America," Savage continued. "Mothers and fathers feel very insecure when they cannot give their children the things their parents gave to them. I've heard it said time and again that there is no way, for instance, they could buy a recreational boat for water skiing or fishing as they were given by their parents when they were growing up. I know that some families never were able to afford such luxury, but the point is, those who could afford them in the past cannot do so in this era.

"It often takes both parents working, one to pay the family's expenses and the other to pay all the taxes that are piled upon them. And a good portion of the taxes they pay goes to provide help and assistance to those from foreign countries who are on our shores taking away the jobs which should go to Americans and not paying taxes on their earnings. This has simply got to cease.

"And for a family to take an extended vacation is out of the question although when in their youth their family quite often took off for a couple of weeks each year.

"These things played a huge part in keeping the family structure together just some 20 years ago. It is not happening today. In this day and time, mothers and fathers give their kids a few dollars and send them off to the movies or to the mall, most of the time by themselves or with friends. Hardly ever is there a family outing. The financial abilities of the family unit today are having a tremendous effect on the relationships between mother and daddy and their kids. The breakdown of the family structure is often due to the financial deficiency of the breadwinners.

"And you don't see that the President has let down the public as it relates to family values?" Bosch asked.

"Yes, I feel that way. However, he is not alone in this. He has had much help from those who make the laws of our country. Now, shall I continue?" inquired Savage.

"Yes, please do."

"Not too long ago, moms and pops were able to assist their kids with a down payment on a small home when they married or at least help them with furnishings. Now, they are tied down so tight with trying to keep their own lives floating there are simply no funds to assist anyone else. And for many families to think in terms of sending their kids to college at todays enormous cost is almost totally out of the question.

"People are frustrated beyond reason. Now, here is a small, insignificant problem that has to be changed at the Federal level but it will point out the frustration of the average man on the street. We all have gone into our local post office and find two or three clerks behind their work stations and all moving at a snail's pace. A long line of customers will be waiting patiently to be 'next' while countless numbers of employees can be seen milling around in the background seeming to be doing nothing more than passing time.

"Quite often, there are another six or seven windows with no employees in attendance. Yet they are equipped with the latest computers, scales, and other paraphernalia which we, the taxpayers, have purchased.

"And recently they have adopted a slogan and have strategically placed posters proclaiming, 'Our goal is to serve you within five minutes.' The next time you are in line and read this statement of their goals, look around you and I'll bet you do not see a clock displayed within the entire post office. I wonder how they feel missing their stated goal numerous times each and every day?

"You may also notice in many post offices they have installed play tables complete with toys and games to keep the children happy and content while their parents stand in line, for what seems like forever, awaiting the bureaucrats to finally get around to them. While such frustrating things like these go on all day, every day, the Postal Department still has the gall to continue to raise the cost of postage and occasionally holds a press conference to tell the world just how great its service is. They continue to spend millions of our dollars on television advertisements that try to counter and combat the private sector's achievements in competitive service. Still they have failed miserably, and when they do they simply raise the cost of postage which penalizes each one of us for their inefficiency. When are we as citizens going to catch on that postage does not need to be raised when the department says in 1995 it profited more than $3.1 billion, and that's with a b.

"The next time you are at a window, ask the attendant about the actual delivery time for their advertised two-day program. I can assure you that you will be told this does not mean your package or letter will arrive at its destination in two days. If they are honest with you, they will tell you they will attempt to get it delivered in two days. Still they use taxpayers' money to advertise otherwise.

"And, Bosch, I don't need anyone to call your show and say this is not a taxpayers' expense and that the post office operates on income derived from postal receipts. Don't you think for a moment their employees and the expenses of operation are not a cost to every taxpayer in this country. To try to explain the cost of a postage stamp and their ineptness of operation as not being a tax is a real farce and insults our intelligence.

"And speaking of their advertisements, which are totally false, our Acirema Platform addresses the issue of truth in advertising. We simply will not condone companies that advertise their products or services and do not follow through to provide as advertised. Politicians included."

"Let me butt in for a minute. Do you not think the President of the United States could change the policy of the United States Post Office to provide better service to each of us who has to use the post office and its facilities?" asked Bosch.

"Of course I do. I know that it can be changed. However, why should he alienate the employees of the Federal Postal System? Why should he get them down on himself when he needs their vote and support?" Savage countered. "That's the real answer."

"Because he should be more protective and concerned about those who have to stand in long lines and watch this flock of lazy-ass Federal employees do just as they please. The reason behind it is they have a gigantic union which protects them," Bosch shot back. "Would you like me, right now at this very moment, to start a stink, a rumble if you may, concerning every local post office across this land?" Bosch asked.

"I don't think I know what you're getting at," Savage said.

"Well, let me show you. Now, ladies and gentlemen, pick up your phones, get out your pens and paper, and contact your Congressman and inquire as to the salary of those employed by the post office. Ask your Congressman why they are being paid such outrageous salaries. Then ask him if he doesn't think for that kind of money, you, the customer, should get better service.

"Now, Mr. Savage, wait until you see the results of what we are about to create. This will accentuate the problems which you have described and perhaps will get some good, positive results."

"You have a way of getting to the depth of the problem, I'll assure you of that," remarked Savage, then continued. "Okay, let's see what you can do about this little bit of a problem. Bosch, isn't it sad that our banks do not give personal service anymore. You are treated as an outcast in most instances, and when you request something as simple as cashing a check they think you have lost your mind.

"We will have a modern and very special banking system in Acirema that will give prompt service, and I will assure you it will lean towards assisting those who wish to go into private, competitive businesses in our state. We are going to create a Commission of Commerce tied directly into our private banking systems and make commerce and development a top priority. It can be done, and I know how to do it.

"And you know, it hasn't been too long ago that we had 'service' stations. I wonder what happened to them? It's sad that a business owner feels it justifiable to sit on his rear end, let you pump your gas, and then you bring to him, in his air-conditioned office, the money to pay for the service that you did not get in the first place. Still, he expects you to patronize him and his business. Don't you think some things need changing?

"Bosch, you turned me loose, and I apologize for this long

drawn-out answer. But you asked what has been going on, so I told you."

"Taylor, I am amazed at your concept of the needs of our taxpaying citizens. The needs, requirements and the day-to-day frustrations of the man on the street. There is little wonder that your program has gotten legs and the vast support which is coming your way.

"Taylor, I want to take some calls, but before we do let me take a second and tell you about my all-time favorite gripe. Have you ever been in a supermarket where they have a checkout counter that is marked 'express lane, 10 items or less?" Well, why management creates such a great marketing idea for their customers, then places the slowest, most illiterate, unhappy employee at that register is beyond me. Know what I mean?"

"Yeah, I know exactly what you mean," Savage answered.

"And another favorite gripe of mine, which runs a close second to the first one, is when I go into a bakery, and you can see from my size I frequent bakeries often, to purchase doughnuts or such. The clerks are trained to use a small paper napkin to gather the products and place them in the bag. Obviously, this practice is to keep their hands from touching the products and thereby possibly reducing the transmission of any germs which may be on their hands. Then, guess what? They proceed to dump the paper napkin right into the sack. Can you believe that?" asked Bosch.

"Certainly, I can believe it. It's called incompetence," informed Savage.

"Okay, let's take a break. No, wait a minute. Let me tell you of another gripe of mine, and perhaps you can do something about it if Acirema becomes a state."

"What do you mean IF Acirema becomes a state. We will become a state, and don't you forget that. Now, what is your third all-time favorite gripe?" asked Savage.

"A couple of years ago I was invited to speak to the Florida Republican Club at a dinner and reception in Tallahassee. The next day before leaving town, Governor Martinez invited me to his office for a visit. While there, I thought I would go to the top of their capitol building. I think it is something like 25 stories high, and get a look over the city. I was told you could see the coast down around St. Marks.

"After leaving the Governor's office, we must have waited 20 minutes to catch an elevator. After one finally arrived, I easily found the reason for the long wait. At every floor a bureaucrat either got on or got off. Now that within itself is not all that bad. However, I began to observe closer, and that is what really teed me off. I would imagine no less than 90 percent of those riding the elevator went only one floor. Now, think about this. These bureaucrats spent precious time, your and my tax dollars, standing there waiting to ride an elevator for only one floor.

"Not only was that somewhat ridiculous, but they halted the flow of daily traffic of folks who needed to conduct business within the building. For God's sake, why couldn't they walk either up or down one flight of stairs? When Acirema becomes a state, as you have assured me it would, will you have a law enacted that any state employee caught riding an elevator in a state building will be called on the carpet and given the royal rear end treatment? Anyway, walking a couple of stairs would be in the best interest of every state employee, and they all should understand this. Okay, now let's hurry into a break, and when we come back we will take some calls. Don't go away."

□　□　□　□　□

"THANKS FOR HANGING around, Taylor. Now, what is next on your agenda. It seems that almost every day something new pops up. What's next?"

"Glad you asked, Bosch. I'll have another important announcement to make at our next full committee meeting. What we in Acirema would like to do is to break all dependency on any form of Federal Government financial aide and assistance. This next announcement will again stir the Federal bureaucracy which will be determined to fight it as they have done on all issues that we have announced and intend to promote.

"When we make this announcement, it will put our Congressmen on the hot seat. They will have to make a quick decision either on the side of the bureaucracy at the Federal level or on the side of what we are going to propose and accomplish right here at home without Federal assistance."

"Let me interrupt you, Taylor. It seems to me that as you develop your program from time to time you share another plank of the Platform with us, and when you do you always seem to place the Federal Government, especially the Federal bureaucracy, on the spot. Is this your game plan?''

''Bosch, it may just seem like that. And obviously it should, for that is exactly what we are doing and there is much more to come. You are well versed in your appraisal of the situation. I applaud you,'' Savage answered.

''Well, it is very obvious that you have written the Platform for Acirema to hit the hardest at their softest spots,'' observed Bosch.

''Thanks, I take that as a compliment. Now, let me continue with what I was explaining. What we are going to announce may well set a trend across all corners of our nation. It also may well establish a trend for other matters that need to be addressed in a similar manner. Our elected officials will have to either choose the role of being statesmen or continue to be nothing more than politicians. Our next announcement has been well thought out and designed. It's fundamentally sound, but as with all new innovative ideas it will receive its share of criticism.

''If those who control the Federal bureaucracy really care about the taxpayers, they will not fight this next proposal.''

''You mean to tell me you are coming forth with even more reasons for the Feds to fight you, or at least the Federal bureaucracy to fight you?''

''This is true, but you have to understand the Federal Government, as it relates to the President and his Cabinet, is not fighting us on any issue. It's the ingrained, entrenched bureaucrats who are resisting change of any sort.

''We are going to reveal our program and our Platform and continue to make announcements that will force our elected officials to either take a stand on behalf of a free enterprise system of government or the position advocated by the bureaucrats who want to run the country. And better than that, we are exposing these situations so that all potential voting citizens can see for themselves just where our elected officials stand on every subject, on every issue at hand.

''Bosch, it is amazing just how much of our tax dollars are spent annually fighting against the wishes of the people. The people themselves are actually providing the funds for their own government to fight them. Isn't that unreal? Isn't that a horrible way to have your own government function?

"With our next announcement I will challenge the Federal bureaucracy to the extent that, if they fight our proposals, then they best not use any tax revenue funds which have been generated by those who will reside within the 19 counties of Acirema. I am also under the opinion that the great majority of all taxpaying citizens across the entire country will also resent the fact that their Federal Government would try to use tax dollars to fight something that the citizens themselves want to accomplish. Something which will have a lasting effect on each of us by allowing all our citizens to have an opportunity to better themselves and to find a more reasonable, more secure, and happier life. It will be interesting to see what position the Feds will take in this regard. I can hardly wait.

"Bosch, let me make sure that you understand where we are coming from. In many, and probably most, instances we just want to be left alone, not bothered. Big Brother, please just go away. We will not need Federal money in Acirema, and we don't want to pay to them any of our hard-earned income in the form of taxes for them to squander on their many social programs which are, for the most part, absolutely not working. When you learn of our next announcement, you will understand where we are coming from and where we are headed. For instance, what we are going to propose is not a social program. However, it would resemble the Social Security program in many ways.

"And speaking of Social Security, you may be surprised to learn about the large percentage of Americans who would rather use these funds, which are now mandated by law to be paid into the Federal Government in the form of Social Security taxes, to personally invest in their own retirement program. What is really happening is the Federal Government makes us fund the cost of generating thousands of jobs to administer a system of government which is failing and bankrupt by all accounts and standards.

"We don't need or want the type of government which promises us roses, and then when it's time to collect, it has nothing more than thorns to offer. We can do better, we can do a hell of a lot better. And in Acirema we will show you what we speak of. You just wait and see.

"Again, with our next announcement, we will see if our

elected officials are more statesmen-like or simply a diminutive form of politician,'' roared Savage.

"You know that you are preaching to the choir when you are talking to me about that form of government, don't you?'' responded Bosch.

"I hope so, and I hope that your listeners will grab hold of what I am saying. This country has got to make some very definite changes in the way we conduct our business. We have got to do something,'' Savage said.

"Okay, why don't we take a few calls. Here is Joanne from Houston, Texas. Thanks for calling Joanne. What's on your mind today?''

"Bosch, I'm a first-time caller and very nervous.''

"You're doing fine. Just speak your mind. I'll let you know when you are wrong or say something stupid. Just kidding, my dear. Go ahead and ask Mr. Savage your question.''

"Mr. Savage, I really admire what you are doing and the stand you have taken.''

"Thank you, Joanne, that's always good to hear.''

"What I want to know is how you plan to accomplish some of the things like crime eradication and at the same time talk about building a new state around old-fashioned values? It does not seem to match up. How do old-fashioned values and today's criminal element play towards each other? How does that work?''

"Thanks for asking that question, Joanne. I am delighted to tell you a short story which will better explain the answer to your inquiry, much better perhaps than I could. If you have kept up with my proposed program, you know that I have spent the better portion of the past five years preparing for the referendum which will create Acirema and bring us to Statehood. During the past five years I've researched many items including this story. I've told it many times, so let me just speak of the major points.

"On February 15, 1933, President-elect Franklin Delano Roosevelt was giving a short speech in Miami. He was taking a few days' vacation after a hard-fought campaign. He had about an hour between the time his ship landed in Miami and the time he was to catch a train. He decided to greet a group of supporters with a short speech.

"The Mayor of Chicago, Anton Cermak, had also been vacationing in the Miami area and wanted to speak with Mr. Roosevelt and was advised to meet him at the Bayfront Park. After Roosevelt's speech a small man took a pistol from his pocket and opened fire. Several were hit, the President-elect was not, Mayor Cermak was.

"The would-be assassin, Giuseppe Zangara, was immediately arrested and was arraigned before Judge Collins the next day and charged with attempted murder. Mayor Cermak died on March 6th. A trial was held and the transcript sent to Florida Governor Sholtz on March 11th. The Governor signed Zangara's death warrant and set his execution for the week of March 20th. Sheriff Hardie took him from the Dade County Jail to Raiford State Prison on the same day the Governor signed the warrant. Zangara was executed for the murder of Mayor Cermak on March 20th.

"The time which elapsed between the shooting and the execution of the murderer was only 33 days, and just 14 days after the Mayor died. This is, in part, what I speak of as 'old-fashioned values.' Today, murder is still murder as it was on February 15, 1933; crime is still crime today as it was on that date. The death penalty was in effect at that time, and it is today. What happened on February 15, 1933, was a pure and simple act of murder, and the State of Florida exercised its privilege of justified punishment.

"Today, our left-wing, liberal Justices of the United States Supreme Court have painted us, the law-abiding citizens of this nation, into a corner and wrapped us tightly with comments such as 'criminal rights.' Now, if you folks want to believe, as I do, that those who have committed major criminal acts should forfeit their rights, all of their rights, then we can change the system not only in Acirema but also in the entire country.

"I believe that it would make a great deal of difference if a person who went into a convenience store or into someone's home, office, or business and knew if he committed a murder that within 33 days he himself would sit in 'Old Sparky' and forfeit his own life, I think he would have second thoughts before committing such a crime.

"However, criminals today think little of the consequences because they have a battery of legal minds who are protecting them, and they fully understand that if they are caught the worst thing that could happen is a few years behind bars with three full meals per day, a place to sleep, color television, recreation room, library, medical and dental care, no taxes to pay, no rent to pay, no payments for child support, no alimony payments. Get the idea?''

''When the Warden at Florida State Prison asked Zangara if he would like to speak a last word, he answered, 'Pusha da button''. Joanne, I say to you, and to all of those listening to this show, that if we exercised more persistence and expediency in pushing 'da button,' we would have a hell of a lot fewer criminals walking the streets of this nation, and our homes and businesses would be much safer.

''This is what I feel as it relates to the eradication of crime and old-fashioned values.''

''That was a great answer. Thank you Mr. Savage, and thanks for talking my call.''

''Thank you, Joanne. Goodbye.''

''Taylor, I really think that you hit a nerve with that answer. Let's take another question before we break. We will go to Wilson in New York City. What's on your mind, Wilson. What's your question?''

''Thanks for taking my call, Bosch.''

''Thank you for calling. What do you have for our guest today?''

''What I want to ask Mr. Savage is why there are more blacks given the death penalty than whites?''

''I am not going to get into any comments concerning racial issues at this time,'' said Savage. ''I am concerned about stopping crime in an area that 1.4 million people will call Acirema. While I will not involve myself with percentages of classifications of those sitting on death row, I will answer that to me it matters not the color of the criminal's skin as all criminal elements of our society should be eliminated. If there are more of one race awaiting execution than another, then I would have to assume there are more criminals of that race than another. Regardless of which race it is.''

''Okay, let's go to Cecil right here in New Orleans. What have you got to say, Cecil?''

''I have a question for Mr. Savage. Mr. Savage, I cannot envision just how large this new State of Acirema will be. Give me some idea. I'll hang up and listen.''

"Thanks for your question, Cecil. Acirema will be approximately 19,500 square miles. This will make us the 42nd largest state relative to land area. We will be larger than Maryland, Vermont, New Hampshire, Massachusetts, New Jersey, Hawaii, Connecticut, Delaware, Rhode Island, and the District of Columbia. Population-wise, we will be the 37th largest State, larger than Maine, Nevada, Hawaii, New Hampshire, Idaho, Rhode Island, Montana, South and North Dakota, Delaware, the District of Columbia, Vermont, Alaska, and Wyoming.

"It is interesting to note that the Federal Census Bureau is estimating the State of Florida will have another 1.1 million residents by the year 2000 and still another 6.5 million by the year 2025. Can you imagine the chaos and crime that 7.6 million more people will bring to Florida? These new people moving into Florida would increase the population by about 50 percent. For every two people you encounter at crowded shopping malls today, you will soon encounter three instead. For every two vehicles that are in front of you at a red light, you soon will have to contend with three.

"The Federal Census Bureau warns, 'Some States, particularly those expected to gain large numbers such as Florida, will need to plan for adjustments in facilities and services, including schools, roads, protection from the criminal element, etc.'

"We are going to solve this problem well before we get into a situation which is not manageable.''

"Okay, let's take another call. Here is David in the heart of our nation's capital, downtown Washington, D.C., crime capital of the world. What's on your mind, David. You have a question for Mr. Savage?

"Yes, Sir. Mr. Savage if you could name one primary fault with America today, what would it be? Name a fault that you and your committee could possibly have some meaningful input to make a positive change. A change for the better.''

"David, that's a real good question. There is a lot wrong in our country today, but before I go any further let me make sure that you and all who are listening understand that even with all our faults there is no better or greater country on this earth. While we do have faults, it is in the best interest of all of us to try to improve on those faults and create a better place for all of us to live, worship, play, work, and enjoy our family.

"To answer your question would be to pick possibly one of perhaps eight or ten faults which could all be called the number one shortcoming. Why don't I give you my answer to just one of those which I have a problem understanding. One of the major problems in America today is incompetence. Incompetence including all classifications and categories of individuals. At home, in the work place, at school, at play, everywhere.

"When you see a television commercial that may feature the owner of an automobile dealership who proclaims his make of car is better than the rest and, for sure, his service department cannot be topped, then you start to believe him. Then you purchase his car, and sooner or later you take it in for service or repairs, and guess what? The owner of the dealership apparently forgot to tell the service manager and the mechanics what he has convinced you would happen. You wait in long lines. They finally get to you. You have to rent a vehicle because your car may be in the shop for days. When you get it back, they may or may not have fixed the problem and the reason for taking it in the first place. And quite possibly you will find something else wrong that was created while they had the car in their possession. Incompetence!

"Take the commercial for your local bank. You would think things could not be more peachy if you dealt with them. However, they too forgot to tell their loan officers and the tellers. Incompetence!

"When the President of the United States makes a statement pertaining to almost any subject, let's take something like a tax deductible item for higher education or something similar, guess what? He forgot to tell your accountant or the IRS or a combination of both. Incompetence!

"Go into a large electronics store and ask a question of one of the intelligent-looking young men or women who are there to wait on you. Most likely, they have little idea what you are talking about. And worse than that is when they feel they need to give you an answer, and it is not even close to being correct. Incompetence!

"Call any government office and inquire about something. Chances are that you will be given an answer that most likely will not be correct. Their employees have not been trained. And if you are trying to find a person who may have answers to your questions, you will be given a dozen or more folks to speak with and after explaining your needs in full to each one then they will let you know you need to speak to someone else. Incompetence!

"These are just some comments I have pertaining to just one of the perhaps 10 top problems wrong with our country."

"Now, here is a sweet southern voice from Centerville, Georgia. What's on your mind, Dianne?"

"Thanks for taking my call, Bosch".

"You bet. You gotta question for Mr. Savage?"

"Yes, and a comment as well. Mr. Savage, I have kept close tabs on the news accounts of what you plan for Acirema, and I'm very much aware of your feelings towards the bureaucrats of our country. My question is this. Over the past few days, have you paid any attention to what Senator Lauch Faircloth of North Carolina has been saying about his investigation of Federal employees using on-the-job time to play games on their computers while they should be working?"

"Well, quite frankly, I have, and the Senator is a personal friend of mine and a great Republican Senator, I might add. Although I know the story, I've got a feeling you are getting ready to tell your version to the entire nation, and I would rather hear it from your point of view. Please continue," he advised.

"Our morning paper ran the story and noted the Senator wanted to do away with all computer programs which gave access to computer games that are part of the programming package on federally owned computers. He noted that we taxpayers are picking up the tab for the cost of wasted time and expense by these employees and quoted the price to be in excess of $10 billion, and that's with a b, $10 billion annually.

"Now, get this. What's so sad about the situation is the Congress had a study done and came to the conclusion that it would cost that much or more to remove the games from the computer programs and felt the best thing was to just leave it as is. That is my statement and now for the question. Why doesn't someone at the federal level have the balls, excuse my language, but have the intestinal fortitude to simply put a note in everyone's pay envelope which states that if they are caught playing games on government time, they will be fired on the spot?'' she asked.

"As I thought, you pegged it just right. You hit the nail square on the head, and your frustration with the issue certainly overrides your graphic description, which I personally like very much. Dianne, this type of waste of taxpayers' funds is not the exception; in fact, much of it is the rule. So often what you have in the workplace at all levels of government is an attitude that has been accepted by upper management of not really caring one way or the other. A large percentage of bureaucratic government managers logs in their 40 hours each week and every payday receives a fat check and starts all over on Monday morning doing the same sloppy job. These things have got to cease. Thanks for asking that question, Dianne. It is most important, and your response and observations are totally correct.''

"Well, let me add my dittos to each of you on that one," said Bosch. "Okay, Taylor, let's take another question and go to Derek in Burlingame, California. What's on your mind Derek?''

"I also have a comment for Mr. Savage and then a question.''

"Go ahead. What's your comment?''

"Mr. Savage, politics stinks. The word 'politics' comes from two Latin words, 'poly' meaning many. And 'ticks' meaning blood suckers. Are there any clean politicians in any level of our governments?''

"Whoa! That's the first time I ever heard that description," stated Bosch. "That's a bit rough, and I'm not at all sure that 'poly' and 'ticks' are Latin words meaning such. But how about it, Taylor. Are all our politicians 'blood suckers'?''

"No, not at all, Bosch. We have some fine public servants, but on the other hand there are those who are only in office to feather their own nests. There are those who are there to do nothing more than to get fat at the public's expense. Just to have a job which they wish could be a full-time, forever, lifetime job. We simply will not have this in Acirema.''

"Thank you, Taylor. We have taken up the entire hour with your comments and the calls from our listeners. I have even made the one exception which I have never made previously, and that is I did not interrupt you even once with a commercial break. I want to again thank you for visiting with us today by phone from the studios of WCOA radio in Pensacola. Give the good people at the studio my very best.

"You and your comments have been well-received by our audience, and please understand that you are welcome here as often as you would grace us with your presence. Please keep us posted as to upcoming events, announcements, and the progress of Acirema."

"Thank you, Bosch. It has been a real pleasure visiting with you today. Thanks for your time. Goodbye."

SAVAGE WAS PLEASED with those who called the show, and he had positive answers to every question that was asked. From all accounts the entire country seemed to be willing to give Acirema a chance.

THIRTEEN

ON MONDAY MORNING Governor Woods called a meeting of his chief advisors, the Little Cabinet, which was made up of the Secretaries of all major agencies of the state. Through an earlier memo he had requested that each be prepared to offer his or her comments pertaining to any suggestions they might have concerning the Taylor Savage issue.

In addition to those who worked directly for the State of Florida, the Governor also requested that Melvin Cooper attend. Cooper directed and managed both of the Governor's successful campaigns for Florida's highest office. Rather than accept a position within the Administration after Woods was inaugurated, he opted to open his own lobbying firm and had done extremely well, especially with issues directly concerned with the Governor's Office.

The Governor was seeking information on all sides of the issue and wanted his staff's opinion as well as the political side of the question. "Good morning," he said, welcoming the group. "Hope you all had a fine weekend and are ready for a hectic workweek. I also trust that each of you will have great news this morning, and together we can solve this nightmare that has been laid at our doorstep by Mr. Savage.

"Our trip to Washington left much to be desired. Governor Foxworth and I left the conference feeling defeated, and the comments by the President's advisors gave us nothing by way of hope. Our four Senators did not seem to be overly zealous

186

concerning their personal support. This morning why don't we go around the table and see what each of you has to offer. I have asked Melvin to come in for this discussion, and I'm most anxious to hear about the possible ramifications as pertaining to his political point of view. Go ahead, Melvin, you lead off.''

''Thanks Governor. And good morning, people. It's good being with you again. Maybe we can find something to hang our hats on, a means to a satisfactory end or at least a position we can live with. You all know that we have to keep the political end of my business out of your day-to-day operations and management of the State Government. What I will offer this morning is simply the political position as I see it, and each of you can form your own conclusion.

''As the Governor mentioned, the President does not seem to want to offer any help to either side. From face value this seems to be a wash. However, don't believe that for one moment. If the President had an inkling of an idea the referendum would fail, he would be on our side and assisting us in fighting it day and night. Unfortunately, this is not what he is thinking. Therefore, this would have to indicate only one thing, and that is he is quite sure the referendum is going to succeed, so he is not prepared to stick his neck out and lose favor with some 1.4 million constituents.

''From my standpoint, I feel much the same way. If I had to bet today, I would bet on the side of Taylor Savage. Now, let's analyze the options. If we continue to go balls to the wall and fight Savage's program and they win, we have lost some 700,000 people and I fear that's just the beginning of several losses we will experience.

''But if we fight it and they lose the referendum and it's a close race, we win. However, we are surely going to antagonize at least half of them, perhaps 350,000 people. So, what kind of win would that be?

''We all know the Governor is thinking about a run for the United States Senate when he completes his term next year. Considering one of his strongholds has always been here in northwest Florida, the alienation of 350,000 would weaken him significantly. If we relax somewhat and offer only token resistance to their movement, then Savage will surely win and we lose 10 very important counties and the Governor loses much of his strong political base.

"On the reverse side, if we do little in the way of an effort against Acirema and they somehow happen to lose the referendum then, the Governor is tagged as a do-nothing Chief Executive and will earn little respect from either side.

"It's kind of a damned if you do and damned if you don't situation. It reminds me of a question I once was asked which goes like this. If an author wrote a book entitled *How To Lose In The Business World* and the book became a bestseller, would the author be a success or a failure? Think about it.

"We have done no polling of our own, and I am not sure that we need to at this time. It appears the poll that Savage's folks conducted shows an 82 percent favorable rating, and quite possibly it has a lot of validity. Governor, that's about all I can report at this time."

"Thanks, Melvin. It's not so rosy, is it?"

"No, Sir, not at all."

"Joe, you're next. What do you see from your Department of Commerce?"

"Governor, it's no secret that Acirema will get the northwest Florida jewels, that is, the Miracle Strip of beaches if they are successful with the referendum. From the Perdido Pass in Alabama to east of Panama City are without a doubt the most beautiful, cleanest beaches in the world. We can talk about Florida's lower east coast and west coast, but what is offered in northwest Florida puts them to shame. And, furthermore, the entire area is ripe for development. It's been waiting in the wings patiently for some time, and its time may be very near.

"When Taylor Savage announced his plans for the Acirema International Global Airport, he included reference to some 50,000 new jobs. Can you imagine what that will mean to a small state like Acirema with its entire population being only 1.4 million and they bring in a new operation which will create 50,000 new jobs?

"He is also going to build a four-lane private highway from their airport to connect with Interstate 10 somewhere near the Loxley, Alabama, exit. This will handle all the traffic problems to and from the new airport complex. Additionally, they will triple their flow of traffic off the Interstate down to their beaches, golf courses, and vacation homes. We have not had time to come up with an exact cost projection of the highway, but $60 million would be close. You think this wouldn't stimulate their economy?

"And with his acquisition of the *Lexington*, he will have a complete floating city. This within itself will provide perhaps 2,000 jobs considering the ship's requirement of personnel as well as those required to support its operations from dockside. I understand that he will be opening his own travel agency to book all passages. He has been quoted as projecting a possible cost of $80 million for renovations of the Lex and says that all work will be completed within the state of Acirema.

"I'm telling you, Taylor Savage is on to something, and it's enormous. There is no way he can financially lose with the detailed plans that we know of thus far. Can anyone here offer me a single reason why those who will be asked to vote in a referendum, given the opportunities that he is providing, would vote against becoming a part of Acirema. I can think of none.

"Now, this may come as a surprise. I learned of it less than an hour ago from a close friend of mine who works in the Mississippi State Department of Commerce. Apparently, there is a move on among several well-heeled Mississippians to have the Savage group consider including a portion of their state from the Alabama line westward to the Gulfport area. This obviously would take in most of their gambling casinos.

"Governor, it appears to me that his program has much on the ball, and I think you would be well-advised to start thinking in terms of 'when', not 'if,' they attain Statehood.

"From what I gather, his overall plan is in a self-sustaining posture. He has already noted that he does not need the approval of either Florida or Alabama."

"Thanks for your comments, Joe. What do you folks from Revenue have to add?"

"Well, obviously, when you lose 700,000 people from a single geographical area, you have to be concerned. Our tax base will feel a deep jolt; on the other hand, our expenses are reduced accordingly. Our current budget for next year will be drastically changed, so it will take considerable work for the legislature to adopt specific changes and alternate appropriations.

"Assuming the referendum does pass, we will lose three major committee chairmen in the House and one in the Senate because their home location will then be in Acirema, not Florida. And this includes Senator Arnold who is scheduled to become President of the Senate if the Democrats retain control, and it looks as though they may.''

''Thanks, Buford,'' said the Governor with a somewhat somber expression.

''Governor, I need to leave for another appointment, but let me say something before I go,'' remarked Melvin Cooper. ''This is a very tough situation, and the more you stir it the more it's going to stink. I would like for you and me to have some time together very soon to discuss more details of the political aspects of the problem.''

''Sure, how about 3:00 o'clock tomorrow afternoon. Can you come by at that time?''

''That'll be fine. I'll see you at 3:00 tomorrow. Have a good day, and I'll see all you folks later.''

After Cooper left the room, the Governor seemed anxious to have the floor. ''Well,'' he said, ''I guess that I have heard enough this morning, but before we go let me tell you folks a short story that came to mind as you gave your reports.

''It is about this King, and Lord knows I can't remember his name. However, considering the mess we are in, let's assume he was King FooFoo. During days of yore, it was the norm for the King to send a rider on horseback to survey his kingdom and report his findings. As the story goes, each time the rider returned from his trips, he reported and explained to King FooFoo there were many problems across his kingdom and something just had to be done and done quickly. This happened time and time again, and King FooFoo became more depressed each time the rider returned and delivered a message proclaiming all the problems throughout the vast Kingdom.

''When the rider returned the last time and upon hearing the latest disastrous news of problems, needs, starvations, medical deficiencies, and such, King FooFoo became more depressed than ever. He had to find a means, a solution if you will, to the countless numbers of problems which were plaguing his kingdom, so he immediately ordered the guards to behead the rider and explained that he would never again hear of such devastating problems now that he had put an end to it once and for all.

"This meeting is adjourned, and all of you take special care of yourselves!"

☐ ☐ ☐ ☐ ☐

GOVERNOR WOODS SET aside two full hours for his visit with Melvin Cooper, his longtime friend and one of his most trusted advisors. From the reports presented yesterday by the members of his Little Cabinet, the possibility of success for Acirema seemed all but certain.

With the Governor's second term of office ending in December next year and this year already slipping into its third month, a decision had to be made one way or the other as to what his future in politics might be, and that decision had to be made very soon. Before Taylor Savage announced his Acirema plans in early January, there was no doubt in anyone's mind that he would seek the United States Senate seat now held my Republican James A. Doyle of Orlando.

Now that Acirema was playing a significant role in everyone's political decisions, some major plans had to be placed on the front burner and very carefully designed. Governor Woods had always run well in the Panhandle and would count heavily on those same votes in either a race for the Senate or for the Governorship of Acirema.

The Governor's secretary, Jackie Smith, knocked gently on the door leading into his private office and announced, "Governor, Melvin Cooper is here. Would you like for me to send him in?"

"Jackie, tell him to wait in the small conference room, and we will meet there. Let him know that I'll be just a minute or so."

"Yes, Sir."

Melvin made himself at home and poured himself a steaming cup of coffee which was always available for every visitor. Coffee and, obviously, orange juice were offered around the clock.

"Good afternoon, Melvin. Glad you had time for a chat."

"Afternoon, Governor. How are you today?"

"Well, I'm in a contemplating mood. Hope you are."

"Why don't we knock around our options?" Cooper suggested.

"I assume the purpose of our talking at this time is to see what plans we need to make for the next race. Am I correct?''

"Oh, yeah. We need to decide on something, that's for sure. Why don't you give me your personal assessment of the Acirema referendum,'' stated Woods.

"Since we have always leveled with each other, I'll shoot straight with you. I think the referendum will pass by nearly 70 percent and perhaps even higher. I know that's not what you want to hear, but that's the way I see it.''

"I'm afraid you are right. Your figures are somewhat higher than I would expect. However, 50 percent plus 1 vote puts us in the same boat as does the numbers that you're throwing around,'' noted the Governor. "Melvin, I need to look at both of the races. We need to analyze my potential for victory in the Senate race as well as the Acirema Governorship. What're your thoughts?''

"Governor, let's start with the basics. I'm thinking you would have a hard time defeating Senator Doyle. With him being a fairly strong Republican and from the populous Republican hotbed area of Orlando, this gives him a real boost and makes him a very tough opponent.

"Furthermore, it is my opinion a Democrat could win the Acirema Governorship. Mr. Haze would give some tough competition in the general election, but I feel a Democrat could prevail. That is my assessment and educated guess.''

"I've given both options a good deal of consideration,'' said Woods. "While we would have some time to waste if I opted for the Senate seat, we have almost no time to kill if my choice should be the Governorship. I have spoken to Taylor Savage about the possibility, and he suggested if I wanted to get in the race to come right ahead, but that I should resign from this office first.''

"You mean you have actually asked Savage his opinion?''

"Yeah, when Foxworth and I met with him down at Seaside. I kinda put it as a 'what if' situation. He was adamant that I resign here prior to his committee sending out the referendum ballots. Otherwise, he said it smelled too political,'' explained Woods.

"From his standpoint I think he is right, Governor. The voters would not like it, nor would they support you if you waited until the results of the referendum were made known before you made up your mind.''

"Yes, I'm with you and Taylor on this one,'' grumbled Woods.

"What is your suggestion, what do you think I should do?"

"If I'm going to be involved with either campaign as your manager, then I want you, or you jointly with your family, to make whatever decision that fits you best. I will adjust, but you have to make the final decision. You have to decide for yourself which road you want to follow.

"This is the first thing you will have to do, and the second thing is that I owe you an honest opinion of my evaluation and that opinion is the Acirema Governorship would be the easiest for you to win, not easy, but easier. And there are other advantages."

"Let me hear all of them."

"Well, should you enter the race and win the Governorship, you could count on being there for six years. At the end of four years, you would have a choice to continue for another two years or seek Acirema's junior Senator's seat, which would be open at that time.

"Should you elect to seek another two-year term as Governor, then the senior Senator's seat would be up for grabs. These are some interesting options."

"Let me point out one more," Melvin insisted. "Should you make a run for their Governorship and lose, then you would still have time to enter Florida's race for the U.S. Senate. However, you will be somewhat wounded from losing their race, and another thing you would have to do is move back here to the State of Florida."

"You have outlined them all very precisely, as usual. Now, what shall I do?"

"You are now asking my opinion, so here it is. I would go home tonight and discuss the options with your family. If the choice is to seek the Governorship, then I would come back tomorrow and sit down with Lieutenant Governor Sanders and tell him what you have decided to do. You owe Dan that much. Then I would prepare a speech to let the citizens of Florida know what you plan to do. Give the speech, resign, and let's get busy with your campaign—and I mean full-time."

"Melvin, I'll tell you what I am going to do. I'll discuss it around home for a few days, and next Monday, March 4th, I'll have a firm answer. As you know, the Platform of Acirema will not allow any campaigning until 60 days prior to the election.

That would mean we could begin actively and have our kickoff campaign rally on September 26th. Although we can't do any politicking until that date, I can make known my intentions. If I make that choice, I will structure my resignation to become effective on September 25th.

"Why don't you come here next Monday morning at 10:00, and I'll give you my decision, and I can promise you it will be a firm and final one."

"That'll be fine, Governor. I'll see you on the 4th. Now you have a lot of soul-searching to do, so I suggest that you get started."

FOURTEEN

IT WAS JUST PAST 8:00 when four Greyhound buses loaded with placard-carrying protestors rolled onto the asphalt parking apron surrounding the Hilton. Following closely behind were several cars, pickups, and motorcycles each blaring its horn and making all kinds of racket. The mass assembled around the front entrances and even obstructed the exit of the hotel overnight guests who were checking out, trying to leaving the building.

Hotel security was well-aware of the possibilities of such encounters with each meeting of the Acirema committee and had alerted the city police, who were on the scene in a matter of minutes. The protestors were told they could do their thing as long as they did not block the entrance and prevent anyone from either entering or leaving the building. They would be permitted to demonstrate as long as they did it peacefully; otherwise, they would again be hauled off to city court.

Hazel Chestnut patiently awaited the arrival of Taylor Savage while making no comments to other members of the committee. She knew what she wanted to say and just who to say it to. Shortly before 9:00 Savage arrived, and as usual he stopped to greet the media. Although not wanting to, he was forced to speak with those gathered in protest.

"Good morning, all. Looks as though you have increased the size of your group. I want you all to know that you are welcome to attend our meeting. However, as usual we would expect you not to interfere with our program. We have a lot to do and have little time to waste."

Hazel Chestnut butted in, "Mr. Savage, when is all this going to cease? When are you finally going to understand that the program you dreamed up is simply not what the people want? These present today can attest to that, can't you see? Don't you understand?"

"Mrs. Chestnut, for the umpteenth time, and let me make sure that you understand what I am saying to you, we are not, and that's spelled n-o-t, going to cease anything. Thus far, I have tried to be nice to you and your group. After this morning I will have nothing more to say on the subject to either you or any protestors. If you feel it necessary to demonstrate this morning, have at it. But this will be the last time I shall give any attention to your antics. Have a good day, Mrs. Chestnut."

"Wait just a damn minute," came the grainy voice of one of the cyclists, a man of perhaps 40 years, dressed in dirty jeans, leather jacket, sun-drenched and leathery face, and pigtails, an earring in his right ear. His only means of identification was the words 'Bone Man' spread across the back of his jacket. "Don't think for a minute that we are going to let you get away with this kind of crap. Man, you're talking about taking some of Alabama, and we just ain't gonna let you. Now if I have to whup your ass right here in front of God and everybody, I'll do it. Many generations of our families have lived in the clay hills of 'Bama, and all toted this here Confederate flag. We ain't meaning to let them down. You understand that?"

"Sir, would you like to come inside and listen to our program, and perhaps you will better understand just what we are planning for this area. Believe me, you and your folks will all be better off after we are successful with the referendum," responded Savage.

"What referendum? You know that we are not going to let you get that far with this thing. Someone is gonna get their ass killed. Don't you know that? We mean business, and we won't let you take our state without a fight, and I mean a real fight, not just some lawsuit in some court somewhere.

"You're talking real trouble, and you need to understand that we all will get behind Miss Hazel to make sure that you don't take our land. You better believe it big shot. And let me tell you something else. A couple of weeks ago you went on and on about doing something about the criminals on death row. Bull crap, you just like all the rest. All you want to do is talk. Let me tell you how to handle that problem. You remember what happened in Oklahoma City last year. That guy McVeigh blew away that whole damn building. Why don't you just get some folks like that to drive a dynamite-loaded truck right down through the middle of the prison. Aim it at the death row, and get rid of all those creeps. It ain't hard to fix that problem.''

□ □ □ □ □

WITH THAT TAYLOR Savage and his staff shuffled into the building, stopping only once to answer a question from a local radio personality.

"Good morning. Thank you all for being here. This is our fourth general assembly meeting, and again everyone is present. I do appreciate your attendance very much. As I am sure you observed, we again have with us this morning a showing of those who would be more comfortable with the status quo than to make a change for the better. I guess we are saddled with this arrangement, so we may as well get used to it. As I mentioned to those gathered outside, this morning will be the last time I comment to those who assemble in protest. Perhaps that should be the order of the day for all of us. However, that is just a suggestion, so please feel free to make up your own mind relative to any comments you may wish to consider.

"Okay, why don't we get down to business. I guess there is no one who does not know what is going on within our program. Since I announced on the Bosch Lemoreaux show last week that I would have a big announcement today, I have been bombarded with questions, as I am sure each of you have been. If it wasn't for the fact that our program is getting such wide coverage, which certainly educates our people, I would have a real problem with all the press everywhere I go. But believe me they are doing a fine job of reporting and everyone knows just exactly where we are headed with what we propose.

"This morning you can see the media is well-represented, and I welcome each and every one of them. I will be available to take questions and hope that each of you will join in.

"I would imagine our committee reports will have to wait until we are finished with the announcement that I have been promising. If the media leaves us some time after the announcement, we will get into the reports; if not, then we will continue with our committee meetings as called by our Chairpersons and report at the next regular meeting which is scheduled for Tuesday, March 19th.

"Now, I want to take some time to present to you a program about which I am truly excited. And, as everything else we do, it will attract much attention. The President and his Secretary of Transportation have released their publication entitled *Moving America, New Directions and New Opportunities*, with the subtitle 'Statement of National Transportation Policy and Strategies for Action.' I wanted to read some of the excerpts from this policy manual, and I quote:

"It is critically important to begin immediately the national effort to implement this transportation policy. During this year and in the following years, the department will work to ensure that this policy is fully implemented. For the longer term the Federal Government must maintain the mechanisms for integrating ideas from all parts of the transportation community that have worked so well to support development of this policy. The nation must invest today to meet tomorrow's transportation needs.

"The next decade can be a watershed in the history of transportation in America. On the threshold of a new century, we have an opportunity to address the challenges of a changing society, a changing economy, new technology, and new roles and possibilities for all members of the transportation community. There is significant potential for increased private sector involvement in transportation, including owning and operating toll roads and transit, and financing a broad range of projects through innovative corporate and joint public-private initiatives.

"We must improve management of transportation systems and facilities in order to accommodate more traffic and to handle traffic more efficiently, particularly in the highway, aviation, and waterway systems where there is congestion today. On toll bridges and highways, approaches such as prepaid passes, toll-free travel for carpools and other high-occupancy vehicles, or automated tolling and billing using electronic systems for vehicle identification that can save the cost and delay associated with conventional toll booths and boost effective capacity. New technologies now in the development and testing stage, such as intelligent vehicle/highway systems, can also improve traffic flow on streets and highways, enhance capacity, and increase trip reliability and safety.

''The range of tools and choices available to state and local governments must be expanded. State and local governments should be given wider latitude to impose tolls on highways and other transportation facilities to raise revenues for transportation, even if those facilities are constructed with Federal funds.

''Projected transportation needs for the 21st century eclipse our present public and private sector programs. We must broaden the base of support for transportation, reinvigorate investment, and tap new sources of ideas and capital to meet growing demands.

''As we face the challenges of a changing society, an evolving world economy, and new technologies, we must restructure the transportation partnership to give other levels of government and the private sector the tools they need to address critical requirements in transportation. All of those who have a stake in efficient transportation must participate—federal, state, and local governments, private businesses, academic institutions, transportation interest groups, communities, and individuals. The measure of our Federal policies will lie in the success of unleashing private resources and of using public resources most efficiently to meet the nations's transportation needs.

''We must ensure that necessary funds will be available to support our transportation system. The Federal Government is prepared to provide the leadership, in partnership with state and local governments and the private sector, to assure an adequate financial base for transportation.

''We need to stimulate increased investment in transportation by state and local governments and the private sector by expanding the range of available tools and choices. Federal policies should provide greater incentives and increased flexibility in financing for other levels of government and the private sector. For example, local passenger facility charges at airports and tolls on highways offer significant potential as financing mechanisms where there is a heavy travel demand. Federal policy should relax restrictions on the use of such mechanisms. In addition, state and local governments and the private sector need greater flexibility to employ innovative financing techniques, such as benefit assessments, joint development rights, and other means of capturing the value of transportation investments in fees assessed on private firms that benefit from transportation services or facilities.

"Innovative approaches to managing and financing transportation are emerging that offer great promise for improving the efficiency with which we use our transportation systems and for attracting additional investment to transportation. State and local governments and the private sector are finding new ways to work together to solve their shared transportation problems. For example, State and local governments across the country are working with the private sector to build new highways as toll roads, with private sector involvement that ranges from financing and managing construction to owning and operating the roads.

"Most recognize the importance of the private sector and market forces in transportation. Although many participants in the outreach hearings looked to the Federal Government for guidance and leadership in addressing transportation issues, their comments also clearly revealed the value and necessity of state, local and private sector involvement and responsibility for many functions in transportation.

"Throughout America, people have ideas for ways their communities, transportation operators, and transportation users could get better use of the existing transportation system.

"There is widespread recognition that the United States will need to rely more on the private sector to finance facilities and services in virtually every area of transportation. During the outreach process, public officials from several states offered examples of successful private investments in transportation. Local governments are also turning to the private sector to provide public transportation service. Many participants in the hearings encourage greater use of innovative financing approaches, including private financing initiatives and joint ventures by private companies and state and local governments. New projects to build toll roads through public-private cooperation and financing were mentioned frequently.

"Financial resources provide a vital tool for meeting transportation needs, including private sector involvement and funding from all levels of the public sector. To address these needs, the nation will have to rely on the initiation and resources of private firms, state and local agencies, and, where necessary, the Federal Government. Not only conventional financing sources but also many innovative financing approaches will have to be involved. The Federal Government will work alongside and in close cooperation with private firms, industrial groups, and state, local, and regional agencies to facilitate the investment that will be required to support the dynamic and efficient transportation system we need for the 21st century.

"Private firms that own and maintain transportation infrastructure and provide transportation services are a vital part of the nation's transportation system. Private lending institutions and other investors also play a significant role in backing transportation projects.

"Government bodies at all levels must encourage and welcome private participation and investment in transportation. Some state and local agencies are already addressing growing traffic demand by permitting private construction and operation of highways and other transportation facilities, or purchase or long-term lease of existing facilities. There are many areas where increased private sector participation in transportation offers significant benefits, for example, in public transit, passenger rail service, airports, air traffic control towers at low-activity airports, toll roads and bridges, and intermodal facilities. The federal government encourages such involvement."

□ □ □ □ □

"THANK YOU FOR your attention; I know that was long-winded. These were joint comments by the Federal Government and the President of the United States, and we in Acirema are determined to take advantage of every opportunity to decrease the cost of government which will save each of our citizens taxes, thereby assuring our citizens that they keep more of their earnings rather than waste dollars on ineffective government. A copy of that statement is available to committee members and also the press.

"As we approach the 21st century, we as a nation, a state, and individual members of a free enterprise society must go forward with new and innovative ideas which will benefit our society as a whole and make the USA a better place for all future generations.

"This morning I want you to listen to a program and a development which we will call The Acirema Parkway (TAP).

"We must learn from the past and face the future with new ideas and new approaches which will redirect our lives today and that of our children as well as their children in the future. Only programs which are good for everyone are programs worthy of consideration. Our TAP fits this description. What we propose is good for the Federal Government, our Acirema State Government, free enterprise, the traveling public, taxpayers, contractors, and many vendors.

"We have to replace the old, antiquated, worn-out ways of doing business and present this generation with new acceptable ideas which will motivate all of us to move forward at a greater pace while keeping in mind the quality of the final product and still remain competitive in the market place. Our TAP program is an idea whose time has come. It is one which, on first glance, seems almost impossible to accomplish. However, the final product will move our traveling public safer toward new goals in this century and not only protect the quality of the final product but also greatly improve on the product as we have known it in the past.

"It was a last-ditch effort during the 1990 Florida Legislative session when the Legislature and the Executive Branch finally agreed on a funding package for new road construction and/or maintenance programs to provide the State Department of Transportation with the necessary funds so desperately needed today to face the oncoming rush of those who will visit or move into Florida each day. Most reports indicate that between 800 and 1,000 individuals move into Florida daily, and we simply must prepare, and do so now, as we can also expect a steady stream of new residents flooding into Acirema.

"The President's new road program states that 'The great American road program is not really a Federal problem at all but a true state responsibility. The future needs for highway construction can and shall be met by state governments.' The President also noted, 'We cannot afford inadequate, inefficient transportation. The national system is beginning to breakdown. The responsibility shall be that of the state—not the Federal Government.'

"Our program, the program which I suggest this morning, will be a joint venture between the Federal Government, Acirema State Government, and free enterprise, one of a complex nature, yet simple in today's terms. It is a program which can be accomplished with total success if all concerned participate in a spirit of solving the problems associated with road transportation industry by using new, innovative means and high technology and leaving the 'antiquated methods' of the past behind.

"We must first realize that our TAP program is one which involves a completely new method of solving the problems associated with one segment of the industry—methods of financing the reconstruction of existing Interstate systems. Not only will TAP solve the problems at hand, but also it will present new ideas and methods concerning the distribution and use of federal gas taxes.

"The financing of The Acirema Parkway will be through a nonprofit corporation which will be named Parkway Management, Inc. Each of you will be a Board of Directors member.

"Our objective is to formulate a program acceptable as a joint venture between our non-profit corporation, the state of Acirema and the Federal Government.

"It will become a pilot, model program to turn Interstate 10, from the Mississippi line to the Apalachicola River, into the world's safest Parkway. This 231-mile segment will become a toll facility. When completed, we propose to add the local name of 'Acirema Parkway' to the present Interstate 10 designation.

"The program assures that only those who make use of TAP will be the ones who pay for that use. There will be no taxes raised anywhere in Acirema that will go toward the building, maintenance, and upkeep of TAP. Again, only those who use the system will pay and do so at the time of that use. This is how our entire state economy will be formulated. Those who use will pay the user fees without burdening others with such cost. Truckers, RVs, and heavy busses will be assessed the proper fare in order to provide the necessary financial resources to maintain the roadway and repair the damage caused by their heavier vehicles.

"This pilot program is a new, innovative idea that will change federal funding of road maintenance as pertaining to the collection of the federal tax on fuel and distribution of the same to the states. Washington will not bail out the states again, and, guess what, we don't want their help. We must find new means with which to solve our own problems, problems that have dogged the Department of Transportation for many years.

"We have no intention of continuing to collect federal gas and fuel taxes and send them to Washington to receive back only a percent of what we submit. We will advise the Federal Government that the taxes we raise on the sale of every gallon of gas and fuel in our state will be used here at home, right here in Acirema.

Let me give you a very short, but to the point, example. Should we in Acirema collect $100 million in gas taxes each year and send this amount to Washington and get in return only 77 percent, then we are losing $23 million. That would be very nice to keep at home, and it is our plan to fight for that right in court, if necessary. Furthermore, we will advise the Feds we will not be asking them for any assistance or help with our roads, either new construction or maintenance of existing ones. We are determined to get Big Brother out of our hair and to do it right away because we will have properly designed plans and programs that are geared for that purpose.

"We are fully capable of handling this situation at the state level and can take care of our roads, bridges, etc., with our local free enterprise contractors. This not only will create new jobs for our local residents, but also will allow us to keep 100 percent of the gas and fuel taxes we will collect and to make use of those funds right here at home. This will improve and increase our economy by millions of dollars annually.

"With the success of this program, we can add a notch in our belt as a megatrend state and lead the nation with conversions of other sections of Interstate around the country.

"The program may seem too difficult from the outset. However, if we all put on the robes of statesmen and leave the pettiness of political infighting behind, we can show the nation this project can accomplish much of what is needed to improve our road systems by using the most equitable manner of financing, and that is user fees.

"Our nonprofit corporation will be a turnkey operation in a partnership between Acirema and the Federal Government for the purpose of total management of this public-owned access highway system. The basis for the entire program is twofold: first, free enterprise can do a more economical job of management than can state and federal governments; second, the user will pay the cost of the system. It is simply not justified when those who are not using the system are still paying the same amount of federal gas tax on each gallon of gas purchased.

"In the past we have often made the 'little old lady' analogy. However, in this case the little old lady may well be the one, such as the retired, that is using the system. Therefore, she should continue to pay the cost to do so. However, the everyday 'working class,' that does not have the time and financial ability for extended vacations or who do not use the Interstate for either daily local or long distance travel purposes, are the ones who are paying the same amount of federal gas tax per gallon and are not receiving fair value for the taxes paid into the system. Again, those who are using the system must be the ones paying for that privilege. This is only fair.

"Our plan will provide many new jobs along the Parkway and create some $205 million of new construction funds which will be scattered throughout the counties along the route. This within itself will be a major boost to the economic well-being of each county, and the annual payroll of TAP employees will also benefit each county's economic base.

"As mentioned, our nonprofit corporation, Parkway Management, Inc., will issue bonds for construction of all toll facilities as well as for reconstructing the entire 231 miles of roadway. Upon retirement of the bonds, all titles of all equipment, buildings, improvements, etc., would automatically vest in the State of Acirema. The bonds will be secured solely by a pledge of toll collections and would not constitute a direct or indirect pledge of the state's credit.

"Let's be innovative. Let's do something different. What we have been doing in the past is clearly not the answer. If this project just happens to stumble, there are many safeguards built in which will guarantee the state and federal governments a better product than what they had before the conversion took place.

"Throughout the President's policy on 'Moving America,' he, time and time again, indicates that the Federal Highway System nationwide is in desperate need of emergency repairs and maintenance. He points out that new and innovative ways must come to light and that it will be the shared responsibility of the federal government, state governments, and the private sector to bring these new and innovative ideas to reality.

"As the President notes, innovative ways concerning the transportation industry must be adopted immediately. It is the position of PMI that the old rules and regulations of the past which dictated policy are to be examined closely; therefore, PMI is pleased to offer our solutions for a 231-mile section of the Acirema Parkway.

"Since our program will generate its own funding, the vast amount of dollars that would normally be required for the renovation of the Parkway can be used elsewhere by our State Road Department on other badly needed projects without having to obligate these funds for continued maintenance and reconstruction of this 231-mile section. Parkway Management, Inc. will provide all funding for our State Trooper unit, which will patrol TAP, and we will beef up the actual number of patrol cars for additional safety on the Parkway. In this manner our Acirema State Trooper Program can use existing funds formerly earmarked for this 231-mile section on other additional manpower needs around the state.

"The Acirema Parkway will be the first picture of Acirema seen by visitors who enter the state. It is our goal to have the most beautiful, manicured median strips and roadsides planted with trees native to Acirema, so that we can offer the driving public a true view of the Acirema countryside when they enter our state.

"We may want to sublease footage on the outer edge of the right-of-way to a tree farming company. This would not only help defray expenses of the maintenance but would also assist in beautifying the entire scenic route. This operation would provide that trees and shrubs be planted, where space is available between the roadways, to add to the beauty of the drive as well as be a safety feature which will lessen the distraction of watching oncoming motorists on the opposite side of the parkway. This is a known safety hazard which we will eliminate.

"Free enterprise contracting will put us in position to eliminate such things as having 15 men, eight trucks, four pieces of
equipment, and two or three foremen on a repair project where, in
effect, perhaps two laborers are actually doing the work. In every
state this is a problem, and we will solve it by using free enterprise
contractors. Our program will truly 'downsize' the cost of
government relating to our Department of Transportation.

"Our PMI Corporation will not be required to own any equipment as we will share the equipment pool which we will set up for
use by the cities, counties, and the state. This will save a
tremendous amount. During the reconstruction phase, we will
contract with communication companies to bury PVC, TV, phone,
cable and other high-tech communication cables along the right of
way for future use. Currently, the Interstate system does not make
use of its right-of-way areas for the highest and best use, but by
this means we in Acirema can take advantage of this large amount
of acreage to create added revenue to ultimately distribute to the
counties along the route.

"PMI will in every respect 'step in the shoes' of the Department of Transportation and relieve them of all duties pertaining to
this section of our Parkway system in Acirema. We will provide
all bonding for the total reconstruction of the roadway and the cost
of constructing all toll facilities, including all computer network
hardware and software. We will totally maintain the entire 231
miles of TAP as well as be responsible financially for all costs of
highway patrol law enforcement.

"Because PMI will shoulder the responsibilities of the Parkway, our State and the Federal Government will have no further
responsibilities for this section of Interstate other than to certify
that all paving contracts have been completed according to the
specifications of the State and Federal Governments.

"To hasten the flow of traffic, we will use a system similar to
that being manufactured by the AMTECH Corporation of Dallas,
Texas. This is a window sticker system which allows computer
scanning that reads traffic flow up to 45 miles per hour as the
vehicle passes through the facility. Anyone, such as a business
traveler who travels TAP often, can place a cash deposit in his
System Account Management account, and SAM will deduct the
toll fee automatically as the vehicle passes the exit facility. In this

case there would be no need to slow down below 45 MPH. We will set up a credit card and/or credit program for those using the system on a regular basis whereby the automatic system would deduct charges from a prepaid account.

"SAM will print out information relative to excessive speeding and will collect the fine on site as they exit. This could be paid in cash, charged against the credit balance in an account, or charged to a personal credit card. This system will save countless hours of time for the court systems as well as the time which would be required for an officer to have to appear in court for the purpose of giving testimony. And most of all, it will create the world's safest 231 miles of high-speed highway.

"At all times SAM can provide the exact number of vehicles, by classification such as auto, bus, semitrailers, motor homes, etc., that are on the Parkway. This information will provide the figures which will assist in designing those areas which may need additional strength, etc., in order to keep the base and surface course from excessive wear and tear. This will provide an exact computation of traffic flow and detect the need for repairs and maintenance, as well as preventive maintenance, to a troubled area well before such a problem could erode into a costly major repair.

"John Naisbitt, in his book *Megatrends*, points out that we are now in the 'Information Society.' We should be prepared to capitalize on all information available and make use of it for the purpose of cutting costs. Keeping this in mind, we will work toward an agreement with Florida State University to make use of their super computer for the network of information needed to make this project work in the manner in which it is intended.

"All vehicles that are registered in the State of Acirema will be permitted to purchase an annual SAM vehicle window bar graph decal for a fee. This fee will allow the vehicle access to TAP without additional toll charges for a period of one year. For passenger vehicles the annual fee may be $25.00. The fee for trucks, trailers, busses, and other vehicles will be determined by you, as a member of our Board of Directors.

"At the time you purchase your SAM decal in your home county, you will make your choice of your 'companion' county by choosing either the county on your east or the one on your west. SAM will allow your vehicle to travel, toll free, between these two counties. The only counties that would be adversely affected by this rule would be Mobile County, as it has no Acirema county on the west, and Jackson County, as it has no Acirema county on the east. Those purchasing SAM decals within these two counties have only one 'companion' county option. Should your trip take you a distance greater than your 'companion' county, then you pay the toll from the point of origination to the final point when you depart TAP.

"There will be no toll charge for any official U. S. Military vehicle using TAP.

"Our program provides that year-end net toll revenues be pro-rated between the 19 counties within Acirema. A distribution policy will be adopted whereby income will be distributed depending on the population of each county. Year-end toll revenue funds received by each county will be earmarked by that county to be used only for their local road construction projects.

"As previously noted, our program provides many millions of dollars for both reconstruction and new construction. Local contractors throughout the northern Panhandle will benefit greatly as likewise will the local economy of all 19 counties.

"Larger vehicles, such as semi-trailers, busses, motor homes, etc., need to share a greater burden of the cost due to the fact that the weight of their vehicles adds so much more to the cost of repairs and maintenance than do passenger vehicles.

"We will construct all toll facilities to facilitate the handicapped and hire these individuals in as many positions as possible. In this way we can help reduce our welfare and unemployment rolls by providing good jobs to the handicapped who may otherwise continue to be a direct drain on the economic base of our state.

"Our employees will be trained to understand they are the 'first line ambassadors' for many thousands of visitors each day. They will be trained to be kind, personal, and courteous to all. So often we find this is not the case on other Parkways throughout the country.

"The President notes that safety on our highways is essential. Safety always must be foremost in our consideration of any innovative plans for the future. Although we cannot accomplish and accommodate all items of advance safety from day one, we will build four medically equipped helicopter stations along the route to ensure the traveling public that we do have the safest Parkway in the country. This program will be added at a later date as revenues permit. When completed, we will contract with all 19 counties to offer this helicopter service to each for a nominal fee.

"It will be asked of us, why should the State of Acirema and the Federal Government choose private enterprise to do this program rather than have our Acirema Department of Transportation do the same program 'in-house?'

"First, we want to 'downsize' state government. We will reduce any efforts right up front, well before we hire Department Managers thereby stopping an attempt to increase the size of Acirema's government. Here are a few other major reasons why we would not allow the program to be Managed by our Department of Transportation. The DOT would feel compelled to add personnel for the program. Our program will actually allow the DOT to reduce its personnel as we will use outside consultants for much of the needed expertise.

"We will eliminate hundreds of thousands of dollars annually for the purchase of construction and maintenance equipment due to the 'downsizing' effect of sharing equipment between all agencies around the state. This is a major expenditure which can be reduced greatly. Obviously, this will not make the heavy equipment sales companies happy. However, it is good for Acirema.

"Private enterprise can simply do it better and save dollars. And as I said earlier, we will not have six foremen, eight truck drivers, and 10 operators standing around watching two men do the actual labor on a project.

"We would totally eliminate 231 miles that the DOT would not have to concern itself with, thereby reducing its budget.

"Acirema will have limited bond liability as we will issue all construction funding bonds through our PMI nonprofit corporation and/or possibly a joint county bond pool.

"We will eliminate one level of state bureaucracy.

"Our program will assist local governments in providing road dollars from revenues received, thereby reducing the number of dollars the state normally sends back to the counties. These dollars would be available more quickly and will increase annually with the increased flow of traffic supporting TAP.

"We will generate several millions of dollars through construction contracts scattered throughout Acirema.

"Free enterprise can hire and fire employees who are not fully performing their duties, thereby reducing the cost of operations and passing these savings on to the counties at a greater rate of return.

"Free enterprise can negotiate with contractors not only for the reconstruction conversion but also for annual maintenance and receive a better unit price by choosing the proper time frame for letting of work.

"People, The Acirema Parkway is a new innovative idea whose time has come.

"Now, let me offer you some data and statistics that are most important. The length of the project from the Mississippi line to the Apalachicola River is approximately 231 miles. We will have to construct a facility for each entry as well as exit station. Since the existing Interstate is constructed with more access roads than a normal toll road facility would have, the number of stations needed will be greater.

"There will be six full-scale rest stations. The annual revenue from commercial leasing of rest stations is estimated to be $945,000 which is a figure that well may increase with positive negotiations.

"The annual revenue from communications companies, $1.6 million annually is a figure which is just an estimate.

"The amount of bond issue required is $205 million, and the associated bonding fees of three percent should be sufficient.

"The cost of each toll station is estimated to be $750,000.

"The cost per mile for reconstruction of pavement is estimated to be $550,000.

"The cost per mile for maintenance is estimated to be $12,114.

"The annual cost of nonadministrative salaries is estimated to be approximately $5 million.

"We expect $75.1 million as annual toll revenue, $2.82 million from local window passes, $1.6 million from lease of easements, and $945,000 from comfort station leases.

"This program was developed to coincide with our overall Platform and will address our intent to be a leader in new and innovative ideas and to meet the needs of an ever-growing demand for public financing of the conversion of the Interstate System into privately managed toll facility Parkways.

"Our project is one which deserves a lot of attention and merit. The opportunity for its approval is at hand. Let's make no mistake about it. We have a huge mountain to climb with high peaks and deep valleys. There's a snake behind every rock. However, the time for this program is now, and when we succeed the rewards will be tremendous. Every county within Acirema will be financially better off due to jobs being created and income derived.

"We are starting down a road, one which has never been traveled. Our plan to convert 231 miles of Interstate into a privately managed Parkway has never been attempted. This will literally take an act of Congress. I feel that if presented correctly and it has the strong local support of the citizens of Acirema, we can accomplish our goal.

"We will be putting together a financial group, the developers so to speak, to fund the initial phase of our study. And as I have described, we will operate as a nonprofit corporation under the title of Parkway Management Inc. The developers will share equally in the fees received from all bonding issues, etc. You, the Board of Directors of PMI, will govern the actual day-to-day activities of the program.

"With the completion of TAP, we will then be in a position to refuse any further Federal highway funds from Washington. Not only will this refusal apply to TAP, but also to all Federal funds that are normally returned to the states for the purpose of road and highway construction. By the same token we will discontinue to send to Washington any Federal taxes on gas and other fuels sold in Acirema. There simply cannot be any argument against our position by the Federal Government and bureaucrats. We will not require any assistance from them relative to highway construction and maintenance; therefore, why should those who use roads and highways within Acirema pay taxes to send to Washington that would not benefit us whatsoever.

"When this announcement hits the air waves in an hour or so, I would imagine the bureaucrats will raise holy hell about our latest plans. However, they haven't a leg to stand on. I promise you.

"I will now field some questions, and I have asked David Hickman, President of Hickman and Hickman engineers and a committee member to join and assist me with technical aspects of the program. David has thoroughly reviewed the basic outline of TAP and is most familiar with what we envision to be a very sound program.

"What I think we should do at this time is open the floor to the media, and if you don't hear the answers to your questions, then please jump right in and ask away."

"I have a question," said a lady holding a CBS mike. "What makes you so sure your program will be accepted by the Feds?"

"Well, the reason I spent so much time earlier reading comments by the President and his Secretary of Transportation was to educate each of you as to what they are thinking in their publication *Moving America*. If they are serious in what they have publicized, then there is no way our program can be deterred or questioned and certainly could not be eliminated. On the other hand, if the bureaucrats start to fight us, then what has been described in *Moving America* has to be refuted not only by their Department of Transportation but also by the President of the United States. The bureaucrats then would have little difference with us, but a very real problem with the White House. All our program really does is to take them at their word as described in their own publication," Savage answered.

"And how long do you think the program will take to complete in full?"

"I don't want the tail to get too far in front of the dog, so let's wait until the referendum issue has passed. Then we can be more specific on questions such as you have posed. But to give you a rough answer, I would expect us to finish within two years."

FIFTEEN

FOR THREE DAYS TAYLOR Savage and Chad McQua, Governor of Mississippi, had played phone tag, but late Friday afternoon they finally connected. The Governor was in his office at the State Capital in Jackson and Taylor at the Opry Land Hotel in Nashville. He and Sheery were on a joint mission of attending the 61st Tennessee Quarter Horse Show and Exhibition and the Satirday night late show at the Grande Ole Opry. They both were most fond of today's modern style of country music, but neither could handle the older version of twang and screeches.

"Hello," answered Sheery.

"Hello, may I speak with Taylor Savage, please?"

"May I ask who is calling?"

"Yes, this is Chad McQua."

"Hold, please. Honey, it's Governor McQua."

"Thanks, hello."

"Hello, Taylor. This is Chad McQua. How are you?"

"Fine, Governor, and you?"

"Just great. Sorry we've had such a hard time tracking each other down," said McQua.

"Yeah, that seems to be the way it has been. How are you? What are you up to?" Savage asked although he knew the answer to both questions.

"Taylor, let me get right to the point so you can go back to enjoying your weekend. When can you and I along with our two Senators, Walter R. Clegg and Hank Shawn, sit down for a short conference?''

"Well, just about any time. I'll be here in Nashville until midmorning on Sunday, then we'll fly to Raleigh. I'll leave there on Wednesday morning for Washington and a couple of meetings. Would you want to try to get together while I am in D.C. or wait until I'm back in Florida? I'll be back there on Thursday afternoon, and we could schedule lunch on Friday if you like,'' answered Savage.

"That'll be fine. Why don't we meet then?''

"Can you come over to Pensacola?'' Savage inquired.

"Sure, we'll be glad to visit with you there.''

"Okay, let's do it Friday at noon. I'll have my office make reservations at McGuire's Irish Pub on east Gregory Street. McGuire Martin will be pleased to have us as guests. We can meet in the comfort of the Tap Room in the privacy of the Irish Politicians Club, have quietness, conduct our business, and at the same time enjoy a great lunch. How does that suit you and the Senators?''

"I'm sure that I can arrange for them to alter any plans they may have, as we all three are most anxious to sit down and discuss with you something which is of interest to the three of us, and I trust will be to you also. I'll make arrangements with Walt and Hank this afternoon, and I'll call your office to confirm.''

"That's fine. Call my Pensacola office and speak with Laura. Tell her of our conversation, and she will arrange to have you picked up at the airport and brought to McGuire's. I'll also confirm it with her later today,'' Savage advised.

"We will look forward to seeing you on Friday next. Now you have a great weekend and enjoy your trip to Washington.''

"Thanks. I'll see you in Pensacola on Friday. Goodbye, Governor.''

□ □ □ □ □

SHEERY AND TAYLOR had enjoyed the great Tennessee weather since arriving on Thursday. It was always a pleasure for him to get out of the pressure cooker and just let his hair down. Thursday afternoon they had driven down to Lynchburg and toured the Jack Daniels Distillery. Although Taylor was extremely familiar with the wine country of California, since his corporation had invested heavily in that area, this was his first visit to a sour mash whiskey operation, and he was much impressed with the giant vats filled with the fermenting liquid.

After a late night at the Opry, they slept in on Sunday morning and did not awaken until it was time for the special brunch which is served throughout the massive entrance halls and the lobby of the hotel.

With lunch behind them, they visited the Greenbriar Stables where Taylor had started negotiations to purchase several fine quarter horses for what would soon become Savage Stables in Acirema, near the Gulf Shores area. They had planned to spend no more than an hour with 'Rod' Hinning, the owner, but it soon turned into almost three. However, time was of little concern as they were flying the company's newest aircraft, a Cessna Citation X, with a cruising speed of 528 knots. They would float down to Raleigh on the cool afternoon breeze, making a very smooth and beautiful flight.

□ □ □ □ □

MONDAY MORNING TAYLOR left Sheery at his home so she could begin her measurements and planning for refurbishing the 23-room mansion which sat in the middle of 1,800 acres of lush lawns and hardwood trees. He had two meetings scheduled with two separate bonding firms to discuss their participation in funding the construction and renovation of the Acirema Parkway, the building of the Acirema International Global Airport, and possibly underwriting the renovations to the Lady Lex.

Both of the firms were most interested in working with Savage on the Airport project, and especially on his unique idea of the Parkway which might change the face of the transportation systems across every state in the country. Each fully understood the possibilities if his firm was successful and what it would mean to several other projects which would spring forth after the Acirema Parkway was completed and in operation. A ground-floor position at an early date could mean millions in fees to the company that won the contract to structure the best financial format of funding these projects.

□ □ □ □ □

SHEERY AND TAYLOR SPENT Monday afternoon and all

day Tuesday working on her ideas for refurbishing "Savage Place." Wednesday morning they again boarded "CC," the name Savage had given the Cessna Citation, and were off to Dulles Airport just outside Washington.

When they arrived, they were met by Ike Francis, the chief lobbyist for the International Prevention of Crime Committee and a longtime friend of Taylor's since they roomed together at Harvard. He had been instrumental in organizing the IPCC and looked forward to having Savage address the group over lunch.

Savage and Ike dropped Sheery off at the Willard Hotel, the chosen hotel for the evening. During Washington trips Savage equally divided his time between the Willard and the Mayflower. Both were first-class hotels, each providing excellent rooms and tremendous service, which was very much to his way of life. While Savage worked the crowd at his luncheon engagement, Sheery busied herself making all the arrangements for a small, intimate, breakfast meeting Thursday morning that included Florida Congressman Drake Hill and his wife Keesh and North Carolina United States Senator Mark Donner.

Taylor was looking forward to meeting with Francis' committee because it not only would offer a good deal of information, but also play a strong role in the anti-crime prevention program that he had in mind for Acirema.

Although Francis had no idea, this trip to Washington and the meeting was an on-site, personal interview and evaluation of him to head up what would soon be known in Acirema as the Anti-Crime Commission, assuming, of course, the referendum passed. Savage, as usual, was way ahead of the game; everyone was playing a part with none having any idea of what was actually happening. He wasted no time, no motion. Everything he did was calculated with precise emphasis on being successful in every phase of even the most minute detail of any business transaction.

At the conclusion of the luncheon, he paid a courtesy call on both of Alabama's and Florida's Senators on Capital Hill. He had not spoken with either since their last joint meeting and felt there may have been some feathers ruffled and this was not his personality. He had every intent to see the referendum pass and for Acirema to obtain Statehood. However, he did not want it to happen at the expense of losing friends. As much as Savage disliked politics in general, he was, without a doubt, the most polished politician of this generation.

With his business out of the way, he returned to the Willard where he and Sheery would again share a long-standing tradition, an afternoon hour together over a fine bottle of wine. Today they would visit the quaint, historic Nest Lounge on the second floor where the walls had pictures of several Presidents and many historic landscape paintings. The Willard had long been noted as a favorite meeting place for generations of national leaders, both American and foreign. It was here that President Lincoln had spent several nights before his inauguration and eventual move into the White House.

Over the past four years this afternoon tradition had become a very special hour they reserved for each other and looked forward to at the end of each day. During times when they were apart, the absence of this hour wore on each and made for a very long and lonely afternoon.

This evening they would dine at Mr. K's, one of Washington's prominent Chinese restaurants, and later take in a play at Ford's Theater. Although Savage was the ultimate businessman during the day, his evenings proved him to be a most romantic character, full of fun, laughter, and life.

☐   ☐   ☐   ☐   ☐

IT HAD ONLY been three weeks since Congressman Hill had returned from his eight-day space flight in the spacecraft "Superior." His flight marked only the third time an elected official had been selected by NASA to fly in space. The Congressman, Chairman of the House Space and Science Committee for the past three years, was most qualified mentally, physically, and politically to complete such a mission—of which many were most jealous, especially Taylor Savage.

The Congressman's wife, Keesh, was a longtime friend of Sheery's since both attended the University of North Carolina where they were sorority sisters for three years. Sheery, a year older, had been Keesh's big sister since she enrolled at UNC and was accepted into the sorority as a freshman.

Both Taylor and Sheery were looking forward to spending

some time over breakfast with these old friends. Having Senator Donner, who was Chairman of the Senate's companion Space and Science Committee, and the Congressman together over breakfast certainly was no accident.

The first four years after Sheery's graduation from UNC, she had served on the Senator's staff with duties assigned to the Banking Committee, of which he was a long-standing member and Vice-Chairman during that time.

Always a stickler for time, Savage and Sheery came downstairs early and were having their first cup of coffee when the Congressman and his wife arrived. As usual the Senator was late. When the five were finally together, they carried on small talk for almost half an hour before Savage got to the purpose of the meeting. "Sheery and I really want to thank the three of you for spending some time with us this morning. In this fast-paced world it is always great to slow down a bit and visit with old friends.

"I wanted you three to know that in our early plans for Acirema, we are looking at a special project which you two men in your capacity as Chairs of your House and Senate S/S Committees will have a special Congressional interest and perhaps a personal one as well.

"We are going to build a privately owned, free enterprise space port in Acirema's Panhandle. We are looking at an area called Crooked Island which is just to the east of Tyndall Air Force Base near Panama City, and just to the west of Mexico Beach.

"Congressman, you have expressed an interest in the past, when you are finished in the Congress and again become a private citizen, of pursuing a leadership role of perhaps directing the Cape Canaveral Space Center. We both know at the best this is an iffy situation as many retiring Congressmen are looking at the same position. In reality, this may or may not happen, and the odds are that it probably won't.

"I wanted to bring us all together this morning to let you two Congressional leaders know of our plans and to see what interest Drake may have in our private program.

"Drake, your Congressional district includes the Canaveral area and a good portion of the east coast of Florida. I thought this possibility may prove very interesting to you. And Senator, we are going to need your help on your committee. While there would be no tax dollars spent on the project, the Senate and the House will have to approve our plans, which would include launching missiles in the vicinity of Tyndall AFB. Thus the reason for discussing the program this morning.

"It appears to me that Cape Canaveral is going to be doing some advance testing for the X-33 prototype which will feature new avionics and new heat-shielding components that may reduce the cost of launches. They have several other items on their menu which may well keep their plate full.

"However, we plan to be in a position to build and launch more cost-effective missiles with expendable boosters for the use of our commercial market enterprises. The United States has great advantages over other countries at the present time, and we seek to improve and expand on that advantage by developing this program in the private sector. While we would have no intent to compete with the Cape for moon missions, we, as free enterprise individual companies, can do much better at a far less cost per launch to assist those who are interested in putting satellites into space for the benefit of the private commercial market.

"I do not ask for any commitments this morning. I just want all three of you to do some soul-searching and come up with your own personal comments at an early date."

"What about me?" asked the Senator. "Don't I get a job?" he mocked in a playful gesture.

"Senator, you already have a job. A very big job. But let me assure you there is always a place in Savage Worldwide if and when you ever decide to retire from the United States Senate."

"Just kidding. You know that I am just kidding," responded the Senator and continued. "You are right on target with a private space port and launching facility. I understand your reasons about flying near Tyndall but see no real problem that cannot be overcome. I'll be more than pleased to work in your corner on this one."

"Thank you, Senator. Now, let's forget business and have some breakfast."

☐ ☐ ☐ ☐ ☐

THE SAVAGE FAMILY had long been a financial supporter

of Senator Donner and contributed heavily to his three previous Senate Campaigns as well as his initial run for Governor of North Carolina. Taylor's father had been Donner's campaign manager for his first successful Governor's race back in 1972.

As had become habit, every time Savage and Donner crossed paths, Savage let it be known that his family was looking forward to continuing its support should Donner choose to seek a fourth term in the United States Senate and, as usual, reiterated, as he has done time and again, just how much he appreciated the Senator's first introducing him to Sheery.

□ □ □ □ □

SAVAGE WORLDWIDE Corporation's office was a beautiful waterfront complex on Pensacola Bay, downtown on Cypress Street at the foot of Spring. Taylor Savage spent the majority of his time in Pensacola, his Southeastern Division Headquarters with its home office in Raleigh. He and his personal staff occupied the top floor with his office on the south side overlooking the bay where the view was spectacular. Throughout the day there was a constant flow of pleasure craft, skiing rigs, sail boats, commercial tankers, and shrimping boats vying for space on the busy waterway. Across the bay at the end of the three-mile bridge lay the northern shore of Gulf Breeze. From his windows he could see this cozy community and its many beautiful homes. If he could see past Gulf Breeze, he would be almost in a straight line with his home which was on the inland waterway side of Santa Rosa Island. This entire area of the upper Gulf Coast is a beautiful and restful area.

Across from his office his secretary, Laura, kept tight rein on both his business and personal affairs and attempted to keep his daily calendar. However, he often made appointments without her knowledge. With the development of Acirema she found it necessary to hire herself an assistant. June Ferris, a graduate of Ole Miss with tremendous secretarial skills and a degree in computer science, had come highly recommended. Her qualifications would do just fine in the Savage Organization, even more so considering the fact she, in a personal way, was looking for a position to latch onto and ride to the top of the ladder of success.

While she was being groomed by Laura to become better

acquainted with the way Savage wanted things done, she still had a lot to learn. The phone rang, and she offered a friendly hello in a very Southern voice, "Good morning. Mr. Savage's office. May I help you?"

"Yes, young lady, you may. I would like to speak with Taylor Savage, please."

"Mr. Savage is not in and will not return to the office until later this afternoon. Perhaps I can assist you."

"I really need to speak with Taylor. Could you tell me when would be a good time for me to call back?"

"We do not know exactly what time he will arrive at the office this afternoon, and tomorrow he has a full day with the Governor of Mississippi and its two Senators."

"Is that right? Well, that's interesting. Perhaps I should try again later this afternoon. Would that be what you recommend?"

"Please hold and let me let you speak with Laura Rings, who is Mr. Savage's personal assistant."

"Hello. This is Laura, may I help you?"

"Yes. This is Walker Baldwin over in Pass Christian, Mississippi. When would be a good time for me to talk with Taylor by phone?"

"Mr. Baldwin, is Mr. Savage acquainted with you? Does he know what company you represent?" she inquired.

"He may or may not remember me. Remind him that we met in Raleigh in '92 when he hosted a fund-raiser for President Clinton. I think he'll remember who I am. Tell him I am a retired Vice-President of Westinghouse Corporation."

"Mr. Baldwin, perhaps you could call again later this afternoon. He is expected in the office sometime after 3:00 o'clock."

"Will you let him know that I called and will do so again later today, and that I represent a group of businessmen from the Mississippi Coast who would like to sit down and discuss the possibility of some connection of our area with the Acirema movement. Your receptionists tells me that he is meeting tomorrow with Governor McQua and Senators Clegg and Shawn. I would like to talk with him before that meeting."

"Mr. Baldwin, I'll be sure to tell him that you will be calling again this afternoon, and thanks for calling."

"Thank you, Miss Rings. Goodbye."

As soon as she hung up the phone, Laura went straight into June's office. "Did you tell Mr. Baldwin that Mr. Savage was meeting tomorrow with the Governor and Senators from Mississippi?"

"Yes. I thought since he was from Mississippi it would be all right."

"Let me tell you one thing, and don't you forget it. Mr. Savage's business is his business and cannot be discussed with anyone. Do you understand this?"

"Yes, ma'am. I understand."

"I want to make sure that you completely understand. Is there any question whatsoever about what I just said?"

"No, ma'am."

"Well, it is most important. Don't you ever again tell anyone of any meeting which Mr. Savage is holding, either here in the office or elsewhere. Is that clear?"

"Yes, ma'am."

"If there is ever a question, you just need to relay the call to me and let me handle it."

"Sure, that's fine. I'm sorry for the confusion."

"It's okay. Now just remember what I said."

SIXTEEN

FRIDAY NOON, RIGHT ON schedule, Laura arrived at McGuire's with the three Mississippi VIPs. McGuire Martin, owner of McGuire's Irish Pub in Pensacola, McGuire's in Destin, and Flounder's on Pensacola Beach, was on hand to welcome the Governor and his two United States Senators. McGuire, a natural at entertaining and being a fabulous host, had that very special trait of knowing exactly what to say and when to say it. He was a most polished and successful entrepreneur.

After a quick tour of the brewery, he led the trio to the Tap Room of the private Irish Politicians Club where they found Taylor Savage, as usual, on the phone.

The IPC had been founded several years ago and counted among its membership the political movers and shakers of northwest Florida. It was a private club somewhat hidden in the rear northwest corner of McGuire's, a restaurant with a long and proud history of being named time and again the recipient of Florida's Golden Spoon Award which denoted the State's most outstanding restaurants. Every politician of any magnitude who sought office was always most pleased to be invited to attend a reception at the IPC, and those who had been elected to office often returned to renew and keep their contacts solid with this most important and prestigious element of the local political power structure.

Over the years many state and national politicians had paid their respects by visiting the IPC, including United States Senators Bob Graham, Connie Mack, Sam Nunn, and Bennett Johnson.

Governors Reubin Askew, Lawton Chiles, Claude Kirk, Bob
Martinez, as had other notables such as Vice-President Al Gore,
former Attorney General Ed Meese, and former Majority Leader
of the House Dick Gephardt.

The Tap Room was the perfect setting for a small business
meeting, and over the years it had been well-seasoned for such
occasions. It was completely private, secluded, and sealed away
deep within the IPC. A drawing on the south wall was a sketch of
one of the founders of the club, the late Bert Brown. The presence
of his picture seemed to be portraying a sentry safeguarding the
many deals which had already been made or would be finalized in
the future by members of the IPC. The eight-place table was set
for only four, which afforded the VIP's plenty of room to dine and
spread their work sheets and other documents they deemed important.

Savage hurried through his call and turned to greet his visitors.
"Welcome, people, to Pensacola, the Western Gate to the Sunshine State, where thousands live the way millions wished they
could and others remain only dreamers until their chance comes to
live in Acirema."

"Wow! That's great. Thanks for inviting us three Mississippians down to your beautiful Gulf Coast," responded Governor
McQua.

"Would you care for a cocktail before lunch? You know it's
Friday, and I'll lead the way. Will you join in?" asked Savage.

Both Senators ordered scotch on the rocks while the Governor
opted for a martini, up. Savage immediately sensed their nerves
were on end, which was quite pronounced by their ordering such
strong drinks at midday. He chose a glass of chardonnay.

"OK, what's on your agenda?" Savage asked, which seemed to
be the standard question as of late.

Senator Clegg, the senior Senator, was obviously going to take
the lead and started right in. "We have kept close watch on what
you have proposed for Acirema. I am personally amazed at your
perception and have immense political interest, especially since I
Chair the Senate Highway Committee. Your thoughts about I-10
becoming the Acirema Parkway make much sense, and I wish you
well.

"Governor McQua, Senator Shawn, and I wanted to discuss a

matter, and I would ask this meeting be between only the four of us for discussion purposes. Can you agree to this?'' asked the Senator.

''Certainly, Senator Clegg. If that's the wish of you three.''

Sandy, the club director, served their cocktails and inquired if they were ready to order lunch. Always the perfect maitre d', she catered to and pampered all visiting VIP's and was most delighted to be waiting on such notables. Savage asked her for a few minutes to enjoy their cocktails, advising he would buzz her when they were ready.

''Go ahead, Senator. Sorry for the interruption,'' said Savage.

''That's quite all right,'' responded Clegg. ''What I am getting at is the question of this meeting being just between us guys.''

''Again, you have my word on it,'' Savage assured.

''Thanks, I hope that you understand. Now for the purpose of all this. We want to look at the possibilities of Mississippi becoming the western approach to and a part of Acirema,'' he said.

''Does that mean you three would support, without question, a number of your counties joining with us if we can reach some type of agreement?''

''Yes, Sir, that's exactly what we mean,'' answered Governor McQua. ''We are talking about six counties, namely Pearl River, Hancock, Stone, Harrison, George, and Jackson. These six counties would include the entire length of the Mississippi Gulf Coast from the Alabama line to the Louisiana line. With their inclusion it would add another 378,505 people to Acirema, making your total population about 1.8 million. It would also add another 3,520 square miles of prime real estate which would increase the size of Acirema to 22,988 square miles, quite a large state.''

''And you three will gladly support the idea of Mississippi losing its entire Gulf Coast. As I understand it, you are offering to do the leg work and the necessary politicking to assure this area would vote positive in our referendum should we make an agreement to include these six counties. Is that what I am to understand?'' asked Savage.

''That is correct,'' said Senator Clegg. ''Also, you would want to know there are approximately another 75 miles of Interstate 10 that you could add to your Parkway.''

''You seem somewhat surprised at what we are offering,''

remarked Senator Shawn. "What the hell is the big deal? Why the strange look on your face?"

"This is a most important offer, so again let me make sure I understand what you three elected officials of the State of Mississippi are offering to Acirema. You three will support our program and do whatever is necessary to bring your valuable coastline into Acirema although you will remain behind as Governor and Senators of Mississippi. Did I hear you correctly?"

"Taylor, you heard us right," answered Governor McQua. "But let me make a few other comments in support of our position and our offer."

"Yeah, you had better fill me in. You have no way of knowing that I was born at night, but you can be reasonably sure it wasn't last night. I want to know what the catch is?" Savage said sarcastically. "But before you go any further, let me explain to you that I had previously considered the possibility of Mississippi coming along for the ride. However, with gambling interests so ingrained in your coastal area, I thought our citizens from both Florida and Alabama would not be as happy with the situation as they might be if we did not include the area.

"Quite frankly, I had decided not to consider it any further. However, keeping the option open for the possibility of annexing a few counties after Acirema has gained Statehood is of interest to me. After our people have spoken on the referendum, then would be the proper time to decide if they were interested in annexing this area, considering the gambling and all.

"In fact, I am on record of fighting against the gambling boats that have been allowed to operate off the shores of Florida. I think they do more harm daily than they could ever do in a helpful, meaningful, and positive way. As you know our primary concern for Acirema is a crime-free society. I just don't know if we would be interested in whatever your proposition may be, but I am willing to hear you out."

Governor McQua jumped right in. "We understand your position. However, we have had no criminal problems at all on our coast, and that is worth much consideration.

"And to continue with our suggestion, let me say that we can deliver the votes we promise, and you can count on that happening. There is no doubt about it. Nothing funny, no dishonesty on the part of anyone. But like you have done with Acirema, we also have a plan that we have been working on which makes an abundance of sense to all of us, and we would appreciate your attention."

"Okay," said Savage. "Let's hear the rest of the story."

Governor McQua continued, "This is my last year in the Governor's Office. I cannot run again as I will have had two full terms. Senator Clegg will complete his third term in the United States Senate at the end of next year. He wants to come home and hang around the coast at his home in Gulfport. In exchange for our delivering to you our support and the Gulf Coast of Mississippi to become part of Acirema, we have a couple of suggestions whereby we will need your support in return.

"When Senator Clegg resigns from the Senate early next year he would like to be appointed to head the Acirema Gaming Commission that will obviously control all gambling within Acirema. As Mississippi's sitting Governor, I will then appoint myself to his United States Senate seat and fill out his unexpired remaining months and then seek a full six-year term thereafter.

"Quinton Brooks, my Lieutenant Governor, will automatically become Governor of Mississippi on the day I resign. Our constitution does not provide for replacement of a Lieutenant Governor under these conditions. Therefore, the next person is line is the President of the Mississippi Senate, who is Senator Ross Brickton.

"Additionally, Senator Shawn, who lives in Biloxi, which would become a part of Acirema, wants to return home from Washington and run for Governor of Acirema. He will resign the Senate at the appropriate time in order to do so. We note thus far there is only one Republican in the race, and that is Ray Haze. I think Senator Shawn will have an excellent opportunity for victory."

Savage summarized, "When Senator Shawn resigns the U.S. Senate to seek the Governorship of Acirema, then Governor Brooks will appoint himself to fill Senator Shawn's remaining term and go to Washington to represent Mississippi. And if I am following your line of the plot, State Senator Brickton will then become Governor of Mississippi. Did I follow it correctly?" asked Savage.

"You are right, absolutely right," answered Senator Shawn.

"So, this is what you folks want. Anything more?" asked Savage in a very bitter tone.

"Oh, yes, I almost forgot," said Senator Clegg. "As Chair of the Senate Highway Committee, I'm sure I can convince my colleagues of the worthiness of the Acirema Parkway. Wouldn't that make you real happy?"

"Yes, that would make me real happy. However, I am still puzzled as to why the three of you are so eager to deal. Could it have anything to do with the fact that your constituents are pressuring the three of you concerning the criminal elements of the gambling business along your coast?

"Could it have anything to do with the fact that your neighboring state of Louisiana has had such a horrible experience with gambling it is ready to vote it out?

"Or could it be that you just want to rid yourself of several miles of problems associated with gambling, and this would be a great way of doing it? Or more so than that, could it be that with the arrangement which you have carefully laid out, you think that you can control the gambling and its criminal elements in a manner that could financially make the three of you very rich individuals?

"Come on, fellows. Let's not do this to me today. This is Friday, and I really want to enjoy my weekend. Certainly, you have not come this far without better news than that."

"Taylor, I am much surprised at your indifference to our offer," growled Senator Clegg. "Where do you get off with talking to us like that. You are a wise person, and you know exactly how politics are handled. We have made you a dynamite offer that you simply should not refuse. If you have any thoughts of getting your precious Acirema Parkway through the Congress, you may well want to reconsider your attitude expressed this hour."

"Okay, people settle down," Savage admonished. "Let's not get in an uproar. Now, Senator, you seem to want to threaten me with your influence on the Highway Committee. Yet, the three of you come here in a veil of secrecy and make these ridiculous requests. Somehow I figured each of you to be much smarter than you're demonstrating.

"Anyway, Senator Clegg, your brother-in-law, Phil Walker of Foley, will be greatly displeased if something happens to the Parkway and, therefore, the proposed four-lane highway that will be constructed southward down to our new airport. I am sure you know that he and I are negotiating on a deal for Savage Worldwide to purchase some 8,300 acres of property that is part of his family's estate for the access right-of-way required for the project.

"Obviously, you folks have given a lot of attention to what we are planning for Acirema. However, somewhere along the line you missed the number one basic point, and that is we are not doing political business as usual. We are not interested in the ways and means of politicking to just get the job done. I totally reject your ideas, every one of them, and wish you well. If that is all you came to discuss, then we can adjourn this meeting immediately."

"I am real sorry that it had to come to this," said Governor McQua in a loud and boisterous voice. "I think it best that we move on down the road."

"Would you like to at least wait and have your lunch?" asked Savage.

"No, thanks," snorted Senator Shawn. "I'd just as soon be leaving immediately."

"Okay, if you will give me five minutes I'll have Laura take you back to the airport. Sorry for your trip down, gentlemen, and I apologize if there are any bruised personal feelings and hurt egos, but we are simply not going to conduct business as you have suggested."

Savage eased out of his chair and picked up the cellular phone on a nearby table to call his office and returned to announce, "Laura knows to pick you up here at the side door. This is only an exit door so you can leave without anyone else knowing of your presence. Hope that you three have a good flight back to Mississippi."

Begrudgingly, the four shook hands, and the three visitors left through the side door without any further comments. The drive back to Pensacola Airport was a quiet one. All three men were thinking of what their next move might be, their next offer assuming there would be another.

Savage pulled the exit door tightly closed, and while tipping his glass to down the final drops of chardonnay, his eyes made direct contact with Mr. Brown's portrait. He would later tell the committee the complete story of the visit by the Mississippi delegation and swear to them that he was almost certain there appeared a new and confirming smile on Mr. Brown's face.

SEVENTEEN

SINCE THE LAST General Assembly meeting, Taylor Savage had traveled extensively from Nashville to Washington to Raleigh, often with three or four meetings each day. After the fiasco with the Mississippi delegation, he was ready for some quiet time.

Late Friday afternoon, he and Sheery drove to Seaside where they were able to spend a long three-day weekend alone enjoying the sand and surf, some great food, and fine wine. He even suggested they unplug the phone where no one could locate them, but Sheery's mother had been quite ill so they thought better.

By Tuesday morning, he was up and ready for the fifth General meeting. As usual, the reporters and media again flooded the Hilton, and a smaller group of protestors was present seemingly content in just waving their signs and being noticed by the press.

The entire committee had arrived, but no one had seen Savage. There were concerns because he was always a fanatic for promptness, so the media immediately set their cynical thoughts toward the possibility of interference by a few of the more active protestors. Perhaps something had happened to him after he left his home on the island, they began to speculate openly.

A couple of minutes before 9:00, he called Laura on her mobil phone. ''Good morning, Laura.''

''Good morning, Mr. Savage. Where in the world are you?''

"I'm stuck in traffic on the Bay Bridge where there's been a terrible accident. Tell the committee to go ahead with breakfast, and I'll be there as soon as possible."

"Well, as you may expect the media is trying their best to make something out of your tardiness. Even speculating the protestors may have harmed you in some way."

"Please go outside and let them know what's going on. I swear I've never seen a group of folks who are so thirsty for news they make up whatever seems to suit their fancy. Will you do that? Just go outside and calm them down. Thanks, Laura, and I'll see you just as soon as this traffic moves."

The committee had completed breakfast and the media allowed to file into the room. It was almost 10:00 when Savage arrived.

"Good morning to everybody. Sorry about the delay. There was a horrible three-car accident on the Bridge. I'm almost certain some folks were hurt real bad."

He looked straight at William Hartmann and said, "They could have used your product, Mr. Hartmann. William just happens to be on the agenda this morning with a new innovative idea which could have been most useful on the bridge.

"Hope all of you had some energized time to do your committee work since we were last together as well as reserving some good, solid, quality time for yourselves. Today, I want to congratulate each and every one of you. Can you begin to imagine what you have accomplished since we started this program just 55 days ago? Here it is April 19th, and it seems as though we kicked this program off just a week ago. People, you have done a simply marvelous job. Again, I congratulate each one of you. And thanks.

"Certainly all of you have been keeping a keen eye on the news. Our movement has been headlines since we first announced our intentions on January 23rd, and I see no slacking up on the coverage. It has been my privilege to have appeared on several radio and television shows, and our message, I can assure you, is getting out all over the country.

"A week ago yesterday I had an outstanding meeting with some bonding people and put together the financing for the Parkway, Airport Complex, Industrial Park, and its component facilities, and while I was at it completed final plans for the refurbishing of the Lady Lex.

"You may imagine that no matter where I go or with whom I am talking, the Lady Lex seems to find her spot right up front to headline the multitude of questions. Quite frankly, that project is going to do very well, and I am looking forward to its renovation, right here in Acirema.

"Last Wednesday I met in Washington with Ike Francis, Chief Lobbyist for the International Prevention of Crime Committee and had a very good discussion pertaining to its program and how it would fit into our platform. In the near future we will be hearing some good ideas from Mr. Francis.

"While in D.C., I also dropped in on Florida's two Senators, Bilinda Hansen and James Doyle, as well as Senators Craig Bennett and Van Wells from Alabama. While we are on different sides of this issue, I still very much respect their position, and we do not want to ruffle any more feathers than is necessary.

"Sheery and I had the opportunity to visit over breakfast with an old family friend from North Carolina, Senator Mark Donner and Florida Congressman Drake Hill and his wife. The Congressman is looking at something we discussed which may well come about in Acirema, and I feel he may have a real personal interest.

"This past Friday I was asked to meet with a delegation from Mississippi to discuss their interest in Acirema. Unfortunately, their assessment of what we were doing did not exactly match with what they had envisioned, thereby spoiling any future participation which may have been anticipated by them.

"This morning I want to announce three new tenants who have signed on the dotted line for our new industrial park at the airport. Before we hear from two who are present, I will announce the third. For some time now I have been negotiating with all three of these new occupants, and while in Nashville last week I nailed down the final one. He could not be with us today, but gave his blessings for this announcement and sends his best to each of you.

"For several months, 'Skylor,' yes, the entertainer, has looked for a place to construct a first-class recording studio that would have easy access to an airport, and what we have to offer is just exactly what the doctor ordered. Furthermore, he will also be moving his Play/Lease company into our facilities.

"Let me tell you a bit about him and what he does in addition to being a world-class entertainer. David Carpenter, Skylor if you will, grew up on the coast between Pensacola and Mobile, his birth city. At an early age his family knew that one day he would become an entertainer, but never envisioned the success which he has claimed. He fashioned his music around the sounds of Elvis and modeled his energy after Garth Brooks. Early in his career he changed his name to Skylor Crisp and, as his popularity grew by leaps and bounds, he soon dropped the last name and became known simply as Skylor. He had several gold singles and a couple of gold albums well before he turned 20.

"Unlike most entertainers, he also used his built-in, self-controlled, God-given personal abilities not only for making money in the entertainment business, but also he invested well in another field. He wisely used his earnings from entertainment to make sure his capital worked hard for him. It took only three years for his contracting company, Play/Lease, Inc., to generate millions on its own. Play/Lease is a company that contracts with homeowners to construct either tennis courts, basketball courts, or handball courts on their private home property then Play/Lease leases the facilities back to the owners.

"With no money down and very low, affordable monthly installments, the income derived from each installation almost triples the cash market price, could the family have paid for the construction in full when completed. However, this is not an option when dealing with Play/Lease.

"For security, Play/Lease retains a lien on the property, including a second mortgage. Occasionally, due to foreclosure, it cashes in on a property at a bargain price. When this occurs, Play/Lease converts the foreclosure into a rental property which provides a tremendous profit margin.

"With millions to invest, Skylor has been looking for a place on the golden upper Gulf Coast to build his world-class recording studio, and we had exactly what he was searching for. It is truly a pleasure for us to welcome both Skylor and Play/Lease into our growing family of happy tenants at our Airport Industrial Park.

"Now, second this morning, we want to welcome one of our own committee members, William Hartmann, to come forward and introduce us to his line, or lines, of products that he will manufacture, market, and distribute from our Industrial Park. And folks, you will readily see where this product would have come in handy this morning while I was stuck in traffic on the bridge.''

"Thanks, Taylor. And you're right, it would have helped considerably and perhaps saved a life. It is truly a pleasure to become involved with the very latest in innovative thinking relative to the newest Industrial Park on the coast and, more importantly, a park right here in what will be the newest state of the Union. When we open for business, we will be in our new 30,000-square-foot plant. We expect to employ about 150 people and commence operations within six months of groundbreaking. We estimate our personnel to climb to around 400 by the end of the second year of operation.

"Let me tell you a little about a new patent product of which we are very proud. I have recently received word from the U.S. Patent Office of approval for our new Emergency Life Saving Vehicle (ELSV). We have patented a vehicle which takes advantage of and uses what is now totally wasted space on every bridge in this nation. We have turned this wasted but very valuable space into a true lifesaving lane. Our ELSV will save countless numbers of lives when accidents occur and provide a means of prevention to keep thousands of other accidents from ever happening in the first place.

"When an accident does occur, the width of the bridge becomes a vital factor. Every inch is important and at a premium. Our ELSV makes use of inches which are not available to any other type EMS vehicle. We use the only portion of the bridge not being used for traffic and turn it to lifesaving advantage.

"I'm pleased to introduce to you our Emergency Life Saving Vehicle.''

Laura passed out to each member copies of 10-by-14-inch color photos of several views of three different models.

"The ELSV is a complete medically equipped, high-tech, emergency vehicle which will ride on or straddle an existing lane, the dividing concrete monorail median strip, or adapt to ride on the retaining side rails and walkways of any bridge. In situations where there are two separated structures, it will straddle the area between the bridges and ride on the inside walkways of both bridges, providing service to all lanes of traffic.

"When an accident occurs on any bridge, all vehicles which are following the vehicles involved are confined and trapped, preventing traffic flow for the standard EMS type vehicle. Most always, the flow of traffic on the opposite side of the bridge is stopped to allow an EMS vehicle to use those lanes. In such cases the EMS vehicle has to travel to the opposite end, turn around, and then return to the scene of the accident. This takes away precious time and medical assistance from those injured. Needless to say, when this happens, all traffic in both directions is halted, and a tremendous traffic jam occurs on each end of the bridge. When an accident occurs on any lane of a bridge where there are two separated structures, then the problem of getting the standard EMS vehicle to the scene is magnified. We simply solve this problem with our ELSV.

"The primary purpose of the ELSV is to render medical attention and assistance to accident victims and hasten their removal from the accident scene in order to get them safely to a hospital emergency facility. We have taken special care to develop the ELSV in a manner whereby the operation is simple after a brief instructional period, provided by our staff. The ELSV is totally equipped with all necessary emergency needs to immediately assist the injured where it is needed most, at the point of the accident.

"Our ELSV has the same equipment as does the standard EMS vehicle, and more. It is not our intent to replace the EMS services, but to render immediate assistance to the injured when it is most needed. Many are the times when an accident victim will be removed from a vehicle and left lying on the roadway surface until the EMS arrives simply because there is no better facility available. Our goal is the elimination of lost time. Precious minutes are those which save lives time and time again.

"Our ELSV totally solves the problem of bad winter weather in states where roadway and bridge surfaces freeze over, thereby preventing emergency traffic from speeding to the accident scene. The ELSV is not affected at all by any adverse weather. It simply performs all of the functions of its design without concern for the elements, which in itself causes most accidents in the first place.

"The ELSV carries an ample capacity of both gasoline and

diesel fuel so it may service stranded vehicles and get them on their way prior to the possibility of a pileup accident which may take several lives. Currently, a wrecker service or other provider has to be called, and precious minutes are wasted delivering fuel to a stranded vehicle, one which could easily be the cause of a very serious accident and the loss of life. This type requirement has been antiquated, and our high tech ELSV vehicle will solve this problem before lives are lost.

"In addition to other safety features, the ELSV design includes a telescopic arm which will extend outward, enabling it to drop a cable to the bumper of a disabled vehicle and pull it from the bridge before an accident happens.

"There are many ways in which the ELSV project will provide savings to the federal, state, and local governments. Our primary objective, as previously mentioned, is to save lives and prevent accidents from happening which would cause the loss of lives and collateral. Our high-tech system replaces the old, worn-out, antiquated ideas of the past. The following is a classic example of how millions of dollars could have been saved.

"Had the ELSV system been available a few years ago, we could have saved the State of Florida nearly $8 million which was spent to expand the width of the Pensacola Bay Bridge to include an emergency lane which is too narrow for the purpose. The ELSV system simply would have eliminated this costly expansion. The ELSV system will be used nationwide to eliminate costly expansion projects such as this example by altering the antiquated method and substituting a more efficient high-tech solution.

"The purpose of the expansion was to give drivers a place to pull out of the lane of traffic when their vehicle is disabled. What has been the result? They now can exit the lane of traffic, but still remain on the bridge, still in harm's way, still there to cause an accident which might well take their lives or the lives of others, still sitting there waiting for a wrecker to come to their service. On the other hand, our ELSV can service stranded vehicles which run out of gas or remove them if they experience mechanical trouble within minutes. To wait for a wrecker, which itself adds another dangerous traffic hazard, is to leave a stranded vehicle in a most dangerous situation which could possibly take the lives of several.

"The ELSV is housed in a building at the end of the bridge closest to the emergency hospital facility. An extension of the monorail center span or side rail from the bridge will be extended into the building for this purpose. The building will consist of a solar panel roofing system which will supply constant power to the batteries to prevent the possibility of delay or downtime. There is a diesel-powered emergency generator for use in case of local power failure, such as during a hurricane or typical bad weather conditions.

"When a bridge is damaged and out of commission, as was the case of the Pensacola Bay Bridge when it was hit by a runaway barge, it obviously is closed to vehicular traffic. There would be no need for the operation of the ELSV system during this downtime. Depending on the extent of the damage, it is quite possible that our ELSV pedestrian unit would be able to operate and move pedestrians across the bridge during the entire downtime.

"The configuration of this type unit seats four individuals side by side on bench-type seats, bus style. The units are constructed of different lengths which would determine the number of persons it could carry per trip. The needs of the community and the number of individuals who would need to cross the bridge daily would determine what length unit would be temporarily installed.

"During the down period of the Pensacola Bay Bridge, it would have been perfectly safe to operate a pedestrian unit 24 hours per day. The standard size unit would provide for seating of 40 individuals. Computing only 12 hours per day, 40 passengers per trip, 10 minutes between trips, full capacity both directions, this unit could shuttle a total of 5,760 individuals during this time frame. If need be, a three-unit system could be used, train style, which would move more than 17,000 individuals per the same time frame.

"Well, that is what is happening with our ELSV. I am very proud that we can associate with the Industrial Park and make use of the commercial shipping capacity of major airlines to distribute, not only across America but also around the globe. Thank you for your attention."

"And thank you, William. I am most impressed with your new vehicle and certainly look forward to your being a satisfied tenant at the park.

"Now, let's welcome our third new tenant. Please give a warm welcome to Mr. Rolf Bartum, President of Bart-Matthews Company of Bay Minette, Alabama. Mr. Bartum."

"Thanks, Taylor. And good morning to all of you. First, let me express to each of you my special thanks for all the hard work you have put into the committee with the goal of creating Acirema. I can hardly wait.

"I bring you warm greetings from the folks around Bay Minette. I think you will be surprised at the support you will receive from that area when the results of the referendum are counted. I personally will do everything I can to make sure it becomes a reality.

"I appreciate the committee giving me a few minutes to tell you about our new product line which we will manufacture, assemble, and ship from the Acirema Industrial Park. I, too, as was expressed by Mr. Hartmann, am looking forward to having a good working location whereby we can manufacture and ship around the globe from the same general business address. The Global Airport will be of great delight to the hundreds of local companies that will use it to increase sales and take advantage of all its assets.

"Now, to our MAXCAPS patented product line. Ask any lady of the home if she could change or add to the structure of her home an item to make it more functionable, what would that item be? In our recent survey nine out of 10 women stated emphatically it would be more storage space. After giving this answer some thought, the 10th lady also agreed that would be at the top of her list.

"There are hundreds of cubic feet of wasted space within each of our homes and business offices that could be put to better use. To increase the amount of storage availability is the basic concept of our MAXCAPS systems. Families are not moving as often as they once did. They have to make do with the home they occupy. While families are expanding, the size of their home feels as though it is actually shrinking. More space is always a much-needed consideration.

"Since the first home was designed, the emphasis has always been on square footage. Everything revolves around how much square footage is delegated per a certain area of the home. Not until our design has anyone taken advantage of the wasted vertical space within every home. We limit the square footage that is required for a MAXCAPS system and take full advantage of vertical space which, thus far, has been totally overlooked and wasted.

"All models take full advantage of vertical space and reduce the use of valuable square footage floor space which can more economically be used for the purpose of increasing the useful living area within each of our homes. Therefore, our primary purpose for this innovative new product is to use space in a home or office that is currently being wasted and convert that space into a useful area.

"We have several models. The CLOSET requires only a six by six foot area of floor space. In a two-story home we can design this area to store an amount equal to 10 normal-size closets. All items are retrieved at the touch of a button. The PANTRY is obviously for storage of items within a kitchen, including food products, dishes, glassware, silverware, etc. Our SHELF model is for storage of books, picture albums, and various reading materials in the family room, den, or great room. The GARAGE model stores items normally found in the home garage or shop, such as patio items, tools, outdoor cooking items, footballs, fishing gear, pool equipment, holiday decorations, etc. Likewise, the LINEN is for storage of sheets, blankets, towels, linens, and other similar items. We offer a WINE storage and retrieval area as well as a storage system for countless numbers of a variety of glasses. Our STORM is a unit that stores all the things that may be necessary while waiting out a storm. It includes drinking water, water for cooking, safety kit, blankets, batteries, flashlights, radio, can goods, packaged foods, nonperishable foods, etc.

"All models have been designed with every family member in mind, including the elderly and those who may be handicapped in any capacity. Items are retrieved at the level desired. The systems are operated by electronic panel selection buttons. Each individual installation can be designed to provide access from any number of locations, including either side or both sides of a first floor, second floor, third floor. On the other hand, the design of an installation may dictate the access to be at only one or two locations depending on the design of the home. A normal installation includes control panels and inside electric lighting for a two-door installation. Should the owner or contractor choose to have more than a two-door access, this would be an additional cost option.

"A unique opportunity to save time and effort is to design the new home to have an access door into the laundry room. With this option, the lady of the home or the maid can quickly hang all items of clothing on the proper racks for each individual family member rather than waste expensive time climbing stairs and distributing clothing in several closets.

"We will offer an option that will include a scanner unit similar to those used in grocery stores. The scanner will keep track of each item that is placed in the PANTRY as well as each item that is removed. It can be interfaced with your home computer, and at week's end print a grocery list representing all items that have been removed from the pantry since the last printout.

"Maybe there are no better opportunities for the primary uses of all models than in the apartments and condominiums of our nation. In such units additional space is always a luxury item. In the kitchen area, it is impossible for a handicapped individual or elderly person to reach into the top cabinets, and totally out of the question to reach above a refrigerator into the standard cabinets normally installed in today's homes. All models of the MAXCAPS system are designed for fingertip operation with convenient access level. Individuals who are handicapped to any degree, especially those confined to a wheelchair, will have access to every item which is normally stored in kitchen cabinets, the closet, bookshelves, or shop/garage area and do so at the touch of a button. The stored items are simply rotated to their level whether in a standing position, in a wheelchair, or whatever. All items 'come to them' rather than their having to stretch, get on a chair or ladder, etc.

"We also have a second line of patented products which we will be manufacturing that we call BEHIND THE WALL SYSTEM (BTWS). Behind every wall, between the studs of every wall in every home and business, there is an abundance of wasted space. If you will take a moment and look up from where you are sitting to observe the walls around you, then you will realize of what I speak. The walls contain space which you could be using for a special purpose when you build-in our new, innovative, modern-designed system.

"We take full advantage of all vertical space within an area between the studs and behind the walls. There is no limit to the number of units which can be installed in a residence or business. In a mobile home, motor home, or a large boat, storage is always at a premium. In every manufactured home there is a great need for more storage space. Each of these cases represent special applications. Our BTWS design will store a great many items and make those items available to the user at the touch of a button. This will eliminate some of the necessary cabinet space which now takes up a good portion of each type vehicle/boat. The BTWS will operate off standard D/C electrical power as do other appliances on board. Again, security is a factor when designing such applications.

"Our system is offered with or without fireproof protection and with or without locking or security-designed options. The units will be constructed of sheet metal, wood, plastics, and fiberglass or a combination of any or all.

"Well, that just about sums up our product line, and I thank you for your attention."

"And thank you, Rolf. What an interesting set of designs. I know a certain lady who comes around my home who will be calling on you as soon as you are in production.

"People, these are a few of the type firms which we will have as tenants in our new industrial park. Good, clean, no smokestack type industries. I am really charged up and ready to hit the road and sell some more footage.

□ □ □ □ □

"OKAY, OUR NEXT general meeting was scheduled for two weeks from today, April 2nd. However, I propose that each committee chairperson schedule his or her own committee meetings, and we will not hold a general meeting on that date. We will convene for our next general meeting here in this room on Tuesday, April 16th, at 9:00 sharp. Thanks for coming. Meeting adjourned."

EIGHTEEN

AS THE DEADLINE FOR qualifying neared for the Governor's race, two United States Senate seats, and the three House seats, time began to grow short for several possible candidates. There was much jockeying for position among those who were thinking in terms of throwing their hats into the ring.

A special provision in the Platform allowed the election of the first two United States Senate seats to take place at the same time since there were no previous officeholders; therefore, there was no concern for altering or staggering the election terms. The provision dictated the terms and conditions of the initial Senate elections as well as the format for all future elections to these two offices.

The initial election provided that both seats were open, and every party, no matter the number, might choose to participate and make its nomination of a candidate known for each seat. This would provide a field of four candidates from the two major parties, and it appeared as though there may be an independent candidate or possibly two who might also enter both Senate races.

The rules of the Platform for the initial election assured that the candidate who got the greatest total vote would be declared winner without a runoff election and would serve for a term of six years and be designated the senior Senator from Acirema. The second highest vote getter would be declared the winner of the second seat for a term of four years and would be designated the junior Senator, again without a runoff election.

At the end of the first four-year term, an election would be held for the junior Senator's seat for which he could again choose to be a candidate. The Platform provided this election would be for a full six-year term of office, and should the junior Senator be reelected his total years in the Senate, at the completion of his second term, would be 10.

Furthermore, the Platform provided a maximum of 12 years total for any Senator. However, because of the short term of the first election of the junior Senator's seat, it would be possible that he could run for a third term of six years, and, if elected he possibly would have a total of 16 years in the Senate.

The Senate races had stirred much interest and would draw a field of candidates with good name recognition. The Platform provided that any candidate serving in any elected office in either Florida or Alabama who represented an area with 50 percent or more of their district falling within the proposed boundaries of Acirema would qualify to run for any office in Acirema provided they first resigned the office which they already held and did so 30 days prior to the election day of the referendum.

This 30-day buffer was designed to give the citizens of the 19-county area an idea of who would be seeking office and who would choose to participate in the initial election process. A shallow field of individuals that may not be well-qualified could possibly turn a number of voters against the referendum, and for sure Taylor Savage was not going to let that happen at all. Everyone knew that Savage would play a hands-on, active part in seeking well-qualified citizens to run for Governor, the U.S. Senate and the U.S. House. The population of Acirema dictated that there would be three members in the U.S. House. The initial election process for those who ran for the House seats was to follow the same pattern as in all other elections by other states, which was for a two-year term. The Platform of Acirema limited the total number of years of service to 12.

RAY HAZE AND Peaches Lamont were enjoying another evening doing what they enjoyed most, discussing politics. "We need to find out who our opponents are going to be, to narrow the field, and reflect on what our options are," she said. "I think it would be well if you called each of the potential candidates and query them about their intentions. You will not need a definite answer, but I am sure you can get a feel for what each is thinking. Anyway, I think it important that you display some personal feelings towards each of those who just might become a challenger."

"You're correct, of course. I'll make the first appointment with Andrew Wright. What do you think?"

"It matters not who, what, where, or why at this point. What really matters is that we begin to find out who is in, who is out, and just who may be willing to support you and your campaign."

"You're right. I'll get up with Andy on Monday and see if he and I can sit down for a little man to man."

After a weekend of fun, frolickin', and the usual, Haze was rejuvenated and ready to make another splash outside his coveted home playground. He made the call to Andrew Wright, and they agreed to spend some time together. While Haze was willing to meet him any place, Wright suggested that he would enjoy driving down to Point Clear tomorrow where they could visit in private.

When Wright arrived, the two men walked the long wooden dock and boarded Haze's boat where they relaxed inside the snug, well-appointed rear cabin.

"I appreciate your visit. Thanks for driving over. Like I said on the phone, I wanted to discuss with you face to face about what your intentions may be concerning the Governor's race. Just about everyone thinks that you will enter. How are you feeling about it? Are you going to make the race?" Haze inquired.

"As you note, there has been much speculation from many that I will. However, not even I know the answer to that question at this moment. I have had many, many folks call to offer their support, but I simply have not made a decision either way. Obviously, I would have to start filing all those miserable monthly reports the moment I officially threw my hat into the ring, and I'm just not ready to do that quite yet. I'll make the decision in due time which obviously will have to be fairly soon."

"Well, you are right about the formalities and paper trail. It is a horrible experience, and everything has to be kept just so, but I am in and plan to run as hard as I can," acknowledged Haze. "I personally think my chances are very good, especially considering the counties that I carried my last time out.

"Now, getting back to you," Haze continued, "I have had several people mention to me that the real reason you are thinking about running is in hopes of becoming Governor so that you can get back at Regions Power Company for firing you. Could this be right?"

"That certainly is not the primary reason. However, the Governor and Cabinet of Acirema will have an impact on Regions' plans for building its new power plant on the Perdido River," Wright boasted.

"Regions Corporation and its President, Sidney Kattzs, have always been good, strong, top-notch financial supporters of mine," Haze countered. "I hate to see the two of you get crossed up, especially by airing dirty laundry in the middle of the Governor's race."

"Ray, let me be quite frank with you. Should you be elected Governor and hold the highest elective office in Acirema, the Chief Executive of the State, would you not believe it necessary and prudent on your part to expose some of Regions' officials if you had proof their top executives were involved in criminal activities?"

"What? Do you have such proof?" Haze stuttered.

"After holding the position of chief lobbyist for Regions for more than 23 years, don't you think I had a good feel about what was going on?"

"I have no idea of what you speak," said Haze. "But if some shenanigans were occurring, then you would have to expect they knew you were in a position to expose them. If this is true, then why on God's green earth did they fire you? It would seem to me this would be the last thing on their minds. Their exposure would be so great and, with your knowledge and loose cannon attitude, your firing just does not make any sense at all to me."

"Yes, you have a great point. I have given that question many hours of thought. The only thing I can come up with is the scenario, as you just explained, would be a significant argument in their defense should it be necessary in a court of law."

"Do you feel free to discuss with me the suspicions and facts which you think you have uncovered against Regions?" Haze asked.

"I don't know. With the possibility that you may become a candidate, and with the knowledge they are strong financial supporters of yours, I feel this information just might fall into the wrong hands."

"Then you don't trust me. Is that right?"

"It's not that, exactly. It is simply the understanding that you will most likely look favorably on the Perdido River project should you become Governor, and it would be one of my objectives to see the project is never built."

"Then, this has to be the backbone and conclusive reason for your entry into the race, should you make that decision, for the sole purpose of stopping their expansion project," Haze insisted.

"No, like I've said, that's not entirely true. If there are criminal activities going on in their company, then I feel a strong obligation to do all within me to see those who are involved are prosecuted. This also should be your objective should you happen to prevail in the election. But how could that come about if, in fact, your campaign is tainted with donations from corrupt officials within their organization?" asked Wright.

"You've been around long enough to know that all campaigns, all elections, and most elected officials are tainted in some way by campaign contributions, either with or without the candidate's personal knowledge. There has always been an element of contributors who seek to have an inordinate amount of influence on those who are elected. This is a fact of life. This is reality, and you may as well accept it as such," preached Haze.

"So, if I reveal to you the information which I possess and you assured yourself it is correct, would you still take political contributions from Regions?"

"I guess it depends on what level within their organization, what level of executives, have been tainted," Haze answered.

"Well, let me assure you that it goes to the top, to the very tiptop. This includes their corporate headquarters in Birmingham and each company President and most Operations Executives at each company level. I can tell you for sure it touches Regions Power in this area, Volunteer Power in Tennessee, Mid-South Power in North and South Carolina, Delta Power in Mississippi, Peach State Power in Georgia, and Sunshine Power in South Florida. It is widespread. Now what do you think?"

"Wow! What do you plan on doing with this information? Would you use it in your campaign? Turn it over to the Feds for Grand Jury action? Blackmail Regions in some manner?"

"I am not sure. However, the blackmail part is out for certain. The only thing I am sure of is that I intend to stop this corruption dead in its tracks. You can count on that and also count on the Perdido Project not being built."

"And again, you don't feel that you can discuss the information you have obtained with me?" Haze asked in a fatherly tone.

"Let me answer that with these questions. If you knew what I know, would you expose them? Would you opt not to take contributions from them? Just what would you do with the information if you had knowledge? And who would know where you got such information? Would you expose to Regions that I know the truth?"

"Well, I can see where you are coming from," mocked Haze. "Perhaps I don't need to know the details. Let me ask you this. Would you have an interest in not entering the race and supporting me if I commit at this very moment to appoint you to a position of authority where you could have a free hand in the pursuit of your goals aimed at Regions?"

"Be more specific with me, Ray. Get to your point."

"If I am elected Governor, how would you like to be appointed my Secretary of Environmental Regulations where you would have the final approval on issues such as licensing for any type of new facility that might have a potential impact on the environment, such as their proposed plant may have on Perdido River?"

"Now, let me get this straight. You are suggesting that you would commit to appointing me to a position that would regulate the licensing of facilities such as Regions and, therefore, give me the opportunity to deny their request for permits for construction. Is that what I am hearing from you?"

"Yes, that is exactly what I said and exactly what I will commit to you."

"And still, you will continue to accept campaign contributions from them and double cross them with my appointment. Is that what I understand?"

"Andy, those words 'double cross' are very powerful and graphic, but, yes, you would have the final approval, no matter what."

"And what if you, as Governor, decided the pressure was too much from old Sidney Kattzs, and you caved in. Where would I be? But, let me answer my own question, and I'll tell you where I would be. You would have maneuvered me out of the Governor's race with this commitment, and I would then find myself at the low end of the totem pole with nothing to hang onto after Kattzs applies his pressure. Now that's where I would be, wouldn't I?"

"That will simply not happen," Haze argued.

"And just how do I know that?" responded Wright.

"You have my word on it."

"Your word! Oh, well! Perhaps, I need to fill you in on every minor detail, and if I do that, then I will have an obligation to explain to the voters that you were well aware of the entire sordid affair, and still you insisted on cuddling up to them for campaign contributions."

"Wait just a damn minute, that's not fair," screamed Haze.

"Pardon me! What's not fair?" Wright said in a raised voice. "That you want to be Chief Executive of Acirema and that you still want to hold hands with those shiftless bastards."

"Why don't we forget that we ever had this meeting and conversation," Haze suggested while rising to his feet.

"No, no, let's not do that. Let's see just how much real truth and honesty you have in your character," Wright countered.

"I think it's time we end this meeting. It's time for you to leave. Begone from my sight, leave my boat and home."

Haze opened the door to the rear deck and escorted Wright to the highly polished teakwood railing which was raised to provide an opening to the dock and motioned with a single hand for him to leave. The two men did not shake hands or speak. As quickly as Wright walked away, Haze retreated back into the cabin and immediately reached for the phone.

THE DEEP SOUTH Group was a well-organized, effective, and efficient conglomerate giant in the electrical power generating business, well respected for its abilities to find solutions to problems, no matter how great or demanding. In each state where it had an operation and did business, its presence and political participation was well known by all candidates who sought any office, either local, state, or national. You could count on its employees always being the number one contributor to every winner in the United State Senate races, Governors' contests, State elections, as well as all movers and shakers who were elected to local office.

Lesser-ranking corporate executives were assigned to participate in and keep their ears to the ground in every local election in every community. Deep South intended to make sure it had input on every issue, especially those which might, even minutely, have an effect on their corporate structure at any political level of government.

It did its homework to assure that local citizens were aware of their civic duties and involvement. It was community minded and very open and upfront with its desire to assist in any way possible by contributing to the welfare of its customers. The average man on the street had the utmost regard for the company's multiple participation in almost every civic endeavor and hadn't a clue about their under-the-table dealings which had made millionaires of many of its top level executives.

For years Sidney Kattzs and perhaps eight to 10 other top executives had taken millions in cash kickbacks from coal producers, suppliers, dealers, and/or brokers. The habit had become so routine they became sloppy and sometimes loose with comments, some of which were best kept to themselves.

Andrew Wright had been suspicious for some time. Three years ago when Joe Harkins invited him to come along on a political trip to D.C. for the purpose of lobbying against acid rain legislation that was being discussed in the Congress, he had found definite reasons to shore up his suspicions.

After dinner the second evening over a couple of nightcaps, Joe and three other high-ranking executives were paying little attention to what they said and made a few interesting comments that could not be misunderstood by Wright. While one of them even suggested they let him in on their secret, the others, although somewhat under the influence themselves, had enough sense and presence of mind about them to quiet their associate and move on to another subject. The next morning Wright cornered Harkins before they all gathered for breakfast and demanded to be brought up to date on their little secret.

Although Harkins was reluctant, Wright insisted that he be briefed, or he would find out what he needed to know direct from Sidney Kattzs should it be necessary. Harkins sat down on the side of the bed and spilled many details without naming names. While he would not identify who was on the take, he did indicate it went to the top of the ladder, which had to mean Sidney Kattzs, President of the Deep South Group.

□　□　□　□　□

"HELLO," CAME THE voice in a sweet Southern drawl, "Mr. Kattzs' office. May I help you?"

"Yes, this is Ray Haze. Is Sidney available?"

"Mr. Haze, Mr. Kattzs is in a conference at the moment. Can someone else assist you, or would you prefer to leave a message and a number for him to return your call?"

"How long will he be tied up?" Haze grumbled.

"This meeting is scheduled to last for only 20 more minutes, and then Mr. Kattzs will leave for Memphis."

"Please tell him that I called, and it is urgent that he call me back before he leaves town. Is that clear?"

"Yes, sir, Mr. Haze. Where can you be reached?"

"Tell him to call me on my boat. He has the number."

"Certainly, I'll make sure that he gets your message."

"Young lady, this is most important. You need to give him this message as soon as his conference is over. Do you understand?"

"Yes, sir. And thank you, Mr. Haze. Have a good day. Goodbye."

Haze walked down two steps into the galley and poured himself a stiff scotch and soda and waited patiently for the phone to ring. After what seemed to take an hour or so, the cellular phone finally came to life.

"Hello," Haze squawked

"Ray? Sidney Kattzs here. How you doing?"

"Fine, I think. I've got something to discuss with you. We need to sit down and talk. When are you returning from Memphis?"

"This seems critical. What's bothering you?"

"Well, it's more about what may come to be a bother to you, not me. I just finished a lengthy meeting with Andrew Wright, and he tells me he has some mighty strong information and evidence that you and your associates may have a great deal of interest in knowing. We do need to talk and talk right away. When are you returning to Birmingham?''

''Oh, I'll be back here tonight. You want to come up? What do you suggest?''

''I don't want to come to Birmingham, and maybe you should not come down here. Why don't we meet at the Atlanta Airport in the Delta Crown Room tomorrow. Can you arrange your schedule?''

''I can in the afternoon, say around 3:00. Will that work for you?''

''Sure, and you need to come alone,'' Haze demanded.

''That's no problem. I'll see you at 3:00 at Delta's.''

''I'll be there,'' said Haze. ''Goodbye.''

Haze placed another phone call to Mobile Executive Flights and arranged for a charter to Atlanta. He had too much on his mind to be concerned with flying himself and did not want to waste time on an airline. After several more cocktails and a sleepless night he was up well before sunrise and began making notes to assure himself that he would cover all the bases during his visit with Kattzs.

□ □ □ □ □

ANDREW WRIGHT HAD horrible dreams all night about the conversation and meeting with Haze. Over breakfast he told Cait, his wife, the entire story. They jointly decided they should let Taylor Savage know the facts about the Deep South Group and the conversation.

Andy and Cait had been married after a two-year engagement while they were both juniors at the University of Kentucky. Not only was their marriage an ideal one, but they were truly each other' own best friends. Their commitment to each other early in the marriage ensured that neither would ever make a major decision without discussing it together, and then they would agree on the course of action that would be taken jointly.

Since Savage had been so determined to insist on a good, clean, wholesome, and crime-free atmosphere for Acirema, they thought he should be made aware of this potentially devastating problem, especially since it would involve at least one and possibly two of the major contenders for the first Governorship of the nation's 51st state, and both were members of the Acirema Committee.

After breakfast Wright made a call to Laura Rings and set up an appointment to visit with Savage the following morning. The meeting was confirmed for 10:00 at Savage Worldwide offices on Cypress Street.

Savage was shocked to learn the details and just how high the corruption flowed toward the top of the executive ladder of the Deep South Group. Wright explained the purpose of his making Savage aware was twofold. First, Savage needed to know just what kind of person he was dealing with in Ray Haze as well as with the upper management of Deep South. And second, he was afraid that something might happen to himself because of the knowledge he had about the corruption and the apparent length of time it had been going on throughout the corporate structure.

He told Savage that he had discussed the situation with Cait but did not want to concern her with the remote possibility that harm may in some way come to him. She just did not need to be exposed to that worry since she was three months' pregnant with their third child.

Savage was outraged when Wright told him of the treatment by Haze during their meeting aboard his boat. While there was no direct tie-in that they could prove, both men suspected that Haze was probably involved with the Deep South Group to a great degree and was starting to try to cover his tracks.

"Are you really concerned about your safety because of what you know?" asked Savage.

"I don't really know just how I feel about it. Sometimes I think this just couldn't be happening, and on the other hand look at all the political problems that have tormented candidates for countless numbers of office across the nation. There is no telling what may come of this, to what degree some may go to see their side win an election."

"Well, your personal health and peace of mind is the most important thing above all else. However, I personally would like to see you become a candidate for Governor, and if you do, then I will, at this very moment, pledge my complete and unconditional support to you.''

"Taylor, you don't know what that means to me. I appreciate it more than I could ever express. And obviously, you know how I feel about your leadership role in putting Acirema together. That was and is a marvelous idea, and you can rest assured it's gonna fly. Over the next couple of days let me talk to Cait. and with your permission I will let her know that we can depend on your support. Would it be okay to reveal your pledge?''

"Certainly. I want the two of you to feel good about whatever decision is reached. With you in the race I think we can be victorious. And let me run something else by you that I have given much thought. How would you feel about Brookman and Daniels running for the United States Senate seats?'' Savage asked.

"I think that would be simply magnificent. Do you realize what effect the three of us could have on good, clean, and honest legislation if the people of Acirema elected us to represent them in the Governor's Office and the United States Senate?''

"Of course, I do,'' answered Savage. "Wasn't it I who just made the suggestion?''

□ □ □ □ □

HAZE ARRIVED IN Atlanta at the Crown Room right on time and, as usual, Kattzs was late. It was almost 3:45 before he got there, explaining he had a late departure from Birmingham. They huddled behind closed doors in a small conference room and assured each other this was a safe place to speak their minds without any interference of snooping eyes or ears.

"Now, what's this about your conversation with Andy Wright?'' Kattzs asked.

"We met on the boat yesterday to discuss his interest in running for Governor. I had no idea he was so dead set on stopping Regions' expansion plans on the Perdido. How in the world did you two get so crossed up?'' Haze inquired.

"When we let him go, it struck hard on him. In fact, I really felt sorry for both him and his family, but now it's a different story. He apparently is determined to take his revenge out on us by throwing his weight around concerning the Perdido Project. What did he say? Tell me exactly what he had to say.''

"He would not commit one way or the other if he was or wasn't going to be a candidate. However, he is adamant about stopping the project. Now, the real kicker is that he says he has some real inside information which will send you and some of your top brass to prison,'' Haze remarked.

"What in the hell could he possibly be speaking about?'' asked Kattzs.

"I don't know. He wouldn't elaborate, but I can tell you this. He is dead serious. If he has something to say as important as he thinks he has, then why on earth did you folks fire him?'' Haze wondered.

"That's a long story, but to make it short, we were assured we had our asses covered and that we also held a trump card over his head. However, since we let him go, the information which we were depending on has proven to be false, or at best unreliable.''

"Sidney, you need to level with me. What's he got on you? What is he holding over you and your executives?''

"Okay. All right. Do you remember Joe Harkins?'' asked Kattzs.

"Oh, yes. Your financial officer who died last year of food poisoning.''

"That's right, such a tragedy. Well, it seems that Joe's tongue got loose one evening in Washington, and some things slipped out that should not have. Anyway, it appears that Wright got wind of the situation with the coal suppliers.''

"Holy, hell. You mean he knows?'' screamed Haze.

"I'm afraid he does, and I assume that is what he was speaking of during your meeting.''

"My God! Do you think he knows about the part Joe Harkins played in laundering campaign funds from the coal people to my last campaign?''

"From what you've said, it doesn't appear he is aware of that situation or he would not have let you know that he had some hard information on us. Isn't that how you would read it?'' asked Kattzs.

"That would make sense. Now, let me tell you something, and you best listen carefully. If the half million dollars which you folks laundered for me comes to light, then Katie bar the door because all hell will break loose. Do you get my drift? Do you fully understand what I am saying?''

"Yes, I think I do."

"No, there can't be any 'I think so.' You had better know so, absolutely so. Is that clear, Sidney?" Haze snorted.

"Yeah, yeah, that's clear. Now that we think we know of the potential problems which Mr. Wright may cause, we need to make some careful plans to keep him quiet," stated Kattzs. "Are you sure there is nothing that could be offered to him, position wise within a Haze Administration, that would be of interest to him, provided you are elected, of course?"

"I don't know. I've already tested him with that, and he did not bite. In fact, I offered him a commitment as Secretary of Environmental Regulations so that he could have input pertaining to licensing for your plans for the Perdido Project. As you know, all plans would have to be approved by that department. He turned me down flat."

"And how, my friend, were you possibly going to handle that commitment had he accepted? Were you going to turn him loose against the project?" Kattzs asked in an unhappy tone.

"Of course not. I would sidetrack him after I made his appointment, during his confirmation hearings. You know just how easy it is to eliminate anyone during those hearings. A negative vote would send him back into oblivion. His name would never surface from the committee recommendations."

"Okay, let's look at that option. Assuming that happened in the way you describe, he then would be madder than a wet hen, and we haven't solved anything. There has got to be a better answer than what you suggest," Kattzs insisted. "We have to find a permanent solution."

□ □ □ □ □

BEFORE LEAVING ATLANTA on his charter flight back to Mobile, Haze called Peaches and said he would come by her condo somewhere around 7:00 o'clock. He asked her to run down to the 'Takee-Outee' and pick up some Chinese and a couple of bottles of wine.

Her condo was an upscale model in a good neighborhood, the historical district in downtown Mobile. Haze had purchased it perhaps five years earlier, and Peaches had made it her home for the last two. He used his pass card to open the security gate and fumbled with several door keys, finally giving up and laying down heavily on the front-door buzzer.

"Why didn't you use your key?" she asked.

"Don't bother me with that crap right now," he groaned.

"How was your flight, your meeting?"

"The flight was fine, the meeting sucked."

"Jeeze. How about a chardonnay?" she asked.

"Make mine a scotch, a double scotch. In fact make me two doubles, one for each hand."

"Sounds like your meeting really did suck. Wanna talk?"

"I'm here, aren't I?" he growled.

"Now, wait a minute. Wait just one damned minute. Look, don't you dare come in here and get short with my ass. I didn't have such a wonderful day myself. Now, if you wanna talk, let's talk. If not then just sit there and sulk."

After small talk and a second cocktail, Haze opened up. "You remember all the campaign contributions that were sent our way by Sidney Kattzs in the last election?"

"Yeah, they got in bed with you real close," she recalled.

"You remember that almost a half million came through the employees of Deep South Group and their various companies?"

"Yeah, I knew that. I remember. Sidney raised some serious funds for you. What's this all about?" she insisted.

"I didn't mention it to you last night when we talked, but my meeting yesterday with Andrew Wright got well out of hand."

"What happened. Is he in the race or not?"

"The Acirema race right now is the least of my worries. During my last campaign when Kattzs raised that $487,000, it did not come from his employees as you may or may not have known. He raised it from a lot of his friends who are in the coal business. Some very powerful friends. Some were owners, others were dealers or suppliers or otherwise connected to the coal industry.

"Kattzs raised the funds in cash, and had his executives distribute the money to a large number of their employees who made their personal checks payable to my campaign. In order for the employees to get motivated, they were allowed to keep 20 percent for their troubles. You may recall a good many contributions were for $2,000. There was a donation of $2,000 from the wife and another $2,000 from the husband. Each of these families had been given $5,000 in cash and they kept $1,000 for themselves.

"Hell, man, that's not shocking. This is done hundreds of times daily across the entire country and in every race, local, state, or national. What's the problem? Hasn't Sidney covered his own ass on this?"

"The problem is, when I met with Andrew Wright, it appears that he knows the story," Haze explained.

"Damn. Think he will use it on you?"

"Well, he apparently has found out that Kattzs and others have been taking cash under the table for several years for their own personal use. Sidney and I don't know if he only knows about the cash kickbacks to executives or if he also knows about the campaign contributions to me. We tend to feel that he may not know of my involvement. It would appear that he would have mentioned it to me had he known that I had played a part in obtaining that type of contributions."

"Possibly," she said. "But what if he is setting you up. Letting you get all primed and cocked for the race and then knocking you on your butt with a press conference which would stop both you and Deep South Group dead in the water."

"Think that could be it?" Haze mumbled.

"Don't know, maybe so," she answered. "Do you have any idea if there are other candidates who may have previously taken some DSG dollars that are now thinking of making the race?" she asked.

"Not that I know. However, Brandon Woods got a lot of financial help from somewhere at the last minute during his reelection campaign. I would bet it came from the same sources. His involvement would not spill over on this race as he surely is going to run for the Senate seat in Florida and not for Governor of Acirema."

"But what if for some strange reason he decides to make a run at the Governorship? Our sources, as you know, say he is strongly considering it," she reminded.

"Well, if that's the case, then Andy Wright could kill two very big opponents with a single press conference, that's for sure. Peaches, what is your suggestion. What should I do now?"

"Let's eat and talk about it later," she advised.

"No, no, I'm not hungry. You go ahead. I'll have another scotch."

While Haze mixed an extra-strong double, she excused herself to the ladies room then returned to open a package of small white containers and lined them up in a neat row across the counter. When she began to nibble, the smell of hot Chinese immediately drove Haze into each of the six containers with both hands and little concern for the weight he was attempting to lose.

"What should we do, Peaches?"

"As I see it, you have two options. Either throw in the towel right now and sit back and worry yourself to death, or choose the second option and assume that nothing is going to come of this and go forward full speed ahead with your plans to become the first Governor of Acirema. That is, as full time a pace as is allowed by the Platform. We can start buying television and radio time and planning print commercials in all the papers and magazines. We can have much done and be ready on September 26th and have one hell of a kickoff campaign. This decision is strictly in your hands. You, and only you, have to choose the course you are willing to take," she said.

"Peaches, I am scared to death. This could really have some far-reaching consequences. We're talking about a bunch of financial hurt and possible personal jail time if the past is exposed. And I am really concerned about what Sidney said at the end of our meeting. He remarked we had to 'find a permanent solution' to the Andrew Wright situation."

"No, no. No, no, no. You don't need to be taking part, or even thinking about taking part, in anything as drastic as that or even listening to anyone with such outrageous ideas. Do you believe Sidney is actually thinking in those terms?" she asked.

"I'm afraid so," muttered Haze. "I'm definitely afraid so."

NINETEEN

A LARGE BROWN PAPER envelope well sealed with scotch tape on all edges came in the mail addressed to Andrew Wright and was marked personal and confidential. This was not unusual, not out of the ordinary, since a great deal of his mail over the years had come with the same notations. However, in the past it always had to do with issues relative to his former position as Chief Lobbyist for the Deep South Group.

Cait Wright placed the envelope in a mounting stack with all of his other mail with no thought or concern of any importance. When he and his three companions returned later that afternoon from a four-day bird hunting trip in Costa Rica, he would tend to the mail and his other chores as usual. These shoots began as annual affairs nine years ago, and the close-knit foursome had scheduled a second trip in another couple of weeks during the height of the hunting season.

☐ ☐ ☐ ☐ ☐

THERE WAS NO MAIL opened nor any other duties taken care of upon his return except spending some time with Cait and their two sons, Cliff and Mitchell, both middle school students. The next morning, after sleeping in an hour later than normal, Cait woke him with a hot, steamy cup of coffee. The four gathered around the breakfast table for their daily morning chat before the boys left for the bus stop. Before they left, Andy and Cait committed to take them and a friend each out to dinner that evening, and they could choose the restaurant, which most likely would be Kooter Brown's.

About midmorning, leisure gave away to the chore of going through, opening, and taking care of four days of mail and paying any bills which had arrived. From the first day of their marriage, it had become customary for Andy to assume this task so Cait never had to concern herself unless something was marked for her personal attention. As if he was opening a Christmas present, the largest item was always opened first. Inside he found a crude, handmade note consisting of single letters and words made up of clippings from all sorts of print materials, exactly like you may see in a movie.

Without yet reading the note, its demeanor indicated without question it was something that he did not want Cait to see. He quickly reinserted the note in the envelope and finished opening the remaining pieces, then left the breakfast table with only the suspicious one.

Retreating into the nearest bathroom, he locked the door without making a sound and pulled the note from its hiding place. He knew before reading that it would be nothing but trouble. With both large and small single characters and words pasted together, it conveyed a message that was sloppy but could be easily deciphered. He read slowly and precisely, "Stop your searching for information concerning DSG. It will only lead to personal trouble for you and your family. If you don't believe me, then have the body of Joe Harkins exhumed and you will find he died of poison, but not food poisoning."

Wright could not believe what he had read. There was no doubt that DSG meant the Deep South Group. Time and again he read and reread the same words. They never changed. Folding it back neatly inside the envelope, he knew he had to take it to the authorities and had to do so right away.

His first instinct was to call Taylor Savage and reveal the note to him so it would confirm he not only was in serious trouble but also on a hot trail of some very valuable and most important information. He also wanted someone to know of the note just in case some harm came to himself.

His mind was in a quandary as to what to do first, call Savage or the police. For sure, he didn't want Cait and the boys to know. If he called the authorities, their home would soon be flooded with officers, and the note would be exposed. He called Savage Worldwide and was informed by Laura that Savage was due back in the office around 2:00 that afternoon and his schedule was open until 4:00. She booked Wright for 2:00. He assured her that he would be there on time and to tell Savage, should he call in, the meeting was very important and most urgent.

□　□　□　□　□

"THIS IS VERY SERIOUS business," Savage noted. "We have to take this immediately to the police, don't you agree, Andrew?"

"Yes, of course. Who should we call? The City police, the County Sheriff, the FBI? Who would be responsible?"

"I suggest we call the Sheriff. At least he can get the ball rolling."

"Taylor, can we call from here and maybe have them come here to your office? I need time to talk with Cait and the boys before they get wind of this."

"Sure. That's no problem at all. Laura, get Sheriff Davis on the phone."

It was only a few minutes before two deputies walked into the Savage Worldwide complex. After being shown into Taylor's private office and introduced around, they at once began asking questions of both Wright and Savage and wanted to see the note as well as the envelope. After a few brief questions, the officers took both pieces and announced they would be back in touch later in the afternoon.

Savage suggested that Wright return home and tell the family everything he knew about the situation, to be sure he knew where the boys were at all times, and to keep a close watch around the house. Frank Marsh, senior attorney for Savage Worldwide, volunteered to be the contact person for the time being and would be the go-between for Wright and the authorities.

Before Wright reached his residence in Cantonment, Marsh had already called and left word for him to return the call as soon as he walked in. Wright had not noticed, but the envelope had been sent from Memphis, and Marsh wanted him to know, since the evidence came from another state, the FBI would soon be involving itself in the investigation.

The FBI involvement suited Wright just fine as he always thought the local authorities were not up to the high degree of expertise and efficiency which may be required in special cases—and this indeed may become a very special case. Already there was a threat of harm to Wright and his family, and according to the note a murder may have also been committed.

A couple of days later, on Friday afternoon, after being well-educated and informed about the details of the note, Joe Harkins' widow, Mary Jane, agreed to have his body exhumed for an autopsy. Should foul play be found, she and her family stood to gain financially if it were determined that any employee of the Deep South Group played even the smallest part in the death of her husband.

After a weekend of studying Mrs. Harkins petition to the Court to exhume his body, Judge Warren Wakeshift gave his approval by issuing an order at 10:00 A.M. on Monday morning. The order included a demand that a full report of the findings of the autopsy be filed with the Court immediately upon completion, although it was understood after the autopsy procedures were finished it would take another couple of days for the lab results to be analyzed and the doctor's written statement completed as to the determination of the actual cause of death.

On Wednesday morning, a week almost to the hour since the suspicious note was first opened, Wright's phone rang, and attorney Marsh informed him the autopsy did in fact reveal the cause of death was due to cyanide poisoning. Apparently, as the note had insinuated, Joe Harkins had been murdered.

The doctor's statement read in part, "Human hair is, for many things, a time line. It is a repository of what circulated in the body. If cyanide was administered to a body, then what will grow from a head will be a strand of hair on which a tiny portion will have a bit of cyanide."

When the autopsy report was made public, major shock waves were felt across northwest Florida and south Alabama with vibrations touching every executive officer of the Deep South Group throughout their massive corporation. Almost instantly, every news organization started digging, each demanding an interview or comment from officials of the Deep South Group.

From DSG came a general statement issued by a low-level public relations employee which highlighted an assurance that the company would keep abreast of the investigation and report to law enforcement any findings they, themselves, might uncover. In the late afternoon Sidney Kattzs made a public declaration that full cooperation would be forthcoming from any and all employees of DSG regardless of their rank and position with the company.

□ □ □ □ □

OVER THE NEXT 48 hours Andy Wright talked, pleaded, and begged Cait to take the boys and the three of them go for a visit to her parents in Dallas. He finally got through to her on Thursday evening when Cliff, their oldest son, broke down and revealed that several motorcyclists had often harassed him and Mitchell as they waited for their school bus.

"Why haven't you said something before now about this?" demanded Andy.

"Well, you know. I just didn't want to bother y'all with it. There seems to be so much going on right now," Cliff responded.

"And how long has this been going on?"

"About two weeks, I guess."

"Two weeks! And you haven't said anything to us about it."

"Dad, you know. We just didn't want to bother you and Mom."

"Mitchell, why haven't you come to us with this?" he shouted.

"Cliff said that we shouldn't say anything. That's all. That's why."

"Well, you three are out of here tomorrow after school. No more conversation about it. Is that clear? You three will leave tomorrow for Dallas. I'll drive the boys to school in the morning and pick them up. You best be getting your things together 'cause you're outta here."

After a call from Wright, Savage arranged to have them flown on CC with destination unknown to anyone except his most trusted pilot and co-pilot. It was agreed that Wright would not call Cait unless he did so from a pay phone, and Cait would not call him at all. Their whereabouts was most important to keep secret.

Savage had adopted a close and special concern for the Wright family and met them at the hangar to assure them everything would be just fine. He took a few minutes to introduce all the Wrights to his chief pilot, Kolt Legions, and co-pilot, Rod King, since he knew Cait had always been apprehensive about flying, and these new circumstances just added to her concern for leaving Andy at this most critical time. Her fears and emotions surfaced, but she was willing to take this step as Andy was sure it was the correct thing to do.

From the ground the two men waved at the passengers until the executive jet streaked off the runway into the late, clear afternoon skies. As the aircraft banked left and headed westward, Wright finally felt safety for his family for the first time in four days.

"What are you doing tonight, Andy?" Savage asked.

"Thought I would go home and relax, nothing more, nothing planned. Why?"

"Why don't you come to the beach, and we will do a little bacheloring. Sheery is out of town, and you have nothing to do. We can throw some steaks and lobster tails on the grill and have a couple of cocktails. There is no need to drive back to Cantonment."

"That sounds like a great idea. I'll take you up on your offer. And Taylor, let me again thank you for all the concern you have shown for my family and me. Your help is and has been most appreciated."

"Think nothing of it. Let's take both cars so you can go home in the morning. Why don't you follow me."

□ □ □ □ □

THE TWO MEN lounged around the cedar-decked porch overlooking the bay, cooked on the grill, played with Hot and Toddy, and in general enjoyed each other's company. They, being alone, had the opportunity to really discuss in detail some of the more interesting points of what Savage had planned for Acirema. He emphasized time and again that he really wanted Wright to be elected the first Governor and was dedicated to doing everything in his power to see that it came about.

Saturday morning after coffee and rolls, the two men took the two Huskys for a long walk down the sugar white sands of Pensacola Beach. Taylor assured Andy that everything was going to work out all right, and sooner or later the entire truth about Deep South Group and Ray Haze would be known to the world.

Wright assured Savage that he felt much better now that his family was out of town and told him that he was considering taking his second planned trip back to Costa Rica on Monday for another bird shoot. Savage urged him to do just that, to get away from town for a few days.

☐ ☐ ☐ ☐ ☐

AFTER LEAVING THE beach, Wright made his way through Gulf Breeze, across the three-mile bridge, and north of Pensacola to Cordova Mall where he ran in to pick up three new suits he had purchased and had been notified the alterations were complete. In 20 minutes or so, he pulled into the three-car garage at his spacious home set almost in the middle of 22 acres of beautiful oaks. At once he noticed the single door at the rear of the garage, leading to the patio and pool cabana, was standing open. Ordinarily, this would be no real concern because the two boys often left it open. However, he distinctly remembered closing it after loading his Ford Explorer to take the family to the airport yesterday afternoon.

He closed the door and squeezed past the front bumpers, which hugged the wall in front of the three vehicles, and climbed the four brick steps to the landing of the door leading into the kitchen area of the home. On the third step his leather shoe soles gave off the squelching sound of crushing glass. He instantly knew what the sound was and what had happened. The lower left hand glass pane of the door had been broken and the knob offered no resistance to the pressure of its turn.

After walking through every room downstairs and the three upstairs bedrooms, he found no evidence of anything missing, broken, or out of place. He reached for the phone and punched "2", the number he had programmed into the phone system so that Cait and the boys could quickly reach the Sheriff's Department if needed.

"I would like to speak with Lieutenant Don Hamilton, please."

"The Lieutenant is not working this weekend and will be off until Monday morning. Can someone else help you.?"

"How about Sergeant Joe Hill Springer?"

"The Sergeant is on patrol. Would you like me to radio him?"

"Yes, please see if you can reach him and let him know this is Andrew Wright, and I need to speak with him. I'll wait on the line."

After making contact, the Sergeant arrived at Wright's home in about 15 minutes. The two men again toured the home and were convinced that, while there had been a break-in, there was no evidence other than the broken glass and an unlocked door. The Sergeant inquired if Savage had looked around the pool and cabana house or the workshop near the rear of the property. The answer to both questions was no, so they began to walk. Nothing seemed out of place around the cabana area, the equipment room, or the cedar-lined steambath or weight room.

About 50 yards from the main house, Wright had built a wooden garage-type structure which served as his workshop where he maintained and restored several antique automobiles. Outside on the south end of the building, he had constructed a fenced area perhaps 100 feet square which was home to his four bird dogs. Their accommodations were first-class and included a swinging access door that led into a special cordoned area inside the building to shelter them from inclement weather.

As the men approached the building, Wright knew for sure something was wrong. Even his presence would set the dogs into howling frenzies, and a stranger would most certainly send them into a rage. With the weather being almost perfect, the dogs would surely be romping outside the building, but none were to be seen or heard. Wright triggered the remote control which sent the garage door folding into the ceiling area. His first concern was what he heard—absolute silence, nothing at all. Not a peep from any dog signaled what was instantly obvious, what had happened. They found all four dogs lying motionless.

The men left the building and walked to the outside fence where they found a large piece of white wax wrapping paper with some small remaining traces of ground meat. Returning to the home, Wright called his friend, Dr. Mort Cascane, a local vet, who lived just down the road. After a quick examination of the dogs and odor testing of the fragments of meat left behind, there seemed to be no question but that the dogs had been poisoned.

This set of circumstances brought on a new wave of speculation and criminal involvement, Wright assured himself. He now knew that something was going down which might well affect him and the safety of his entire family. He placed a call to FBI Special Agent Carl Adams who was heading the investigation team looking into the possible involvement of the Deep South Group. The agent was off for the weekend, but Wright insisted that his office contact him and have him return the call.

Within the hour Agent Adams called, and all information pertaining to the break-in and the poisoned dogs was discussed. The Agent insisted that Dr. Cascane deliver the dogs to the Federal Lab where a full analysis could be performed as to the type of poison used. Before noon the following day the report was complete, and the agent told Wright the poison matched the exact same as had been found in Joe Harkins' body. For all apparent reasons the agent assumed it left no doubt, at least in his mind, there was a connection between the murder of Harkins and the death of the four dogs.

□ □ □ □ □

WITH ALL THE assumptions and criminal activities, Wright's three fellow hunters talked him into keeping their second scheduled bird shoot in Costa Rica. Wright agreed, thinking his being there would probably be safer for him than hanging out around his home by himself. Anyway, he really needed to replace some of the drudgery which had cluttered his life with some laughter and fun. One of his hunting companions, Boogie Bates, would make sure the foursome had their share of entertainment. Boogie, Waddell Bates' younger brother, was always ready for a party. Everywhere he went, so went his ever-present guitar. Country music was his 'thang,' and it mattered not if there was a crowd or just a few gathered; he was going to 'pick and sang.'

By midmorning on Monday the four friends had gathered at the Pensacola air terminal an hour or so before their flight was to leave for Miami at 10:42 A.M. After checking through security, Wright made a pay phone call to Dallas using coins and not charging it to his credit card as was the norm. All was well in Texas and everybody safe.

Their flight from Miami connected with the Costa Rica airline with little time to spare. The foursome had made this trip a number of times over the past several years, and it seemed as though each trip brought the group closer, friendship better, all much tighter. These four men were very special to each other.

In addition to all the game birds anyone would want to shoot, Costa Rica was also noted for other forms of entertainment which proved easily available to any and all who wanted to participate. It would be a fine time and place for these four to get their minds off the day-to-day grind of life's reality. Returning to the States after each trip, the men could always attest to their activities by showing their black and blue shoulders; it was not unusual for each to expend an entire case of bird shot in a relatively short period of time.

TWENTY

AS THE LATE COOL winter months began to give way to what appeared to be an early spring along the absolutely beautiful Gulf Coast of Florida, people began coming out of the woodwork, coming from behind closed doors, and enjoying walks down the sugar white sand. Kids and adults alike were seen up and down the beach flying brightly colored kites high into the cloudless skies, taking advantage of the winds of March.

March and April continued to bring cool days and nights on the coast, and the residents of the beaches still experienced winds which forced them to dress appropriately while trying desperately to begin another season of enjoying one of Mother Nature's most prized places on the earth, the upper coast of the Gulf of Mexico.

Few homes on the beaches had been built with fireplaces, so during the depths of winter some of the permanent island residents favored patronizing restaurants and lounges that prided themselves with having a roaring fire for most of the entire "off" season. This scene frequently looked out of place when you sat down to dine at the beach with a roaring fire on one end of the room and out a window you could watch the seagulls frolicking along the cold white sands with the waves lapping at their webbed feet.

Early in the year, brave young men and women began to test the waters with their sail boats, catamarans, and two-person rigs. The colorful masts could be seen catching the winds both on the Gulfside and bayside of the Santa Rosa Island peninsula. Strong

271

March winds afforded those who chose to sail in the Gulf a chance to romp with the magnificent dolphins that are always eager and delighted to chaperon them up and down the island. Those who sail catamarans often experience these stunning animals positioning themselves between the two pontoons and following along mile after mile. As the sailors headed west down the coast, around the horn at historic Fort Pickens, and into the Sound, their swimming companions would turn back, leaving them as they prefer the Gulf waters to the calmer bay.

◻ ◻ ◻ ◻ ◻

THROUGHOUT MARCH AND most of April the various Acirema committees labored feverishly to complete their work on the Platform so it could be mailed on schedule. They put in long hours at their general assemblies and in meeting after meeting doing committee work, often late into the night. With each passing week they were more assured their efforts were going to pay off and began to think in terms of being the front line of a well-oiled machine that had been working tirelessly to bring to their region of the country a new and wonderful experience which all would soon enjoy.

Taylor Savage had been a whirlwind of activity since the first announcement in January. He not only labored to guide the committee through the Platform, alter it, change and improve it, but also to make it acceptable to the average man and woman who would find themselves a part of Acirema should the referendum find success at the polls.

Savage spent considerable time between committee meetings in meetings with his architects, who were working overtime with the design of the Acirema International Global Airport and its Civic Center, Industrial Park, Hospital and Shopping Mall. And plans for the Acirema Parkway were coming along nicely and would be taking shape in the not too distant future.

He fully understood the financial risk involved in jumping into the design stages of these projects before the vote on the referendum was taken. However, he also understood that, in part, his promotion for the acceptance of Acirema by those who would cast their vote was based on his ability to accomplish just exactly what he said he would do, and he did not intend to fail. There was no time to kill, and if design and planning had to wait until after the vote they would just be that much further behind. He was willing to take the financial risk based on polling results that his organization was gathering on a regular basis.

From time to time the committee had some genuine disagreements among themselves pertaining to certain planks of the Platform, but did a marvelous job of compromising in every area of dissension.

Peaches Lamont, with her years of experience and expertise in mass mailing political campaign materials, took on the task of generating the computer mailing list of every potential voter within the 19 counties. The committee spent countless hours assembling information that would be mailed to each voter and realized, early on, the wording of the packet had to be just right and not lean one way or the other pertaining to either the Republican or Democratic point of view nor the liberal or conservative persuasion. This was to be a full bipartisan referendum and hinged primarily on one element only: to have a better place for every family to live in a safe environment and to operate their commercial businesses free from crime and corruption. Nothing more.

□ □ □ □ □

WITH THE RISING sun the morning weather was great, perfect for the occasion. The birds would be on the wing in a short time. Andy and his three companions finished their morning coffee and piled into the old Jeep where José, their hunting guide of many years, was waiting patiently to drive them back to the same fields where they had experienced much success on numerous other shoots. Perhaps 15 minutes into the hunt it happened. With his first shot Andy's Remington 12-gauge automatic exploded, totally disintegrating the shotgun and literally tearing off the entire right side of his face and the top of his head.

His friends knew instantly something dreadful had happened as the sound was much more like the exploding of dynamite than a 12-gauge number eight shot. From across the open field they all came running, and in unison each turned away and became sick from the horrible sight.

José radioed for the authorities who in turn called for an

ambulance, although the latter was really of no use. As in any similar circumstance, all guns and ammo were confiscated by the Costa Rican authorities, and Wright's body was taken to a local funeral parlor where nothing would proceed until further instructions were received from his family or U.S. State Department officials.

During the flight from Miami, Wright had talked about Cait and the boys being on a trip, but did not elaborate to his friends where his family might have gone. Arthur Dick, one of the foursome and the Wrights' next door neighbor, was aware of his closeness to Taylor Savage. He decided the only thing he knew to do was to call Savage, who possibly could use his staff and other means to locate Andy's family.

Before taking this action, he called his wife to explain the tragedy and to inquire if she may have some idea where Cait and the boys had traveled. This option proved to be negative so he placed a call to Savage.

□ □ □ □ □

TAYLOR SAVAGE ARRIVED at the Pensacola Hilton right on time for the 9:00 general committee of the whole meeting. Apparently, the media had finally learned to wait for his appearance in the meeting room and did not bother to clutter the outside as had become standard practice.

"Good morning, it's great being together with all of you again. I trust that over the past two weeks, each of the standing committees has put in some good, hard work and is ready to report your findings this morning.

"Before we get down to business it is imperative that I make a few comments about all the activities which have occurred over the past four weeks since our last full committee meeting on March 19th. It appears that a couple of our committee members have already started sparring about the upcoming governor's race. As we all have agreed, we need to have spirited debates, debates that are real debates and to discuss the issues which will affect all of us so very much.

"While I will not direct my comments personally toward anyone in particular, I want to make an open and general comment to all of you. If any of you choose to throw your hat into the race for any position, be it the United States Senate seat, House seat, the Governor's race, State Cabinet races, members of the Legislature, or any other position, either state or local, then do so with all of our full blessings.

"However, if any of you who choose to be a candidate feel that your personal life or any aspect of a personal nature concerning your personal life would in any manner deter your effectiveness on this committee, I hope that you would resign as a committee member. This is not to say that we hope that you drop out of any political race that you may be considering; just please resign from this committee whereby we, the remaining members, can still function without an inside squabble among our membership.

Now, just a few more comments and observations. We all are acutely aware of the happenings concerning Andrew Wright and the note which he received and its contents pertaining to the Deep South Group. This entire situation is simply appalling and very stressful to me personally as I'm sure it is to each of you.

"We all learned just six days ago that the result of an autopsy on a former DSG employee, Joe Harkins, apparently proved to the authorities that he had been poisoned, and it looks as though a murder may have been committed. As you may have noticed, Andrew Wright is not attending our meeting this morning. He and his family have taken a few days away from the city, and I may add it's a much-needed rest for all of them. He has been under much stress and strain since finding the note.

"This morning I expect there will be a mountain of questions from the media concerning this pathetic set of circumstances. But if you will hold your questions and let us get through with our agenda, I will be more than glad to stay as long afterwards as is necessary to answer any inquiries which you may have of me. However, I want to caution each of the media, as well as each of our committee members: the innuendos and allegations which have been heard are not aimed at this committee or the goal we seek. There is no tie-in whatsoever, and I will not address any questions or allegations so assuming.

"There is a concern on my part that this situation, and I mean the receipt of the note, may well have been intended to dilute the positive strength of our movement simply by taking the momentum away from our goal and focusing it on the note and possibly a tragic murder.

"Now, let's get down to some things more pleasant. Let's get down to the business of Acirema. The skipping of our last committee of the whole meeting two weeks ago afforded me some time to do things which I really needed to finalize. I can report to you this morning I have in hand signed contracts for lease space at our Industrial Park by the Skylor Company, the William Hartmann Company, and the Bart-Matthews Company from Bay Minette, Alabama.

□ □ □ □ □

AS SAVAGE CONTINUED with his comments, a hotel bell captain approached the head table and whispered to Laura Rings that her office was on the phone, and it was urgent. Laura took the call from her assistant, June Ferris, who reported she had a Mr. Arthur Dick on the phone, and he was demanding to speak with Mr. Savage.

Laura insisted that Miss Ferris convince the caller that Savage was in a most important meeting and could not be disturbed, but he wasn't buying it. Laura gave in and told June to connect her to Mr. Dick.

"Mr. Dick, this is Laura Rings, Mr. Savage's assistant. Is there something that I may help you with?"

"Ms. Rings, I must speak with Mr. Savage, it is urgent."

"Can I convey a message to him? He is in the middle of a committee meeting and really does not like to be disturbed."

"Ms. Rings, are you aware of all the happenings over the last several days concerning Andrew Wright, his family, and the Deep South Group?"

"Yes, Sir. Does this concern itself with that?"

"Yes, it does, and I must speak with Mr. Savage and must do it posthaste."

Laura decided the call was apparently as important as Dick was making it out to be. She returned to the committee room and communicated to Savage he needed to take a break, and that it was necessary he come to the phone immediately.

"Ladies and gentlemen, please excuse me for a moment. Let's take five minutes. I'll be right back."

While walking, Savage questioned Laura about the urgency of

the call, but she could only tell him the caller was a Mr. Arthur Dick who said it had to do with Andrew Wright and the Deep South Group, and he said it was most urgent to talk with him straightaway.

"Good morning. This is Taylor Savage. How may I help you?"

"Mr. Savage, my name is Arthur Dick. I am Andrew Wright's next-door neighbor, but more important than that, Andy, myself, and two other friends are in Costa Rica on a bird shoot. There has been an accident, and I am aware that Andy's family is out of town. I thought perhaps you can assist in finding them."

"My God, what has happened?"

"Somehow, Andy's shotgun exploded while he was shooting. It was a fatal accident."

"Jeeze! Holy crap. Look, I am at the Hilton in downtown Pensacola and will leave immediately for my office. I'm going to let you talk again with Laura. Please give her the number where you are, and I'll call you back in a very few minutes. Please stay where you are, and I'll be right back with you. And thanks for calling."

Savage turned to Laura and explained, "Andy Wright's had an accident and has been killed. Get the number where Mr. Dick is located while I tell the committee. We will be going back to the office without delay. I want you to call Sheery at my home in Raleigh and have her come to Pensacola immediately. If she can't get a good flight, then send a plane for her. I want her here."

Savage quickly returned to the podium. "People, there has been an accident. Andrew Wright has been killed while hunting in Costa Rica. That's all I know at this time. We are adjourning the meeting, and please understand that I simply cannot take questions from anyone. Later this afternoon if you will get in touch with Laura, she will let you know everything we find out."

SAVAGE HAD LAURA call the company's airport hangar and locate Kolt Legions, his chief pilot who had flown the Wright family to Dallas. After a lengthy conversation Kolt could not remember anything that may have been said which would lead to finding out exactly where her parents lived. She and the boys had been picked up at the airport by her family without giving any address or phone number. However, and for reasons unknown, sometime during the flight Cait had mentioned that her maiden name was Adkinson.

With this bit of information, Frank Marsh and his entire legal staff when to work. Savage called the Texas Attorney General's office and requested their assistance. In a couple of hours every home and business with the name Adkinson had been called. Finally, a Herman Adkinson, who lived midway between Dallas and Fort Worth, seemed to have some association. He was not willing to do much talking but was perfectly willing to listen.

Adkinson obviously knew the reason his daughter and grandsons were visiting with him and his wife but was not about to admit they were there and certainly would not discuss details with someone who just happened to be calling on the phone looking for them. The secretary in the Attorney General's office, who made the call that apparently found the right Adkinson, talked him into a way to verify that she was exactly who she said she was. She asked him to look up the Texas Attorney General's number in the phone book and to place a call to that number and ask for the Attorney General personally. She in turn would make sure the AG would speak with him and explain what was going on.

The secretary hardly had time to get from her desk into the AG's office when the phone rang. She took the call and turned Adkinson over to Milton Rolin, the Attorney General.

"Hello, is this Mr. Adkinson?" inquired the AG.

"Yes, this is Herman Adkinson."

"Mr. Adkinson, this is Milton Rolin, Attorney General of the State of Texas. Since you looked up our phone number in the directory and made the call to my office, are you convinced that you are talking to me, an official of the State of Texas?"

"Yes, Sir. Now, what is the purpose of your contacting me?"

"Mr. Adkinson, we have been trying to locate a Mrs. Cait Wright and her two sons, Cliff and Mitchell. Do I have the correct Adkinson?"

"Yes, Sir. She is my daughter, and they are my grandsons. Is something wrong?"

"Mr. Adkinson, there has been an accident involving Andrew Wright. He is your daughter's husband, is that correct?"

"Yes, Sir. Her husband is Andrew, my son-in-law."

"Mr. Adkinson, as my office understands the situation, Mr. Wright had a hunting accident in Costa Rica. I hate to bring you this news, but it was a fatal accident."

"My God! My God! No! It can't be. What happened, Mr. Rolin?"

"Mr. Adkinson, I have no details. I know nothing more than it was a fatal accident. I am sorry."

"Were others hurt? Were others killed also?"

"Mr. Adkinson, I really have no answers. I wish I could tell you more."

"When did it happen?"

"It is our understanding it happened early this morning when they were first in the bird fields. Mr. Adkinson, I am sorry that I don't have more information for you, but that is all we were told.

"Is it okay if we give your phone number to a Mr. Taylor Savage in Pensacola, Florida. I understand he is a friend of the family and has an airplane standing by to fly to Dallas to pick up Mrs. Wright and the boys."

"Sure, please do. I'll need a few minutes to locate my wife, Cait, and the boys. I'll be gone from home for maybe 30 minutes. Have Mr. Savage call in about a half hour. And thank you, Mr. Rolin, for your help and concern."

"Mr. Adkinson, please convey my condolences to your daughter and your family. Goodbye."

"Goodbye, Mr. Rolin."

Within the hour Savage was talking with Cait Wright. She simply did not know what to do. She had yet to tell the boys and did not look forward to the ordeal. She could not think straight and was not concerned or eager to return to Pensacola immediately since she was with her parents who offered the support she really needed.

Savage committed an airplane to bring them home when she made whatever decision she would eventually make. She asked about how Andy's body would get from Costa Rica back to Pensacola, and Savage gave her his assurance he would have his staff make all necessary arrangements for the return if she would like for him to do so. His offer was quickly accepted and was most welcome.

All of a sudden, things had really gotten out of hand. The emphasis had shifted from the daily news of Acirema becoming the 51st state to the news of criminal activities and wrongdoings at the Deep South Group, which now included the possibility of two murders and a tremendous amount of trouble for a good many top executives and perhaps a few politicians.

□ □ □ □ □

SAVAGE BEGAN TO THINK about the old saying, "When it rains, it pours." Sheery had received a distressing call from her father in Goldsboro telling her that her mother had passed away only moments after Laura called her with the bad news about Andy Wright. Her mother had been ill for a number of months, and while her death was not a real shock it still was very much unexpected. She did not know how she could possibly go to Florida and give the support Savage needed knowing that her presence was also much demanded by her father and younger sister.

Like the "fixer" he was, Savage understood and comforted her the best he could through long distance phone calls. He would leave this afternoon and fly to Goldsboro to spend the evening with her and her family, return tomorrow to meet the Wright family upon their arrival from Dallas, attend Andy's funeral services, then return to Goldsboro on Sunday for the services of Sheery's mother, Mrs. Helen Carol Goss. Sheery would remain in Goldsboro until Tuesday afternoon and join Savage at his home on the beach that evening.

□ □ □ □ □

ALL ARRANGEMENTS FOR the return of Andrew Wright's body to the States were made through a joint effort by Florida's senior United States Senator, Bilinda Hansen, and the U.S. State Department. Local and national news carried the story and tried in every instance to associate it with events and happenings relative to Acirema, but they simply could not find any connection, no matter how hard they tried.

All members of the Acirema committee attended the services as did many friends and former co-workers of Wright's from the Deep South Group, including President Kattzs and several top executives. Throughout the services there were mistrustful glances in every direction from everyone attending. The entire congregation resembled a group of potential criminals who were sitting in a line-up with long, somber, and agonizing faces. Everyone tried to shield his or her glances from each other but to no avail.

Savage could not help but think that most of the Deep South executives were there to try to lessen the possible guilt of their past and certainly not for the purpose of the service. Before taking a seat each walked down the isle to the solid bronze, closed casket and paused briefly. An 8 by 10 color portrait of Andy was resting midway on the casket in the middle of a spray of his favorite flowers, yellow roses.

Cait, Cliff, Mitchell, and both of Cait's and Andy's parents were seated in a private section to the right of the room behind properly positioned vertical wooden blinds which afforded them full view of the service without their being observed by those sitting in the chapel. Savage had been invited by Cait to sit with the family, but he politely refused, saying this was a time that should be reserved for only the immediate family.

Florida Governor Brandon Woods was shocked to learn of the accident but was as much, or more so, concerned about the rumors and news accounts of criminal activities aimed at the Deep South Group. He, along with every other potential candidate for office, attended the 10:00 funeral services and wrapped themselves in their usual political mannerisms of long, sad, and somber faces.

☐ ☐ ☐ ☐ ☐

AS SOON AS THE SERVICES at Oak Lawn were over, the media tried in vain to obtain statements from several officers, directors, or executives of DSG, but none was willing to make any comment. A statement by a public relations director did express the deep sorrow of the entire staff and management of DSG and spoke of deep sympathy for Mrs. Wright and her sons.

An anchor woman with the local ABC station was finally given a comment by Taylor Savage. "Our sympathy goes out to the fine family of Andrew Wright. He was an honest, honorable family man and a very decent human being. We who have come to know him as of late will miss his shining personality and his constant wit, wisdom, and up-beat attitude."

"Mr. Savage, will you comment on the note that was sent to Mr. Wright and your opinion of the set of circumstances which may have contributed to his untimely death? And are you sure it was a murder and not just an accident?" the reporter continued.

"While the authorities have yet to say if it was an accident or not, I personally feel most certain that it was no accident. And to that possibility I hope the law enforcement agencies that are in charge of this investigation will move swiftly to identify and apprehend the responsible party or parties and see that they are brought to justice and given their due punishment.

"I could care less about the personal status of any individual who may have had a hand in this horrible episode. I will personally fund a cash reward payable to anyone who may be instrumental in bringing to justice any and all of those who may have had the slightest bit of involvement in this sordid affair. That is all I have at this moment. Thank you."

After the chapel services and burial at Bayview Memorial Park, Savage accompanied the Wrights back to their home where friends and neighbors had prepared a feast of food and desserts.

□   □   □   □   □

SINCE THE ACCIDENT, or murder, Governor Woods had spent considerable hours with both Melvin Cooper, his campaign manager, and his financial campaign advisor, Sue Upton. After reviewing countless numbers of pages of campaign contributions, they determined that more than $285,000 had been given to his reelection campaign by those with direct ties or association with the Deep South Group.

Although this information was public record, thus far no one had inquired or tried to associate these contributions to any criminal element involving DSG and his campaign. If it were to come to light, it would be most embarrassing personally and devastating to any future campaign he may choose to enter. The three conspirators bound themselves to complete and total silence of the facts surrounding any and all contributions.

□   □   □   □   □

THE LEAD STORY in all the media was a quotation made by a special agent of the FBI, "From all early and preliminary investigative reports, it appears that Mr. Wright was killed by a high grade level of explosives that was reloaded in a shotgun shell and placed among several full boxes in his possession. When the shell was fired the explosion occurred, killing Mr. Wright instantly.''

Although the FBI was questioned time and again by the media, it would not confirm or deny that other shells were found in Wright's provisions which may also have been tampered with or altered in some manner. The ammo which had been confiscated by Costa Rican authorities had now been turned over to the FBI field office in Miami where more tests were underway.

The FBI was very sensitive to the feelings of Taylor Savage but insisted he sit down and go over all he knew about any aspect of the story which may have taken place just days before the accident. Savage informed them he would be more than anxious to cooperate and would be available at 10:00 o'clock on Saturday morning and would either come to their office or they could visit with him.

☐ ☐ ☐ ☐ ☐

WITH ALL THE preliminary greetings and usual comments out of the way Savage and three special agents settled down in comfortable chairs in the second-floor conference room of the Federal building. This room was strategically located on the southwest corner and provided the only area of the building where smoking was permitted for obvious reasons. The cross ventilation of open windows, when necessary, allowed nervous witnesses to enjoy the pleasure of their habits while undergoing cross examination.

A tape recorder was activated to preserve for the record all questions and answers. Special agent Carl Adams inquired, ''Mr. Savage, I understand that Mr. Wright called you and asked to see you the afternoon after he and Ray Haze met on Mr. Haze's boat at Point Clear. Is this correct?''

''Yes, that is right.''

''And did Mr. Wright detail to you what was discussed between himself and Mr. Haze?''

''Yes, he did.''

''And can you tell us what he said about that conversation?''

"Andy was very nervous. I had never seen him like that. As I understand it, Mr. Haze had called a day or two earlier and wanted to sit down and talk politics with Mr. Wright. This was the purpose of their visit. Andy said that Haze wanted to know if he, Andy, was or was not going to enter the Governor's race in Acirema, and Andy explained to him that he had not made a final decision.

"Mr. Haze questioned him about the purpose of his entering the race. He, Mr. Haze, thought that Andy's real reason may have been that he wanted to find an avenue of retribution toward the Deep South Group, and if elected Governor he then would be in a position to take any form of action he may choose."

"And what, if you know, would be the purpose of any retribution against Deep South Group? Why would he have an axe to grind, so to speak?"

"Mr. Wright was fired by Deep South."

"Do you know why he was fired?"

"I only know what Andy told me."

"And what was that?"

"He apparently had found out about some under-the-table, cash kickback dealings involving some of the executives at DSG. That, I assume, may have been the rub or the major problem."

"Did Mr. Wright tell you what he knew, what he suspicioned about these cash kickbacks, under-the-table dealings?"

"Andy told me that about three years ago he was with a group of executives from Deep South who were visiting in Washington for the purpose of lobbying against acid rain legislation, and at some point in time one of the men had too much to drink and started talking about things which he should have kept to himself."

"Did he tell you who this person was?"

"Yes, it was Joe Harkins."

"This being the same Joe Harkins whose body was exhumed recently, and the autopsy proved that he had been poisoned?"

"That is correct," Savage said.

"Did Mr. Wright indicate to you who was involved with what he termed 'under-the-table dealings' or 'cash kickbacks'?"

"Andy had been told by Joe Harkins that several executives from the Deep South Group had been taking cash payoffs from coal suppliers and dealers over a number of years.''

''Did he name any names of those employed by Deep South?''

''No. He did not. However, he indicated that Joe Harkins told him that the fraud went all the way to the top.''

''And what did you think 'all the way to the top' meant?''

''I have to assume it would have to mean to the very top of the executive ladder, to the President of the company, Mr. Sidney Kattzs.''

''Now, during your meeting with Mr. Wright, did he tell you that he had any suspicion that Mr. Haze was involved in any manner with these 'under-the-table' dealings?''

''He and I both spoke in terms that it was a good possibility. However, we were just venting our own suspicions to each other.''

''At any time did Mr. Wright indicate to you that he thought his own life might be in danger?''

''Yes. He was very concerned.''

''And did he take any action to combat that concern?''

''Well, after he received the note, certainly sending his family out of the state was a positive action. He became very concerned for the safety of his entire family as well as himself.''

''And, Mr. Savage, did Mr. Wright indicate to you that he had a fear of any one person? Did he name anyone?''

''No. That is no one at DSC. However, I personally felt he was holding back and that he was concerned about someone, but he never said who that person was. And let me tell you this. We were much concerned about several members of a motorcycle gang that were harassing his two boys. It seems they were taunted a few times while they awaited their school bus. Andy told me about this, and it was actually the final straw that convinced him to send them for a visit to her parents home in Dallas.''

''Yeah, we were aware of that, and we have located and questioned three riders. A call came in from the principal of the school who reported they were hanging around across from the schoolyard on several afternoons and seemed as though they were following one of the busses when it left the apron. We're on top of that.

''Mr. Savage, I am sure we will have more questions for you, but for now let me thank you for coming in this morning. We will be back in touch if we need you.''

"Let me say to you, one and all, I want this murder solved. I will take whatever actions that you suggest in order to do everything within my power to see this crime is solved and those who have played a part are incarcerated. I want you people to suggest to me how big a cash reward for information I should fund. I'll fund whatever is necessary."

"Thank you, Mr. Savage, but that will have to be a decision of your own. We simply cannot play a part in a reward fund from a private citizen. I am sure you will reach the proper decision," said agent John Wilton.

"Mr. Savage, I would like to change the subject and make a comment off the record. Would you agree?"

"Certainly, what's on your mind?" asked Savage.

Agent Adams announced on the record that the inquiry was finished, then turned off the recorder. "Completely off the record and a personal comment of my very own," continued agent Wilton, "I sincerely wish you well in your efforts for Acirema. Here in our northwest Florida office we have only 16 employees, and last week we conducted a straw ballot. The vote was 13 for Acirema with only three opposing. I think that is remarkable, and I wanted you to know of our support."

"I appreciate that very much, and you can rest assured you have my total confidence in your off-the-record comment. Now, let me ask the three of you a question. Do you think this miserable set of circumstances in which we have found ourselves will have an effect on the results of the vote for or against the referendum?" Savage asked.

"No, I do not think so," answered agent Prince Hartfield. "I think your conduct and personality is above reproach. Obviously, there will be some skeptics. However, I do not think this unfortunate situation will have any effect, but if so, it will be very insignificant."

"Thank you all, and have a good day," Savage offered while leaving the room.

The FBI had now taken full control of the investigation, and at the top of its list of those it wanted to interview were Ray Haze and Sidney Kattzs. Testimony thus far had indicated that both men were under suspicion. The FBI was most concerned about their clandestine meeting at the Atlanta Airport, especially since it was the day after Haze and Andrew Wright had an argument aboard his yacht.

Furthermore, the agents were keeping a close watch on several of the bikers who were among those assembled during early protest rallies and had been seen milling around the school attended by the Wright boys. Of special attention was ''Bone Man,'' who previously had several minor run-ins with the local authorities.

TWENTY-ONE

THE TRIO OF AGENTS were completely satisfied with the Savage interview and were more than anxious to have Ray Haze come to Pensacola to answer a few questions. Agent Adams placed a call to his home in Point Clear and was informed by Hattie, his maid, that he would be returning in the next 15 minutes. He had taken Peaches' advice and had set a three-times-per-day course of heavy walking in hopes of getting into better shape for the upcoming Governor's race.

Shortly before noon he sauntered in the front door, exhausted and completely out of breath. "You had a call from the FBI, and they want you to call them back in Pensacola as soon as you can," she said.

"From who?"

"He say the FBI."

"Did he leave his name? What did he want?"

"He say his name is Agent Carl Adams, and he just wants you to call him."

"How long ago did he call? When was it?"

"Bout half hour go."

"Did you tell him that I would be coming back soon?"

"Yes, Sir. I told him that you would be back in about 15 minutes. It was bout 11:30 when he called."

"Damn," proclaimed Haze.

☐ ☐ ☐ ☐ ☐

"HELLO, MAY I SPEAK with Agent Adams, please."

288

"Yes, Sir, may I tell him who is calling?"

"This is Ray Haze in Point Clear returning his call."

"Certainly, please hold, Mr. Haze."

A few minutes passed before Agent John Wilton came to the phone. "Hello, is this Mr. Haze?"

"Yes, this is Ray Haze. Is this Agent Adams?"

"No, Sir. This is Agent John Wilton. Agent Adams has stepped out for a bite of lunch. Mr. Haze, Agent Adams, Agent Hartfield, and I have been assigned to a case, and we have some questions which you may be able to clear up for us. We would like to schedule some time on Monday morning for you to drive over and visit with us. Can this be arranged?"

"Well, this is quite sudden, isn't it?"

"Not really, we just have some things that we need to talk to you about. How about 10:00 on Monday morning here in our office?"

"Well, I have my schedule somewhat full for Monday. Can we do it later in the week or perhaps the following week?"

"No, Sir, I think we need to talk on Monday morning. Can we expect you here around 10:00?"

"Agent Wilson. You did say Wilson, didn't you?"

"No, Mr. Haze. Close but not quite. Its agent Wilton, John Wilton."

"I'm sorry. Look, agent Wilton, are you sure that this cannot wait until later in the week?"

"No, Sir. Can we expect you on Monday morning around 10:00?"

"Well, let's make it 11:00 so I can take care of some things that I had planned for the morning. Will that be okay with you folks?"

"Sure, Mr. Haze. We'll schedule you for 11:00 o'clock Monday morning. Do you know where we are located?"

"I assume that you are in the Federal Building, and, if so, then I know how to find you."

"That's correct. Just take the elevator to the second floor. I will advise security to be expecting you. Thank you, Mr. Haze. I'll see you on Monday."

"Wait just a moment, Agent Wilton. Should I be represented by an attorney? Will that be necessary?"

"That is your decision, Mr. Haze. If you feel more comfortable with legal representation, feel free to have one present. Only you can make that determination.''

"Okay. I'll see you on Monday morning. Goodbye.''

"Have a good day, Mr. Haze.''

□   □   □   □   □

IT WAS ALREADY PAST 11:30 on Monday when a call came to Agent Adams' office from Haze explaining that he got a late start, and a wreck on Highway 90 had caused further delay. He apologized and said he should arrive right around noon. He inquired if they would like to go ahead with their lunch hour before the meeting, and if so he would come in around 1:30. The agent informed him they had rather proceed with the meeting as scheduled as soon as he could get there.

□   □   □   □   □

ABOUT 11:45 SECURITY called upstairs informing them that Haze had arrived and was on his way up. When he got off the elevator, Marcia, the agency secretary, greeted him and escorted him down the hall to the conference room situated on the southeast corner of the well-worn building.

After formal introductions, the four men got right down to business. "Mr. Haze, for the record this meeting is being electronically recorded. Do you understand this?''

"Yes, Sir. That is perfectly all right with me,'' he answered.

"Mr. Haze,'' spoke agent Wilton, "when we talked on Saturday you indicated that you might bring along an attorney. Have you waived that right?''

"Yes, I have given it a lot of thought, and I cannot possibly see what you folks might want with me that would require an attorney. When we talked on Saturday, it was such a surprise that I guess I just automatically inquired if I would be needing one.''

"That's perfectly okay with us, Mr. Haze,'' responded Agent Adams. "Why don't we get right into the purpose of the meeting. Mr. Haze, it is our understanding that you had invited Mr. Andrew Wright to visit with you at your home on the 26th of March. Is this correct?''

"Well, yes and no. I did meet with Andy. However, it was he who called and wanted to come over for a meeting.''

"I see," said Agent Wilton. "And you did not make the call and invite him. Is that correct?"

"That is true. It was he who called me and scheduled the meeting," Haze assured.

"Okay, could you tell us the purpose of the meeting? What was it that Mr. Wright wanted to discuss?"

"He had two things on his mind. First, he wanted me to drop all interest in running for Governor of Acirema. Second, he told me of having knowledge of some serious wrongdoings by top executives of DSG."

"And what do you mean by DSG?" asked an agent.

"Oh, yeah. That is the Deep South Group. Sorry," said Haze.

"And were you surprised at the comments he made?"

"Of course. I was shocked at the allegations he was speaking of concerning DSG, but I gave little concern about me dropping out of the Governor's race. That's just politics, you know."

"And can you explain to us about his comments concerning what you refer to as DSG?"

"Yes. I was shocked to learn that he was apparently going to use information which he said he had obtained against DSG and blackmail them because they had fired him. He said that several top executives had been taking cash kickbacks from coal suppliers, dealers, and others who had some connections or interest in the coal industry."

"And he told you that he intended to blackmail them. Is this what we are to understand?"

"Yes, Sir. That he was going to see that Sidney Kattzs, President of DSG, was to pay for firing him. Furthermore, he made sure that I knew that any dollars he collected from the blackmail operation would be used to finance his campaign for Governor, and he assured me there was no way I could raise funds equal to what his war chest would ultimately become."

"And did you take him seriously. Did you think that he really would blackmail DSG?"

"I have known Andy for several years, and in the past his word has always been on the up and up. I had to assume that he would do as he said he would. His word had always been his bond."

"Now, please tell us about the rest of your conversation with Mr. Wright during his visit to your home."

"Well, our meeting was actually on my boat, which is docked at my home."

"So the meeting we are discussing was on the boat and not at your home?" asked Agent Wilton.

"Yes, that is correct. He came to my home and we decided to meet aboard my boat."

"That within itself is somewhat strange, isn't it?" inquired Agent Hartfield.

"No, not at all. I have many meetings aboard the boat. Some while docked at home, and others while enjoying Mobile Bay or just cruising the intercoastal. Anyway, I like to have a cigar from time to time, and I have a lady friend who despises the smell of smoke in the house so I often go down to the boat to sit around and enjoy a drink and a smoke. Are you trying to make something of that?"

"No, Mr. Haze. I just thought it strange since you live in a grand home that you would hold a meeting down at the end of a dock in a boat. But go ahead with your story. What else did Mr. Wright have to say?"

"Say, is it permissible to have a smoke in here?" Haze inquired.

"Sure. I'll just crack the windows," answered Agent Adams. "Agent Hartfield will probably join you sooner or later."

"Thanks. Now where were we?" asked Haze.

"You were about to tell us what Andy Wright had to say. Please continue."

"Oh, yes, Andy was adamant that he was going to see the Perdido River Project, which is in the planning stages by DSG, stopped dead in its tracks. When I inquired as to why, he again insinuated that it was in retribution for his firing."

"And what else did he elaborate concerning any wrongdoings pertaining to the Deep South Group?"

"He was not more specific. He did not tell me whom he was speaking of, and, quite frankly, I did not want to know. It was none of my business what he may or may not have suspected. I have known Sidney Kattzs and many of his upper-level executives for many years, and I have never known them, any one of them, to be anything except good, clean, law-abiding citizens who have their customers' interests at heart at all times."

"Let me ask you this," inquired Agent Adams. "Have you or your campaign, to the best of your knowledge, ever received any campaign contributions from the Deep South Group or any employee of their company?"

"Certainly I have. Did I not just say they have the best interests of their customers always as their top priority. This company is for good, responsible government at all levels."

"Well, let me ask you in a different way," the Agent continued. "To your knowledge, have you ever received any campaign funds from any source other than the name which is listed on a check for the purpose intended?"

"I don't think I follow your line of questioning. What are you speaking of? What do you mean?" asked Haze.

"I'll be more than pleased to clear up the question. Have you ever, to your knowledge, received any campaign contributions from any individual, company, or corporation, as represented by a check from an account which contained the contributor's name and address, with the knowledge the contribution was given to your campaign but was actually funded from another source?"

"I am afraid I still do not understand what you are getting at," said Haze. "What is it that you are trying to find out? What are you searching for?"

"Okay, let me get right to the point," said the agent.

"Please do," Haze stated in a sarcastic voice.

"It is our belief that possibly some of your contributions were made by employees of the Deep South Group at the urging of one or more of their superiors. In turn, the employees may have received cash funds from others to cover their contributions. Do you know anything about a situation such as this?"

"I have no idea what you're talking about," responded Haze.

"Would you consider this to be wrong and inappropriate if, in fact, such did occur?" he was asked.

"Yes, I would assume there would be some implications of wrongdoing on both the part of the contributor, the receiver, and those who may have funded the contribution. Especially if it was done through a cash reimbursement," answered Haze.

"And again, Mr. Haze, you have no knowledge of any of your previous campaigns ever having received any such contributions as we have detailed?"

"No, Sir, not to my knowledge," Haze mumbled while speaking between clenched teeth that were biting hard on a very moist stogie.

"Okay, let me ask you this," inquired Agent Wilton. "Would anyone in your political organization, such as your campaign manager, your comptroller, your director of finance, or any others, have such knowledge that this, or something similar to this, may have occurred?"

"I don't think so. However, you would have to ask them as to what knowledge they may or may not have. I simply do not have a better answer to that question," Haze noted.

"Okay, let's move on. It is our understanding that the following day, March 27th, the day after meeting with Andrew Wright, you flew to Atlanta and met with the President of Deep South Group, Sidney Kattzs. Is that correct, Sir?"

"I don't have my appointment book with me. I don't know if that date is correct or not," answered Haze.

"Well, do you know if you flew to Atlanta to meet with Mr. Kattzs the day following your meeting with Mr. Wright on your boat?" inquired Agent Adams.

"Yes, that is correct," Haze responded.

"And can you tell us the purpose of that meeting, the urgency of the meeting?"

"It was a meeting that Sidney Kattzs and I had planned for some time. The purpose was to keep him informed about the Acirema Committee and just how our progress was going pertaining to the polls concerning the upcoming referendum. That's all there was to it."

"What was the purpose of going to Atlanta to do that? Why did the two of you not meet either at your office or his? Why the clandestine atmosphere of such a meeting in a distant city which has nothing whatsoever to do with the boundaries of Acirema?"

"Mr. Kattzs was to be in Atlanta for other meetings, and it just worked out this was a good place for us to get together," Haze countered.

"And you had made plans to have this meeting some time ago. Is that correct?"

"Yes, it had been previously scheduled," Haze retorted.

"And, Mr. Haze, if we were to inform you that our investigation revealed that you made the appointment on the afternoon of March 26th shortly after Mr. Wright left your boat, then could we assume this was the time frame which you speak of in terms of it being scheduled for 'some time'? And when we interview Mr. Kattzs, will he tell the same story that you are telling us?''

''Look, I don't know what you folks are getting at. I had to meet with my longtime friend, Sidney Kattzs, to keep him abreast of the activities of the Acirema Committee, and, yes, I also spoke about what Andy Wright had said concerning the Deep South Group. Is this a crime?''

''No, Mr. Haze, meeting with Mr. Wright or meeting with Mr. Kattzs is not a crime,'' explained Agent Adams while rising from his chair and leaning forward placing all 10 fingers spread evenly on the table top, forcing his fingertips to become blood red from holding his entire upper body weight. He gazed direct into Haze's eyes and said, ''I am the agent in charge of this investigation, and it is my duty and the duty of Agents Wilton and Hartfield to get to the bottom of this situation, and we have every intent to do just that. We hope to have your full cooperation.''

''Certainly, I understand. This entire affair has been so very stressful. Please continue,'' Haze responded.

''May I inquire,'' asked Agent Wilton. ''Mr. Haze, you stated earlier that you had known Andy Wright for some time. How long have you known him?''

''Heck, I'm not sure. He was the lead lobbyist for Deep South for several years. Perhaps I have known him 15 years or more,'' he said after exhaling a larger than normal cloud of white smoke.

''Mr. Haze, perhaps you and I can change sides of the table if you don't mind. On this side I think your smoke may find its way through the window. Do you mind?''

''No. Of course not,'' Haze agreed.

''Thanks,'' said Adams.

''Now, were you and Mr. Wright close friends?''

''I guess we were better business acquaintances than what you might call close friends.''

''Had he been to your home on occasion?''

''No, only the time in question. The meeting down on my boat.''

''The meeting of March 26th. Is this right?''

"If that was the date, yes that would be the time, the only time he has visited at my home."

"Have you ever visited at his home?"

"Not that I recall."

"Do you know where he lives?"

"No. I have no idea."

"Would you like to rethink that answer?"

"Well, no. I don't recall ever being in his home, and for that matter I don't think I know where he lives."

"Mr. Haze, our investigation reveals that you have been to his home in Cantonment, Florida. Do you know where Cantonment is?"

"I have a general idea. I know that it is north of Pensacola and that you have to drive through there when headed north to pick up I-65."

"And Mr. Haze, do you not recall being in Mr. Wright's home for a fund-raising event for your campaign when you last ran for Governor of Alabama?"

"You know. I think you may be right. Yes, Andy did bring some people together for an event at his home. Yes, he did indeed. I had forgotten about that."

"Mr. Haze, I'm somewhat curious as to why someone living in north Florida would throw a campaign fund-raising event for someone living in and running for Governor of Alabama. How did this come about?"

"I recall, now that you mentioned it, Cort Locke, who is President of Regions Power here in Pensacola, had some folks in town for a regional managers' meeting. In the late afternoon Andy had invited me to join them for a cookout. I had spent most of the day in the Atmore area campaigning, and so I drove down. As I recall, it was just a short drive south."

"And was this a fund-raising event for you and your campaign?"

"I guess you could call it that, but it was mainly just an outing for a number of their managers."

"But you did leave the cookout with some donations in your pocket and more pledged for later, did you not?"

"Yes, I recall there being some checks given to my campaign. Yes, you are right."

"And was there any cash given you or your campaign at this event?"

"Look, what are you folks getting at? Hasn't this line of questioning gone far enough?"

"We only have a couple more," responded Agent Hartfield. "Concerning the death of Mr. Wright, would you have any information or personal opinion who may have been involved with his untimely death?"

"No. I have no earthly idea who could have possibly wanted anything to happen to Andy Wright. He was a fine person, and yes, we did have an argument during our last meeting, but you can rest assured that in no way did I have anything to do with his accident."

"Do you have any idea who may have gained from his death. Who may be better off with him dead rather than alive?"

"No. Again I have no idea about any facet of his passing," Haze assured them.

"If we had reason to believe that one of your friends may have gained by his death, would you have any idea about whom we would be speaking?"

"Absolutely not. I have no knowledge of anything to do with the death of Andrew Wright. How many times do I have to tell you this?" he questioned in a harsh and demanding voice while pounding the table. "But I'll tell you one damn thing. You should be looking into those hippy bikers. Everyone saw on national television where they said someone was bound to be killed if they continued with the Acirema movement. Why don't you go ask them?"

"Believe me, Mr. Haze, we have that under control."

"Mr. Haze, would you be more comfortable if we recessed this inquiry which would give you some time to reconsider if you would like to have an attorney present when we next continue?"

"Based on where it looks like you are trying to go with your questions, I may well need to do just that. I am guilty of nothing, nothing you hear. If this is going to turn into a witch hunt or possible charges against me which would have no merit, then, yes, I will come back with my attorney."

"Mr. Haze, as of right now we do not have any idea where this line of questioning is going or where it may end. Why don't we continue this until Wednesday morning at 10:00 and let's again meet here in this office. That will give you almost 48 hours which should be sufficient time for you to decide if you would like to secure legal representation. Is that enough time for such a decision?''

"Yes, that will be most sufficient," Haze responded.

☐ ☐ ☐ ☐ ☐

TAYLOR SAVAGE HAD called a special meeting of the general assembly to try to catch up on items that had fallen behind schedule. The Platform was to have been mailed on Tuesday, April 23rd, yet there still was additional work to finish before sending it across the 19 counties.

As the members gathered in what had now become known as 'The Acirema Room,' their personal meeting place at the Hilton, each filed in with somber faces and low voices.

"Good morning." Savage said, opening the meeting. "Needless to say, we've lost a dear friend of this committee, someone whom I admired greatly. This is a very personal loss to me and Sheery. I said a few days ago that I would comment this morning on Andy's death. I have been besieged with questions from the media, and it appears that most of them are trying very hard to connect his unfortunate death with our plans for Acirema. There is no connection, and as hard as they may try, they are simply wasting valuable time which could be better used in a more positive direction. I would hope you, the media, will pay close attention to what I am about to say.

"The death of Andrew Wright has not one inkling of association with our movement. And don't you find it strange that we have no protestors with us this morning? From what I have gathered, learned, and expect, Andy's life may have been taken to keep him from exposing what he may have known about certain activities concerning high level executives within the Deep South Group. These suspicions may relate to extortion and cash kickbacks pertaining to the coal industry which supplies each of their electric generation plants across the Southeast.

"As you know, the examination of the exhumed body of Joe Harkins indicated foul play; it now has been proven that he died from a dose of cyanide poisoning. It is my personal opinion that

Mr. Harkins was murdered for the same set of reasons and circumstances as was Andrew Wright. Again, this is my personal opinion and does not reflect on any other member of this committee but me. It does not take much smarts to recognize the associations of these two deaths.

"The media has now drifted away from factual reporting by taking this dreadful situation and blowing it completely out of proportion. It is my fondest wish that you of the media drop your search for an elusive connection and revert to responsible reporting about Acirema and the activities of our movement. Please report about where we were prior to this horrendous act and where we are still headed and just how we plan to get there.

"We will go forward with renewed, concerted efforts to see that the referendum passes, and it will if that is the wish of the good people of these 19 counties. Furthermore, we, each of us, should dedicate ourselves to the memory of Andy Wright with a new commitment of finishing this job, a job which he was most determined to see come to a positive conclusion.

"After we obtain Statehood, I think it more than fitting to erect a monument to Andy and his dedication to our goals. That will be all of my remarks about this tragedy. After the committee meeting is completed today, I then, and only then, will take questions from the media. Now let's finish up with Acirema."

□ □ □ □ □

THE COMMITTEE FINISHED its agenda and was most pleased with the final product. "That's about it," said Savage. "Remember we all will gather here on Thursday evening to acknowledge your hard work in putting together the Platform. On Thursday afternoon, and only two days late, our Platform of nearly a million copies will be mailed to every registered voter within the 19 counties. In the evening we will symbolically drop one copy in the mail chute here at the Hilton and have a reception to celebrate this first milestone.

"Thank you all for attending today and let's all look forward to coming together on Thursday evening. Good day."

□ □ □ □ □

AFTER BEING GRILLED by the media, Savage was approached by Prescott Daniels and Hoppy Brookman who wanted a few minutes of private time. The three men retired to a fourth-floor suite which Savage Worldwide kept under lease for those who visited the city on company business.

The conversation quickly turned to whom they now were going to support for Governor since Andrew Wright was no longer in the picture. Both men demanded adamantly that Savage take up the slack and become the candidate.

"Both of you fully realize that I can do so much more from the outside. Anyway, I would be betraying what I have already announced and committed to, and that is I would not be a candidate for any office or accept any appointment to any office," he reminded them.

"But the situation has drastically changed and through no fault of yours, ours, or the committee. Circumstances are very different now. The public will understand, and we truly need your leadership," begged Brookman.

"It's out of the question. We've got to move forward with someone else to fill the void. It cannot be me, and that is that" he said with a final certainty.

After another hour or so of haggling back and forth, they finally accepted him at his word. None of the three could think in terms of supporting Haze, not just because he was a Republican, but because of the potential disaster they all assumed would surely come his way. Anyhow, Savage really was angry about the way Haze had treated Wright during the boat visit.

Several ideas were kicked around, and the better one which kept creeping back to the top of the list was committee member Martin Parker, Chairman of the prestigious Law firm of Parker-Adams of Destin. The discussion of his age seemed to be a sticking point among the three, and all agreed that should he be receptive to entering a race they all thought he would probably opt for a run at a United States Senate seat rather than the race for Governor.

It was agreed that Savage would approach him about any interest he might have in either race and offer him the option of his choice.

Prescott Daniels assured both men it certainly would be in his own personal interest, and the interest of the coalition, if he entered the race for one of the U.S. Senate seats since he had already served eight years as Governor of Florida. He was concerned that the voters from the nine Alabama counties which would be joining Acirema might have a problem with someone who had been Governor of Florida for eight years and now wanted to be Governor of Acirema for another eight.

On the other hand Hoppy Brookman was on the fence and could be easily persuaded to go for either the Senate or Governorship. At this time it mattered little to him which office he would seek, and he was more than pleased to have both the financial and personal support of the Savage family with either decision.

The trio continued to kick around several ideas, and all three spoke favorably of and acknowledged their high regards for Cole Williams, President of the University of West Florida, as a possible candidate for one of the three positions. They felt he most likely would have a great interest and certainly would be an attractive candidate.

All decided they would first approach Parker, and if he would become a candidate for either office then Brookman would run for the remaining position and Daniels would enter the race for the second Senate seat.

Savage made some calls and arranged for Parker and his wife, Rose, to meet him and Sheery for a late afternoon dinner the following Sunday at Shagg's near Seaside.

□ □ □ □ □

ON WEDNESDAY MORNING Ray Haze and his attorney, Jobe Patson, left Point Clear and drove to the Cracker Barrel Restaurant on Pine Forrest Road near I-10 for breakfast. Time and again they plowed through questions and answers that surely would be asked by the Feds. After coaxing by his attorney, Haze was convinced that he could face this inquiry with little problem.

Arriving at the Federal Building at five minutes to 10:00, the security officer guided them up the single flight of stairs and directly into the conference room. Haze introduced Patson to the investigators who began immediately with their questions. "Mr. Haze, I see from our phone records that you had called the office and advised our secretary that you would be bringing Mr. Martin Parker to the hearing as your attorney. Were we incorrect in that assumption?"

"No, Sir, you are correct. You see, Mr. Parker is a friend and a member of the Acirema Committee, and I assumed that I would be using his services. After making the call to your office, I talked with Mr. Parker and found that he felt it might be a conflict of interest should he represent me since we both are committee members. It was my mistake by not asking him prior to notifying your office, and I apologize for any trouble it may have caused.

"Mr. Patson will be representing me during today's hearing and in the future should there be a need."

"Very well, Mr. Haze, that is perfectly acceptable. Shall we now continue?"

"Yes, of course," said Jobe Patson, "but first I want to inquire as to the reason for the line of questions posed to my client during his first meeting relative to the death of Mr. Wright. It seems that you folks want Mr. Haze to answer questions about something which he has no information. Is there a reason?"

"Mr. Patson, I assume that you are not trying to influence the line of questions we plan to ask. That is not your intent, is it?"

"I simply am concerned why you are pushing my client relative to facts that may relate to the death of Mr. Wright. I understand that he has testified that he has no knowledge whatsoever about the facts of the accident. Is that not the way you understood his answers?"

"Again, Mr. Patson, as we explained to Mr. Haze previously, we are going to conduct this investigation in accordance with the path we seek to follow. If you or your client has any problem with this line of questioning, so be it. We will eventually get to the bottom of all aspects of Mr. Wright's death as well as any possible participation of your client relative to his relation with the Deep South Group. I suggest we get this meeting underway."

After two hours of questioning, both men left the building and were besieged immediately by the media. They declined to answer all questions except one. Haze commented, "Yes, it is my understanding that Mr. Sidney Kattzs, President of the Deep South Group, will be questioned here at the Federal Building tomorrow morning. That is all I have for you. Good day."

☐ ☐ ☐ ☐ ☐

THE FOLLOWING MORNING AT 9:00, Sidney Kattzs and

three other men, apparently attorneys, did show up as predicted by Haze. It was after 12:30 before they were seen leaving the building, and Kattzs declined to answer any questions posed by the media. However, one of the men who accompanied him, introducing himself as Charles Hampton, an attorney, did offer a statement, ''Mr. Kattzs was pleased to visit with the FBI investigative team that has the responsibilities of looking into several aspects of a number of serious allegations. Mr. Kattzs and other executives of the Deep South Group have pledged their full support to the FBI and will cooperate with the investigation in every area of which they may have any knowledge.''

With that statement the four men hurried into a waiting sedan and sped off without responding to any further questions from the sea of reporters.

□　□　□　□　□

''THANK YOU ALL for coming out this evening,'' said Taylor Savage. ''This is truly an historic occasion. I'm sure you all have reflected, as I have, about this moment being the very first time in the history of our country when a movement of this magnitude has made it this far.

''In years past, I would imagine many has been the time when the various segments of our society have grown weary and wanted to do whatever they could to improve their station in life, but until now we are the only committee to actually take an active movement to this level.

''By tomorrow afternoon thousands of voters will begin to receive their copy of the Platform. And pending the level of the efficiency—Ha! Ha!—of the United States Postal Department, every registered voter should have his or her copy in hand no later than Monday afternoon.

''Before we begin our celebration, I would like to read a letter from one of our members, Ray Haze. Mr. Haze is not with us this evening and asked that I read the following statement which was delivered to my office this afternoon. This is a letter addressed to me as Chairman of the Acirema Committee.

''Dear Mr. Savage and committee members. It is with deep regret that I resign as a member of the committee. This is to become effective immediately. I wish you well and look forward to working with each of you during the months ahead. While time does not permit me to continue with membership on the committee, I will pursue my candidacy to become the first Governor of Acirema. I ask each and every one of you for your vote and support of my candidacy.

"It is signed, Ray Haze, Candidate for Governor."

□　□　□　□　□

THE TWO COUPLES met at four o'clock at Shagg's, one of the fine restaurants in the Seaside area. This was the first time Sheery had met Rose, and the two ladies seemed to hit it off right away. They had a lot in common, and after dinner each detailed her interest in home decorations, remodeling, and restoration work while their men found the right time to excuse themselves and walk outside towards the edge of the shore to consider the question which Savage would pose.

"Martin, you have been such a friend to me and my family and have done so much for the Acirema Platform with your support, comments, and your legal advice. I really want to thank you."

"Taylor, you know that I believe in what you have proposed for Acirema, or I would not have given my support, at least to the degree which I have. And thank you for your compliments of me."

"I've got another favor to ask of you," Savage said, kind of sheepishly.

"Just name it, I'm yours," responded Parker.

"A select few of us want to urge you to run for Governor."

"Whoa! No, no, no. That I cannot do."

"Now, don't be so quick. You know you have every bit of ability, and those who would support you would go to the wall in every way to see that you are successful. We'll raise the dollars. You won't have to concern yourself with finances."

"Taylor, that's just not in the cards, believe me. That just can't happen. I hate to refuse you, but let me beg off of this one. Anything but that."

"Okay, you're off the hook. Now, I have another question."

"I'm scared now. You've shell shocked me. But what could be more shocking than your first question? How could you top that?"

"Would you be more at ease, more comfortable, with a run for a United States Senate seat?''

''Jeez, you did find a more sobering question after all, didn't you? Taylor, I can't. I simply cannot.''

''Martin, we need you in one of these races. We will support you, and you can win. The option, the choice of the race, is yours to make. We truly need your leadership and experience.''

''Taylor, you flatter me, you really do. But can I speak very, very frankly with you? Strictly man to man without it going any further than between you and me?''

''Of course. Whatever you say will not leave this beach. No one will know but us.''

''Thank you. I have a serious medical problem. I just learned of it two days ago. I'm still searching for a way to tell Rose. I had planned on talking with her tonight and probably will. Let's you and I end this conversation with these two words and nothing else. Prostate cancer.''

Would the hurt, the pain, the madness never end, Savage wondered? Did it always have to pour when it rained? The two men turned and walked slowly without speaking a word, back into the restaurant where they rejoined their ladies for coffee and dessert.

When the couples parted, Savage, totally out of character, asked Sheery to drive them home. He sat very somber during the trip, his mind full of negative thoughts. What else could possibly happen, what was lurking in the shadows? First, Andrew Wright. Then Sheery's mother. Now Martin Parker. Who was next? What was next?

□ □ □ □ □

THE FOLLOWING MORNING Savage reported by phone to Daniels and Brookman about his conversation with Martin Parker without divulging their personal secret. The three agreed that Savage should approach Cole Williams to find out about any interest he might have and decided to do so immediately.

Later in the afternoon, the two men met at Savage Worldwide. Williams convinced Savage he was most interested and thanked him for offering support. He was most flattered to be considered, but was not at all certain of his ability to conduct the type of statewide campaign that would be needed to be effective and successful.

Savage knew there was no room for a candidate in any race who was not completely sold on himself, as this was the very first cardinal rule of politics. Williams' comments left little room for discussion, as he could not now change his attitude and suddenly become a new person who possessed all the required traits to become a candidate who could win over the voters and gain their undivided attention, confidence, and support.

Their meeting ended with Williams saying that he wanted a couple of days to think about the offer. With this response Savage knew for sure he was not their man and so stated. Being a man of action, Savage knew there was no time to put off the inevitable.

TWENTY-TWO

SINCE IT WAS ALMOST certain that his name was among those who might be called before the Grand Jury, Ray Haze felt that continuing a quest for the Governorship of Acirema was nothing more than a waste of time and, in all probability, a losing battle. His campaign had already reserved many hours of airtime on both radio and television along with print media space in several publications and most major newspapers. Although no candidate could actually advertise his candidacy until the beginning of the 60-day cycle, it was permissible to reserve such media buys, and Haze, at the urging of Peaches Lamont, did a very wise thing hoping it would curtail others who might be thinking about entering.

With Haze the only Republican candidate in the race with any possibility of being successful, rumors of the grand jury action really put a crimp in the spirits of the Republican Party. While the Republican hierarchy searched frantically to come up with a candidate who could carry their banner, Haze and Peaches were themselves well into announcing their substitute candidate.

After managing and establishing a winning record in many campaigns, Peaches was well versed in exactly what needed to be done and done without delay. There was still ample time to do all the right things, to position and keep a challenger on the front burner, and to scare off any other potential competitors from their own party while concentrating on a formidable battle with the Democratic candidates.

It was most obvious, they both agreed, that something had to be announced to the media right away. Peaches faxed a flyer to all media reps that Haze would hold a news conference the following day at high noon on the Mobile County Court House steps, south side. The media, already in a feeding frenzy, could hardly contain themselves to hear what more he had to say. Everyone believed that he would argue his innocence and ask his political supporters to hold firm until he had an opportunity to prove as false any charges or allegations which may be levied against him.

At the hastily called news conference, Haze again accomplished his goals as usual by springing on his potential political and judicial opponents a set of new circumstances that was way beyond anyone's imagination. "Thank you all for being here today. As we all know the Federal Government and its Grand Jury are once again flexing their muscles. They have issued several subpoenas, and, in all probability, are going to issue some number of indictments before this is over.

"Although I personally have been a subject of interest to those conducting the investigation, I have no concern whatsoever that I will be involved other than as a point of information for their purpose. However, to put to rest any thought of concern by any of my supporters who might question that I may have committed any element of wrongdoing, I have chosen the option of not continuing as a candidate for Governor of Acirema."

The media could not contain themselves. Hands were waving for attention, and everyone wanted to speak at once.

"Hold it just a minute. Please give me a moment to finish my announcement, and I will answer your questions. I promise.

"Thank you. Furthermore, I want to take this opportunity to announce that Peaches Lamont, in a ceremony earlier this morning, became Mrs. Ray Haze.

"The name of Haze has strong political connections across Alabama and North Florida and will continue to play an important political part. Today I would ask all of my loyal, longtime supporters who are already on board my campaign and all of you who love this area and who truly want good, clean government to give strong consideration of support to the candidacy of the first Governor of Acirema...my wife, Peaches Lamont-Haze."

The reporters could not believe their ears or eyes. It was

obvious Haze was pulling a sneaky one. Was this shades of George and Lurleen Wallace all over again? Each reporter immediately wondered just how much power would Ray Haze have if, in fact, his wife was sitting in the Governor's chair. Again Haze quieted the crowd and spoke up. "I would ask you to give Peaches the opportunity to say a few words. Peaches."

"Thank you, Ray. I know that my candidacy is quite a shock to some of you. I am only prepared today to announce my intentions and will hold a formal news conference next Friday at noon. The conference will be held here in Mobile, my home city, at the Holiday Inn on Government Street. At that time I will make a statement, offer my platform for office, and answer any questions you may present. This will be the extent of my comments for now. Thank you."

Dorothy Palmer, a local radio talk show host, insisted on asking a couple of questions, and Peaches, while knowing better, agreed. "Mrs. Haze," asked Palmer, "was your surprise marriage one of convenience and was it for the purpose of entering the campaign with a name which does carry much political recognition and at times also much political baggage?"

"Ma'am, I don't know if you have been following the committee meetings of Acirema or not. However, if you have, then you will read the transcripts where I have insisted that campaigning within the proposed new state be limited to the issues and not involve itself with personal attacks or personal comments. I think that your question is most inappropriate," she responded and began walking away.

"Well, Mrs. Haze, perhaps you can tell us what amount of power your husband will have in any official capacity should you be elected Governor?"

Peaches stopped dead in her tracks and looked the reporter square in the eye. "Everyone of you reporters, and especially you, young lady, need to understand at this very moment there will be no personal comments or questions acknowledged from any member of the media or anyone else for that matter. If you will understand this up front, we can get along. If not, then there will exist a very cold relationship between myself and any media person who tries to break this personal rule of mine."

With that, Peaches and Ray Haze swiftly walked to their van

and sped away. Among the media the talk was about the very tart and stinging candidate for Governor, and they wondered out loud just how long she could possibly think this kind of talk would hold their attention.

□ □ □ □ □

THE MORNING AFTER Mr. and Mrs. Haze made the announcement that Peaches would become a candidate for Governor, Sheery, while walking Savage to his car, asked what time he thought he would be coming home that evening because she wanted a couple of hours of quiet time, explaining she had something to talk with him about, something that was of personal importance to both of them.

Years earlier his father once told him that it was not wise to put off anything that needed discussing. Do it now, get it over with, get it behind you. Adhering to this bit of wisdom, he quickly said that he had time right now. She countered that she would rather do it that evening over a bottle of wine, possibly in front of the fireplace if it was cool enough.

All day Savage concerned himself greatly about what this important matter could possibly be that it required a bottle of wine and a romantic fireplace. Once, while at Harvard, a roommate had received a phone call from a lady friend with much the same message. Savage really was not quite ready for such a surprise.

At the end of a long and tension-filled day, he arrived home to find Sheery preparing some snacks and noticed a bottle of wine being chilled near the hearth. However, only a single paper log was simmering as it was not near cool enough to have a roaring blaze.

"Want to change into something more comfortable. Get out of your blazer and tie?" she asked.

"Yeah, I want to, but I'm more interested in sitting down with you."

He slung his coat over the back of a leopard skin, designer sofa, kicked off his shoes, loosened his tie, popped the cork, and poured just the proper amount of wine in two long-stemmed red glasses, then sat down in "his" chair which faced "her" chair, both centered on the custom-built Tennessee stone fireplace.

"I've got something I want to discuss with you," she said.

"Fine, let's hear it," bracing himself for the worst.

"Can we sit on the sofa? You seem so far from me," she said.

"Certainly," he agreed, as they both moved to the sofa and rested their glasses on the large, square coffee table. From their first date Savage always insisted that she sit on his left and would never explain why. In turn, she always did and never asked for a reason. The only time there ever was an exception was when he was driving a car and she was the passenger.

She continued, "You have been busting your buns for many weeks full time over Acirema. You set aside almost five years of your personal life to perfect the planning stages before making the first announcement."

This really got Taylor's attention and immediately brought him back down to earth where the air was easier to breathe and where he could listen with much more attention. He felt as if he had dodged a bullet.

"Taylor, I am so very proud of you I don't know what to do. Not only are you my boyfriend, lover, and best friend, but you are someone that I truly admire, trust, respect, and adore."

"You are making me blush, Sheery. But I like it when you recognize what I am trying to do. Your being here is enough. It's not necessary for you to say those things."

"Wait, I'm not through. Just wait a minute. Yes, I've been here for you, and I shall continue to be. I want Acirema to succeed as much as you do, if you could visualize that.

"Although I've been at your side, I still don't think that I have contributed as much as I could have, and I want to contribute more, much more," she insisted.

"Honey, what more on earth could you have done or could do that you haven't already done?" he asked shyly.

"Will you please hear me out? Will you listen to what I have to say? Let me find the words and finish, then say whatever you may."

"Of course, please continue. I didn't mean to interrupt you."

They both reached for their glasses and tipped down the first offering. As he did the honors of refilling, she continued. "Okay, here goes. I've had this speech prepared for a week or more. Now, let me see just how it begins. God, am I nervous!"

"Sheery, what in the world could make you so uptight? What

is wrong?''

"Nothing is wrong," she assured him as she left the sofa and began to pace back and forth in front of the fireplace. "Just let me continue," she pleaded. "I'm 38-years old and not a bad-looking broad, huh?''

"You got my attention, all of it," he confessed. "Go ahead, you're on a roll.''

"I'm a college graduate with a degree in political science and earned four years of valuable training as administrative aide for Senator Donner. In addition to my Capitol Hill experience, I have also started my own business, and thus far I have been successful. I consider myself a businesswoman who knows what it means to meet a payroll, and I am fairly well versed in the tax structure of both the federal and state levels of government. I have a tremendous amount of self-respect, poise, pride, and I'm more than self-motivated, a selfsstarter and well read.

"I've been with you for more than two years now, and while I love all the attention and material things you can provide, I am still my own person. While I love you dearly, I am not mesmerized by you, your presence, or your wealth. Like you told your father after graduating from Harvard, you wanted to go into the Navy and get your wings before you would consider joining Savage Worldwide. Then you let him know that you wanted to do something on your own, thus your plan, your own personal plan, for Acirema. I applaud you for your reasoning, your line of thinking, and your independence.

"Not unlike you, I want also to do something on my own. However, what I want to do definitely will require your help and that of many others, and tonight I ask you for your help and as many people as would pitch in to assist. And if I can have both your blessings and assistance, I would be most appreciative.''

Walking over to Savage she looked down at him, took his hand, looked deep into his eyes, and said in a very clear and distinct voice, "Now, to the point of all of this. I want to be the first Governor of Acirema!''

You could have bowled Taylor Savage over with a feather. He sat there staring straight at her and did not speak for what seemed to her an eternity.

"I cannot believe what my ears just heard. Are you serious?''

he asked loudly as he rose from the sofa.

"I've never been as serious about anything in my life. I hope I haven't disappointed you, and please just say what's on your mind. Say it now and get it over with."

"Sheery, I am totally surprised, amazed, astonished, flabbergasted, not to mention very relieved," he answered.

"Relieved about what?" she questioned.

"Oh, nothing. Nothing at all worth discussing," he declared.

"Well, are all those words you just spit out good, positive adjectives, or are you totally disappointed?" she asked with a somewhat inquisitive and trembling voice.

"You know, I cannot believe after putting in countless numbers of hours after hours after hours of planning and planning, and the solution to one of my biggest worries was right here with me. Yes, of course, I'll support you with no equivocations whatsoever. Do you know how good this will be to have you heading the ticket and how important it will be to have you, a well-respected, first-class, beautiful lady working strongly for the referendum? What else could I possibly ask for? We need to make this known as soon as possible—within the Platform rules and regulations, of course.

"Sheery, I couldn't have planned it better myself. You truly upstaged me in every respect. What a great, tremendously great idea," he said as they held each other in a loving embrace.

"I only wish Mom could be here when we make the announcement," she said.

"Yeah, I know, honey, I'm sorry," he assured her as their faces touched lightly while warm tears from her eyes found their way over and around the crest made by their two cheeks.

"You know, I had been thinking of this since we lost Andy Wright, but I didn't know how to approach you with it," she said. "Yesterday when Haze and Peaches made their announcement, I knew if I was going to talk with you, it had to be today. When do you think we should make it public?"

"God, this is such a surprise, I don't know the answer to that at this moment. Let's talk tonight about details, and we'll meet in the morning with my staff and do some planning. Sheery, I am so very proud of you, I am delighted. This adds a very personal dimension to the entire Acirema program.

"But let me make sure that you know exactly what you're getting into. This is a rough business, and the opponents, however many it may turn out to be, will give you pure hell. You do understand this, don't you?"

"Yes, certainly. I know what I am in for, and I can and will go the distance if I know at the end of the stretch you and Acirema will be there."

"I cannot wait until we make the announcement. Can't you just see old Ray and Peaches when they learn. How about a toast?"

□ □ □ □ □

THE NEXT MORNING Savage called his office and told Laura to bring together his inner-circle of top-level executives for a 10:00 o'clock meeting and to have plenty of coffee as it would take a couple of hours. When he and Sheery arrived, a small group of his most trusted executives of the Southeast Division of Savage Worldwide had already found their way into the conference room.

"Good morning," he said while shaking hands with each. "We've got another project to undertake, and we'll need your help."

"You mean another one in addition to Acirema?" asked Andrea Walton, Director of Finance.

"I'm afraid so. However, this one will not be as detailed but just as important. Sheery and I have an announcement to make this morning."

All five executives froze in their seats thinking only one thing, marriage. Savage quickly read the expressions on their faces and immediately recognized that what he had said had been misread. "No, no. Not what you are thinking."

Dilbert Yanks, who had recently transferred from the Dallas office to Pensacola spoke. "Taylor, I have not had the privilege of meeting Sheery although I have heard a lot of nice things about her."

"I'm sorry, Dilbert. Sheery, say hello to Dilbert Yanks who is our Southeastern Director of Operations. He has been with us, how long now Dilbert, perhaps 20 years?"

"In June, it will be 22. My, my, how time flies when you're having fun."

"Dilbert, you haven't seen nothin' yet. Wait until you hear

what we are about to lay on you.

"When I left home yesterday morning, Sheery remarked that she had something she needed to discuss with me when I returned in the evening. Obviously, I was a nervous wreck all day. She said she wanted to do it over a cool bottle of wine in front of the fireplace. Now, if that won't make you fidgety, nothing will.

"To make a long and most interesting story short, it is Sheery's desire to be the first Governor of Acirema, and I, we, will do all we can to see that she is victorious."

What a surprise for everyone! All stood and congratulated her and wished her well, with each pledging his or her personal support and proclaiming this might just be the ticket to put the icing on the cake for Acirema.

"The reason I wanted all of you to come in this meeting was to give us a chance to go around the table, and each of you offer your thoughts and comments pertaining to how the public will react, how the media will react, etc. In effect, I want to create our own in-house think tank and begin to prepare Sheery for some of the more difficult questions that she will surely have to face.

"Why don't we ask some of the questions the media will be asking, and Sheery can respond as if in a real press conference. Who wants to be first?"

"Let me start it off as I have been involved in more than a couple of campaigns," stated Frank Marsh. "A campaign of this sort will have to begin with some deep down soul-searching. We will need to establish right up front that there will be some very tough questions from the media, and you have to know and trust that everyone in this room is your friend and will help guide you through those times. And when we bring up an issue to you, it may seem as though we are picking on you, but what we are really doing is nothing more than preparing you for what is to come.

"We also need to have a complete understanding that we all can speak our minds without hurting anyone's feelings. Again, it is only for the reason of preparing you for what is to surely come from the press and other media. Is this agreeable with all?"

Everyone agreed with a nod of the head, and Sheery added, "I completely understand, and I want all of you to know just how much I appreciate this vote of confidence. I want you all to put me through the paces, and let's, together, come out on top. I want to win this election.''

"Great," continued Frank. "Now let me ask you a question. You are a very beautiful young lady, slender but not frail. You do not seem the type who would seek political office, at least not the top executive office of a state. We often see tough old birds like Janet Reno when we think in terms of women in politics. Are you sure you are up to this challenge? Do you think that you can handle the scrutiny which will be coming your way?''

"First, thanks for the comment, and second the answer is yes. I completely understand politics. During my tenure on Capitol Hill with Senator Donner, much came across my desk, and the pressures were great at times. I know what you mean and have given this much consideration even before I first mentioned it to Taylor.

Harvell Mahan, Director of Personnel, spoke next. "As you know, in my position with the company I am most aware of the comments of a personal nature made by all employees. I can come up with a variety of questions that I think the media will immediately ask.''

"Okay, Harvell, let's take them one at a time. Sheery why don't you respond to each question, and we will offer any constructive criticism we have," Savage suggested.

"All right. Are the two of you living together?'' asked Mahan.

"No. I have a home at Seaside. When we attend functions or have to travel together, we often stay in each other's homes. But my personal residence is at Seaside," she offered.

"And how often do you two share each other's homes? How often do you stay together?''

"Without being rude, let me say right up front that is none of your business. It does not pertain to the issues of this campaign, and I will not answer any questions of a personal nature.''

"That's fine. Do the two of you plan to marry and, if so, any time soon?''

"We have known each other for just over two years. Marriage has not been discussed.''

"Is that all you're going to say about that?''

"That's correct," she responded.

"Okay, let's shift gears. Why do you want to be Governor, and are you qualified to be Governor?''

"I think that I can do a lot for this brand new state. Women today are taking part in the business community and the world of politics more than ever before. I understand the role of Governor and have had experience in the business world. I do not see this position as requiring a lot of experience based on past political knowledge. Today, we are fast moving into a world of electronics and computers, and, right or wrong, we are leaving behind many of the old customs of the past. I am ready to be Governor, and I know I can and will be good for Acirema."

The questions and answers went on for almost two hours. All were satisfied with her answers and knew for certain that she could face the press and handle herself accordingly. After a lengthy discussion, it was agreed that a news conference would be called by Savage on Friday, and nothing would be revealed to anyone until that time. The conference would be at the Pensacola Hilton and would be held one hour before Mrs. Haze was scheduled to meet with reporters in Mobile.

□   □   □   □   □

LAURA RINGS HAD faxed a press release notifying the media that Taylor Savage would have an important announcement to make on Friday at 11:00 A.M. at the Hilton. With all the action and speculation about the grand jury, plus the continuing advancement of the Acirema movement, the media was not sure what else could be so important.

For the purpose of the conference and to water down preconceived ideas, Savage brought his upper management group along to accompany him and Sheery. This would give the appearance of a cadre of well-dressed, highly intelligent, and polite individuals who would apparently be the staff behind the candidate.

Laura had arranged with the hotel to have the room partitions opened to accommodate the large number of reporters and their equipment. The front table was set up with seven chairs and a podium centered midway.

Savage opened the meeting. "Good morning. We are back once again. Let me report to you that we have had tremendous response from the citizens who have received their copy of our Platform. It was necessary that we set up a battery of phone lines and operators to answer some of the questions although most were of a minor nature. Those who called apparently were satisfied with the answers we provided, and we expect to carry the Statehood vote by a very respectable margin on August 5th.

"We all have been surprised concerning the recent news about the Federal Grand Jury actions. I bring this up now and indicate to you that I personally will not address any questions which deal with individuals who may or may not have been called before that body. Please do not ask me to indulge in answers to questions where I really have no answers in the first place.

"Today I am here with these ladies and gentlemen pertaining to the Governorship of Acirema. As we all know, Mrs. Haze will be addressing the media in Mobile in about an hour from now. She has already become a candidate for governor, and we wish her well.

"We have no idea who else may jump into this race, and, quite frankly, we could not care less because this morning I am going to make known the candidate whom I will support to be the first Governor of Acirema. This person is someone who is dedicated to seeing that Acirema gets off the ground with a good, solid foundation. Someone who thinks good, clean government should be the order of business from the day Acirema draws it first breath. Someone who can be trusted. Someone whose word you can carry to the bank. Someone who indeed will be good for Acirema.

"Ladies and gentlemen of the media, let me introduce to you the first Governor of Acirema, Sheery Goss."

As she stood the media scampered in every direction to take pictures and place their cameras in her face. Savage let this continue for a couple of minutes and then suggested she make a few comments.

"Good morning," she said in her smooth Southern voice. "Yes, I want to be the first Governor of Acirema, and I will campaign for that position full time within the boundaries of the 60-day politicking cycle as noted in the Acirema Platform. I am much aware that the deadline for all who may seek office is not until September 25, although I cannot politic until the start of the 60-day cycle, nothing prevents me from announcing early that I intend to be a candidate.

"You all know that Mrs. Haze has entered the race. I welcome her candidacy and wish her well as I would all others who may wish to throw their hats into the ring.

"Rather than give you a long speech this morning, why don't I do something different and let you ask your questions. Surely, through this process you can find out much more about me than I could ever tell you. Who wants to be first?"

Immediately everyone tried to speak at once. "Hold on. Wait just a minute. I am not sure of each of your names, so until I learn to match a name with a face, why don't you permit me today to perhaps point to each of you, and I'll address your questions as asked. Okay, the lady in the blue dress."

"My first question is, and the question that I am sure everyone is waiting for an answer, who are you?"

"Well, that's a fair question," Sheery responded. "I am a resident of Seaside in Walton County. I am single and 38 years of age. I was born in Goldsboro, North Carolina, and I am a graduate of The University of North Carolina with a political science degree. Recently I have moved to Seaside, and before that I lived the previous four years on Amelia Island."

"Ms. Goss, have you ever held public office before?"

"No. But there is much precedence concerning that issue. Right here in Florida you had a candidate for Governor last time who had never held public office, and he came darn near unseating the incumbent. I see this as no big obstacle, and perhaps you have noticed that Ray Haze has twice sought the governorship of Alabama, and to this day he still has never held public office."

"Without a track record, how can we of the media have any possible idea of your credentials and capabilities to run a state government without any previous elected experience of any sort?"

"Acirema is going to be a brand new state with a brand new state government composed of new ideas, new means of accomplishing new goals, and a head of state who will have the ability to lead its citizens into the next century. Look around you at the stories that are currently flooding the news. I personally feel it is an advantage for me and my campaign inasmuch as the people who will be voting for a Governor can be assured I am not tainted in the least.

"Let me turn the table for a second and ask you a question. Would you want one of those who is being questioned by the

Federal Grand Jury to be the top executive officer of your state?''

Another reporter asked, ''And what qualifications do you possess that makes you worthy of being considered a candidate for Governor, and why do you want to become Acirema's first Governor?''

''I am obviously over 21 years of age which makes me eligible. I have a college degree in political science. I had four years of hands-on political experience on Capitol Hill in D.C. working in the office of Senator Mark Donner of North Carolina. I am half owner of a business with my associate, Darlene. The name of our company is Ess-Dee's, and we are interior decorators—and the business is very successful. I have a burning desire to see that Acirema gets off the ground in the proper fashion, and I intend to be at the helm when the doors open.

''Certainly, all of you understand just what a great opportunity we have right here in the center of what will become the 51st state of our Union. What Taylor Savage has envisioned is a state that will be the cream of the crop, so to speak. Like taking the heart from a melon, we are getting the very best of all worlds.

''We have a great coastline which, without question, has the most beautiful beaches in the world as well as great shipping ports. There are vast farm lands and farming communities, and it goes to say we have the best, down-to-earth, God-fearing families that any community could ask for. We do not have the influx of foreigners to contend with as does South Florida, nor do we have their massive overcrowding.

''Crime is lower in this section of these two states than anywhere else within all of Florida and Alabama. And it is our intent to see that we offer our citizens a place as crime free as we possibly can make it in which to raise our families and conduct our businesses. On the upper Gulf Coast, we are blessed with a great deep water fishing industry, and our lakes and streams are clean. We do not lack for potable water as do some sections of the country.

''Perhaps this answers your question as to my qualifications and the many reasons I want to be a part of this gigantic undertaking. I can and will do the job.''

''And what can we expect in the way of a personal platform of yours? What will it entail?''

"Thank you for the question. You know, I could spend a good deal of my time working up a special platform or at least changing some words from the Platform we just mailed to all the potential new citizens of Acirema, but why should I do that? I subscribe totally to the Platform as written for the development of Acirema, and thus far there would be no significant changes that I would suggest."

"By that I have to assume you totally agree with every aspect of the Acirema Platform. Is that correct?" a reporter inquired.

"By and large that is correct. You are right. However, there may be a couple of small differences and perhaps one major difference. One which I am studying and hope to work out."

"And could you detail the major one about which you speak?"

"Without question I would like to see Acirema become self-sufficient and not have to depend on Federal tax dollars and likewise avoid sending any of our tax money to Washington. However, I have yet to prove to my personal satisfaction that this is absolutely possible. I can, however, assure every citizen of Acirema that will be a goal which will have my full attention, and we will work day and night to posture ourselves in a position where we will not have to depend on Washington and federal taxes.

"We simply do not need Big Brother looking over our shoulders, and to shut the door on him and keep him at a distance will be our goal.

"I was reading just this week where the Mayor of a small city in California made a remark something like this, 'Government should stay out of people's faces, but you can accomplish that only to a degree as you have to have a social structure, now that everything has become so regulated and politicians love regulating. That's part of the whole power structure.' In Acirema we intend to correct that attitude.

"As I just explained, there is only one major aspect of the Platform which I have questioned, but on the other hand the remainder of the planks of the Platform I absolutely agree without any question or difference of opinion whatsoever. One of the planks pertains to the death penalty and capital punishment. I will not hesitate as Governor to sign as many death warrants as necessary to assure our citizens that we intend to make Acirema the safest state of the Union. Any criminal who commits a capital offense within our state will surely have to pay for his crime and do so at an early date.

"It will be my position to become personally active relative to any Judge or Justice of our Acirema Courts who tries to stand in the way of or slow down the legal process of capital punishment.

"Recently, I have watched the Governor, Cabinet, and other officials of Florida hunker down under the dictates of our own Supreme Court when it issued rulings to release thousands of hardened criminals to walk the streets of this state. I see no reason why the Governor and other elected officials who are in leadership positions within this state are not still fighting the release of those hoodlums. One of the core purposes of any state government is to be concerned for the protection and safety of its citizens. The Governor has simply shirked his duties. This I cannot and will not permit or accept as Governor of Acirema."

"So by your remarks, are we to assume that you would fight your state's Supreme Court if such happened on your watch?"

"Without question, and you can chisel that in stone and while doing so you can include the United States Supreme Court as well. I can think of nothing more important than the protection of our people.

"And while we are speaking about courts, judges, and justices, let me tell you that I am totally in favor of the election of all judges, including those on the Supreme, Appellate, Circuit, and County courts. In Florida some are appointed by the Governor, but I firmly believe that those who are allowed to dictate so much of our lives should be hired by the people in the same manner as is our legislative body."

"Okay, let's change the subject," said another print media reporter. "What about Mrs. Haze entering the race. What do you think about that?"

"As I said previously, she is most welcome. She, as well as anyone else, can run for any office. I have no other comment on that subject at this time nor will I revisit the subject in the future."

"Ms. Goss, I would like to know about the relationship between you and Mr. Savage," asked a reporter holding a channel 9 mike.

"Sir, my relationship with Mr. Savage is not germane to the

purpose of this news conference. It also has no bearing on my candidacy whatsoever. Next question, please."

"I would like a follow-up to my question if you don't mind. Why is your relationship with Taylor Savage not germane in your opinion?"

"I have already answered that, and I will not continue with that line of questioning. If there are no other questions, we can conclude this conference."

"Yes, Ma'am. I think there are many more questions, and as far as I am concerned you are certainly within your rights to place your personal life outside the realm of this political race," stated a print media correspondent. "However, I would have another question which is germane. What is your opinion of the possibility of Acirema actually being granted Statehood?"

"Well, while not trying to be amusing, I would have to answer your question with a question. Do you think that I would be standing here announcing my candidacy for Governor had I any thought Acirema would not become our 51st state?"

"Does that answer mean that you will be working actively to assure that Acirema gains Statehood? Will you give speeches across the 19 counties in support of the Platform and the program in general?"

"You can count on that. I will do everything I possibly can to accomplish the goals which have been outlined by Taylor Savage."

"Okay, that's a fair answer. Now let me ask you this. What problems do you foresee between Florida and Alabama working with Acirema should it become a state?"

"It would be nice to think there will be none. However, that is just wishful thinking, I'm sure. It is my understanding that both Governor Woods and Governor Foxworth have pledged their support toward a smooth transition should the referendum pass on August 5th. On the other hand, they have vowed to fight the referendum issue tooth and toenail in hopes that it fails. I cannot blame them for that attitude as they properly should represent the remaining balance of their respective states," she answered.

"Within 10 minutes or so, Peaches Haze will be holding a news conference in Mobile. What do you expect her to say pertaining to your news release of this hour?"

"No comment."

"What do you mean, no comment. Don't you have any answer to that question?"

"I hope each of you will learn that when I answer a question, as I already have, I will not revisit it. Again, and final, let me tell each of you that anyone who wishes to get into any political race should make that decision for himself or herself. It does not concern me, and I will not continue to waste any time answering questions pertaining to that subject."

"Ma'am, I want to again ask you a question about Taylor Savage. One that is most certainly germane. Assuming for a moment that you are elected Governor of Acirema, then what role would Taylor Savage play in your Administration?"

"Sir, if you have followed the Acirema committee meetings or have read any newspaper accounts, listened to any radio talk shows, or. watched any television stories, you would certainly know that Mr. Savage has said time and time again that he would not be a candidate for any office or accept any appointment should one be offered. Does that answer your question?"

"Somewhat, but will he play a part in your Administration should you be elected?"

"You can be assured I will be calling on him in the same capacity as I will call on several others who could lend input and direction to our Administration."

"Thank you, Ms. Goss."

"Okay, are there any other questions?"

"Yes, I would like to know if you are a registered Democrat or a Republican?" asked an AP reporter.

"I am a Democrat, and I will be entering this race as a Democrat."

□   □   □   □   □

WITH THAT QUESTION the news conference was concluded. Sheery, Taylor, and his staff hurried back to his office at Savage Worldwide and tuned into the CBS affiliate in Mobile to listen to what Mrs. Haze had to say.

TWENTY-THREE

RIGHT ON CUE, PEACHES Lamont-Haze and Ray entered
the crowded conference room. She had called the hotel earlier and
arranged to have the meeting moved from the ballroom into a
smaller room so it would appear there was a greater crowd, a well-
used political trick she had learned many years ago. Knowing that
she would be besieged by reporters inquiring about Sheery's
announcement just an hour earlier, she had prepared herself well
and was ready for whatever might be thrown at her.

Since Ray had made a formal introduction a couple of days
earlier, it was not necessary to do so again. "Thank you all for
attending. We have already had a morning full of excitement, and
I can assure you it is just beginning.

"My assistant, Dorris Fé, will pass out a written platform and
policy statement that will be the backbone of my position papers.
It is my intent to run a positive campaign based on the issues that
are important to those who will be living in Acirema. We will not
deal with mud-slinging or name-calling in any manner, so let me
get that out front and on the top burner immediately.

"I could not care less about any other candidate who may enter
the race or what his or her personal or political stance on the issues
may be. I will be conducting this campaign in an appropriate
manner without regard to what any other candidate may do or say.
If you will take the information which I have prepared back to
your office and study my position papers, I am sure you will have
full knowledge of where this candidate stands on every major

325

issue.

"Now let me address your questions."

"Mrs. Haze, I have a couple of questions," responded a young man wearing a Grateful Dead loose-fitting tee shirt. "What name will you be using? Ms. Haze? Mrs. Peaches Haze? Just what name?"

"That one is easy. My birth name is Patricia Anne Lamont. For years my friends have called me Peaches. Since I am now married to Ray Haze, I choose to be called 'Peaches Lamont-Haze.' Now, let me ask a question of you. Are you a reporter, and if so what organization do you represent?"

"I am the editor of a gay paper that we call *Our Choice*. Do you resent my attendance today? Do you wish that I would leave? Does my being gay bother you?" he shot back.

"You are as welcome as all the others. You simply seemed to be dressed somewhat differently, and I wanted to know if you were a reporter or not."

"Can't a reporter dress as he wishes? Do you favor a dress code for the media?" he insisted.

"No, no. Look, let's not start this. Let's not continue with this line of questioning. You are most welcome. Are there other questions from anyone?"

"Yes, did you watch the news conference earlier when Sheery Goss announced her candidacy?" asked a middle-aged reporter from a local station.

"Sure did."

"Any other comment?"

"No."

"You mean you have no comment about her entering the race?"

"I have no comment about any other candidate. Period. As I said just seconds ago, I will run my campaign, and they can run theirs. I believe that is the same answer which Sheery gave earlier this morning. That's a good answer for the both of us. However, I would warn you about any candidate who might try to make the people believe he, or she in this instance, has the market cornered as the Southern distributor for integrity."

"Mrs. Lamont-Haze, let's look a bit into the future. What would be your position should Ray Haze be indicted by the Grand

Jury?''

"What do you mean, 'my position'?'' she inquired.

"I mean he is your husband, and I would like to know if you will stand by him under such circumstances? That's not a difficult question to answer.''

"Of course, I will. Haven't you heard in America that everyone is considered innocent until proven guilty? Does that ring a bell with you?'' she answered tartly.

"Certainly, it does. However, how can you actively participate in a political campaign that I assume will be based on honesty and integrity in government, if in fact, your husband has been indicted by the Grand Jury?''

"You seem to be assuming a great deal. To be indicted does not mean guilty.''

"Yes, ma'am, I understand that, but if he is indicted, will he continue to be making campaign stops with you, promoting your candidacy and your position on honesty and integrity in government?''

"That will be his decision. You will have to speak with him about that.''

"And Mrs. Lamont-Haze, will you abide by the Platform of Acirema which details the limitation on campaign contributions for all candidates, or will you think it permissible for Mr. Haze to contribute funds in your behalf?''

"Look, I have been in several campaigns, and not once have I ever heard of the candidate or the candidate's family not contributing personal funds,'' she stated.

"And you think those funds could be accepted in addition to the limitation placed on all candidates above and beyond the agreed platform limits?'' he pressed.

"I personally would see no reason they should not be perfectly acceptable,'' she preached.

"And Mrs. Lamont-Haze, should Mr. Haze be indicted by the Grand Jury, would you then return to him any funds which he may have contributed to your campaign?''

"Hey, I think we are getting off the track, don't you?''

"No, ma'am, I don't and would like an answer to my question, if you will?''

"I will be glad to answer your question. I would keep any

contributions he may contribute to his wife who just happens to be a candidate for Governor. Does that answer satisfy you?''

''Yes, so are we to understand that you will travel across the 19 counties gladly boasting about your full campaign chest of which a large part was given by a person who is under indictment by the Grand Jury. Is this what we are to believe?''

''If you would like to put it that way, that's your decision,'' she answered. ''I'll take only one more question.''

''Will you endorse your Republican opponent should he or she beat you in the primary election?''

''Yes. And I trust that my opponent would endorse me should I prevail,'' she assured.

''Please give me a final follow-up question. Mrs. Lamont-Haze, I have attended several Acirema committee meetings, and if I'm not mistaken, you are a committee member. Is that correct?''

''This is true.''

''And have you missed any meetings or attended all?''

''I have been able to attend each meeting and all committee meetings which were called. Why do you ask? What is your question?''

''It is my understanding, but I will go back and check the minutes of the meetings. However, I understood the Platform to state in this first election there would be no runoffs, and the candidate who leads the ticket of each major party would automatically be in the general election. Is that how you remember it?''

''You may be right. I'll also have to check the Platform.''

''Then you're telling us that you are qualifying as a candidate for Governor and do not even know if you will or will not have to conduct a run-off campaign to reach the general election?''

''I'll get back with you on that. This will conclude this press conference. If you have any more questions, please contact Dorris Fé and she will prepare the proper response. Thanks for being here. Have a good day.''

Returning to their suite of rooms on the fifth floor, which would serve as her campaign headquarters, she was livid, steaming, hot under the collar. No sooner than the door closed, she began, ''Damn you, Ray Haze. The press is already all over my ass just because of the stupid things that you did. Not me. You. I am not going through this campaign when at every stop I'm going to be asked about your crap.''

''Whoa. Whoa, right there. You know this marriage can be undone just as easy as it was done. I ain't going to be talked to like that, and you need to get that through your thick skull right now. You hear me, woman?''

''Well, for sure something has got to give. I cannot run a campaign with your political baggage that may drag me down. What do you suggest?'' she screamed at him.

''What I suggest right now is that you go to hell while I go back to Point Clear. That's what I suggest.''

BY THE END OF THE day both press conferences had given the media much to ponder over the weekend. While the Saturday morning papers mentioned the stories but detailed little, the Sunday editions of every major paper in Florida and Alabama devoted several pages to these two ladies who were seeking the Governorship as well as the intriguing goings-on of the Grand Jury including several speculations about things which might occur in the very near future.

BY MONDAY MORNING things were beginning to hop around the Federal Building. With each new day, more and more speculation appeared in print and on all television and radio talk shows.

Sue Upton, finance director for the last two campaigns of Governor Woods, began to have some deep personal concerns for her own well-being pertaining to any part that she might have played without having any knowledge one way or the other concerning unlawful or possible illegal contributions. She had made one mistake, but hadn't decided if she would report it or not. Although it bothered her, she had mixed feelings about disclosing it to anyone as she was almost certain nobody else knew.

She called in sick so that she could have the day to herself to mull over the situation and think about what she really needed to do. Needing to get away from it all, she drove down to St. Marks, perhaps 30 minutes due south from Tallahassee, to have lunch and a couple of beers at Posey's, a local restaurant with a long-standing tradition of offering a fine selection of great seafood dishes and a perfect spot to linger and reflect on personal problems.

After lunch, she walked the waterfront docks for a couple of hours, beer in hand. Commercial boats unloaded their catch-of-the-day, while pleasure crafts with families just enjoyed a day of leisure on the river, soaking up the fantastic weather. Nearing 5:00 o'clock she had finally decided to call the authorities and request a time and place where she could come to give a personal statement.

With Pensacola being in the Central Time zone, she knew she had another hour. Making use of a pay phone just outside Posey's, she dialed long distance information and then the FBI. A secretary quickly determined whom she needed to speak with and transferred her call to Agent Adams.

"Good afternoon, this is Special Agent Carl Adams. How can I help you, Ms. Upton?" he asked smoothly.

"Mr. Adams I think that perhaps I need to come in and have a conference with you or whoever is looking into the case concerning the Deep South Group," she volunteered.

"I assume you feel that you might have information which would be germane to our investigation. Is that correct?"

"I'm not sure. However, I am concerned that I personally may be involved somehow, someway, and I just need to talk with someone. I just want to clear the air, so to speak."

"When would you like to come in?"

"I forgot to tell you that I live in Tallahassee, but I could drive over in the morning. Would that work for you folks?"

"We will make it fit our schedule. How about 11:00? Considering the hour you gain driving this way, it should be a comfortable time frame for you. Is that good for you?"

"Sure, that'll work. Where should I meet you?"

"Just come to the Federal Building on Palafox right in downtown Pensacola. We are on the second floor. Joining me in the meeting will be Agent Wilton and Agent Hartfield. I will advise security to be expecting you a few minutes before 11:00."

"Sure. I'll see you in the morning. Goodbye."

"Goodbye, Ms. Upton, and have a safe drive over."

She walked back into Posey's and ordered another Miller Light, lit up a menthol filter tip, then drifted to the rear of the building through a swinging door opening onto an outside patio. She leaned heavily with both arms on the badly worn wooden railing and stared down at the swift-moving current. Had she made a mistake about calling the Feds, she wondered? Was volunteering information to the FBI what she should have done? Unanswered questions kept taxing her mental capacity. Was she right or wrong in her approach? Who could she talk to? Whom should she talk to?

Driving back into Tallahassee, she kicked around the thought of calling Melvin Cooper. Or maybe she should talk with Governor Woods before going to the Feds. There were a million details, and she kept thinking the number one thing to do was to take care of herself. She knew that she had done nothing wrong, and, if she had, it was only because she was following orders from her superior. Was that a crime?

She tossed and turned all night. The alarm went off at the appointed time, and with very little rest she hit the floor but was still much concerned about this being the proper thing to do.

□ □ □ □ □

IN HER BRIGHT RED Mustang convertible she eased down Gregory Street and turned south as had been advised. She could not miss the Federal Building on her immediate left.

"Good morning, Ms. Upton. I'm Agent Adams. These men are Agent Wilton and Agent Hartfield. We appreciate your appearance here this morning. The three of us were quite surprised to receive your call yesterday, but rest assured we are most eager to have your statement. Would you care for a cup of coffee or a cold drink?"

"No, thank you. I've had all I need for awhile."

"Okay, fine. Then shall we begin?"

"Yes, Sir."

"Ms. Upton, your statement and our questions are being electronically recorded. Do you understand this?"

"Yes, Sir."

"Okay, for the record please state your name, occupation,

address, and phone number."

"My name is Jerrie Sue Upton. I am known as Sue Upton. I am the comptroller for Mavis Automotive Company in Tallahassee. I live in the State House Apartments, number 106. My phone is 904-555-1533."

"Thank you, Ms. Upton. Now, why don't you just sit back, relax, and tell us what you came to talk about."

"Yes, Sir. Obviously, everyone knows of the Federal Grand Jury's actions and those who have already been called to appear. It is thought, according to media reports, that others may also be called to testify. I feel that I have some information which could be helpful, some information which may have been overlooked by the U.S. Attorney and his investigative staff."

"And does this information involve your employment at Mavis Motors in Tallahassee?" asked Agent Wilton.

"No, Sir," she responded. "It involves my part-time employment as campaign financial director for the two Gubernatorial campaigns of Governor Brandon Woods."

"Okay, please continue."

"I am personally concerned that someone might consider my position as finance director of these campaigns to have some criminal intent on my part. I have done nothing wrong and have nothing to hide, thus my appearance here today. However, while I was employed in that part-time capacity, I did learn of some facts and information that possibly should come to light.

"Since reading about all the charges that have been exposed in the papers, I felt I needed to let you know some additional facts. The reelection campaign of Governor Woods included campaign contributions in the vicinity of a quarter million dollars that came to us from employees of the Deep South Group. I know for a fact these dollars were laundered by DSG and originated as cash funds which were sent to Deep South by those associated with the coal industry."

"Let me interrupt you for a moment, Ms. Upton," said Agent Adams. "You just said a phrase, 'came to us.' Who is 'us,' and are you referring to the campaign when you said 'to us'?"

"Yes, Sir. I am referring to the campaign in that respect."

"Now, did Governor Woods know about the circumstances that you just described?"

"For the longest time I was almost certain that he did not. However, since the death of Mr. Wright, he asked both Mr. Cooper and me to dig through files to calculate the actual amount that was received from employees of Deep South. I now have no doubt that Governor Woods knew exactly what had been going on pertaining to these contributions."

"How did you come to know the full story? Did the funds come directly to your attention? Directly to your desk, so to speak?"

"No, Sir. They were given to me by Melvin Cooper, and I was told to list them as contributions in accordance with the name and address on each of the checks."

"And for the record, Ms. Upton, please tell us who Melvin Cooper is."

"Melvin Cooper is an independent lobbyist, but during the time frame of which I am speaking he was the paid campaign director for Governor Woods' reelection campaign. Previously, he had served in the same position when the Governor was first elected four years earlier."

"So, Melvin Cooper delivered the checks to you. Is that correct?"

"Yes, Sir."

"And what evidence would you have that Mr. Cooper had any earthly idea or knowledge about the origination of these funds?"

"Well, about midway through the reelection campaign, I made a comment to Melvin, uh, I mean Mr. Cooper, that the bundle of checks he had last given me were all in the same amount, $2,000 each. We often got contributions of that amount, but never that many at the exact same time.

"He told me each was from an employee of Deep South, and they often gave similar contributions to several major campaigns. When I continued with my questions, noting there were at least 142 checks in that amount and wondered out loud just how could so many folks afford such large contributions, I was told it really did not cost the employees anything.

"Mr. Cooper explained to me these contributions were being covered by the coal industry cartel, and each Deep South employee was reimbursed for his check. I later learned that executives of Deep South had given each family $5,000 in cash; then both the husband and the wife wrote a separate check to Governor Woods' campaign for $2,000 each, and they kept the balance of $1,000 for their trouble.

"During the reelection campaign we had a situation come up that really concerned Mr. Cooper. One of the contributors apparently thought he had found a way to gain financially himself. Both he and his wife called the campaign headquarters and told me they had decided not to support the Governor and they wanted their contributions reimbursed.

"Since I knew how the funds had originated in the first place, it was not hard to understand they were in a position to spill the beans if we did not return the value of their check. Mr. Cooper was quite concerned to think what may happen if a number of the contributors started a rush on the funds."

"And, Ms. Upton, did you return the check to the contributor?"

"The checks, all of them, had been deposited. I was told by Mr. Cooper that we did return the value of the contributions. However, I personally was not the one to do it. I assume he did."

"And did any other employees of the Deep South Group ask that their contributions be returned?"

"No. I was told, again by Mr. Cooper, that he had solved that problem, and we would not have to be concerned with others asking for their donations to be returned."

"Do you know how he 'solved the problem,' so to speak?"

"Mr. Cooper told me that he discussed it with Mr. Kattzs, and there would be no more difficulty. No one else would ask for his donation to be returned."

"What more can you tell us, Ms. Upton?" asked Agent Wilton.

"That's about it. I have been very concerned about my personal part in this situation, and I thought that I should bring this to your attention."

"Let me ask you about the first campaign," said Agent Walton. "Do you have knowledge that contributions were made to Governor Woods' first campaign in a similar manner as you have described concerning his reelection campaign?"

"One time I distinctly remember that a number of checks came to me in a folder, all of which were for $2500 each. These also were handed to me by Mr. Cooper. I thought little about it since this was my very first political campaign; perhaps something was going on back then about which I had no knowledge. I just don't know."

"Is that all? You have anything more to offer?"

"No, Sir. That's about it."

"Again, thank you very much for your comments. We really appreciate your help and your attitude. For the time being we would ask that you keep this conversation to yourself. Is that agreeable?" questioned Agent Adams.

"Most certainly, whatever you say."

"If you have nothing more to add, then you are free to go, Ms. Upton. And again, thank you."

The three agents walked her to the elevator, and while they waited, she spoke again. "There is something else. One more thing that I want to tell you."

Returning to the conference room, she again sat facing all three federal agents and began to weep.

"Would you like a glass of water?" asked Agent Hartfield, handing her his handkerchief.

"Yes, Sir. Please."

"Would you like a few minutes to gather your thoughts?"

"No, Sir. Let me get this over with. During the last campaign one of the checks which came in the large stack of checks that was handed to me by Mr. Cooper was dated, signed, and made out for $2,000. It did not include the name of the campaign, no payee listed at all. I was working full time at Mavis and doing this campaign job on the side. I hardly could make ends meet. I took the check, put my own name on it, and deposited it in my personal account. I knew it was wrong, but I was up against the wall and decided to take the chance."

"Was it ever revealed? Did anyone ever find out that you took the funds for your own personal use?"

"No, Sir. Not yet."

"And how did you cover the account?"

"It was simple. As I said, many of the checks came from both a husband and a wife in the same family. I only deposited the check from a Mr. David Shue, and the one from his wife was the one I deposited in my personal account.

"We had a routine where the governor would personally sign a thank-you letter to each contributor. When I wrote the letter for the checks from the Shues, I simply wrote one letter to Mr. and Mrs. Shue, not one for each check. We had made it a rule not to mention the amount of the contributions in any letter, so upon receiving our letter I assume they thought both checks had been used in the campaign.''

''And they never found out? They never called you on it?''

''No, Sir. I guess after the check cleared the bank, perhaps she never looked to see what name was typed in. The check from Mr. Shue was typed, so I typed my name in as payee on hers. Nothing was ever said about it.''

''Is there anything more, Ms. Upton?''

''No, Sir. That is all. Am I in bad trouble?''

''Well, we will make this a part of our investigation, but I won't comment any further than that,'' answered Agent Adams.

□ □ □ □ □

SHE BADE THE agents goodbye, then Agent Hartfield walked her to the elevator. Returning, he and the other agents began going over the facts and this new wrinkle. With the interviews of Taylor Savage, Ray Haze, Sidney Kattzs, and now Sue Upton complete, they knew they had strong and sufficient evidence to present to the Grand Jury.

□ □ □ □ □

ONLY 10 DAYS after Lady Goss and Lady Lamont-Haze threw their bonnets into the political ring, every front page headline in all the papers and the lead story on every news network carried the same message: ''Several Politicians and Executives to be called before the Federal Grand Jury.''

After six weeks of extensive investigative work by the FBI and other Federal authorities, the U.S. Attorney for the Northern District of Florida and the one for the Southern District of Alabama had issued more than two dozen subpoenas in what appeared to be a widespread dragnet designed to get at the core of two possible murders as well as possible political corruption involving several top ranking executives, elected officials, and some candidates for high office.

Among those summoned by the Grand Jury were Sidney Kattzs, President of the Deep South Group, along with several executives of DSGK's subsidiaries, including the Presidents of Regions Power, Volunteer Power, Mid-South Power, Delta Power, Peach State Power, and Sunshine Power.

Other notables called included Governor Brandon Woods of Florida and his former campaign manager, Melvin Cooper, Alabama Governor Lance Foxworth, and former Alabama gubernatorial candidate Ray Haze and his new wife Peaches Lamont-Haze. Many other lesser-known political figures were expected to be called later.

It was also reported that another list, several pages long, would be released the next day which would contain the names of hundreds of individuals who were employees of the Deep South Group or one of its subsidiaries. It was thought the list would contain the names of those employees who had made political campaign contributions to various candidates. It was expected these people would also be called before the Grand Jury in the coming weeks.

□　□　□　□　□

THE VOTERS THROUGHOUT the 19 counties received their personal copy of the Platform and eagerly awaited an opportunity to attend the six Public Hearings that had been scheduled. The first was to be held on May 21st and, thereafter, each Tuesday through June 25th. Taylor Savage and the entire committee, with no exceptions, attended each hearing, strategically scattered across the entire width and breadth of what might soon become Acirema. Every gathering was well-attended, and the press could not believe their eyes and ears as to the positive acceptance the crowds gave at every event. Even the protest group organized by Hazel Chestnut had dried up.

Of the many issues that were to be made part of Acirema, the only one which gave the committee any problem was the issue of gambling and casinos. The issue was put to rest during the third hearing when the committee members decided they would not consider discussing any further the possibility of taking in the area of Mississippi that had been offered by the Mississippi Governor and the state's two United States Senators. Acirema simply did not want anything to do with gambling, especially those wretched floating gambling boats.

After the committee sat through the first three extra-long hearings and answered questions of many individuals, several civic clubs, and business groups, they were convinced more than ever the referendum would pass overwhelmingly.

A week after the second hearing, a joint effort by Governor Woods and Governor Foxworth to rally support for the anti-Acirema movement failed miserably. These two powerful Southern Governors held their only scheduled hearing at the Pensacola Civic Center in anticipation of an over-flow crowd. However, if you counted the media and the staff members of each Governor's organization, there may have been just over 200 people in attendance.

A poll conducted by the Savage group immediately after that hearing indicated the points in Acirema's favor exceeded their previous high mark and was nearing the 80 percent level. Political pollsters across the country all proclaimed that any social movement of this nature which could attract such high positive numbers was absolutely magnificent, and the chances for its passage were almost without question.

□ □ □ □ □

INSIDE THE FAMILY quarters of the White House, the President and three of his political advisors were finishing lunch and were in deep discussion about just how well the Acirema movement was going. "I'll bet you the referendum passes by better than 80 percent," said the Chief Executive.

"No, no, Mr. President. Not that much. I see it passing, but never by 80 points."

"And why not? What's going to keep the numbers down? There is not one reason for those folks, more than a million four hundred thousand, not accepting the program that Savage has prepared for them. It's a godsend. Why on earth wouldn't they take advantage of it?" he insisted.

"Mr. President, have you given much attention to that Grand Jury action? Have you seen the list of all the folks who have been called? It's going to create real havoc in both states."

"Yeah, it will, you're right. But guess what? Mr. Taylor Savage is going to reap all the benefits, you just wait and see. He could not have it any better. My reports indicate that those two

dumb, backwoods Governors have thrown their position to the
wind. They can't even begin to draw a crowd. This should be a
real lesson about the politics of the past and where the country is
headed in the future, the immediate future. Savage is onto
something that not only is going to reshape Florida and Alabama
but also will rock the establishment around the entire country.
You mark my word.''

"Perhaps you are right, Mr. President. What will be your
comments to the press as the date for the referendum nears?''

"Look, I'm going to be me. I don't have a dog in that fight. Let
them duel it out, and old Savage will be the winner. There is no
way you are going to draw me into this situation, and you can
count on the Congress feeling the same way. You should never
take a position unless you are forced to take a position. I'm not,
and I won't.

"Just let the will of the people speak loud and clear. And those
who, sooner or later, make up what could be known as Acirema
should not be taken lightly. We are going to be needing them in
our next campaign. You realize that, don't you?''

"What next campaign? Mr. President, this reelection will be
your last term. There won't be another campaign.''

"Don't be too damn sure about that, Daniel,'' spoke the President. "Don't be too sure of that. With me in the White House, a
Southerner from Arkansas; the Vice-President, a Southerner from
Tennessee; the President of the Senate, a Southerner from Mississippi; and the Speaker of the House, a Southerner from Georgia,
just about anything can happen and probably will. I'm not at all
sure that Mr. Taylor Savage hasn't already calculated well beyond
the meager intellectual and psychological capabilities of each of
us mortals. Just you wait and see. The ballgame is a long way
from being over. You just mark my word.''

FOR MONTHS THE campaign chairman for the reelection of
the President had kept a keen eye on Taylor Savage and how the
movement was shaping up. The President was much aware of the
part he should play pertaining to his own reelection and had not
until this time taken sides either for or against Acirema. There
simply was no way the President or his staff was going to alienate

1.4 million citizens with a negative response on either side.

On the other hand, the percentages were so greatly in favor of Acirema, the President began to look for a position which would also benefit him in accordance with the wishes of those of this potential new state. While he had a plan in the offing, it was way too early to spring it on the voters, especially those who could really make a difference, the prevailing side.

☐ ☐ ☐ ☐ ☐

WITH THE PUBLIC hearings behind them, the committee met its schedule of preparation and mailing of the petition ballots. For very special and obvious reasons, the committee had chosen to mail them on July 4th. Since the Post Office was not open on that date, the ballots went into the mail on the 3rd with anticipation of some voters receiving them on the 5th. The instructions gave voters 30 days to fill out the petition and return it to the Supervisor of Elections in their respective county no later than midnight August 5th, the first Monday of that month.

Since there were some delays by the post offices due to the holiday, the large majority of the petitions were delivered on Monday, July the 8th. While the voters had a full 30-day turnaround cycle to complete and return the forms by Friday, July the 12th, more than half had already been returned to their election supervisor's office. Savage and his pollsters thought this to be a very good and meaningful indication they were going to be quite successful.

To make certain each voter had all the information needed to make a positive decision, the committee had arranged to have three volunteers present each day from 8:00 A.M. until 5:00 P.M. at each county's Supervisor of Elections Office. Should a voter need someone to visit in his home to explain a certain plank of the Platform, all he needed to do was make a request and a volunteer was there in no time.

Both the Democratic and Republican parties supplied volunteers and spent countless dollars to ''get out the vote.'' Each party knew just how important it was for this nonpartisan referendum to pass and do so by a wide margin. During the final week before the deadline, each county's volunteer committee was given a computer printout of those who had not yet voted. Without exception, each household was visited and urged to return their ballot as soon as possible and for certain not to miss the deadline of August 5th.

The national news services were reporting they thought the return would be the highest percentage of any political movement or election in the history of the country. Most were predicting a return of between 85 and 90 percent.

□ □ □ □ □

IT HAD BEEN ALMOST a week and a half since any significant development had been heard from the Grand Jury, not a single squeak. Speculation grew with the dawning of each new morning as the ''gang,'' a name they bestowed on themselves, gathered at Cobb's, a turn of the century restaurant across the street from the Courthouse. This morning the ''gang'' was abuzz as each of them interpreted the headlines with their own personal slant.

Cobb, no one seemed to know or care about a first name, had rented the building more than 50 years ago from a local realtor whose father had left him and his brother several medium-sized structures in old ''Downtown Pensacola.'' Cobb knew that he had paid for the building several times over, but renting seemed to be a good idea back in the mid '40s when he had left his job as a cook on a steamer, and it apparently continued to suit his purpose today. A purchase with a mortgage and commitment, was completely out of the question.

Although he retained a good leaseholder relationship with the owner, it often took weeks or more to make simple repairs which were clearly the owner's responsibility. Midway on the right side of the building, the seeping rains often found their way down the side of the plastered wall. About twice a year a roofer would be called in to work on the problem which had been caused almost 30 years ago when a distraught woman leaped from her lawyer's office on the 10th floor of the adjacent building. Her heavy-framed body went completely through the roof, and she wound up on Cobb's floor, but lived to tell the story.

This morning the gang, many of whom were often seen loitering around the Courthouse, City Hall, or Federal Building, began to assemble around the usual hour of 8:00. It was a strange assortment of retired lawyers, judges, has been politicians, businessmen, and young attorneys who wished to be accepted into the old-timers' power structure. Still others were present who simply were nothing more than "wanna-bes" who had little chance of even being noticed.

The gang was always very dedicated and retained a passionate interest for following such actions as were developing in the potential of Acirema, as well as the actions of the Grand Jury. They were not the least bit concerned about the lack of activity from the Grand Jury over the past couple of weeks and thought this lull not at all strange; each assured the other that something was soon to break and, when it did, it was going to be big, very big.

Some of the "wanna-bes" sat with their own groups scattered throughout the restaurant, while the gang of men—no women—always found their spot at the rear of the building around two red and white checkered wax-cloth tables. Hanging above seemed to be an invisible sign which might have noted, "Gang Members Only, No Outsiders Welcome."

Morning breakfast only offered eggs, cheese grits, link or patty sausage, and either wet or dry toast, no biscuits. Over the years coffee remained at a nickel a cup but Cobb always seemed to be ahead of the game as the regulars tipped in excess of the norm to make up for the obvious loss. During the lunch hour, from 11:30 until 1:30, the blue-plate special was a choice of fried chicken, chicken-fried steak, or meat loaf. Each plate included mashed potatoes with gravy, green beans, and a roll. No menu was necessary, as the only other option was the very best home-cooked burger in town, known far and wide as "Cobb-Burgers."

In the rear left corner stood an old pot-bellied stove that served its purpose during the dread of winter, always offering the gang warm memories of their past. On cold mornings many would linger around the welcome heat several minutes before finally taking their place at their table.

Down the hall, just past the restrooms, old "You Boy" occupied his own special corner of history. Only two years after Cobb opened, "You Boy" became a fixture and was widely accepted as the best 'shine' in town. A simple old-fashioned, two-step stand with well-worn dark green leather seats became the "seat of knowledge" for many politicians. As the black vote became more and more relevant to the election process, "You Boy" was well ahead of the class and often counseled those seeking office about the political temperature of the black community—and he was seldom wrong.

Many years ago, and no one wanted to claim responsibility or even discuss it, one of several wooden benches that sat in the wide hallways of the Courthouse made its way across the street and into the rear of Cobb's. Countless numbers of political races were started, and ultimately won, by those who would choose to linger for hours on "the bench," as it had become known over time. And the acceptance of wise teachings by those who would listen often prevailed and made the difference in elections, of which many were otherwise considered too close to call.

The elders of the gang were well at ease with the name of "You Boy." While such names as this had been commonplace in years past, "You Boy" made known his full acceptance by the standards of today's society by explaining that his father had tagged him with "You Boy" as far back as he could remember. Still, some of the younger "wanna-bes" who got a shine each week, whether they needed it or not, insisted on calling him by his initials, "YB". This did not set well at all with the older establishment.

"You Boy" possessed what many politicians wished they had, the ability to listen. He was a great listener and only spoke when he had something to say, and when he did it made a great deal of sense, far beyond his formal education of only four years of grade school.

Since the day Taylor Savage had made the first formal announcement about Acirema, "You Boy" had kept close track of the movement and now was especially interested in the proceedings of the Grand Jury. He was always fond of saying, "Thunder always follows rain, then lightning is just around the corner." For two days now the entire Panhandle of Florida had suffered under continued downpours which kept "You Boy" on his toes just waiting for the thunder and the lightning which would surely follow.

□ □ □ □ □

ON TUESDAY MORNING THE headline of the *Pensacola News-Journal* read in dark, bold capital letters, "GRAND JURY INDICTS SEVERAL." What many had speculated and envisioned had finally come about. Everyone was sure this was going to be the beginning of numerous other indictments, in addition to those listed in the paper, and each one would have far-reaching implications across the political and business communities of both Florida and Alabama.

The paper wrote of the alleged murders of Andrew Wright and Joe Harkins and other matters concerning potential political and business transactions relative to the Deep South Group, then noted the names of those indicted:

Florida Governor Brandon Woods, Alabama Governor Lance Foxworth, Melvin Cooper, former campaign manager for Governor Woods; Ray Haze, businessman from Point Clear Alabama; Mrs. Peaches Lamont-Haze, candidate for Governor of Acirema; Sidney Kattzs of Birmingham, President of the Deep South Group; Cort Locke of Pensacola, President of Regions Power Company; Deke Mallory of Montgomery, President of Mid-South Power Company; Kirk Lane of Nashville, President of Volunteer Power Company; Reginald Miles of Tampa, President of Sunshine Power Company; Rhodes Ashby of Atlanta, President of Peach State Power Company; and Ryan Warner of Jackson, President of Delta Power Company.

After these indictments, the liberal media continued their ruthless pursuit of trying desperately to find a connection of the two murders and the cash kickbacks with that of the Acirema movement. The liberal press was determined to keep their anti-Acirema position on the front page with hopes of finding a means to narrow the gap and defeat the movement, and was working overtime to come up with any story. with little regard to its credibility if it would assist them and their goal.

☐   ☐   ☐   ☐   ☐

IT WAS A VERY WARM afternoon the last Saturday of July when Garrett Lewellen and his wife Samantha hosted a garden party for 22-year-old Monica Sims, the daughter of their best friends, Dr. and Mrs. Hank Sims. More than 300 invited guests attended the social event of the season at the Lewellen's 800-acre farm and ranch on the outskirts of Georgiana, a small Southern town in Butler County, Alabama. Although the event did not commence until 6:00, the thick late afternoon air was almost super-saturated with steamy hot humidity lingering from a day that saw the temperature reach 98 degrees in the shade.

The Lewellens were most pleased with the turnout, and everyone seemed to be enjoying their grand style of Southern hospitality, especially the absolutely magnificent spread of the finest foods and beverages. Many of the guests were the age of the soon-to-be bride and groom and spent most of their time enjoying the fast-moving music provided by two bands and four well-stocked bars scattered throughout the gardens.

The parents and older guests found refuge on the veranda under slow-turning ceiling fans which pushed cooler air in their direction. They enjoyed mixing and mingling with old friends, some of whom they had not seen for quite some time. While the younger generation enjoyed their style of partying, they had nothing on their elders who were sipping their favorite, the old Southern tradition of mint juleps.

Although the invitations indicated the reception was from 6:00 to 8:00, it was almost 9:30 before the crowd realized they had almost worn out their welcome. After the last guest left, the Lewellens suggested to Dr. and Mrs. Sims that the four of them should have a nightcap. These old friends had spent many evenings together and truly enjoyed each other's company. Little did the Sims know this would be the last time they would ever see their friends alive.

□　□　□　□　□

IT HAD BECOME A ritual for the Lewellen daughters, both married and living in Virginia, to call their parents each Sunday morning before the three families left for church. Neither daughter could come home for the reception, and each decided on her own that perhaps her parents were sleeping late this morning, so they would wait until after lunch to call.

Lisa and Dawn had called each other back and forth all day to report no success in reaching their parents at their home or on their mobile phone. Although it was only a few minutes past 7:00 in the evening, they had become very concerned and finally agreed to call their uncle Fred, who lived in Greenville, less than an hour from Georgiana, to ask if he would drive over to check on them.

When he arrived at his brother's home, he had little concern as every light in the house seemed to be on and the gardens were also well-lit. After getting no response from ringing the bell and knocking on the front door several times, he walked around to the rear of the home and did his best to get some attention by banging on the two sets of double doors, one leading into the kitchen from the veranda and the other to the garage. Through the glass panes of the garage door he could clearly see that both cars and Garrett's Chevy pickup were parked inside as usual. Nothing seemed out of place which gave reason to think that they should be answering his many knocks.

He began to concern himself and retrieved a hidden key which was kept over the inside door of the greenhouse. Entering, he called aloud several times and heard no response. After quickly scanning every room downstairs, he eased up the winding staircase to the private quarters on the second floor.

In the master bedroom there was no evidence of either Garrett or Samantha. With hesitation—and the feeling you sometimes get when you know down deep that something is wrong—he slowly pushed open the bathroom door, being careful to not touch the handle. Stepping inside, he found his 73-year-old brother and sister-in-law both lying nude, half-submerged in the sauna bath full of hot, bubbling red water.

□ □ □ □ □

ACCIDENTS AND GOSSIP seem to go hand in hand and flow quickly throughout small Southern towns. No sooner had Fred notified the Sheriff's office than friends and neighbors began flooding the front lawn. Law enforcement agents hardly had time to rope off the area before several were already milling around all sides of the mansion.

What at first appeared to be nothing more than the horrible murder of a well-respected, financially secure couple in a small Alabama community would raise unlimited suspicions in a matter of an hour or so. On the 10:00 o'clock news it would be the lead story across the South.

It did not take the media long to learn that Lewellen was the same person who had been President of the Deep South Group and had retired eight years ago when he handed control of the conglomerate over to Sidney Kattzs. Could this be the knot the media had been waiting for? The one that could ultimately tie all the loose ends and coincidences together, or would it be just another chapter in what was quickly becoming a very weird, complicated set of circumstances involving many in high places and now perhaps a third and fourth murder, all linked to one source?

□ □ □ □ □

MAXWELL RANDOLPH, THE U.S. Attorney for the Northern District of Florida, had arrived at his office at the normal hour of 9:00 o'clock on Monday morning. Before he had time to get his first cup his secretary announced that a Mr. Jobe Patson, an attorney from Mobile, was on the line and insisted on speaking to him.

"Good morning, Mr. Patson. This is Maxwell Randolph. What can I do for you?"

"Yes, Mr. Randolph, good morning. Mr. Randolph, it's been some time since we have seen each other. You will remember that I represented Dailey Freight Lines years ago in a case which you handled. Do you recall?"

"Certainly, Mr. Patson. How've you been?"

"Doing well, staying busy. Look, Mr. Randolph, I am representing a client whom you would know, Mr. Ray Haze from Point Clear."

"Oh, yes. I know of Mr. Haze. Who wouldn't know of someone who ran for Governor of Alabama twice and now is married to a candidate who wants to be the first Governor of Acirema. What's this all about?"

"Mr. Randolph, Mr. Haze has asked me to see if the three of us could sit down together this afternoon and discuss a little business. Would you have a half hour or so?"

"What's the purpose? What is this in reference to?"

"Well, I'd rather not say right now. How about 3:00 this afternoon. Will that work for you?"

"No, that won't work. How about 4:00?"

"That'll be fine. We will see you in your office at 4:00 sharp. Goodbye, Mr. Randolph."

As soon as Randolph hung up the phone, his secretary buzzed him with another call. "Pick up line three. It's Mike Fitzwater, and he says he needs you."

"Good morning, Mike."

"Good morning to you, Maxwell. How was your weekend?"

"Way too short. I hate these Monday mornings. What's up?"

"Oh, not too much. Look, just a few minutes ago I got an interesting call from a Mr. Charles Hampton in Birmingham. He says he is representing Sidney Kattzs, and they want to come in this afternoon and spend a bit of time. You have any idea what could be going on?"

"Well, that's strange. I just hung up the phone talking with Jobe Patson. He is representing Ray Haze, and they also want to come in this afternoon for a discussion," responded Randolph.

"That is indeed strange. Let's see now. Both men have been indicted by the Federal Grand Jury, and one is President of the Deep South Group whose former President was found murdered yesterday. The other dropped out of the race for Governor of Acirema, and his new wife stepped into the race, and she too is under indictment.

"And bright and early this morning one called the U.S. Attorney for the Northern District of Florida and the other called the U.S. Attorney for the Southern District of Alabama. Something is getting ready to happen, wouldn't you say?" asked Fitzwater.

"You got that right. What do you think is up?" responded Randolph. "Looks to me like we might be seeing a couple of rats trying to find a hole, wouldn't you say?"

"Could be. Maybe it's a race to see who can convince the Government he is telling the truth and is seeking immunity from prosecution. Think so?"

"I think you may have something there. Let's meet with them as they have requested and touch base as soon as we know something. Agreed?"

"Yeah. Right. Let's do just that."

"Listen, Mike, is there anything new on the Lewellen case up there in Georgiana?" Randolph asked.

"Not that I know of. I got a report last night but nothing more this morning. Perhaps I need to touch base with Sheriff Ezell over in Butler County just in case there have been new developments which we should know about before our meetings this afternoon. I'll do that and be back with you as soon as I know something. What time are you meeting with Haze and his lawyer?" Fitzwater asked.

"They are due here in Pensacola at my office at 4:00. What time is your meeting with Kattzs?"

"They are going to meet here at 2:30. Let me see what I can find out from Georgiana, and I'll call you around 1:00."

"Great, I'll talk with you then. Thanks Mike."

TWENTY-FOUR

SINCE THE MAILING of the referendum ballots on July 4th, Taylor Savage and Sheery Goss had made it their goal to visit every city and township within the 19 counties and to spend the final 30 days of the crusade visiting with those who were leaders of the movement within their home communities. Although they traveled into an area together, which made a more interesting news event for the day, they soon would separate and go in different directions.

The active supporters were most appreciative that they would spend these final days drumming up votes for Acirema and bringing the campaign directly to the people, directly where it counted the most: into their homes and businesses. Each morning, noon, and evening small groups would gather for a meal in a supporter's home and discuss just how important it was that every person vote and to be sure to return the ballots no later than August 5th.

While the Platform restricted any candidate for office from politicking until September 26th, Sheery knew that her touring with Savage and drumming up support for the referendum was the very next best thing to campaigning for her own political future.

During each day the two would go their separate ways and speak at gatherings and often visited in the homes of those who were unable to get out for one reason or another. In each of the 19 counties, they made sure their tours included every hospital and nursing home. On Sunday, each would speak at a different church at the morning services and another in the evening, making certain they did not leave out any religion. Each Friday evening they visited a Jewish Temple.

They wanted every person who was eligible to vote to participate in the election process for Acirema. Each understood just how important it was to win and to win big. Early on, someone pointed out to them that during George Wallace's second campaign for Governor, he had visited with as many individuals as he could find without regard if they were rich, poor, or middle class or black or white. After he was elected, he later commented that he even asked little old ladies for donations as small as a quarter for his campaign, knowing that if he got their money, no matter how much or how little, then he would surely get their vote. This was a hard lesson for Wallace to learn. However, after losing his first attempt to win the Governorship, he made all the proper adjustments.

At the end of each day, Taylor and Sheery would go their separate ways and into the homes of those who would put them up for the night. They were very cognizant not to differentiate between any class of supporters and made sure their hosts were as much at ease with them as they were as a guest. It was amazing just how much political knowledge and savvy they both had absorbed and just how well tuned-in to the exact way to use this self-taught awareness.

Over the 30-day period, from the time of mailing the referendum ballots to the date they were to be returned, Taylor and Sheery estimated they had spoken personally to no less than 60 percent of those eligible to vote. Between the two of them, they had spoken at more than 30 church services of all denominations and had eaten no less than 180 meals at the homes of key supporters and their invited guests.

Several times during each day, supporters and nonsupporters alike would often ask about the Grand Jury actions, subpoenas, and indictments. Savage was extremely careful not to make any comments about any individual and always answered any inquiry by assuring those who asked that any information would have to come from other sources. And Sheery answered each question by stating since she was going to become a candidate for Governor, she would not involve herself with the actions of the Grand Jury.

It was safe to say by the end of 30 days of ''around the clock campaigning,'' they were ready for some rest and relaxation. They ended their tour on Sunday afternoon, the day before the ballots were due back in each county's Supervisor of Elections Office. Returning to the beach from the last leg of a fantastic trip, each made a pact with the other that no politics would be discussed this evening. They simply would relax on the outside deck, have a cocktail, play with Hot and Toddy, and enjoy one of Voncile's home-cooked meals.

□ □ □ □ □

AFTER DINNER AND warm showers, they propped themselves up on several pillows on the king-sized bed in his master suite, and, as usual, Savage began to channel surf, a habit Sheery still had not gotten used to. Finally, he stopped on Channel 5, the CBN affiliate, just in time to catch the start of the 10:00 o'clock news.

''Alex Simonton reporting. By this time tomorrow evening, after all the ballots have been counted, it would appear, and we predict, that Acirema will become the 51st state of our nation and, rightly so, will head the alphabetical listing of all the states. We expect Acirema to grow, mature, and excel by leaps and bounds above and beyond many other states that have long since become lazy and decadent in their ways of governing.

''Never in our wildest dreams could we have imagined that something like this movement could have taken place and actually succeeded. Taylor Savage has shown the world that pure guts, instinct, management skills, and planning and execution of those plans could truly make a difference and change this world of ours in an extraordinary and marvelous direction.

''We certainly anticipate that several other areas of our country may well follow suit if a favorable Acirema vote, as we expect and predict, becomes a reality tomorrow evening.

''There is no question in our mind that Taylor Savage will be nominated 'Man of The Year,' and I would expect if Acirema controls crime as he has planned, then surely a Pulitzer Peace Prize award shouldn't be far away.

''Who is to say that a personality such as Taylor Savage couldn't become an overnight top-rated candidate for the Presidency of the United States, should that hold an interest for him.

"So, until the results are in tomorrow night, we will leave you by stating unequivocally that these past 10 months have been some of the most interesting, enjoyable, and memorable reporting hours that I personally have ever encountered. To report on and work with a personality who has had such a dynamic impact on the future of our country, and especially the section of the country which may become Acirema, is to acknowledge that we have truly been pleased to have played a small part in this magnificent story.

"Years ago some very wise person once said, 'There is no power on God's green earth that can keep a first-class man down, or pick a fourth-class man up.' Good evening."

□ □ □ □ □

"WELL, THAT WAS interesting, wasn't it? Savage remarked.

"Sure was. I've always liked Alex Simonton," she responded.

"I wasn't speaking directly about Alex. Think you'd be comfortable in the White House?" he questioned.

"Oh!, go to sleep."

"How about the Lincoln bedroom? Think the bed is bigger than this one? I understand it's lumpy."

"I said, go to sleep, Taylor."